W9-BRY-706

OF
BEAST
AND
BEAUTY

ALSO BY STACEY JAY

Juliet Immortal

Romeo Redeemed

Princess of Thorns

OF
BEAST
AND
BEAUTY

STACEY JAY

EMBER

This is a work of fiction. Names, characters, places, and incidents either are the product of the author's imagination or are used fictitiously. Any resemblance to actual persons, living or dead, events, or locales is entirely coincidental.

Text copyright © 2013 by Stacey Jay
Cover photograph (girl) copyright © 2013 by Wojciech Zwolinski/Trevillion
Cover illustration (city) copyright © 2013 by Angela Harburn/Shutterstock

All rights reserved. Published in the United States by Ember, an imprint of Random House Children's Books, a division of Random House LLC, a Penguin Random House Company, New York. Originally published in hardcover in the United States by Delacorte Press, an imprint of Random House Children's Books, New York, in 2013.

Ember and the E colophon are registered trademarks of Random House LLC.

Visit us on the Web! randomhouse.com/teens

Educators and librarians, for a variety of teaching tools, visit us at RHTeachersLibrarians.com

The Library of Congress has cataloged
the hardcover edition of this work as follows:
Jay, Stacey.
Of beast and beauty / Stacey Jay. – 1st ed.
p. cm.
Summary: When nineteen-year-old Gem of the Desert People,
called Monstrous by the Smooth Skins, becomes the prisoner
of the seventeen-year-old Smooth Skin queen, Isra,
age-old prejudices begin to fall aside
as the two begin to understand each other.
ISBN 978-0-385-74320-4 (hc) – ISBN 978-0-307-98142-4 (ebook)
– ISBN 978-0-375-99100-4 (glb)
[1. Toleration–Fiction. 2. Kings, queens, rulers, etc.–Fiction.
3. Mutation (Biology)–Fiction. 4. Monsters–Fiction. 5. Fantasy.] I. Title.
PZ7.J344Of 2013
[Fic]–dc23
2012034854

ISBN 978-0-385-74321-1 (trade pbk.)

Printed in the United States of America

10 9 8 7 6 5 4 3 2 1

First Ember Edition 2014

Random House Children's Books supports the First Amendment
and celebrates the right to read.

To Riley and Logan

But he that dares not grasp the thorn

Should never crave the rose.

—Anne Brontë

OF
BEAST
AND
BEAUTY

IN THE BEGINNING

IN the beginning was the darkness, and in the darkness was a girl, and in the girl was a secret. The secret was as old as the cracked cobblestone streets of Yuan, as peculiar as the roses that bloom eternally within the domed city's walls, as poisonous as forgotten history and the stories told in its place.

By the time the girl was born, the secret was all but lost. The stories had become scripture, and only the very brave–or very mad–dared to doubt them. The girl was raised on the stories, and never questioned their truth, until the day her mother took her walking beyond the city walls.

In the wilds outside, a voice as fathomless as the ocean spoke to her of a time before the domed cities, before wholes became halves and bargains were made in blood. It told of a terrible choice and even more terrible consequences. It begged her to listen, to live. . . .

In the early days, I was one, the voice whispered. *I was this world and this world was me, and the dance was seamless and sweet.*

Then the ships came from a faraway world. They came belching smoke and fire, stinking of space and beings living and breathing, loving and hating, hoping and despairing in close quarters for too many centuries. I watched the humans spill from their ships, blinking in my sun, marveling at my moons, weeping as they set foot on land for the first time, and I was . . . curious.

I teased my magic between their spindle fingers, into their seashell ears, around the pulsing heads of their babes, finding them as delightful as my native creatures, but soft and unprepared for life on our world. Knowing they would die without my help, I began to touch them, to transform them. It was what I had done since the beginning, when I was only the land and the sea and a longing for something more to keep me company.

But the humans were afraid of my touch, of the magic that caused their smooth flesh to scale and their bodies to bunch with unfamiliar muscle. They cursed me. They praised me. They retreated into the great domes they had built and hid themselves away, locking those already touched by my magic outside their gates and calling them Monstrous.

They made promises and offerings and dangerous bargains, pulling at me until I was no longer one but two: the Pure Heart and the Dark Heart, something both more and much, much less.

The Dark Heart, my shadow self, soon developed an equally dark hunger. It told the Smooth Skins in the domed cities of its longing, promising them safety and abundance in exchange for blood and pain, for the voluntary laying down of a life, the ultimate act of devotion. It gave them magic words to speak and took their rulers as offerings, and in each city, in the place where the sacrificial blood was spilled, enchanted roses grew, a symbol of the covenant between the Smooth Skins and their new god.

Decades passed, and the Dark Heart fed and grew powerful, stealing vitality from the planet, determined that none but its chosen few should thrive. And so the Smooth Skins in the cities learned to bleed, and the Monstrous outside learned to hate, and I faded away, stretched thinner with every passing year, until only a precious few heard my voice.

Finally, I realized I had to reach out to the Smooth Skins in a new way. Before it was too late. Using the power of transformation upon myself for the first time, I took the form of a Monstrous woman with long black hair and white robes, a body to give the Smooth Skins one last chance to show compassion.

I went from city to city, introducing myself as an enchantress, a priestess of the planet. I begged to be allowed inside. I begged the Smooth Skins to abandon their dark worship and accept the gifts of their new world. I begged them to make me whole, to restore the innocence I'd lost when they had begun to call me god and devil.

But the gates of the domed cities remained shut. The Smooth Skins had no concern for the rest of the world, so long as their own desires were met. They spit harsh words through the cracks in their walls. They shot weapons through slots in their gates. Arrows pierced my chest, and my new blood spilled onto the ground.

I stumbled into the wilds, seeking shelter, but in the camps of the

Monstrous I found no aid. Sensing I was not truly one of their own, they bared their teeth, called me witch, and turned me away.

My new body dying and my hopes for peace shattered, I gathered the last of my magic and sent a curse sweeping across the world. I cursed the eyes of the Monstrous to run dry, never to know the release of tears, but I cursed the Smooth Skins even more terribly. From that day forward, a precious few of their babes would be born kissed by the Monstrous traits they despised. The rest would be born with missing pieces, trapped in bodies as twisted and wrong as the Dark Heart they worshipped.

The Dark Heart managed to spare a few of the city dwellers—those from the families who had spilled blood for their god—but my curse had its way with the rest. The rest of the Smooth Skins became more monstrous than the creatures they feared, and no amount of blood spilled in their royal gardens could make them whole again.

There is only one way to undo the curse: if even one Smooth Skin and one Monstrous can learn to love the other more than anything else—more than safety or prejudice, more than privilege or revenge, more even than their own selves—then the curse that division has brought upon our world will be broken and the planet made whole.

For a time, I had hope that my last act of cruelty would sway the humans in a way my pleas for mercy had not. But as time passed—hundreds and hundreds of years slipping away as I tossed on the wind, a ghost haunting lands where I used to live and breathe—I saw I had accomplished nothing. The world outside the domes continued to die. The land and the creatures upon it cried out for aid, but I could only watch as elders suffered and young ones starved. I had nothing left to give. I had lost everything but my voice.

And what good is a voice when so few will listen?

Will you listen, child? the Pure Heart of the planet asked the girl. *Will you do what the others would not? There is proof of the story I tell. I can show you where to look. I can help you find the truth.*

The truth had been hidden away, the voice told the princess, but she could find it, if she was brave.

The girl wasn't brave. Her fifth birthday was still three months away. She wasn't a hero with a sword; she wasn't even allowed a knife to cut her food, for fear she'd sever a finger. But still, the voice haunted her dreams. It cried out for justice, but the girl learned to cry louder, to stand on her tower balcony and howl, terrifying the common people living in the center of the city.

She screamed and fought the servants who were sent to care for her. She clawed at her father's face and bared her teeth at him in rage. She wept and ripped her dolls to pieces—heads and arms and legs pulled asunder, every dress torn in two, every tiny crown bent and broken—but she never spoke of the secret. She never admitted, even to herself, why she was so angry. And sad. And afraid.

Months passed, and eventually the Pure Heart spoke to her no longer. The girl's misery and rage slipped away, and the secret sank like a stone,

deep,

deep,

deep

inside her, until the truth was as forgotten as hope and beauty and all the other things given to the darkness.

AUTUMN

ONE

ISRA

THE city is beautiful tonight. I can tell by the smells drifting through Needle's open window—the last of the autumn flowers clinging to their stalks, their perfume crisper and cleaner than the summer blossoms that came before; fruit sweet and heavy on the trees; and above it all, the heady fragrance of the roses blooming in the royal garden.

I will be out among it all soon. The tower holds me by day, but by night I am a wanderer, a good fellow of the moons. The yellow moon, the blue moon, even the red moon, with its beams that cut angrily through the dome when the Monstrous

light their funeral fires in the desert. I call the moons by secret names; they call me Isra. I am not their princess, or their
mistress, or their daughter, or their prisoner. I am Isra of the
wild hair and quick feet clever in the darkness. I am Isra of the
shadows, my secret made meaningless by moonlight.

I am ready to see my moons, to see *anything*.

It's been four endless nights since I visited the roses.

The Monstrous draw closer to Yuan than ever before.
There are city soldiers everywhere, prowling the wall walks,
fortifying the gates, testing for weaknesses in the dome, padding the trails from the city center to the flower gardens to the
orchards to the fields, and back again, in their soft boots.

They would never survive in the desert outside. Their
boots are glorified house slippers, their feet soft and vulnerable beneath. I'm certain I have more calluses on my feet than
any of Baba's soldiers, rough spots on my toes and heels that
catch and hold on stone.

I can practically feel the stone of the balcony's ledge digging into my skin now, grounding me as I hover in the hungry
air at the edge of the world. . . .

My toes itch. My tongue taps behind my teeth. My skin
sweats beneath my heavy blanket. Just a few more minutes.
Surely Needle will put out her light soon. My maid insists it's
impossible to smell wax melting from across the room, but I
can smell it, and it keeps me awake, even when I'm not biding
my time, waiting for the chance to escape.

An untended flame is dangerous, and this tower has
burned before.

I dream about that fire almost every night—flames blooming like a terrible flower, devouring the curtains and the bed, licking at my nightgown. Baba's strong hands throwing me to the ground, and my head striking the stones before the world goes black. And finally, the door splintering and my mother's cry as she hurls herself from the tower balcony.

That night is my clearest memory from the time before. One of my only memories. I don't remember my mother's face or the color of Baba's eyes. I don't remember romps in the garden or holiday dinners at court, though Baba swears we had them. I don't even remember the sight of my own face. My mother forbade mirrors in the tower, and after her death, I had no need of them. My eyes never recovered from the night Baba saved me from the flames. For a day or two, the healers thought they might—I saw flashes of light and color in the darkness—but within a week it was obvious my sight was gone forever. I've been blind since I was four years old, the year my mama joined the long line of dead queens.

"Terribly unfair," I've heard people whisper when they don't realize the figure in the garden with the cloak pulled over her head isn't another noble out for a walk, "that the princess should lose her mama and her eyes all at once."

I want to tell them my eyes are not lost. *See? Here they are. Still in my head.* But I don't say a word. I can't reveal myself. No one knows what the princess of Yuan looks like these days. I haven't been knowingly allowed out of the tower since my tenth birthday. If the Monstrous breach the walls, Father is certain I'll be safe here until the mutants are destroyed. There

13

is only one door leading into the tower, and Baba and his chief advisor, Junjie, are the only ones who know where the key is hidden.

They have no idea that I don't need a key. Or a door.

I only need my sentry to put out her light and go to sleep!

I muffle a frustrated sigh with my fist. She's probably sewing in bed again. Needle has sewn me a dress each month for the past year. This one is green, she told me.

Lovely, I said, and rolled my eyes. As if I need another dress. I'm drowning in dresses. I've begged her to stop—or at least make something for herself—but she won't listen. One would think she's deaf as well as mute. If *one* didn't *know* better. If one hadn't been caught sneaking out of one's bedroom a dozen times, betrayed by the squeak of the bed frame or the crack of an anklebone.

That's why I have to wait. I have to be sure. . . .

Another half hour ticks away with maddening slowness. I've decided Needle has indeed forgotten to put out her candle—*again!*—and am about to throw off the covers, when I hear the *shup* of the silver cap smothering the flame, and catch a whiff of smoke and the tail end of Needle's soft sigh as she curls beneath her blankets. Needle doesn't make many sounds, but of those she does, that sigh is the saddest.

Sigh.

I'm suddenly ashamed of myself. Poor, tired Needle, the common girl without a voice, sworn to serve the princess without sight.

When I'm queen, I will give her a better job. Something far away from me and the burden of my misbehavior. When

I'm caught sneaking from the tower—and I will be caught, no matter how careful I am; there are only so many precautions a blind girl can take—she will be the one who's punished. I know that, but I can't stop. I need the night. I need the feel of my hair lifting from my shoulders as I run.

There is no wind in Yuan. Wind is a fairy tale, a magical, invisible force that stirs the planet, assuring living things that the world still moves. Under our dome, the air is too still. It smothers, clutches, a hand tightening into a fist that will some-day crush the city to pieces.

It's been nearly a millennium since those outside the domes were mutated by the toxic new world, but the past two hundred years have been the most devastating for the people living in the cities. All but three of the original fifteen settle-ments have fallen to the monsters in the desert. The messenger birds from the king of Sula and the queen of Port South come less and less frequently. One day they will stop altogether.

Or perhaps our birds will be the first to have their free-dom. Either way, Yuan is living on borrowed time. Though probably not as borrowed as mine. . . .

I wait a few more moments—until Needle's breath comes slowly and evenly—before slipping out of bed and eating up the thick carpet between my bedroom and the balcony with eager feet. Seventeen steps to the bedroom door; twenty-seven down the hall, past the sitting room, through the music room, and out onto the balcony; then three more and the careful fall to freedom. Careful, so I don't follow in my mother's footsteps. Careful, so my escape is only for the night, not for forever.

I brace my hands on the balcony ledge and push off the

15

ground with bare toes, drawing my knees up to my chest, landing atop the parapet in an easy crouch. My fingertips brush the cold marble; my cotton overalls draw up my shins.

The overalls are an orchard worker's suit with wide legs and deep pockets. I stole them from a supply shed near the apple orchard two years ago. Now the legs grow too short. I am seventeen and very tall for a person. Very, *very* tall. I am taller than Baba, taller even than Junjie, whom I've heard called "an imposing man." I am long and tall, and my skin is coarser than any other I've touched. Even Needle's work-roughened hands are softer than mine, the princess she bathes in cream, washes only with honey soap. My rough, peeling flesh was my greatest clue, back when I was still sorting out the mystery of myself.

Now I understand. I know the real reason I'm locked away from my people.

"I may be tainted, but I'm not a fool," I whisper into the too-tranquil air. It gobbles up my words and swallows them deep, smug in its assurance that the quiet order of the dome will never be disturbed. Seconds later, I bare my teeth in my most ferocious smile, and jump from the ledge.

The night comes alive. Cool air snatches my hair, lifting it from my shoulders, tugging at my scalp. It rushes up my pant legs, shivering over my belly and up my neck. My blood races, and my throat traps a giddy squeal. The tips of my toes beat with their own individual heartbeats as they make contact with the curved edge of the first roof and I take a running leap for the second, deliciously alive with fear.

I've made this descent a thousand times or more, but still

a taste of the original terror remains. The first time, my feet didn't know the dips and curves and footholds for themselves. The falls—the six curved roofs below the tower balcony—were only a story told by Baba as we sat in the afternoon sun. My fingers and toes are my eyes. I couldn't see the truth of my way out until I was already over the edge, dropping the ten feet to the top of the first roof. But it was there. Just as my father had said. As were the second and the fourth and the sixth, and the last tumble into the cabbage garden.

I plop down on the hard ground between the cabbage rows—no fertile patch of land is wasted in Yuan—and fold back into a crouch, staying low as I shuffle back and scatter the dirt with my hands, concealing the two deep prints from my landing. There is rarely anyone this close to my prison, but I don't set off right away. With all the guards milling about, Baba surely has a patrol stationed near the tower.

I wait, squirming my toes, ears straining in silence broken only by the faint buzz of the hives at the bottom of the hill. The bees are quieter at night but still busy. I like the hum, the evidence of nonhuman activity. We used to have wild birds under the dome, too—all different sorts, some night singers, some day—but the last of them died years ago. Father said it was an avian epidemic.

"Why didn't it take the messenger birds, then?" I asked him at the time. "Or the ducks and geese by the orchard pond? Why did only the wild birds die?"

"Wild things don't always survive under the dome," he said.

There was something in his voice that day. . . .

It made me wonder if he knows I'm not as biddable as I pretend to be, if he knows I'm wild, and doesn't hate me for it. Or at least doesn't blame me. It's not as if I asked to be born this way, with a taste for defiance and a longing for the hot desert wind, the wind I felt only once, the day my mother took me for a forbidden walk outside the city walls.

I'll never have that wind again—if I left the city for any length of time, I would die of thirst or sun poisoning, if the Monstrous didn't get me first—but I can have my night runs. I can have the autumn smells, the satin of rose petals between my fingertips, and the sweeter sting of the roses' thorns.

My mouth fills with a taste like honey and vinegar mixed together. The rose garden. How I love and loathe it. How I need it and hate the needing. But still, I'll go there first tonight. I want to see the color of the sky, know which of my moons hangs heaviest above the dome. I am efficient in my darkness, but how I crave the moonlight!

It's hard to wait, but I don't move a muscle, don't twitch a nostril, even when my nose begins to itch in the way noses never fail to do when you're not able to scratch them. Two minutes, three, and finally my patience is rewarded with the soft, rhythmic scuffing of leather boots on stone.

Scuff, scuff, scuff, scuff. I am a soldier, this is my song, and I shall scuff it all the day long. I am a soldier and these are my boots, the biggest shoes for the biggest brutes.

My lip curls. Soldiers. Ridiculous. Yuan needs a third as many, and those should be stationed at the Desert Gate and

Hill Gate and around the wall walks, where the rest of the city won't have to bear witness to their strutting about.

Our only hope is to keep the mutants out. If they make it inside, the city will fall. If we've learned anything from the destruction of the other domed kingdoms, it should be that. The Monstrous are bigger, stronger, with poison seeping from their claws, and skin as thick and hard as armor. They can see in the dark and live on nothing but a daily ration of water and cactus fruit. They are brutal beasts determined to destroy humanity and take our cities for themselves.

But our bounty will never be theirs. If they kill the keepers of the covenant, Yuan will turn to dust like the other cities and the land beyond our walls. Magic is loyal only to those who have bought and paid for it. With blood. Hundreds of years of blood, blood enough to fill the riverbed beneath the city and carry us all to the poison sea.

As soon as the soldier scuffs away, I scurry between the rows of cabbages on tiptoe, leaving as little sign of my passing as possible, counting the eighteen steps to the road, the four steps across it, the fifteen steps down the softly sloping hill—also planted with cabbage; oh, the cabbage I have eaten in my life—and into the sunflower patch. My fingers brush their whiskery stalks, feeling the heavy flowers bob far, far above me.

They are unusually tall this year. No matter how high I reach, I find only more prickly stalk and leathery leaves. I am nearly two meters tall, and my reach is another half above. They must be three meters, maybe more. I bet their heads are bigger than the moon.

"Moon. Moon, moon of mine," I sing softly as I skip the

19

thirty skips through the sunflower patch, up the rise to the city green where the children play. Seventy more steps—it is the widest green in the city, and the grass is still damp from the groundskeeper's hose—and I am in the orchards that surround the royal garden.

Dried grass sticks to my wet feet as I carefully tread the last fifty steps that separate me from my destination. There are snakes in the orchards. They hide beneath the grass clippings, lurking in wait for the rodents that feed on the apples the orchard workers miss. More than once, I've felt a strong serpent's body brush my bare foot, heard a rustle and a hiss as a viper slithered—

Shish. I freeze, ears pricking. My ears are very large, too. They hear more than average.

Yes . . . *shish* . . . a faint stirring in the grass to my right, but then nothing. Silence. After a long moment, I continue on my way.

Luckily, I've yet to step on any hidden squirmy thing. Snakes don't strike unless they have no other choice. Given the opportunity to flee, they will, and so I force myself to move slowly, no matter how the roses' perfume urges me to run. The smell is so strong, I can taste it, like the filling in the rose honey candies Baba brings me on the winter solstice. The sweets are terrible—bitter, and as enjoyable as sucking on a perfume bottle—but I eat them anyway. I save them up for treats on days when Baba is too busy to visit and Needle and I are alone and the silence threatens to drive me mad. The rose candies never fail me. I slip one into my mouth to melt, and taste freedom. Every time.

I pull in a breath and hold the sticky air inside me as I step onto the paving stones. The path is still warm from the sun. The stones kiss the bottom of my feet, whispering sweet things about how nice it is to see me again.

I stretch and smile and run. And run and run and *run*.

It's safe for a blind girl to run here. The path goes in a perfect circle, the roses stay in their bed except for a spill of vines on one side that I've learned to avoid, and there is never anyone here at night. If I am of the mind to eavesdrop later this evening, I will have to continue farther down the path. The royal garden is the most beautiful of Yuan's gardens but also the most tragic. It is a place of death, and the living avoid it when they can. They say they feel watched here, as if the roses have eyes.

They have no idea.

The roses have more magic than anyone, even my father, understands. I am the only one who knows their secret, who knows that they are more alive than other flowers, that they see and hear more than anything else on our world.

I throw out my arms, running faster and faster, until my heart beats in time with the slap of my feet, a layer of sweat coats my skin, and the giddy feeling inside swells so big that I have to leap and twirl, to spin with my head thrown back, the wind I've created whipping my hair. I want to scream with delight. I want to howl like the dogs on hunt day. I want to announce to the world that I'm free, free, free!

Instead I leap onto the ledge of the central bed, where the oldest roses' roots dig deep into the ground, where vines as thick as human arms twine through ancient trellises, snapping the brittle wood. Where flowers as big as melons bloom and thorns as long as fingers warn, *Don't touch! Hands to yourself! Back, savage!*

I reach out, the pads of my fingers prickling. I never know where I'll find a thorn. The wind never blows in Yuan, and the roses seem to grow like any other flower—though larger and older and always blooming—but the vines move. They *move*.

From one night to the next, a girl never knows when she might—

"*Ssss . . . ,*" I hiss as my finger finds a thorn, a sharp one that glances off my fingertip and slides beneath the nail, piercing the bed. I grit my teeth and fight the urge to snatch my hand back to my chest. We must be connected—the thorn and the flesh—for the magic to work. I hold perfectly still until the sharp pain becomes a mean little ache, until the blood flowing from my cut eases the hurt away with its warmth. I stay and I breathe and I sigh as, one by one, my eyes open.

All one hundred of them.

TWO

GEM

THERE'S a woman in the garden.

No, a girl. Tall but young. She runs like a child. Big, loping steps with her arms held out and her head bobbing like one of the giant flowers.

I've never seen so many flowers. Flowers, plants, fruit, green things bursting out all over. When we first crawled from the caverns, I stumbled in the face of it. I fell, and my hands felt alien against the soft, wet grass. The smells devastate me. I don't have Desert People or Smooth Skin names for them, can't tell where one smell ends and another begins. The land under the glass dome overwhelms with its life.

Fierce, vicious life. Stolen life. Paid for with the deaths of my people.

We're starving. The children first. Their skin cracks and bleeds. They cry until they have no strength left, and their silence is worse than their moans. The tribal medicine men have become death dealers. Better to eat poison root and have the pain over in an instant than to die slowly.

The autumn harvest of cactus fruit has bought the Desert People time, but only a little. We must have the roses. According to our chief's visions, they are the key to the magic that keeps the land under the domes flourishing and abundant.

"Take them at any cost," Naira said when we left our camp a month ago. "Die for them. Kill for them if there is no other way." Our chief is a peaceful woman. But these are not times for peace.

Or mercy. If the girl sees me, she'll scream. The guards will come. They're everywhere. They were here a few minutes ago. I hid in the orchard, but they'll come again, and I might not be so lucky next time. The moons are so bright, it's practically daylight under the dome. I have to act. If Gare were here instead of on the other side of the city, he would have already slit the girl's throat and wrested a plant from the soil, and would be halfway back to the caverns.

It took generations of digging to build the tunnel down to the underground river. It will take generations more to find another way in if we fail, generations we may not live to birth. This path will serve us only once. When the Smooth Skins realize what we've done, they'll shore up their underground defenses, build another impenetrable wall. They already suspect an attack will come. Their guards shot arrows at our scouts as they circled the city. This is our only chance.

Kill her. I hear my brother's voice in my head. *One death is nothing, a drop of water in a sea of the Desert People's blood.*

I flex my hands. My claws grow loose inside the grooves above my nail beds. There's no choice. There's no time.

I step from behind the thick tree, out of the shadows, into her line of sight. I bend my knees and bare my teeth. My claws *slick* from their hiding places as I ready myself for the rush. Her eyes fall on me, huge round eyes in a face so different from my people's, but somehow still so . . . familiar.

I hesitate. I shiver.

I didn't expect the Smooth Skins to look like this. I expected softness like uncooked dough, empty eyes sunk in privilege-rotted flesh. I didn't expect whisper-thin skin peeling like old tree bark, skin so pale I can see the blue blood flowing beneath. I didn't expect a sharp chin or a sharper nose or eyes that seem to see everything.

Except me.

She doesn't see me. She doesn't startle. She doesn't scream. Her gaze doesn't waver. She looks past me, into the orchard. I turn, but there's no one there. I turn back to find her still motionless, her hand in the flowers, her eyes focused on some faraway nothing. The truth hits, and my claws slide back into their chambers with a *shup* so hard, it hurts.

She's blind. I was about to kill a blind girl. Maybe even a simple blind girl. Now that I've seen her face, there's no doubt she's nearly a woman, but she skips and plays in the flowers like a child. No near adult of the Desert People would behave that way unless they were rattled in the brain.

A strange heat creeps up my neck, making my face burn. Shame. That's what this is. Not something I've had reason to feel more than once or twice, but now it curdles inside me.

This isn't the way. No women or children. We're not like the Smooth Skins. They are as soulless as a sandstorm. We are better. We know the power of transformation. This planet has changed us, but its magic is good magic. It would be enough to sustain us all if the Smooth Skins hadn't twisted it to serve their unnatural purposes.

They are the murderers. Their domed cities rob the surrounding lands of vitality. Their prosperity is paid for by the slow death of the desert, and if something doesn't change, it will lead to the extinction of my people. This raid isn't about killing Smooth Skins; it's about keeping them from killing any more of *us*.

I back into the shadows under the orchard trees. I'll wait. The girl will leave eventually, and then I'll–

"Please," she says.

I freeze, skin crawling, claws *slicking* out again. Was I wrong? Has she–

"Show me *this* garden," she begs. "Show me myself. Just once."

She isn't talking to me. There must be someone else. But where? The flower bed looks dense, the thorns dangerous. I ease closer, circling around her on quiet feet, braced for attack. But there is nothing in the shadows beneath the roses.

Only her hand, with a thorn buried deep in one finger and her blood dripping slowly to the earth below.

"You've shown me the nobles' cottages and the soldiers on the walls and the desert outside and the monsters who live there," she says, spitting each word. "But you refuse to show me what's right here. Right now. All I want to see is my face! You promised me. You promised!"

The girl is rattled. No question.

"I hate you," she whispers, sightless eyes narrowing. "I'll set fire to the entire lot of you." She laughs, a cruel laugh, not childlike at all. "I'll do it. I swear I will if—"

She breaks off with a cry as the flowers begin to move. Squirm. Coil like snakes preparing to strike. The giant blossoms roll on their stems, turning to fix me with their alien eyes.

Naira's visions are sound. The roses *do* have magic, greater than the planet magic that touched our people in the early years, granting us size and strength and protection from the sun and our new predators; greater than the blessings our dead bestow as their final flames burn. And the girl knows the magic. She speaks to the flowers.

A plan takes shape quickly. I'll trap the girl, creep up behind her, and hold my claws to her throat. I'll make her dig up one of the bushes and whisper the roses' secrets while she does it. If she's helpful and quiet, I'll let her go. If not, I'll—

"No," she gasps. Her eyes go wide. Her thin chest heaves as her breath grows faster. If I didn't know she was blind, I'd think—

"No!" she says, louder this time. "Help me!"

I lunge for her, but she darts away, leaping off the edge of the flower bed, leaving a smattering of blood behind. "The Monstrous are in the city!" She runs, as fast as the desert wind, around the flower bed and down a stone path lined with more flowers. "Monstrous! In the royal garden! Help me! Help!"

I race after her. I have no choice. I need her silence before it's too late, before–

More Smooth Skins appear at the end of the path, spears raised. I know the moment they see me. I see their silhouettes ripple in the yellow moonlight. I smell their fear. I lift my clawed hands and roar–a warning to my people. Wherever their search has taken them, my father and brother and the others in our raid party will hear me and know I've been discovered. They'll make it to the caverns and into the river before they're caught, but they'll do it without the roses we came for. We've failed. *I've* failed. I let this girl doom my tribe. I should have killed her. I should have slit her throat and lapped the blood from my claws. Now everyone I love will die–my father, my brother, my friends. My son.

He's only six weeks old. He'll be the first on the pyre.

I roar again, a sound so terrible the girl screams and stumbles, falling to the ground. I leap and land on top of her before the guards can throw their spears. They'll kill me sooner or later, but I'll kill this girl first. I'll take her life as payment for the destruction of my people.

I grab her shoulder and flip her onto her back, the better to get at her throat. Her skin gives like water beneath my claws. Her blood is the exact color of the roses, red that swallowed brown and black and holds them prisoner in its belly.

I stare at it. It's beautiful. Terrifying.

I've never killed something so large before. So large or so delicate. I didn't even mean to cut her. I didn't—

"Do it," she whispers, her voice fearful, but angry, too. She trembles beneath me, her long body quaking, her eyes once again without focus. "Do it! Kill me!"

Her words make my blood burn. "You're so ready to die?" I demand in her language. "My people would do *anything* to live. *Anything*."

Her eyes bulge in her narrow face. "You—you—s-speak. How—"

A spear falls next to my arm, and another glances off my bare shoulder, but my skin isn't like theirs, so thin that it's practically pointless to have skin at all. My hide is thick, scaled across my chest, over my neck and shoulders, and down my back. If they want to kill me, they'll have to hit my belly. I lift my head, roaring at the two guards who've dared come close enough to hurl their weapons.

"Wait!" the girl screams. "Take it alive! Don't kill it!"

It.

I snarl into her face. She screams, and her eyes squeeze shut. Her hands cover her mouth, muffling her sobs. Another spear flies. And another, but I knock them away, rage making my warrior's reflexes even swifter.

I am not an *it*. I am a Desert Man. I have nineteen years. I have a son. I might have had a mate if there were no Yuan, no tunnel to dig, no scouting missions to take me away from my tribe over and over again. But Meer chose a different mate, and my son sleeps in another family's hut. Now my son will die and be burned without ever knowing my face. Because of them!

I roar again and hope it rattles the loose pieces of her brain. Stupid girl. Stupid Smooth Skin. Stupid—

"Stop!" she shouts, hands lashing out. Her tiny fists hit my mouth, bruising my lip as they bounce off my teeth. Before I can react, her fingers return to my face, gentle this time, curious. I freeze, too shocked to pull away.

"Hold your weapons," she orders the soldiers. Boots shuffle forward, but she shouts, "I am Isra Yuejihua. My word is *the* word! Hold!"

Yuejihua. The name of the ruling family. It can't . . . Not this girl. This strange one.

The guard closest breathes deeply; another gasps like a woman. A third says, "My lady—"

"My word is *the* word and will one day be law. Hold your weapons." Silence falls. In it, her fingers trace the outline of my lips, discover my nose, smooth around my eyes. When she reaches the scaled patches above my brows, she hesitates, but eventually moves on. She finds the place where my braid begins and smoothes a shaking hand down the ridge to the end falling over my shoulder. "It's soft," she whispers. "What color is it?"

"You saw."

"I'm blind." Her lids flutter. Her eyes are not brown or black like every other pair of eyes I've ever seen. They're dark green, and as strange as the flowers in her garden. They are sightless now, but I would have sworn she saw me before. How else could she have known to run?

"Black," I snap, keeping one eye on the soldiers.

"Like my people." Her breath shudders out. "But you have very large teeth, I think."

"You think?"

"I haven't felt many teeth." Her fingers come to her shoulder, covering the place where my claws pierced her skin. "Will the poison take effect soon?" she asks in a small voice.

"Poison?"

"In your claws."

The guards inch slowly closer, torn between obeying their princess and saving her life. I smile at them, baring my undoubtedly large, bone-white teeth. Now that I know how valuable this girl is, I have hope. Not much, but enough to make my voice smooth when I say, "Take me to the underground river and set me free. Before I go, I will tell you how to rid yourself of the poison."

"And if I don't?"

"You die."

"Maybe I'm already dead," she whispers, her words as haunted as her eyes. "The roses are hungry. I felt it tonight."

She's out of her mind. She makes me . . . afraid. *That's* what I feel when I look into her vacant eyes. Fear, as foreign as shame. Why I should fear a girl I have pinned to the ground, I don't know. She's helpless, fragile. I should be afraid of her guards, and their weapons.

The thought has barely formed when I feel it, the sharp jab of metal deep in the back of my thigh where there are no scales to protect me. I cry out and swipe at the guard with my claws. I graze his leg and reach for the spear, but the guards in front don't give me time. One snatches the girl from beneath me and drags her across the stones while the second—a man with a knife longer than my claws—lunges for my throat.

I knock him away with a growl that transforms to a howl of pain as the man behind wrenches his spear free of my leg. Blood rushes from the wound, and I scream.

"No!" the girl cries. "Don't kill him!"

The guard drives his weapon into my other leg, just above the knee, hobbling me. I wail like the grieving at the funeral fires. It's over. Even if I fight off the guards and get to my feet, I'll never be able to run.

"No! No!" The princess is suddenly by my side, tripping over my arm and falling to the ground beside me. "Take him alive!" she pants, turning to address the air around her, blind eyes wide. "Take him alive. We need him to tell us how to remove the poison. If not, I will die."

My claws dig into the stone so hard, my knuckles ache. There is no poison—these Smooth Skins believe such strange things about my people—but I can arrange for her to die. She's close. I could slit her throat before her guards could make a move to protect her.

My pulse beats faster. The agony in my legs fades to a high-pitched hum of pain that urges me to act. To kill. This is my last chance to take vengeance. This is their princess, the woman who will be queen and continue the devastation of the land until not a single living creature remains outside the domed cities.

I should do it. I *will* do it.

My heart races. Faster, *faster,* until I hear it rushing in my ears. *Faster,* until sweat beads on my lip and my scales move farther apart to accommodate the heat building inside me. *Faster,* until my teeth ache and my brain pulses and colors swim through the night air.

Red for the blood that's been spilled.

Blue for the sky I'll never see again.

Green for her eyes.

Her eyes . . .

They are the last thing I see before black sweeps in, stealing all the colors, all my hope, away.

THREE

ISRA

THERE'S a muffled *kapluph,* and the Monstrous man's arm goes limp. It lolls against my leg, heavy and so hot that it burns through my overalls. He's as hot as fire, as hot as I've imagined the desert sand would be against bare feet.

No human could live through such heat. Not for long. I don't know about a Monstrous, but he certainly wasn't this warm before.

"Take him to the cells," I say, my breath coming fast. "Bring the healers to see him. Find the king and tell him I'll meet him there."

Baba. By the moons, he'll be terrified. And livid. He's already locked me away. What will he do now? When he learns I've been out of the tower and met such trouble? Put bars on the windows? Brick up the stairs? The thought of being any more trapped than I am is almost enough to make me hope the poison in my blood kills me.

I shiver. I asked the Monstrous to *kill* me. *Why?* What was I thinking? I don't want to die. I want to live, I want–

"But, Princess–"

"Do as she says," comes a worried voice from my left. "We need the monster awake. He might be the only one who knows the cure. I'll escort Princess Isra. Hurry!" The air fills with the *scuff, scuff* of soldiers' boots, then grunts and groans as the heavy Monstrous is hauled from the ground and with more *scuff, scuffs* is carried away.

"Let me help you, Princess," the remaining soldier says. His voice is familiar, though I don't know why. I've never spoken to a soldier. I've never spoken to any men at all except for my father, Junjie, and now the Monstrous.

The Monstrous was definitely a man, a man the size of a small mountain, the only being I've ever seen longer than I am. My people are almost invariably small of stature and petite of bone, with nut-brown skin and straight black hair. The Monstrous had similar hair, but he stood a head taller than me, with shoulders the size of boulders, covered in orange and golden scales, like a fish, but dry and smooth.

No, not like a fish, like . . . a snake.

The thought makes me shudder as I take the soldier's hand and let him help me to my feet.

"Are you able to walk, my lady?" His voice pricks at me like one of the needles in my maid's apron pocket.

It's how Needle got her name. The day she came to give me a bath, I had just turned five and was still feral with grief. She started unbuttoning my dress, and I shoved her away, pricking my fingers on the sharps in her apron in the process.

Strangely, the pain calmed me. Needle's gentle touch, her hands like birds alighting on my head, my shoulder, my cheek, communicating concern with every cool brush across my skin, calmed me more. She was only fifteen, but her touch reminded me of my mama's. I let her stay, when I'd sent every other companion away.

I'm surprised to find I want her now. I would very much like to have Needle's slim fingers under mine, making the signs for "Calm down" and "We'll sort this out." I didn't think I was afraid of anything, but now I am. I'm afraid.

My fingers tremble as I touch the torn flesh at my shoulder. I don't feel the poison yet, but I could. At any moment. I try to swallow, but my throat is too tight. I don't want to die. Not like this. It's not fair! I've lived with Death hovering on my shoulder my entire life, but I never–

"Should I carry you, Princess?" The soldier's hand warms the small of my back. My spine ripples as I twist away. His touch is foreign, unexpected, too strange after the night I've had.

"I'm sorry. I shouldn't . . ." The soldier clears his throat. "I was wounded as well."

"You were?"

"The Monstrous tore the skin at my leg." He sounds younger than he did before. Scared.

I reach out, brushing his shoulder with my hand, surprised to find that my arm is parallel to the ground. The soldier is nearly my size, shorter only by a bit. "Thank you. For helping me."

"Please, don't thank me." His hand finds the small of my back again, settling over the knobby bones of my spine. The warmth of him—cooler than the Monstrous but warmer than me, in my sweat-damp clothes—heats my hips. My stomach. My chest. "It was a privilege to defend the life of our queen."

"I'm not—" Before I realize what's happening, soft, hot skin presses against my half-open mouth. I flinch, but the soldier's hand at my back holds me still as his lips move against mine, as his tongue flicks out, bidding a cautious hello.

A kiss. *This* is a kiss. It is . . . slipperier than I'd imagined. His *tongue* is . . .

A *tongue*? Who would have thought?

A part of me wants to laugh at this soldier and the jabs of the slick muscle invading my mouth, but another part of me is . . . fluttering. Something stirs inside me. Something urges me to tilt my head and move my lips, to dart my own tongue out—quick as a wink—for a taste.

Salty. Sweet. Hint of cabbage. Something familiar in the midst of all the unfamiliar feelings that are making my skin warm and my insides as hot as the Monstrous man's flesh.

I pull back, heart beating too fast. "We should go to the cells. The monster might have revealed the cure."

"We should, but if we die tonight, I—"

"No one's going to die," I say with more confidence than I feel. "Come with me." I start down the path, but stop after only a few steps. I've never been to the cells. I've never dared go that deep into the city proper.

I hold out a hand. "Guide me. Hurry."

"Yes, my lady." A second later, his arm is under mine. It's strong and densely muscled, but the bare skin at his wrist is as soft as all the skin I've felt in my life. Much, *much* softer than mine. This soldier is a whole citizen of Yuan.

So why did he kiss me? A tainted girl, too tall and too wide, with skin peeling from the chest down in a frustrated attempt to reveal the scales that lurk beneath the surface? I'm obviously not sufficiently tainted to be sent to the Banished camp, but even the slightest sign of mutation is reviled. From what I've overheard, a whole citizen would rather die than marry someone with Monstrous features, no matter how mildly they might manifest.

He's hardly thinking marriage. He's thinking he's going to die and yours might be the final lips he encounters.

The thought banishes the last of the tingling sensation from my body, expelling it like a fish bone. I lift my chin, holding my head high as we move swiftly toward the city proper. I do my best not to think about dying with the taste of this stranger on my lips.

Dying. If I'm dying, I'll never get the chance to tell my father that I have dreams that live outside the tower, to confess how much I need something . . . more. Tears fill my eyes, but I don't cry. I sip in a breath and hold the air in my lungs.

The soldier pats my rough hand with his softer one. "My name is Bo. I'll stay with you until the healers come. My father would want that."

"Your father?"

"Junjie," he says, his voice dipping and sliding on the last part. That's why he sounds familiar. Junjie's son. "My father's spoken of me?"

"No. I didn't know he had a son."

"Oh." The word is a stone plunking sadly into the water.

"But he doesn't speak to me often," I say, feeling a *little* sorry, despite my fear and the shame still lingering on my lips. "Most of the time he's only at the tower to steal my father away on business."

"Yes. The king . . . I . . ." He sighs, a pained sound that sets fretful things stirring in my stomach.

"What about the king?"

"Nothing." He walks faster. "Your wounds need treatment."

"No. Tell me. What were you going to say?"

"I can't," he whispers. "Your health is the most important thing."

"I feel fine." I do. The scratches still sting, but the feverish sensation is gone. I'm no healer, but it doesn't *feel* as if there's poison in my blood. It makes me wonder . . .

Has my slight mutation made me immune to the creature's venom, or . . . could the texts about the poison in Monstrous claws be wrong? Was the Monstrous lying when he said I'd die without his help, saying whatever he had to say in order to escape to the river?

"The river." My hand tightens on Bo's arm. "The Monstrous wanted me to take him to the caverns where the underground river flows. That must be how they—"

"We know," he interrupts, making me sputter. I can't remember the last time I was interrupted. Have I *ever* been interrupted? "There were three other creatures. Their hair was damp when we captured them. My father guessed where they'd come from. There are guards in place now. No more Monstrous will get into the city tonight."

"Did you kill the others?" I ask, afraid to hear the answer. The Monstrous are terrifying, but they also have language and pain. They aren't the complete savages Baba and Junjie have made them out to be. There's a chance we might be able to make peace with them.

"Not yet." Even in those two small words, his bloodlust is clear.

"They speak our language," I say gently. "They might not be as savage as we've thought."

Bo's muscles flex beneath my hand. "They're worse. They're devils."

"Devils or not, it doesn't make sense to kill them if we don't have to. It will only make things worse for the city." I think of the Monstrous man, how he endured my fingers roaming his face. He could have killed me, but he didn't. He showed mercy. How can we do anything but offer the same?

"It will be up to you to decide, of course." Bo's voice is stiff. "My queen."

"Don't call me that," I snap, wishing I didn't need his arm

to guide me. I'd prefer *not* to be touching this soldier anymore. "I'm not queen yet."

"Yes, my lady," he whispers. "You are."

I am?

I . . . *am.*

The ground turns against me, and I trip over the raised edge of a paving stone. Bo catches me and holds me up by the elbow. His hand is larger than I thought. It circles my bone, making me feel like a child, but I'm not a child.

I am queen. I . . .

That means . . .

"Baba . . ." There isn't enough breath in me to finish the question.

This can't be true. Baba was with me this morning. We had breakfast together, sat on the balcony and talked about the harvest festival and made plans for our private celebration after his duties in the city center were finished. He agreed to allow Needle to make him a hat for the party. He laughed one of his rare, light laughs and asked me to play him a song on the harp. He was so alive.

He *has* to be alive.

"It was the Monstrous," Bo says. "The king was walking the path around the lake. One of the creatures surprised him and his guards. All five of his men were killed, and your father . . ."

"The Monstrous . . ." My mouth is too dry. My lips have gone numb.

"We captured the thing not far from the court cottages. There was blood on its hands. It laughed when it learned some of it was the king's."

Blood. Baba's blood. My baba.

My baba is dead. The monsters have killed him. Now I am alone. And I am *queen*. Queen so much sooner than I ever thought I would be queen, and there is nothing left for me but pain.

"We'll kill them." I dig my fingers into Bo's arm. "All of them. I'll do it myself."

FOUR

GEM

I'm not dead, but I'm burning. Thrown on the pyre. Alive.

No! I try to scream. *Father! Gare!* But no sound comes. My jaw creaks open in a silent wail. My heart shrivels, and all around me the flames burn and burn. The pyre spits sparks at stars crackling in a cold night sky, and fire sizzles through skin, bound for bone, and I am alone with the pain.

More alone than I've ever been.

Why has my family done this? Is it because I failed them? Is it–?

43

A girl's voice startles me awake. "I know you speak our language," she says. "Answer!"

My eyes creep open. The night sky becomes a stone ceiling streaked with green, but the burning feeling stays. It's coming from my legs. Pain. Fever. Shredded muscles screaming. Blood sticky on my skin.

Why? What has—?

"Answer!" the girl shouts, making me flinch.

It comes back in a rush: The woman-girl-princess, the soldier. His spear. Failure. The death of the Desert People on my back, to carry for however long I live.

The memories fan the fever flames. I've had fevers before, but nothing like this. I grit my teeth and turn my head. The greens and reds pulse and bleed. Black slashes like claw marks slide back and forth before my eyes. It takes a moment for the marks to still, another moment to understand what they are.

Bars. A cage.

"Don't pretend to be ignorant." A gray blur behind the black slashes. My throbbing eyes strain, pulling the blur into focus.

It's the princess in her baggy gray clothes, trembling in front of another set of bars. Behind them, my brother, Gare, stands as still as the stone walls, tall and strong in the face of her interrogation, though his cheek is split open and his eye swollen shut.

"Tell me!" she shouts, stepping closer to him.

"No, my queen." A man—shorter than the princess, but

44

with broad shoulders and the hard face of a leader—reaches for the girl's arm and pulls her back. "You're too close."

She turns, and I see her face. It is red and puffy; her cheeks and nose are wet. "Junjie. Please. Help me." On the last word her features crumple, her eyes squeezing shut and water leaking from behind her lids. More magic. I've never seen anything like it. I blink, and her face swims like the air above a fire.

Fire. I'm so hot. Burning.

My eyes close, and the cell melts away.

When I wake again, the cage is dark and quiet, and I'm cold. Freezing. My skin crawls. My scales pull so tightly together that it feels they'll rip away from the flesh. I shiver until my teeth knock with a dull *clack, clack.*

"Gem? Are you awake?" A whisper I can't place, but in the language of the Desert People, not the Smooth Skins, so it must be—

"Gem? Can you hear me, boy?"

Father. I try to speak, but my jaw is clenched too tightly; my tongue is fat and slow. I'm dying. I know it. My body feels cut in half—the top made of ice, the bottom still hot, scattered with knots full of poison.

"Gem, if you can hear me . . ." He draws a ragged breath. "You are our hope. Remember what we came for. Leave a message at the gathering stones if you're able. We'll come back for you if we can."

Come back? Where are they going? Have they found a way to escape?

"If not, you must finish–" A long, hollow scrape interrupts him.

"Silence in the cell," a voice booms in the Smooth Skin language.

Father ignores the warning. "Bring life to our people. Save them, Gem. You–"

"I said silence." There's another scrape, and then footsteps and the clang of metal on metal. "Bring the darts!" Another man answers, and more footsteps fill the room, and my father is still shouting, but somewhere beneath it all, I swear I hear Gare growl that he should be the one to stay behind, that he doesn't need Smooth Skin words to claim Smooth Skin lives.

I try to tell him he's right, to confess my weakness, to tell father I'm dying and it's too late, but I'm already floating away from my body. Up, up, up, until I look down at the slab of meat that housed my spirit, down from the ceiling where the air is silent and peaceful.

I want to keep going. I want to leave my corpse to cool on the stone, but I worry. . . .

Will I be able to reach the land of my ancestors if I die here? Without a funeral fire or the songs of the Desert People singing me into the night? Or will I stay in this hole, a lost spirit, haunting the Smooth Skins for the rest of time?

They deserve a haunting, but I don't want to be the spirit to do it.

I am weak. How could I have ever thought myself strong?

My heart *thu-dums,* and I'm pulled back to the cold and

the hot of my body. To the knocking of my teeth, and the sound of my father crying out in pain as he's shot. When the blackness comes again, I'm grateful.

In and out. In and out.

Days—maybe weeks—pass in a haze. My feverish body is moved from the stone slab to a pallet so soft, I'm sure I'm dreaming it. It cushions me like a cloud. A blanket made of whispers covers my body. Gentle fingers pry open my lips and pour bitter liquid down my throat. I swallow. I don't care if it's poison. I sleep. I don't care if I wake. I'm ready to die. I don't want to live or think or dream anymore.

The dreams are the worst. Even when the sick heat in my legs fades, I still dream of flame, of a pyre where I burn forever to pay for failing my people.

I am more than shamed. I loathe myself.

"Father . . ." The sound of my own voice startles me awake. I open my eyes wide, but immediately slide them half-closed again. It's bright in this room. Sun-filled. I never thought I'd see the sun again. I never thought I'd see *her* again, either.

The princess sits by my pallet, her oval face calm, emotionless, her blind eyes staring through me. "Are you awake?" Her voice is different than I remember. Emptier. She looks different, too.

Her dark hair is coiled on top of her head like a nest of snakes. Her lips are stained the red of a cactus flower. Her body is covered in a dress the color of her eyes, but not a dress as Desert Women know it. Our women's dresses tie with straps at the back of the neck. They end at the knee, with slits up the sides to give their legs room to move. This dress has sleeves that clutch at the girl's arms, holding her shoulders prisoner. It squeezes her chest and waist. I roll my head to see that the squeezing continues all the way to her ankles.

She looks like a worm wrapped up in green silk for a spider's dinner.

"I asked you a question," she says, still calm, unmoving except for her red lips. It feels like we're alone in this room, but she doesn't seem afraid.

I roll my head, forcing my stiff neck to turn one way and then the other. My eyes roam, taking in the stone walls, the barred windows, the heavy wooden door. Still a cage, but not as miserable a cage. And we *are* alone. The princess and the monster.

I turn back to her, watch her pale throat work as she swallows. I could kill her now. I'm weaker than I've ever been, and my legs ache in a way that assures me that standing isn't possible, but I could still take her life. My arms aren't restrained. One swipe of my claws at her neck where the blood flows quickest, and it would be done. She'd bleed to death before the guards could open the door.

"I know what you're thinking." Her lips twitch.

My right hand flexes. My claws descend with a sluggish *lurp,* oozing from above my nail beds.

"It would be a tragedy for the city." Her words float on their own cloud, hovering above us in the crisp air. "I should be married," she announces suddenly, proving she's as rattled in the head as I remember. "Seventeen is young, and I'm in mourning until the spring, but I could do it. I'm sure someone would be willing to risk the bad luck that comes from breaking tradition."

Seventeen. Two years younger than me. Not young at all.

"But then they'd have no reason to humor me." She sighs. "Being the keeper of the covenant only goes so far, you know. I've learned that in the time you've been sleeping. People still feel free to tell a blind girl what to do. My maid had to sneak a sleeping draft into your guards' tea in order for me to be granted a private visit with my own prisoner. Maybe it would be different if . . ." Her empty eyes slide toward the door, her ears lift until the tips are hidden in her hair. "They'll lock me up again if they find me here," she whispers. "Junjie will take my father's place as jailer. I will never be seen again."

"Then . . . go," I rasp.

Her lips curve in a hard smile. "I knew you'd speak to me. Sooner or later." She leans closer, stretching her long neck. "How did you learn our language out in the desert?"

I think about refusing to answer, but I don't want the princess to leave, not until I've decided whether or not I'll take my piece of her. "My mother." I lift my fingers and let them drop, one by one, bringing life back into my hand. "She carried the tradition."

"What does that mean?"

"She carried Yuan words in her mind. Her mother carried them before her, my great-grandmother before that." With a steady movement I pull the whisper-soft blanket down my body. It slips off my shoulders, down my chest. I keep pulling, slowly baring my right hand. "Women usually carry language.

49

They take words faster. But I have no sisters. I was the youngest, so my mother taught me."

"How did your ancestors learn?"

"I don't know." My hand is almost free. My focus is on ridding myself of the blanket. "Mother never told me, and she died four winters . . ." My words trail away as I realize what I've said.

The princess is quiet. I lie still, not wanting her to hear me rearranging the covers. "My mama is dead, too. When I was four years old."

I don't say anything. I don't feel sorry. The Smooth Skins deserve to suffer, this girl most of all.

"Well . . ." She clears her throat. "You speak well."

"Thank you."

Her laughter startles me. My arm jerks, baring my claws in one swift pull. But there is still no sound, and the princess doesn't flinch. Thank the ancestors the girl is blind.

"And good manners," she says. "Strange . . ." Her curved lips droop. "The other Monstrous killed my father."

I pause. Is she telling the truth? Is the king of Yuan dead?

"They cut him open from his throat to his belly. I felt the wounds. Before we put him in the river," she says, her throat working harder. Her bound shoulders tremble, straining the seams of her dress. It looks as if it were made for someone else, some girl even frailer than this one. "He was taking a walk. He was unarmed. He wouldn't have hurt them."

He would have. He did. He hurt them every day that he ruled this city.

But I don't say the words aloud, no matter how much I

want to. Instead I ask, "Where are the others? What did you do to them?"

"If it were up to me, I would have gutted them the way they gutted the king." I let my arm creep toward her neck, remembering how her flesh parted so easily for my claws the first time. "But I told you, being queen only goes so far. My advisor said we should send the others back to your people with a warning to stay away from the city. Junjie could communicate with your leader. They drew symbols on the dirt floor of the cell. Your leader—your father, if he's to be believed—offered to leave you here as a gesture of good faith. He knows we'll kill you if the city is attacked again."

Her words would wound, but I remember what Father said that night I lay shivering in my cell. I'm not a gesture of good faith; I'm a weed in their garden.

"He seemed confident that you'd recover. I wasn't sure." She reaches out. I hold my breath, ready to drop my hand back to the pallet, but her fingers alight on my forehead, not my arm. "But you're cool now." The pads of her fingers trace the slope of my nose, over my lips, sending a strange zinging sensation across my skin.

She continues, over my chin, down to my neck, where her hand curls. Her fingers begin to squeeze, and the zing is banished by the *thud, thud, thud* of blood struggling to flow.

I should do it. Now. Cut off her arm; go for her throat. But I don't. I'm still weak. Not only in body, but in mind. I don't want to kill a motherless, fatherless blind girl. Even if she is my greatest enemy.

"Did you know they would kill him?" she asks.

I think about saying yes, just to see if she'll try to strangle me to death, but instead I say, "We weren't here to take lives."

Her grip loosens. "Why were you here?"

I swallow, throat rippling beneath her fingers. "We're hungry. We hoped to steal food to take back to our people." I can't tell her that my chief's vision revealed that the roses are the secret to the Smooth Skin's paradise under the dome. And I can't kill her. If I do, I'll never leave this room alive.

My arm falls; my claws ease back into their beds. I don't know why I'm alive, but I am, and I must make the most of it. I have to find a way into the garden.

"My people are starving," I say.

She makes an angry sound beneath her breath. "If my father weren't dead, I would feel sorry for you." Her fingers tighten again, until my eyes ache and green and pink spots dance around her face. "I would have put food outside the gate."

"Liar," I grunt, fighting for breath.

"Maybe." She bends close, and I smell her breath, sweet like sticky fruit and . . . roses. "Maybe I *am* lying. The way *you* lied when you told me I'd die without your help. But you'll never know for sure, will you? And your people will continue to *starve*."

She smiles, and I move, faster than I thought I could after so much time in a cage. I snatch her wrist, pull her fingers from my throat. She comes for me with a balled-up fist that hits my chest and glances off without damage, and I snatch that wrist as well, holding tight as she struggles. I am so weak that my heart slams inside my chest and my head spins from even this small effort, but she's weaker. Like a child.

"Release me," she demands.

"You're the one who wanted to fight." I pin her wrists together and hold them, like Gare did to me when I was small and wanted to play rough. I am determined to show her that I won't tolerate her abuse, but she struggles only a moment, before her neck bends and her forehead drops to her hands.

I flinch as her eyes shut and her shoulders begin to shake. Water spills from behind her lids, fat drops that slide down her cheeks to fall onto my bare chest.

It wasn't a fever dream, then.

"What is that?" I breathe.

She lifts her face. Her eyes aren't empty now. They're swimming with misery and pain. This girl wouldn't run through the garden laughing like a child. The death of her father cut that part of her away and left her bleeding inside where wounds hurt the most.

I tell myself it's no less than she deserves, but my voice is softer when I repeat, "What *is* that?"

"What?" Her hands squirm.

"The water." I loosen my grip on her wrists. "From your eyes."

She swallows and sniffs as she pulls her fists to her chest. "Tears?"

"Tears." I remember the word, but only vaguely. It wasn't one that came up often in my lessons or Mother's songs. My people don't tear. Water comes from our skin to cool it, from our body to rid it of toxins, but not from our eyes. We aren't leaky and fragile like the Smooth Skins.

Yet *they* hold all the power. They hold me prisoner. Their ruler smiles as she speaks of my people's hunger; their queen runs her hands over my face and tightens her fingers at my throat, and I must lie here and do nothing.

I smear the tears on my chest away, but some have already soaked into my skin. I can feel them, as if she has marked me, infected me with Smooth Skin weakness.

"Get out," I growl, hatred burning in my belly.

"Not yet. I have—"

"Now!"

"Quiet, or you'll wake the guards," she hisses, her own hatred flashing in her eyes. "*You* don't tell me what to do. Junjie and the other advisors tell me, but *you* do not. Your own father left you here. Forever. For the rest of your life, you are *mine*. If you'd prefer that life to be a long one, you'll do what I say, when I say it."

"I'll cut you open," I snarl through gritted teeth.

"You'll do no such thing." She doesn't flinch, or move away from the bed. "If you were going to kill me, you'd have done it already."

"I nearly did."

"I don't believe you."

"Do you believe these?" My claws are at her neck a second later, the tips puckering the skin at either side. Her lips part and a strangled sound gurgles in her chest, but she doesn't move. She has realized that the slightest twitch will open her throat. "You seem curious about what will happen when

54

you die," I whisper. "Maybe it's time for your curiosity to be satisfied."

She sips air, swallowing like a three-hooved gert picking its way down the rocky slope of a canyon. I tighten my grip. The five puckers on her throat deepen. A little more pressure, and her blood will flow. I tell myself it will be justice, but I'm not thinking about justice. I'm thinking about the way she stuck her nose in the air when she told me I'd do as she says. I'm thinking that I prefer fear in her eyes to any other emotion I've seen.

I'm thinking I would rather be a monster than her slave.

"Your father told Junjie that you were a healer." Each word is careful, formed mostly with her lips, using as little breath as possible.

"I am a warrior." I come from a family of warriors, the greatest family of warriors. At least until *I* was born into it.

"Then you don't know plants?" she asks, a new fear creeping into her voice. "You don't grow and mix herbs for the Monstrous?"

"We are the Desert People."

And my name is Gem, I silently add. *Thank you for asking. Thank you for offering your name before you started giving orders.*

But why would she give her name? In her eyes, I'm an animal. My only hope of becoming anything more, of gaining enough freedom to escape the domed city, is to win the Smooth Skins' trust. So far, none of them have bothered to speak to me. Only this girl. But she is the princess—no, *the queen*—and has power, even if it isn't as much as she'd like. And she wants to know about herbs Father said I could mix. I

55

know certain common remedies, but I've never mixed a true healing pouch in my life.

My father isn't a stupid man. There must be a good reason for his lie. If I weren't on the verge of committing murder, I could probably think of it.

I relax my grip. Almost immediately, my head clears—*grow and mix herbs.* The gardens. Father was paving the way for my escape with the roses, giving the queen a reason to let me out of my cage.

"I know plants. And herbs." I retract my claws. The queen gives a shuddery breath. "Why?"

"I have . . . a field. A large one," she pants, hands fluttering at her neck. "I want you to help me plant it with healing herbs, especially those that the Mon"—she clears her throat—"that the Desert People use to ward off further mutation."

Herbs to ward off mutation? There is no such thing. At least, not that I know of. But just like my lie about the poison in my claws, this lie must serve a purpose. If I agree to assist this girl, I will find out what it is.

"All right," I say. "I'll help."

"Good." She stands, wobbling in her narrow dress. "I'll talk to Junjie and have guards sent to fetch you in the morning. You'll be bound when you leave this room, but the chains will be loose enough to allow you to work." She goes to the door but turns back almost immediately. "When the guards come, tell them nothing about what we'll be growing. I don't want my people to know. Not yet."

"Why?"

She pulls a silver key from a pocket near her hip. The sight of it makes my damaged legs ache. If I were whole, I could rush her and take the key. But I'm not whole. Thanks to this girl and her men.

"You seem like a clever beast," she says, fitting the key in the lock. "I'm sure you'll understand. Sooner or later."

I am not a beast. I swallow the cry pushing at my lips. It would do no good to tell her. I must show her. *Tomorrow I will begin,* I think as she slips out the door as swiftly and silently as a tear down a Smooth Skin's cheek.

Tomorrow, I will serve and obey. I will be on my very best behavior. I will use only Yuan words and keep my claws sheathed. But tonight I will close my eyes and pretend I am not her prisoner.

Tonight I will remember the fear in her eyes and let it fill my mouth with a taste as sweet as her rose-and-sugar breath.

FIVE

ISRA

"YOU were missed at the harvest feast last night." Junjie hovers so close to my side, I can smell the oil he uses to shape his mustache.

Needle tells me his lip hair is as long as my hand from palm to fingertip and as big around as my thumb. I take her word as truth. The thought of asking permission to touch Junjie's face makes me fidget with nerves. Of all my advisors, my chief is by far the most intimidating.

"I wasn't feeling well." I bring two fingers to my forehead, faking the ghost of a headache I never had.

"Then you should have called for the healers," he says. "Your health is too important to the city to take any chances, Isra. You know that."

"I know," I mumble, wishing I had arranged to meet the Monstrous and his guards in the field, instead of coming with the soldiers to fetch the beast.

It has been only three weeks since I became queen, and already I grow tired of my newfound "freedom." Each time I dare set foot outside my tower, fretful, bossy old men shadow my every move. Junjie and the other advisors would obviously prefer that, until I'm married, I pass my days alone in my bedroom surrounded by mountains of pillows. I'm treated like a foolish child with bones made of glass, and I *hate* it.

I long for my walks alone in the garden, for the velvet night sounds and the gentle light of the moons. I long for the time when my ugliness was a secret guarded by the father who loved me. Now no one loves me, and my secret is a scandal that has set the entire city talking.

"I will have a healer appointed to the tower," Junjie says. "A woman, so that she may sleep there with you and—"

"Sleep there? In the tower?" I ask, horrified by the thought of a stranger invading my last safe place. "But where would we put her? Needle and I already share my bedroom."

"She can sleep in your dressing room. There's enough space beside the bath for a small cot, and she can keep her clean uniforms underneath."

"Please, Junjie," I beg. "I don't need a healer sleeping in my dressing room. I'm not an invalid. It was only a headache."

"The kingdom would sleep better knowing a healer is minutes from your side."

"The kingdom is safe. I'll call for someone next time I have the smallest ache or pain. I promise," I say, wishing Needle would hurry and get back with word from the Monstrous's cell and save me from Junjie. The guards went to fetch the creature from the prisoners' floor of the infirmary nearly twenty minutes ago.

What's taking so *long*?

"Very well, but the people need assurance that you are in good health and fit to rule. It's time you dined with the nobles at court, at least during special celebrations," Junjie says, disapproval clear in his voice. I may be queen, but in his eyes I'm still the naughty little girl who threw paint on the king's best fur when she was four years old. "You owe it to the city to honor its traditions."

"I know. I just couldn't. Not last night," I say. "I'm sorry."

When I was younger, I used to beg to be allowed to accompany Baba to the harvest banquet, but he always said no. It seemed wrong to go last night without his permission, without *him*. I'm not ready to face the court alone, and I don't see why I should have to.

We're all in mourning, the entire city grieving the loss of their king. Needle tells me Yuan is painted with loss: tables covered in red cloth, mirrors draped in white, and men with black scarves tied around their arms, and I myself wearing green and only green until the first day of spring, as is tradition for a child in mourning.

"I understand," Junjie says in a gentler tone, reminding me that there is a heart beneath his gruff exterior. "But remember, you are not alone. I am here to support your rule. I served your father well for twenty years; I will serve you just as faithfully."

Though not as long. He doesn't say the words, but I hear them lurking in the silence after he speaks. My mother went to the roses thirteen years ago. The offerings are usually made no more than thirty years apart. In ten years–or seventeen, if I'm lucky and the city's magic holds strong–it will be my turn. If Baba had lived and remarried, things would have been different, but he's dead and they aren't. The fact hangs around my neck like a stone, making it harder to pull myself from the pit of my grief.

The healing garden is the only bright spot in my darkness. When the Monstrous boy's father first told Junjie his son would be helpful in our gardens, I admit I was less than impressed. Our gardens do very well on their own, thank you very much. What captured my attention was his insistence that his son knew how to grow and mix the healing pouches the Monstrous use to ward off further mutation in their young. I did my best to conceal my curiosity from Junjie, but I'm sure he guesses why I fought for a plot of land and the chance to help the Monstrous create a new garden.

For years I've been certain there was no hope for me, but what if there is a way to reverse my mutation? Or at least be certain the peeling of my flesh will never spread? For years, I've had nightmares about waking up to find my face and neck

61

as scaled as the rest of my body. Now I have hope that those nightmares might someday be a thing of the past. I could barely sleep last night, I was so eager to begin.

And now the beast is *ruining* the morning by being difficult. That must be what's keeping the guards. Unless . . .

Unless the monster attacked them. Unless they are even now doing battle with it. If that's the case, I'll have the creature's claws cut out.

I should have given the order yesterday when he dared to put his claws to my throat, but I was afraid Junjie would find the guards asleep at their posts and guess at the stupid, impulsive thing I'd done. If he finds out I was alone with the Monstrous, I–

"In the name of that service," Junjie continues, startling me from my thoughts, "I've scheduled your coronation for the week after next."

My lips part. "Week after next? But I–"

"The plans are under way," he says, interrupting me. Again. It seems Baba was the only member of court who thought a blind girl deserved the right to finish her sentences. "Out of respect for the violent nature of the king's death, the celebration will be subdued—simply a short procession and the ceremonial presentation of the crown and scepter. Afterward, you'll be taken onto the dais to be cheered by the common people, and we'll conclude with a banquet in the afternoon, during which the members of court will be able to present themselves to you personally."

I bite my lip and nod my agreement. I want to beg him to postpone for another month or more, but I know it would do no good. Once Junjie has set something in motion, there is no stopping him. He is inexorable. It's one of the qualities my father valued most in his chief advisor.

I, however, have yet to acquire Baba's appreciation for Junjie's single-mindedness. Persuading my advisor to allow me to work in the new garden with the Monstrous—even accompanied by four armed guards—took every bit of stubbornness I possess and then some. If getting my way as ruler is always going to be so difficult, I'll have to choose my battles carefully, or spend the rest of my life in a state of perpetual exhaustion.

"Good girl," Junjie says, his condescension leaving a sour taste in my mouth. I'm *blind,* not simple. *Seventeen,* not seven. "I'll send word to the court dressmaker."

"There's no need. Needle will make my dress." I'm prepared to fight for Needle's right to ply her namesake—she'd be devastated to miss the chance to design my coronation gown—but am saved from the battle by swift footsteps running down the path leading from the infirmary.

I recognize the rhythm of the run as Needle's even before one small, cool hand takes my wrist and the other begins to move beneath my palm, communicating in our secret language.

The boy is hurt, Needle signs, her fingers trembling.

"What boy?"

The Monstrous boy, she signs, proving that everyone—no matter how immense or terrifying—is a child in her eyes until proven otherwise. Needle is only twenty-eight, but you'd think she was sixty from the way she talks. *The guards are forcing him to walk, but his legs are too weak. He's very pale. He'll faint if they don't take him back to bed.*

"Yes, I would like something to drink," I say in a controlled voice, not wanting to arouse Junjie's curiosity. He's too eager for an excuse to forbid me from taking the monster out of his cage. "Would you care for some lemonade, Junjie?"

"I would enjoy that very much," Junjie says, making my stomach clench. I'd expected him to be too busy to spare time for my imaginary refreshment. "But I have many things to attend to. I'll make my apologies and hope to share a drink with you this evening in the banquet hall."

His none-too-subtle hint that I should *not* take dinner in my tower again tonight doesn't escape me, but I'm too grateful to learn he won't be tailing me inside to be bothered by it. With a nod and a softly murmured "Good day," I loop my arm through Needle's and allow her to guide me slowly up the walk.

As soon as we are through the door—stepping into shadows that cool my flushed skin—she takes me by the hand and sets a much swifter pace. I follow her up stairs and stairs and more stairs, nearly as many as there are in my tower, until we reach the top floor, where the Monstrous has been kept separate from the other ill and ailing.

As we hurry down the hall, I expect to hear sounds of a struggle—growls and snarls—but there is only one harsh voice, shouting, "Move, beast! On your feet!" and a muffled thud followed by a moan so piteous, I understand immediately why Needle called the monster a boy. He sounds like a wounded child.

For the first time I wonder what the creature must be feeling. What must it be like to be abandoned by his family, to be held captive and pressed into slavery to people he loathes? To be alone and hurt with no one who cares enough to insist he stay in bed long enough to heal?

This is my fault. I told the guards to drag the Monstrous from his bed if they had to. A wave of self-loathing rushes inside me, making my stomach lurch and my voice break when I order the guards to, "Stop! Leave the monster be!"

I draw a deep breath, trying to compose myself, knowing the soldiers must be staring. "One of you, go fetch the healers. The rest, give the beast some room." I squeeze Needle's arm as one pair of boots tromps down the hall, the guard thankfully obeying my order without question. I can't always trust the soldiers to do as I say, especially if Junjie is close by. I may be the queen, but Junjie is their true leader. "Take me closer," I tell Needle.

I don't need to add *but not too close*. Needle is nothing if not protective of me. She nearly had a fit yesterday when I ordered her to help me meet with the monster in private.

"Where does it hurt?" I ask the Monstrous as Needle settles me on the stones near where he has fallen. "Is it your legs?" The Monstrous doesn't say a word, not a word, for a long, strained moment. "I only want to help you. . . ."

I hesitate, realizing I have no idea what the Monstrous calls himself. He has language, he must have a name, but in the three weeks since he was captured no one has bothered to ask it. "What is your name?"

"Gem," he says, forcing the word out with obvious difficulty.

"Isra," I offer before I think better of it. A prisoner shouldn't call the queen by her first name, but for some reason that seems like a silly rule at the moment. "I'm sorry. I didn't realize you were still unwell."

The Monstrous makes a sound—a sigh or a laugh, I can't tell which. Either way, the message is received. "Sorry" is a feeble word, and hardly sufficient when a person is brought to his knees by pain.

"I don't want you to suffer any more than you have already," I say, hoping he can tell that I mean it. "We'll postpone our work until you've fully recovered."

"What if I'm never recovered?" he asks, so softly that I know only Needle and I can hear him. "What if I never walk again?"

"You will walk."

"You can't know."

"No, I can't," I say. "But I'll do everything in my power to make certain you do."

He sighs again, a defeated sound. An alone sound.

"I wasn't always blind," I say, strangely compelled to convince him I understand his fears. "There was a fire in my bedroom when I was four years old. My nightgown caught fire and my father threw me to the ground to put out the flames. I hit my head, and the world went dark. It has stayed that way ever since."

"But you still see," he says beneath his breath, as if he knows my moment of sightedness in the garden is a secret. "By the roses."

"Only sometimes," I whisper. "And only since I was ten."

My tenth birthday, to be exact, the last day I was knowingly allowed out of the tower. Before then, Baba and I went to the royal garden every year on my birthday, but that was the first year that he let me explore on my own, let me feel my way around the edge of the ancient flower bed to the place where the vines spill over one side.

I pricked my finger by accident, and the sunlit world rushed up to meet me. The roses showed me the city from high above, all the flowers and the green, green springtime grass, and every tall, white building gleaming in the morning light. It was beautiful, breathtaking to a girl who had nearly forgotten the world of color and light.

I would have stayed there forever, grateful tears streaming down my face, if my father hadn't pulled me away.

As soon as he realized I was bleeding, Baba carried me back to the tower, but the damage was already done. I knew the roses had more magic than anyone else realized. I knew they could be my eyes. I told Baba, but he forbade me to speak of such mad things and refused to take me to the garden again. Months passed, but I didn't forget that shining moment. It took a year, but I found a way out, risking death climbing over the edge of my balcony, rather than returning to the hopeless darkness.

The loss of hope is the worst kind of loss. I don't want to be the cause of that in someone, even if that someone is a monster.

"I will help you recover," I say, with an intensity that surprises me. "I swear it."

"Thank you. Isra." My name is uncomfortable in his

mouth, strange-sounding in that accent of his, but there's something nice about it all the same. Something nice about being Isra instead of "my lady."

Before I can assure him there's no need to thank me, the healers arrive. Needle pulls me to my feet, guiding me down the hall after Gem and the healers, fingers busy beneath my palm as she describes the scene. Two male healers carry Gem back to his room, but it is a woman who runs her hands lightly over his legs, examining the Monstrous with a gentleness that Needle approves of.

"How is he?" I ask when the healer is finished.

"There's no bleeding on the inside, my lady," she says. "But the muscles are still healing."

"But they *will* heal. He'll be able to walk again?" I ask, anxious for her answer.

"I don't see any reason why not," the healer says. "He'll need a brace on the left leg and crutches for a time, but the muscles should mend. If I'd been notified he was to work today, I would have had the aids prepared." Her tone is nothing but deferential, but I feel chastised all the same.

"I'll consult with you before we try again," I say. "How much time do you think he needs? A week? Two?"

"He should begin exercising as soon as the leg is braced," she says. "We don't have anything in his size ready-made, but the brace makers work quickly. I can have him fitted this afternoon and able to work tomorrow, my lady."

Brace makers. Surely Yuan doesn't have need of more than one brace maker to service the thousand-odd souls under the dome? But then, maybe people turn ankles and break wrists more often than I assume. There's so much I don't know about my city, my people.

"What do you think, Gem?" I ask. "Will you be up for trying again tomorrow?"

"Does it matter, my lady?" he asks, mimicking the healer's subservient tone perfectly.

I get the strong feeling that he's mocking me, and I scowl, but clench my jaw against the harsh words on the tip of my tongue. He's hurting, and despite the fact that I didn't intend for him to suffer, that hurt is my fault.

"Yes. It matters," I say. "Do you think you'll be ready?"

"Anything to escape these white walls for a few hours," he says, but there's still something . . . off in his voice.

"We can wait. I'm eager to begin, but I don't want you to be in pain."

"That's kind of you, my lady, but I'm also eager to begin." There's a sneer beneath the words this time, I'm sure of it. The only thing I'm not sure of is whether he's wrong to think me contemptible. Yesterday, there was no doubt in my mind which one of us was the monster, but now . . .

I'm the one who neglected to ask his name. *I'm* the one who insisted he be pulled from his bed without consulting the healers to make sure he was fit to work. *I'm* the one who has treated him like an animal when I know that he has language and at least a certain degree of intelligence.

The thoughts make me feel sour inside. They make me wish I could have a moment alone with Gem to speak frankly. I want him to know that I understand what it's like to be a prisoner. That I know what it's like to walk a road I didn't choose to a destination I fear, and that I will do my best to make his life in Yuan tolerable.

But the guards and the healers would never knowingly leave me alone with a Monstrous, and it doesn't matter anyway. I am Gem's jailer and his enemy. Why should he feel anything for me but contempt? He shouldn't. And I shouldn't care one way or another.

"Tomorrow, then," I say, taking Needle's arm and allowing her to lead me from the room. I have enough misery to bear. There's no need to take the hatred of a beast to heart.

But as I walk away, I can't help remembering Gem's cry in the hall, how desperate and human he sounded, and how much something inside me wanted to protect him from the soldiers.

From Yuan. From . . . me.

GEM

THE healer gives me more bitter water to drink, and the agony in my legs fades to a distant ache. My eyes grow heavy, but I fight the muddying of my thoughts. I don't want to sleep.

I want to lie here and stare at the white wall until my mind is as soft as windswept sand. Then I will bury all my hate deep beneath it, so deep that not even an outline can be spied from the surface. The queen may be blind, but she saw through me. I have to try harder.

She was kind today, open in a way she hasn't been before. She even confirmed my suspicion that the roses' magic gave her the power to see for that moment in the garden. I should have welcomed her confidence. I should have shared a story of my own. I should have done *something* to begin the long journey to earning her trust.

Instead I mocked her. I mocked her because the worry in her eyes hurt more than my legs. Because her promises to help made me hate her more than I did before.

It's too late for kindness. No amount of kindness can change who she is or what her people have done to mine. Her moment of compassion only proved she's worse than I first assumed. To be cold and incapable of pity is one thing; to have compassion and use it only when it's convenient is nothing less than evil.

I hate her so much my body aches with it, but I hate myself more. I hate that I felt even a moment of pity for that little girl with her nightgown on fire, or for the queen whose guards roll their eyes before obeying her commands. No warrior of my tribe would ever treat his chief with such a lack of respect, but the soldiers clearly feel no need to conceal their disdain from the blind queen or her silent attendant.

Or from the monster whimpering on the floor.

They should be more careful. Everything I see and hear is my weapon. Everything. From their disdain, to the way the silent woman's fingers move with words, to the flash of guilt in the queen's eyes.

"Isra's eyes," I correct myself aloud. "Isra."

I practice saying her name again and again, until it sounds the way it did when she said it, until I sound like a Smooth Skin, until I fall asleep with her name on my lips and dream of sand.

Thick, warm sand, rising up my thighs, trapping my chest, spilling into my nose and mouth. Burying me alive.

SIX

ISRA

"HERE. Use the middle fork," Bo says, pressing a utensil with a smooth bone-covered handle into my hand. "The spoon is only for soup."

"Thank you," I mumble, cheeks flaming as I run my fingertips over the heavily glazed duck on my plate, searching for a place to aim my fork. By the moons, I *know* which utensil to use. I was simply trying to spare myself the embarrassment of dirtying yet *another* napkin.

Whoever planned the menu for my coronation should be cast out of the royal kitchens in disgrace. They couldn't have made the meal more challenging for their queen if they'd tried. I've already spilled soup on my dress, sent half a boiled carrot leaping off my plate when I tried to cut it, and dirtied four napkins with my sauce-covered fingers. And there is no doubt that every member of court observed my failure. The banquet hall is positively buzzing.

Buzz, buzz, buzz—the noise in the great room builds like a swarm of bees, rattling my nerves, killing my appetite, stinging the skin on my face, the *only* skin left completely exposed on this momentous day.

The sleeves of my coronation dress fall to my wrists; my skirt brushes the floor. My hands were encased in silk gloves until I was forced to remove them for the feast, and my feet are snug inside new slippers. Even my legs are bundled into thick cotton stockings. If I trip and my dress rises up, Needle and I wanted to be sure every inch of tainted flesh was covered.

We were so careful, with my dress, with my hair—slicked into a bun so tight it's impossible to tell how wild my curls usually are—but all the preparations were a waste of time. I'm still taller than every whole citizen of Yuan. I'm still big-boned and sharp-featured, with hands too large and lips too wide and eyes too sunken.

The common people saw me for the tainted thing I was the moment I stepped out on the dais. They gasped. One shocked collective breath, followed by a silence so thick and terrible I would have turned and fled if I'd been sure where I was going.

The cheering and clapping started soon after, and Needle insisted the people were simply surprised by how "lovely" and "exotic" I looked, but it was too late for her kind lies to make a difference. I know the truth. My people are horrified by their queen. Yuan has never had a tainted ruler. I am the first, the contemptible offspring of the king's mad second wife. Her insanity almost cost the people their lives, and now her tainted daughter sullies their throne.

I'm sure they're all praying I will die before having children of my own. As long as I'm married, the covenant will be secure. My king will be able to remarry, and the poor noble girl forced to wed him will take on the mantle of sacrifice.

Sacrifice. Blood and bones. That's all I am.

The common people cheered, and the nobles have spent the feast flattering me, but the truth is that none of them sees me as anything but a walking dead girl. There have been queens who ruled with wisdom and power, but none of them were tainted. Or blind. Or locked away and hidden from the people. I will have to be truly extraordinary to lift myself above all my failings.

"Should I have the servants bring more sweet wine?" Bo asks, laying a hand on my wrist and letting it linger there too long.

"No, thank you." I pull my hand away, scratching between my sticky fingers to cover my escape.

The more wine Bo drinks, the more familiar he becomes, ensuring that I can't help remembering the kiss he stole when he was the first to know I was queen. In hindsight, that kiss is nothing if not suspicious. For twenty years, Junjie has been the most powerful man in Yuan aside from the king. There's nowhere left for him to rise except to the throne. He's already married and too old to wed me himself, but I'm sure he finds his son an acceptable substitute.

"You are beautiful tonight," Bo whispers, his wine and rosemary breath warm on my cheek. "Your eyes are like springtime."

"Thank you," I mumble, struggling to keep my expression from going sour. There's nothing wrong with Bo's lies. They're pretty lies. Kind lies.

There's nothing wrong with him wanting to be king, either. Someone will be my king. It might as well be Bo. He is solicitous and flattering. Our marriage would make his father happy, and the people relieved. It would fulfill my duty as a daughter of the covenant, and secure the future of the city. All good reasons to relax and let his hands linger, but for some reason my body remains tense no matter how much wine I drink.

"May I walk you to your rooms tonight?" Bo asks, his arm snaking around my shoulders, trapping me in my chair.

Around us, the buzzing grows hushed for a moment before resuming at a more insistent drone. The nobles are talking about me. They've been talking about me since Needle led me to my chair on the raised platform at the center of the room. The hall eventually grew too noisy to pick out individual words, but before it did, I heard more than enough.

Words like "large" and "mad" and "mother." Words like "sad" and "strange" and "frightful."

"Would that be all right?" Bo's fingers grip my shoulder, making my pulse speed. I feel like a rabbit trapped beneath a falcon's claws. Prey. Something to be consumed.

. . . get her married . . .
. . . glad it's not my son . . .
. . . an embarrassment . . .

The scraps of drunken conversation are arrows flying through the roasted-duck-perfumed air, finding their marks in my heart.

I take a deep breath and remember the smell of the newly broken ground in my healing garden. I remember the feel of the plow handles beneath my palms, the sound of Gem's new brace squeaking as he walks, his gravel-and-grit voice telling stories of his tribe while we work the rocky dirt by the Desert Gate.

Dry grass is all that's ever grown there, and I know Junjie doubts anything else ever will, but a patch of land is a small price to pay for an absent queen. And why shouldn't I be absent? It's becoming increasingly clear that no one intends to take me seriously. There might as well be a stuffed toy sitting on the throne, for all the attention my advisors pay me when I dare to speak up during their interminable meetings. There's no point in fighting them. I'd rather leave the running of things to Junjie and the other cranky old men.

And so I have my field and my Monstrous to help me tend it, and four guards to watch over me while I work, and Junjie meets with the other advisors and the nobles and soldiers and farmers and shopkeepers alone, without a blind girl getting in his way.

I find the garden a more-than-satisfying use of my time. The work is hard but simple, and Gem has proven himself capable of making the best of his captivity. He is cordial and pleasant and appreciative of the efforts I make on his behalf. Best of all, with Gem, I never have to worry about what I look like.

Heard she's hiding . . . sickening . . . underneath. The whispers grow louder, harsher.

"Isra?"

Repulsive . . . never . . . large. My fork falls to my plate with a dull clink. *Strange . . . mad . . . unnat—*

I push my chair back, shrugging Bo's arm from my shoulders as I stand. If I don't escape this room, I'm going to explode.

"Isra? Are you—?"

"I need some fresh air." I hold out my hand, grateful when Needle's fingers immediately appear beneath. "I'll be back in a moment. Have them bring more sweet wine."

I squeeze Needle's hand, and she immediately sets off at a brisk but reasonable pace, leading me down the platform steps, weaving between the tables scattered throughout the hall.

Conversations stop as I pass by, and I swear I can feel the nobles' eyes raking up and down my long body, clawing at my dress, hoping to catch a glimpse of the scaled skin they've heard rumors about, eager for me to do something wild and uncivilized.

I hold my head higher and press the tip of my tongue to the roof of my mouth. I won't cry. I won't get angry. I won't give them any reason to bring up the older stories, the ones about how I abused the women sent to care for me after my

78

mother's death, or the way I howled like a Monstrous from the balcony of my tower in the middle of the night, giving the city children nightmares.

I can't remember that time—I was only four years old, by the moons!—but Needle warned me that the stories live on. My people are waiting for a reason to believe I'm still that feral creature, that girl as tainted on the inside as on the outside.

As soon as we're out of sight of the banquet hall, Needle begins to sign.

Are you all right?

"I'm ready to leave."

You can't leave. Not without—

"I am queen. I can do what I wish," I snap, pulling my arm away, only for her to reclaim it a second later. "Leave me!" I demand. "I can find my way from here."

But your guards. They're still at the banquet. They will want to—

"I am perfectly capable of getting back to my rooms without guards," I say, voice rising as I pull away a second time. "Why do I need guards, anyway? Who would dare harm the *sacrifice*?"

Needle sighs her sad sigh but doesn't try to retake my arm, and soon I hear her footsteps hurrying away toward the tower. She knows better than to argue with me. Arguing is pointless. I am stubborn and selfish, and once I've made up my mind, I will not be swayed.

For a moment, I feel bad for taking my anger out on my only friend, but soon I'm too distracted by the pain in my toes to think of anything else.

My slippers are too tight. I told Needle they were too tight, but she insisted they were the same size I've worn for a year, and shoved them onto my feet. Now they pinch so badly, I'm hobbling by the time I near the royal garden. I stop, bend down, and rip them from my feet with a growl that turns to a moan of relief as soon as my toes are allowed to spread on the cool stones.

Ah. So much better. "Stupid things," I mutter as I toss the slippers into the flowers lining the path.

"Good choice," comes a voice from high above, making me draw a surprised breath. "Who needs shoes in a soft world like this one?"

"Gem?" I ask, though I know it's him by the pronunciation of the word "shoes." His accent is changing, but still, no one else under the dome sounds like him. "Where are you?"

"In my new room," he answers. "New *rooms*. There are two. One for sitting, one for sleeping."

"They gave you the apartment overlooking the gardens?" I ask, tilting my face in the direction of his voice.

I gave the order for Gem to be transferred to the soldiers' barracks a few days past. I requested that the apartment with the view of the royal garden be converted to a cell—Gem mentioned that he'd like to see the roses again—but there was some grumbling from Junjie about whether such a prime space could be spared.

I told him to find a way to spare it and left it at that, but I wasn't sure he'd take my order seriously. Junjie seems to treat my commands as suggestions he'll take into consideration. If he remembers. If he approves. If it's convenient.

"They did," Gem says. "Thank you."

"You like it, then?" I ask, craving approval in this night filled with condemnation.

"I do. Very much."

"I know there are still bars on the windows, but . . ."

"It doesn't matter. The view is nice. And I like the books," he says, before adding in an almost shy tone, "I've been trying to read them. My mother taught me your letters and the sounds they make. It's not as difficult as I thought it would be."

"I'm sure you'll figure it out soon," I say, feeling a little envious. "I wish I could read. Being read to is wonderful, but I always thought the stories would go faster if I could see the words myself."

"I'm not very fast."

"You will be. You're clever." He is. More clever than I could have imagined before we started working in the garden together. The past two weeks have only confirmed how foolish I was to underestimate Gem. He has a vast knowledge of plants, speaks our language with the fluency of a noble, and has more stories memorized than I've had read to me in my life.

"Soon you'll have even more stories to add to your collection," I say, trying to smile. "You'll have to tell me your favorites."

"Of course," he says, before adding in a softer voice, "What's wrong? You don't sound like yourself."

I lean against the retaining wall, and reach out, running my fingers over the wilting petals of the last of the autumn clematis. "I've done foolish things tonight."

"What kind of foolish things?"

"I was mean to Needle," I say, tears stinging my eyes for the millionth time since my father died. "I shouldn't have been. She's always so patient with me."

"She'll forgive you," he says, the lack of judgment in his tone making me feel even worse.

"I know," I mumble, wishing I hadn't said anything. No matter how well we've been getting along, or how much more human Gem is than I could have dreamed a Monstrous would be, it was stupid to start confessing things to him. He's not my friend; he's my prisoner.

"What else?" he asks.

"Nothing," I say, lingering when I know I should tell him good night and be on my way. But I'm not in any hurry to return to the tower or Needle, who I know will be waiting by the door with her sad sigh, ready to gently remind me of everything I did wrong tonight.

I know I have to apologize and endure the reminders, but I'm not ready. Not yet.

"I don't believe you." Gem's voice holds a challenge I refuse to take.

"Tell me a story," I say instead, forcing a smile. Storytelling is what built the bridge between Gem and me in the first place. I began it as a way to break the strained silence during our first day in the garden, but Gem soon took the lead. He is a gifted storyteller and obviously appreciates a receptive audience. He has never refused me a story. "A happy story, please."

"What kind of happy story?"

"One of your people's legends. One with wind in it."

He falls quiet, but I don't repeat myself. I know he's putting his thoughts together and that it will be worth the wait. Gem's stories are always wonderful, mysterious and magical and eerily familiar, stories my heart swears I've heard before even if my mind can't remember them.

"Once, long ago, in the early days of my tribe, there was a girl who loved a star," he begins, summoning a delicious shiver from deep in my bones. I pull myself up to sit on the edge of the wall and draw my legs to my chest beneath my dress, grateful Needle gave me a full skirt rather than one of the narrow ones that make me teeter when I walk.

"It was a summer star," Gem continues once I'm comfortable. "And it appeared in the sky just as the summer grass turned brown. It burned a fierce orange and red, and spent its nights boasting of all the worlds it had known and the creatures who had loved it.

"All the girls in the tribe enjoyed gazing at the star, but one girl, Melita, was captivated at first glance," he says, the lulling rhythm of his words easing the last of the tension from my shoulders. "Every evening, she would creep from her family's hut and lie down in the grass beneath the star. They would talk late into the night, telling each other their secret hopes and dreams, their messages carried between land and sky by the west wind.

"The girl told the star how she wished to journey beyond her tribe's lands and see things no Desert Girl had ever seen before. The star told the girl how he yearned for someone with arms brave enough to hold him, strong enough to wrap around him at the close of the day and hold on until morning.

"Eventually, the two grew so filled with longing that the star's wish was granted. The girl opened her arms and called him from the sky, and with a sigh, he fell, burning a trail through the night as his flame went out, leaving only his bone-white body behind."

I drop my chin to my knees and close my eyes, suddenly feeling shy of this story.

It's a love story. Gem has never told me a love story. It feels more intimate than his other tales. Sadder, too. I haven't imagined the Monstrous loving the way we love, but I suppose they must. It makes me wonder if there is someone Gem left behind, a Monstrous girl whose arms he imagines holding him until morning. . . .

"The next morning, the girl awoke to find the star weeping in the grass," Gem continues. "He had already grown tired of the girl's arms. He craved the eyes of every creature of this world and the next and the next. He mourned the loss of his spark and shine and the glory of burning brighter than anything else in the night. He cursed the girl, blaming her for his fall, and left her so he could find his way back to the sky, abandoning her long before the girl's belly began to round with the new star he had put inside her."

I blush so hard, my cheeks tingle. Heat spreads from my face, down my neck, to make my skin itch beneath my clothes. *The new star he had put inside her.* By the moons. Yuan's storytellers would never say such a bold thing. If Needle were here, she'd be scandalized.

The knowledge makes the story a bit more delicious.

"Months passed, and the time came for the baby to be born. It was a cold night, near the end of winter, and both of the tribe's midwives came to the girl's hut, but the girl could not be saved," Gem says. "After hours of suffering, the star baby came from her in a rush of fire, killing his mother as he shot toward the sky."

I lift my head, lips parting in silent protest. Surely this can't be the end of the story, the poor girl dying in childbirth?

"The west wind saw the tragic birth," Gem continues, "and wished he had never carried the girl's whispers to the star father. He plucked the girl's soul from her burning flesh and held her in his arms, offering her a breath of his own magic to prove how sorry he was for the part he'd played. The girl used the magic to steal the language of our people from the stars, ensuring that no other Desert Girl would hear a star's false promises or fall in love with one of the fickle creatures ever again.

"But still, the west wind felt his debt had not been paid. And so, from that day forward, he has continued to share his magic. He still comes to the Desert People as their funeral fires burn, granting each of us one last wish. And that is how we were given death magic, and why our deaths are cause for celebration as well as sadness."

He falls silent, but the air still hums with the power of the legend.

"*That* is a happy story?" I ask after an outraged moment.

"It is," he says, a hint of laughter in his voice. "One of our happiest."

"You're mad!" I protest. "That poor girl. And whatever happened to the star?"

"He became the star of the true north," Gem says. "And, in honor of his mother, he has guided the lost home to the tribal lands for hundreds of years."

"No. I meant the other star, the one who left the girl alone to die."

"He returned to the heavens," Gem says. "He continues to fill the summer sky with orange and red, and unsuspecting women with babies. He put a baby in the harvest moon that has refused to be born for hundreds of years, for fear of hurting its mother, but that's another legend."

I'm about to say how unfair it was for the girl to die and the star to live on unpunished, but I stop myself before the words can leave my mouth. Of course it's not fair, but . . . that's the way life is. Gem and I know that as well as anyone.

Gem and I. We have more in common than I ever dreamed we would. Sometimes, it feels like I have more in common with him than I do my own people. Sometimes, I wish he wasn't my prisoner and that we were more than polite acquaintances. Sometimes, I wish we could be friends.

But we can't. And my only true friend is alone in the tower, waiting for me to apologize for acting like a spoiled child.

"I should go. Thank you for the story," I say, tossing the words over my shoulder as I unwind my legs and start down the path, trailing my fingers along the wall to guide me.

"Good night, Isra," Gem calls, something in the way he says my name making the hairs on my neck prickle.

I lift my hand and wave good-bye as I make my way into the heart of the royal garden, careful to give the rose bed a wide berth. Gem may have guessed that the roses allow me to see, but I'm not prepared for an audience while availing myself of their magic.

I didn't plan to stop here tonight, anyway. I haven't pricked my finger since the night the Monstrous invaded the city five weeks past. The unrelieved darkness weighs on me, but not as heavy as the memory of the hunger I felt pulling at me that night. The roses are tired of being teased with a drop or two of what they crave; they grow eager for a proper feeding.

"It isn't time," I whisper as I pass them by. It isn't. Not for years and years.

I know I'm right, but still, I shiver as I step into the orchard. The air beneath the dome feels colder than it did a few moments ago, and I wish I'd brought the shawl Needle tried to press into my hands as we left the tower.

Autumn is dying, and winter will be here all too soon, a fact I would be wise to remember the next time I'm tempted to throw my shoes into a flower bed or linger listening to stories that have nothing to do with my people or our life beneath the dome.

WINTER

SEVEN

ISRA

"THE ground will be ready soon," Gem says, his words under-scored by the steady *chip, chap* of his hoe as it breaks up the soil that has proven too stubborn for our plow.

I follow behind him on my hands and knees, gathering clumps of grass, rocks, and springy roots in my giant pock-ets. Needle stitched me a new pair of overalls—in mourning green—but I wear them only out here, in the loneliest corner of the city, by the Desert Gate. I like it out here. It's quiet and peaceful, and the guards hardly bother Gem and me at all anymore.

After a month with no show of claws, the soldiers began taking turns at Gem's side. After eight weeks, they watch our progress from chairs at the edge of the field. Bo tells me one of them always has a blow tube and a sedative dart ready, but I'm not so sure. I catch snippets of their conversations, and it sounds like they're more focused on card games than protecting their queen.

No matter how valuable my life is to the city, boredom eventually won out over duty. Knowing Gem as I do, I'm betting that's part of his plan.

He has a plan. A secret. I'd bet my hands on it. I know him better than he thinks I do. You don't spend every afternoon with someone—listening to his stories and teaching him songs—without learning a thing or two about the way his mind works.

"The herbs can be put off a month or two, but not the bulbs." Gem speaks our language like he was raised in the city now. There is nothing growly or rough about him. He is the perfect gentleman. Gentle-Monstrous.

"We need to get them into the ground," he continues. "They should be planted while it's still cold."

"It will be cold forever." A part of me believes it. Spring is a promise that nature doesn't intend to keep.

"It won't be cold forever."

"It will. My nose will never be warm again."

"Good thing blue suits you," he says, making my lips twitch. "Have you spoken to Junjie?"

"I speak to him every day. Several times a day. Whether I like it or not."

92

"You know what I mean."

I sigh. "I do." I sit back on my heels and tilt my face up, soaking in what warmth I can from the weak winter light penetrating the dome. Our great shield is made of ancient glass, designed by our ancestors to block the damaging rays of the sun, specially treated to keep the city from growing too hot during the summer or too cold during the winter. Still, the air is chilly in the winter months.

According to Gem, it's even colder in the desert. If it weren't for the risk of Monstrous attack, it would be possible for a citizen of Yuan to venture outside the city for a short time without fearing sun damage.

But there *is* the risk of attack. Gem's tribe is only one of many. The other tribes—those farther to the east and the south—have left our city in peace until now, but they wouldn't hesitate to kill a Smooth Skin found wandering their lands. I can't ask the soldiers to put their lives in danger, and Junjie will never allow Gem through the gate alone. His people have withdrawn deep into the wilds. They've left our city alone, as they promised, and Gem is the reason. Junjie won't risk having our good-luck charm running off into the desert, never to return.

I would agree with him, but I know Gem's legs aren't healing as well as we'd hoped. He can't stand for more than a few hours at a time—hence the slow pace of our ground breaking. He would never make it to his people's winter camp on foot, but he *could* make it to the mountains where the bulbs we need grow, and back to the Hill Gate. And he *would* come back. He doesn't want to die of starvation in the desert. He's as committed to living as the people of Yuan.

So committed, he nearly has me convinced that he doesn't hate me anymore.

Nearly.

I haven't hated *him* for a long time. I like how steady he is with his work, how he hums beneath his breath when he hoes, the stories he tells, the jokes he makes about Yuan and our abundance of cabbage, even the way he teases me about my big hands and clumsy feet. I like *him.* Sadly, aside from Needle, my monster prisoner is the best friend I've ever had.

"Isra? The bulbs?"

"Tell me a story," I say. "Something scary where terrible things happen to bad creatures."

"If I can't leave the city, I can't get the bulbs or seeds we'll need," Gem says, refusing to play along the way he usually does.

"I know. I've known that since we started." I scratch at my wrist, wincing as paper-thin pieces of myself fall away. My skin is worse than ever. The winter never agrees with it, but this winter has been especially brutal. Needle washes the skin everywhere but my face and neck twice a day in milk and honey, but still, I'm falling to pieces. "Well . . ." I force myself to stop scratching with a sigh. "You'll just have to leave the city, I suppose."

"When?" There's hunger in his voice. Is it hunger for escape or simply for a few hours of freedom? I don't know, and I don't want to know. In the past two months, my time with Gem has become the bright spot in my day. If he were to leave . . .

"Remember your promise," I say softly. "You're to stay here. Forever."

"There's no such thing as forever," he says. "And I promised nothing. No one speaks for me. Not even my father."

"Psh." I pick the rocks from my pocket, chucking them out into the grass at the edge of the field one by one. I'll have to pick them up again later, but I don't care. It will give me more time to figure out what to do about the seeds. "Parents make promises for their children all the time. I was promised to this city before I was even conceived."

"And it's clear how pleased you are by it," he says.

"Don't let Junjie hear you say that."

"Why not? Why not tell him yourself, and let them find another queen?"

My arm falters, and the rock in my hand falls. "That's not the way it works," I say, running my fingers along the ground until I find the stone again. "You know that by now."

He grunts. "Well, then . . . why not leave? The desert wind isn't something any living thing should do without," he says, dangling the words like bait on the end of a line.

"A blind girl. In the desert. Alone. That sounds like a wonderful plan, Gem, but I have responsibilities here," I say, wishing I'd never let him know how much I crave the feel of the wind on my face. I throw my rock. Hard, using the full strength in my long arm. "Besides, I need this garden. A mutant queen isn't good for the city."

95

He's quiet for a long, strained moment that makes my skin start to itch all over again.

"Yes?" I ask, recognizing his "about to say something Isra won't like" silence. "What is it?"

"It's . . . I'm not sure the garden will give you what you're looking for."

I cross my legs, letting my heavy pockets flop at my sides as I tilt my chin up, fixing him with my full attention. "But the herbs and bulbs we'll plant will reverse or inhibit mutation," I remind him. "You've said so yourself. What about the Monstrous babies born with scales covering their eyes? And the boys whose teeth would grow too large to fit their mouths without the herbs your healers administer when they're children?"

"The healing pouches have helped my people," he says, groaning as he settles on the ground across from me. His legs seem to hurt the most when he's standing up or sitting down. "But you are what you are. There's no changing that."

"Maybe not, but there's a chance to stop it before it gets any worse." I drop my voice to a whisper, suddenly very conscious of the soldiers across the field. "I'm . . . growing."

"And?" Gem asks in a way that makes it clear he thinks I'm being ridiculous.

"I'm already the tallest person in the city, and I'm still growing," I say, wishing I had a rock left to chuck at him. "My new mourning dresses are bursting at the seams. I thought Needle had made a mistake in her sewing, but her measurements were correct when she took them four months ago. She didn't think to re-measure. I'm sure she assumed it was impossible for me to get any bigger."

"My people grow until eighteen or older. Isn't it the same for Smooth Skins?"

"No, it's not," I say, though I'm not completely sure, not having been around any growing girls besides Needle and not remembering when my maid stopped stretching. "At least not the way I am. But it's not only me I'm worried about. It's come to my attention that there are others who need this garden even more than I do."

Others who will be grateful for the work I'm doing here, and who will help me prove that I am a true queen, more than a sacrifice or an entertaining source of gossip.

"What others?"

"The other tainted, the ones with more severe mutations. The rest of the city won't tolerate them," I say, anxiety rising in my chest. "Bo says their situation is worse than I knew."

Baba told me about the Banished, but he never told me how cruelly they were treated. Bo was surprised that I didn't know the rules for the outcasts. I lied and told him that Baba rarely discussed city matters with me, but I'm sure Bo guessed the real reason the king kept the worst aspects of the Banished camp from his daughter. He didn't want to frighten me, or make me worry what might have become of me if I weren't so valuable to the city.

If my father had remarried and given Yuan another queen, and if the court advisors had reviewed my case and found me sufficiently tainted, I might be living in that camp today.

"They live on the outskirts, and are fed and watered like

animals." I swallow hard and continue. "They can't own shops or work in the orchards or come near our animals or children. They can't have children of their own or seek help from the healers. Their lives are often . . . cut short. I would like to help them."

Gem growls something in his language, really *growls* for the first time since the day he threatened to open my throat. "And you call *my* people monsters."

I flinch. He's right. I didn't realize how right until I met him.

I had always taken for granted that the texts on the Monstrous were correct and that outer mutation was a sign of a corrupt soul, of being not entirely human. But that clearly isn't always the case. There is nothing hideous about Gem's soul. The same might not be said for all his people–certainly not for the one who slaughtered my father–but for Gem, ugliness is superficial. Surely it could be the same with the people forced into the camp at the edge of the city. If a Monstrous can be so human, surely some of those Banished citizens of Yuan are more human still.

"It isn't fair, I know," I say. "But–"

"And why are these people cast out?" he asks. "Because they have scaled skin or are bigger than the other children?"

"I don't know. It was all decided before I was born. But I *do* know this . . ." I drop my voice again. "Because of me . . . my . . . Some of the nobles worry that mutations might be catching, beginning to infect those who have always been immune. But if I can show them there's a cure . . . or at least a way to slow the process . . ." I clear my throat.

It's difficult to talk about this with Gem. He doesn't realize how repulsive the Monstrous are to my people. He doesn't think it odd that the Monstrous grow plants to impede mutation but use them only for babies born with scales covering their eyes, or in other rare cases where health is threatened. He seems to think his people are beautiful.

"That's why I need this garden," I say, tugging another chunk of grass from the earth and stuffing it into my pocket. "Why the city needs this garden."

"They don't need a garden. They need a queen."

I blink in the direction of his voice. "What does that mean?"

"You have more power than you think. You could put a stop to this with a word."

"I couldn't." I shiver at the thought. I can't even convince Junjie to change the seating arrangement in the great hall so that I don't have to eat on a pedestal at the center of all the gossip.

"Division makes a people weak," he says. "My chief would never allow this."

"You don't understand. I'm queen, but I'm not–"

"Excuses." He grunts as he struggles to stand.

"It's *not* an excuse," I say, not sure whether to be offended or hurt. "I'm tainted. Not as badly as those who are banished, but the whole people still won't listen to me. They'll think–"

"It doesn't matter what they think." The sound of his hoe being flung onto the dirt makes me flinch. "It only matters that they do what–"

"Move away from the queen!" The shout comes from the

edge of the field, making me flinch again. *Bo.* I didn't know he was here. He wasn't with the other soldiers when they arrived with Gem.

But he's been doing this lately, materializing wherever I happen to be. He says it's because his father asked him to keep a "special eye" on me. *A special eye.* I don't like the sound of it.

"It's all right!" I call. "We're only talking."

"We're finished talking." Gem is already shuffling away. The rattle of the chains hobbling his feet makes the skin at the back of my neck bunch. I hate that sound. I hate that I've never had the courage to ask for the chains to be removed. "Tell the guards I'm ready to go back to my cell."

"Are you all right?" Bo squats beside me, his swift breath ruffling the hair above my ear. I want to swat it away like an insect, but I don't. Bo hasn't done anything inappropriate. Not really.

"I'm fine," I say, forcing a smile.

It's not Bo's fault that I'm having a difficult time embracing our impending betrothal. Junjie hasn't said anything outright, but his machinations aren't as subtle as he believes. Bo is always seated next to me at dinner, always the one chosen to deliver messages to my rooms, and the only guard allowed to be alone with me. As soon as my mourning is over, Junjie will be at the tower door with official betrothal documents in hand, asking me to sign away what little freedom I've enjoyed since Baba's death.

Bo is a good man, a good boy—only nineteen, the same age as Gem—but even good men can make cruel jailers. My father locked my mother in the tower for months before she made her fatal escape, and he held me prisoner for years. What if Bo proves to be a king who prefers his wife kept under lock and key?

I know it's my duty to marry as soon as custom allows, but I can't help wishing I had more time to adjust to the idea, to adjust to Bo. He's attentive and flattering, but aside from his opinions on wine and music, I don't know much about him. I can't seem to scratch the surface to find out what—if anything—lies beneath.

Winter, as miserable as it is, can't pass slowly enough this year.

"Are you sure?" Bo asks.

"I'm sure." I brush the dirt from my hands, moving a degree away from him in the process. "Gem's only tired. His legs hurt. He needs an escort back to his rooms."

"Right away." Bo calls to the other soldiers, clearly relieved to be rid of our prisoner. He's spoken to Gem a few times, but never more than a word or two. Gem obviously makes him uncomfortable. I know Bo would welcome an excuse to tell his father I shouldn't be allowed to work with the Monstrous anymore.

That knowledge makes me careful to remain calm as I call—

"Gem?"

"Yes, my lady?" The words are crisp, cutting in their politeness. I'm the one who told him he must call me "my lady" when other people are around, but at the moment I hate the sound of the words.

"Will you come to work tomorrow?"

"You're the queen, my lady," he says. "You don't have to *ask.*"

"I *want* to ask." I mimic his sugary tone exactly, down to the hint of a snarl hiding beneath. "Wouldn't your chief *ask*?"

"I don't know, my lady. My chief doesn't keep slaves." He shuffles away, the rattle of his chains banishing any whisper of protest.

He's right. He *is* a slave. But what can I do to change that, when I'm not much more than a slave myself? I can work on this healing garden and do what I can to help my people, but I will never fundamentally change Yuan. In a city bought with blood, certain things will never change. *Can* never change. If they did, the city and her bickering people and hungry roses would cease to exist.

I fold my arms around myself, cold despite the layers I put on before leaving the tower. I'm always cold, lately. There never seems to be enough fire or hot tea or ginger soup to thaw the things frozen inside.

"What's wrong?" Bo's hand warms my knee. He's settled down to sit on the ground beside me, a strange thing for a soldier to do, but I'm grateful. I'm not ready to stand. "Are you really all right?"

"I told you, I'm fine." I smile to soften the frustration in my voice. "Gem and I had a disagreement. Nothing to worry about."

"A monster shouldn't quarrel with a queen."

"Why not?" I laugh my new bitter laugh. My parsnip

laugh—sour and gritty. "Everyone else does. Even Needle, and she can't speak."

"Do you want a new maid?" he asks, making my heart skip a beat. "I know a wonderful girl, a noble, who mentioned she'd be honored to—"

"No, no," I hurry to say. "I love Needle. She's devoted to me. It's nothing like that. It's . . ." I brush the hair from my face with an angry whip of my fingers. "Forget I said anything. Please. I'm not myself."

"Are you ill?"

"No, I . . ." My stone-filled pockets suddenly feel heavier. "I'm just . . . tired."

"And dirty." Bo cups my chin in his hand. "I've never seen a lady of the court who enjoys dirt as much as you."

"I'm not a lady of the court. I'm a lady of the tower."

"Not anymore," he says.

"Always." I turn my head, breaking contact. His touch still makes me nervous, and his hands feel even softer than usual.

"Isra . . ." His sigh blasts my neck like a wave of heat from the fire. I curl away, brushing my ear with my shoulder. "I need to tell you something. I think . . . I wanted to ask . . ."

My pulse picks up. Have I been wrong about Junjie and Bo waiting until my mourning is over? What if Bo asks me to marry him right here, right now? What will I do? What will I say?

I will say yes, of course, but how? Should I say I hope we'll be friends? That I hope our marriage will be a happy one? That I look forward to our wedding day—but not our wedding night, because I've heard he has a reputation with the ladies at court, and that petrifies me, because how will a girl whose entire experience consists of one wet kiss ever compare to all the girls, and *women,* he's already been with?

No. I can't say that. *Of course* I can't.

I lick my lips, preparing to give him his answer and hoping it comes out right.

And then he asks, "Does your maid take breakfast with you?" and I feel like a fool.

"Excuse me?" My forehead wrinkles.

"Does Needle take food or drink from your tray?"

"No. Needle has her own tray." I don't understand what he's getting at, but I don't see any harm in telling the truth. "It's brought before mine. She wakes early."

"That's what I thought," he says in his stone-plunking voice.

"I don't understand."

"Don't drink your morning tea."

Plunkier still. "What?"

"Stop drinking your morning tea. Get rid of it," he whispers, leaning close enough for me to smell the cabbage on his breath. "Pour it into the plants on your balcony or into your bed pot or someplace no one will think to look."

The casual mention of my bed pot makes me cough awkwardly into the crook of my arm. I'm far from shy, but I've never discussed my bed pot with anyone. *Ever.* "And why should I do that?"

"So that no one will realize you're not drinking it."

My skin crawls beneath my shawl, but I refuse to scratch

it. "Are you . . ." I swallow, shaking my head as I understand what he's implying. "No. No one would try to poison me. I'm the queen. I have no husband, no children. If I die now, the city–"

"Not all poisons kill, Isra." He takes my hand, his thicker, fatter fingers cushioning my longer, thinner ones like ten little pillows. "I may be wrong, but please, indulge me. Pour out the tea for a week, maybe two. That should be enough to know."

"Know what?"

"I think you'll see," he says, a smile in his voice. "I hope so, anyway. I hope many things for you."

"What kind of things?" I ask, a little breathless.

"You'll see," he repeats in that same cryptic tone.

"Bo, I . . ." I pull my hand from his. I want to believe Bo has my best interests at heart, but the idea that someone has been poisoning me . . . it's too strange. I feel *fine,* the same as I always have. Mostly.

Except for the exhaustion. And the creeping certainty that winter will never end. And the troubling stretching of my bones, and the dresses with popped seams.

Could that be it? Could someone be slipping something into my tea to accelerate my mutation? Is that why I grew nearly three centimeters and put on ten catties in the past two months? Gem and I are planning to grow herbs and roots that will impede mutation. It makes sense that plants exist that would amplify the process.

I want to ask Bo if that's what he believes is happening, and why someone might do such a thing, but I can't. I can't discuss my defects with any whole citizen of Yuan. I am the

empress without clothes, and no one can speak of my naked-
ness, not even me.

"All right. I'll do it," I say, rising to my feet. "I'll dispose
of the tea."

"Thank you."

"I should be thanking *you*." I try to smile but can't. I've
gone too sour. I'm past parsnip, bittering to a turnip inside. "I
should change for dinner," I say, backing away.

"Let me escort you."

"Thank you, but I can find my way. I'd rather go alone."
Or as alone as I ever am, considering that the guards at the
edge of the field will be shadowing my every move. Since the
night I slipped away from them at the coronation banquet,
they've been careful not to lose track of me. "I'll find you later.
In the hall," I say.

I turn and walk away, counting my steps to the edge of
the field. I wouldn't *really* rather go alone. I just don't want to
go with Bo. Or any other member of court, or any of the soft,
silky, whole citizens of Yuan.

I'm filled with a sudden longing for Gem. Only with him
is it safe to be the ugly thing I am. He's the only one I can talk
to, the only one who tells me anything close to the truth. And
now I've made him hate me all over again.

But perhaps I can do something to make amends. Perhaps . . .

He craves a walk beyond the walls. Maybe I can give that
to him. The state of the Banished camp isn't the only thing
I've learned from Bo. I've also learned the location of a hid-

den gate, the King's Gate, created to provide an escape route for the royal family if the city were ever compromised.

Long ago, there were other domed cities close enough to be reached on horseback. There was a chance a refugee from Yuan might find sanctuary before falling prey to sun damage. With a little help from Needle, I might be able to sneak Gem through the King's Gate, or perhaps . . . if I'm careful . . . and if Needle agrees to help . . .

I walk faster, eager to talk to my maid. She's as excited about the healing garden as I am. Surely, if I explain my plan and beg and wheedle for an hour or two, she'll see that what I propose is the only way.

I have to escape the tower and offer Gem a bargain he can't refuse, one that will ensure his return from the desert and keep my Monstrous in Yuan, where I, for one, feel he belongs.

EIGHT

DEO

I stand and watch her go, though I would rather be by her side. I like the feel of her hand looped through my arm, the rich tone of her voice when she speaks. Her voice is like music from a faraway city, unfamiliar, but seductive in its strangeness.

Isra is nothing like I imagined she'd be from listening to my baba's stories of the temperamental princess hidden away in the tower. She's nothing like any other girl I've ever met. She is strange and stubborn and graceless. Rough in speech and rougher of skin, and strangely resistant to my attempts to win her affection.

I should find her frustrating. I should pity her. Most everyone else does. The gentle members of court feel sorry for the mad queen's blind, itchy, awkward daughter, and even sorrier for me. My bed has been warmer than usual these past two months. It seems there's always a sympathetic woman—or two—lingering outside the door to my chamber when I quit the great hall for the night.

There's been no official announcement, but every member of the court knows it's only a matter of time. As soon as Isra's mourning is over, she will take a husband. A childless queen cannot be allowed to remain unmarried. If something were to happen to Isra now, with no daughter to take her place and no husband to remarry and continue the royal line, the covenant would be broken. Yuan would have no royal blood to sustain the magic that keeps our land green and fruitful, and our city would fall like so many of the others.

Isra *will* marry, and soon, and there is little doubt who the man will be.

Junjie is the most powerful man in the city, and I am his son. It is only right that I should be king. It's understood that Isra will take me as her husband and I will put aside any distaste I might feel for her peeling skin and odd ways, in the name of service to my city.

No one suspects that the distaste I feel isn't for the girl.

As Isra disappears over the gentle swell of the hill with her guards close behind, a familiar tightness clutches at my throat.

I set off toward my father's quarters with a heavy feeling in my legs.

How have the other kings done it? How have they lived with a woman, even loved her—I've read the poems the fourth king wrote to his first wife, have sung the ballads King Deshi composed in praise of his queen—knowing that her life would be cut short? That her throat would be opened and her blood spilled in the royal garden, often before she reached her thirtieth birthday?

Isra's mother died thirteen years ago. The roses can go unfed for another ten years, maybe fifteen, but no more. They will have their royal blood. Isra will never see her thirty-fifth year. If the crops begin to fail or other evidence is found that the covenant is weakening, she might not see her twenty-fifth.

She has so little time. It isn't right that she should live it in darkness.

I don't care what my baba said, I don't care what the king made him promise before he died, I will not see my queen suffer any more than she must by virtue of her birth. I will see her eyes light up with wonder. I will see her smile as she looks at me and knows I am the one who restored her. I will taste her gratitude in her kiss on our wedding night.

It won't be long. Only two months until her mourning is over. We will be married when the spring flowers poke their green shoots above the earth, long before her garden can bear fruit.

I will put a stop to her playing in the dirt as soon as she is my wife. It isn't safe for the queen to spend time with a Monstrous. The nobles already worry that she's out of her mind to allow the beast out of his cage, let alone work closely with it. The creature has behaved himself, thus far, but I see the way he watches Isra, taking in every movement of her hands, every flutter of her throat. He's a predator waiting for a moment to strike.

He will not have it. I will have my queen, and the monster will be returned to his cage. A proper cage, not the tidy quarters in the barracks that Isra has given him, but a hole deep underground, with stone floors and thick bars.

A place suitable for a beast.

Isra seems to have a soft place in her heart for the creature, but she will forget him soon enough. She will be distracted by my gift, then overwhelmed by my attention, and then, someday soon, big with my child. A baby will be a far more fitting outlet for her feminine affections than a Monstrous pet.

She would know better than to treat beasts as human if she'd spent more time among civilized people. When we're married, we will move into her father's great house near the other high-ranking members of court. We will attend dances and feasts and spend long weekends watching the horse-and-stick matches on the king's green. And when the time comes for her to go . . .

For our children, if they are daughters, to go . . . Or for my second wife and *our* daughters to go . . .

"Bo, I have news from your father." The boy soldier running down the path toward me is out of breath and sweating like it's the dead of summer.

He's a chubby new recruit, no more than fifteen or sixteen. Too young to shave, too green to know better than to call a superior by his first name, even if that superior is only a few years older. Under normal circumstances, I would discipline him, but I'm too grateful for the interruption. I don't want to think of the future. I can't, or I won't enjoy a moment of being king.

"What news?" I ask, settling for a stern look down my nose rather than an official reprimand.

"There's trouble," he pants. "Captain Fai thinks he's found a crack in the dome."

A crack in the dome. The covenant keeps Yuan's shelter strong. If the dome has a crack, it could be seen as a sign that the time for the queen's sacrifice grows near.

"Show me," I order through a tight jaw. "Now. Run. I'll follow."

I set off after the boy, sprinting hard across the green and up the path to the Hill Gate, past fields of stiff cornstalks browning in the winter chill. I run, and try not to think about losing her before she's even mine.

GEM

NIGHT falls early in winter. Sometimes, I light my lamp right after dinner and practice reading or writing with the paper and charcoal Isra gave me—I'm trusted with flint to light the lamp and can ask for extra oil if it burns out.

But most nights I still choose darkness and the moonlit view out my window.

I stand and watch the roses. They are the only flowers still blooming, as obscenely red as they were in autumn when I was captured. When I was first moved to my new quarters, I would watch the path through the garden late into the night, expecting to catch a glimpse of Isra, hoping to learn more of the roses' secrets. But after the evening when I told her the story of the girl and the star, she never came again.

Her absence is disappointing, like so many things about Yuan's ruler.

Now, as I do what exercises I can in my small sitting room, I watch the garden path for soldiers. I memorize the timing of their patrols. I find the weaknesses in their guard. I store away everything I learn and pray to the ancestors that I get the chance to use the information. Taking possession of a rosebush is essential, but getting it to my people is what matters most.

Not if you can't work the magic. If you can't, the roses will be no good to anyone, and you will have failed the Desert People all over again.

I grit my teeth and bend my knees more deeply, squatting up and down with the heaviest of my new books balanced on either shoulder, building the strength in my legs, though my muscles still tremble in protest.

I'll learn the magic. I'll get the truth from Isra. She already tells me more than she knows. More than she should ever tell an enemy.

I tell her nothing that matters. I tell her stories to earn her sympathy and lower her guard. I labor hard beside her and keep my temper in check, slowly winning her trust. I tease her into thinking we are friends. I play the damaged weakling, sighing and groaning and stumbling through my work in the field even though I'm getting stronger every day. By spring I will be completely healed.

If she lets me out to gather the bulbs in a week or two and I return, she will let me out again to gather herb shoots in the spring. *That* is when I will return to my people. I will bring them the roses and hope and life. I will see my son.

I have to believe he's still alive. Our chief knew these months would be hard. She will have had the women dry the cactus fruit harvest so it can be rationed throughout the winter. The men will find small game in burrows beneath the sand; the women will boil poison root until the poison is gone and only the mealy meat remains. The Desert People will live to see spring, and I will bring them hope and magic.

With a soft grunt, I shift the books from my shoulders to the floor, stacking one on top of the other. I stand on top of them, dipping my heels down and up, building the strength in my lower legs, the running muscles.

I will have to be fast. By the time I escape, every moment will be precious. Every moment is precious *now,* but there's nothing I can do. Not yet. The best use of my time is to spend it getting stronger, and gaining the further trust of the queen.

I should have kept my mouth closed today. I don't owe Isra the truth, and the Smooth Skins' outcasts are nothing to me. Let them suffer. They have food and safety, two things my people would give a year of their lives for. And their queen cares for them. In her way. Enough to worry about whether they are soft and pleasing to the eye.

Phuh. Her obsession with Smooth Skin beauty is disgusting. All this from a girl who can't even *see.* She's planting a garden of dreams to cure an imaginary disease she'll never bear witness to, when with a word she could abolish the outcast camp and end the custom that displeases her.

"Queen of fools," I mutter.

It's days like these that remind me why I hate her. I'm grateful for every one of them. I can't afford to forget. I can't afford to enjoy the way she sighs with happiness when I finish a story. I can't afford to admire how hard she works. I can't let myself grow comfortable on the dirt beside her as we share bread and apples from the basket she brings. I can never take her muddy hand in mind and promise her that the winter will end and the pain and loss she feels will fade the way mine did after my mother's death.

I can certainly never tell her that she is out of her mind, and all the rest of her people with her, if they don't see the beauty in her. In her green, green eyes, in her smile big enough to light a room, in the way she walks like she's dancing with the ground beneath her feet, each step careful and graceful and—

"Fool," I whisper as I step off the books and move closer to the window.

I grit my teeth and direct my gaze toward the roses—reminding myself why I'm here—just in time to see a woman creep from the shadows of the orchard. I can't see her face or what she's wearing in the dim moonlight, but I know immediately who she is.

Isra. I recognize her walk, the way her hips sway beneath her clothes, the careful reach of her toes as she moves across unseen terrain. I know her. I do. Even in the dark.

The knock on the door is soft, but it still makes me jump.

I feel like I've been caught doing something worse than staring out my window. Maybe I have. I can imagine what Gare would say about my knowing a Smooth Skin girl so well.

The knock comes again, and I turn slowly to face the door. My evening meal came hours ago. There shouldn't be anyone near my room until morning. The Smooth Skins have great trust in their locks and keys. The only time I'm guarded is when the soldiers escort me to the queen's garden.

So who is here now?

The flap at the bottom of the door swoops open, and a small package slides along the floor. I tense on instinct, my claws shuddering in their beds.

I approach the bundle carefully, keeping an eye on the still-swinging flap of wood through which my meals are shoved. This is the first time something else has come through. I squat beside the package and unfold the linen holding it together. Inside is a piece of paper with simple words written in an even hand, and a thick coil of rope with a large hook on one end.

I begin to sound out the words on the paper, but haven't gotten past "Gem, I need–" before the sound of a key turning in the lock makes my head snap up and my claws extend.

I lift my arms as the door swings open to reveal Needle, Isra's maid, standing on the other side. Her large brown eyes get even bigger when she sees my claws, but she doesn't scream or turn to run. She only blinks and swallows and points a thin finger to the package.

Having my claws out begins to feel . . . strange.

"Ridiculous." That's the word Isra uses for the hated dresses she's forced to wear to the Smooth Skin eating rooms and the endless Smooth Skin banquets. In some ways, Isra is a stranger here, too. I know that. I know that's why Bo treats her like an invalid and her advisors treat her like a child. Still, I didn't expect this note. There are some words I can't work through, but I understand enough to decipher its meaning.

I finish, and I am . . . shaken.

If anyone finds out what she's done, she really will be locked away in that tower of hers. Not even a queen can go against her city's wishes like this and not be punished. At least, not a queen like Isra, a blind, broken queen without the love of her subjects or the trust of her council.

I have to stop her. And if I can't stop her, I will have to help her. I may hate her, but I need her. She's the only reason I'm allowed out of this room, my only chance to steal a future for my people.

I hand the paper to Needle, who wastes no time tearing it to pieces. She's loyal to Isra, then. That's something. Maybe not enough to keep the soldiers from discovering mine and Isra's absence, but it's something. I take the rope with the hook and begin to move past her, but she stops me with a hand on my arm.

117

I look down and down *and down* at her. She is half a meter shorter than Isra and more fragile in every way, but the stubborn glint in her eyes reminds me of the queen.

Her lips move without sound. I watch her, and after a moment I think I understand her silent plea.

Keep her safe. Please. Keep her safe.

Maybe Isra does have the love of at least one person.

"I would never hurt her," I assure Needle in a hushed voice.

She stares up at me for a long moment before stepping back and pointing to the end of the corridor, where a window large enough for a Desert Man to crawl through opens out onto the royal garden. The guards passed down the path outside the barracks only a few moments ago. I should have just enough time to reach Isra, talk her out of leaving the city, and get back to my cell undiscovered.

I don't waste my breath telling Needle more lies. I turn and run.

NINE

ISRA

I step into the garden, shaking all over, but not from the cold. I'm barely aware of the cold. I'm racing inside. My pulse rushes like the river beneath the city, wild and reckless and angry.

And frightened. I'm frightened, too.

I've been frightened my entire life, but that fear was different from this. The former was a monster hiding in the shadows at the end of a long, winding lane. This fear is Death reaching for my throat with both hands, so close that I can hear his cold breath seep from his lungs.

Junjie tried to keep the news quiet, but there was little chance of that. The court is still in mourning. There is no music or dancing or playacting to provide entertainment. The only thing to do is talk, and the ladies and gentlemen of the court excel at that, especially when the subject of discussion is something so compelling.

And terrible.

A crack in the dome. It was all anyone could whisper about: "Is it truly there?" "What caused it?" "How long will it take to assess the damage?" "What will Junjie do to ensure the safety of the city?"

Not, *What will Queen Isra do?* No one thought to seek my council. Junjie was the one they turned to for guidance. My name was never spoken, but I was at the heart of every hushed conversation that drifted to my giant ears. If the dome is cracked, it will be seen as a sign that the covenant is weakening. If the injury can be easily repaired, the panic may pass for a time, but the damage is already done.

I press my fist against my lips to hold back the whimper rising in my throat. I knew the day of sacrifice would come, but I didn't expect it would be so soon. My life can't end now, not when I've scarcely had the chance to live it.

I lean over, resting my palms on the bed surrounding the roses, digging my fingertips into the rough stone. I take a deep breath, grateful for the cold air that softens the roses' perfume. I don't want my head filled with their ominous stench. I wouldn't have come here at all, except it seemed the safest place to meet Gem.

I focus on my breath until it grows smooth and, finally, my heartbeat slows.

I can't lose hope. The crack might not be a crack at all. It could be detritus from the desert stuck on the outside of the glass, a trick of light, or . . . something else entirely. (*Please, please, let it be something else.*) The fissure is too high up for it to be seen clearly, even with a spyglass. The soldiers will have to send a man to take a closer look, which means rigging the rope-and-pulley system the city hasn't used in half a century.

Bo says it will take at least three days to set up the equipment, and that he will be the one to strap on the harness and be hauled out into the void to assess the situation. He promised to keep everyone away from me until then, and to alert Gem's guards that the Monstrous won't be working in the field for the rest of the week. I told Bo I wanted to be alone while I waited to see what effects giving up my morning tea will have on my constitution, but I know he assumed it was fear that made me retreat to my tower.

He seemed afraid, too. His arm shook as he escorted me to my door. His lips trembled when he pressed a kiss to my cheek.

I touch the place now, and swear the patch of skin still feels colder than the rest. It was the first time Bo has dared a kiss since the night he thought we were both infected with poison from Gem's claws.

"Maybe he only kisses queens who are about to die," I say aloud, fighting the sudden urge to giggle. There's nothing funny about the mad thing I'm about to do. There is nothing funny about what will happen if Bo fails to keep his word. If Junjie or his guards enter the tower and discover my absence, they'll know Needle was keeping my disappearance a secret. They'll jail her. Or worse.

Probably worse.

The smile on my lips prunes into a worried pucker. Needle is taking a terrible risk to help me prove I'm a queen with more to offer my people than my blood. I can't forget that for a moment. I will go carefully and quickly, as soon as my eyes arrive.

I'll have Needle to thank for that, too. If she can manage—

The sound of boots scuffing along the path interrupts my thoughts. I pull my shawl farther over my head and crouch down by the wall, hoping the shadows will conceal me. I hold my breath as three soldiers—maybe four, it's difficult to tell— *scuff, scuff* by on the other side of the circular planter.

If they'd taken the other fork in the path, they would have seen me.

My breath rushes out in an unsteady stream, and my legs suddenly feel wobbly. I sit down hard, the paving stones grinding against my sit bones through the padding of my old gray overalls layered over my new green ones. I have on long underwear, too, and a shawl and sweater. It will be cold in the desert.

The desert. I'm going out into the *desert*. This isn't a plan; it's an act of desperation. But what choice do I have? There isn't time to waste. I have to trust my instincts and hope with everything in me that luck is on my side.

And Needle's side. And Gem's.

Gem. What if he doesn't meet me in the garden? What if—once released from his room—he runs for the nearest gate? What if he kills the soldiers guarding it and escapes into the desert, never to return? He's still weak, but there's a chance he might try it. Maybe even a good chance.

I push my shawl back around my shoulders, feeling trapped by the heavy wool, but before I can drop my arms back to my side, I feel it—a vine snaking around my wrist and pulling tightly.

I almost cry out in surprise, but manage to stifle the sound at the last moment. The guards are still too close; I can't afford to make any noise. I try my best to quietly wrench my wrist free, but the roses are stronger than I realized. The vine tugs my arm up and over my head, drawing my hand into the thick of the flowers' nest. I clench my fist—hoping to protect my fingers—only to feel a thorn meaner than any I've yet encountered dig into the thin skin between my knuckles.

"Ah!" I gasp as blood spills, hot and sticky, down the back of my hand, making my true eyes fill with tears even as my borrowed eyes open on the city.

I see a tower—*my* tower—rising from the surrounding fields like some spiny creature from another world. The roses have never shown me the building where I've spent my entire life, but I recognize it immediately: the sharp gold curves of its many roofs, its red stone walls and balcony jutting from the top like a stubborn chin.

My borrowed eyes swoop toward the entrance at the tower's base, where a boy with a silky black braid, high cheekbones, and bow-shaped lips that any woman at court would envy stands clutching a pair of muddy slippers. The boy is Bo—there is no mistaking those lips—and the slippers are mine, the ones I threw into the flowers the night of my coronation.

Bo lifts his hand to knock on the door, while, far away in the garden, my heart beats frantically in my chest. Bo has come to return my slippers, and to demand to know how I managed to lose them in the first place, no doubt. There's an anxious look in his eyes, tension at the edges of his mouth, and an almost guilty twitch in his neck as his head turns from side to side, making sure the other guards' eyes are averted.

I suddenly realize what a good job Bo has done of hiding his true feelings. He cares for me more than I've assumed—there is genuine concern in his expression—but he also fears for my mind more than I ever would have guessed. He worries I'm more than odd. He worries I'm touched by my mother's madness, and that one day the queen he's come to care for may become a madwoman who'll try to kill her children in the night.

I don't know if it's the roses' magic or my own intuition, but I am certain that is what Bo feels. And I'm just as certain that he won't leave my tower without knowing how I managed to leave my shoes in a flower bed only feet from the Monstrous's cell.

I have to go. I have to go back to the tower. Now.

No sooner is the thought through my mind than the thorn withdraws from my flesh and the vine loosens its grip on my wrist. I pull my hand back to my chest, pressing it tightly to my sweater until I feel the bleeding stop.

Breath coming fast, I draw my knees to my chest. I am

preparing to leap up, run back to the tower, and hope I can make the climb up to the balcony without being spotted by Bo or the guards—when the greater implications of what has just happened hit hard enough to make my bones weak all over again.

The roses *knew*. Somehow they knew what I was planning and they don't want me to go. They showed me just enough to make me afraid, before setting me free.

But should I really be afraid? I wonder as I scoot away from the containing wall, out of the roses' reach.

It's late, nearly midnight. Bo knows better than to come to my rooms at this hour. If he finds the door locked and neither Needle nor I answer, he might very well decide to leave and return tomorrow. Tomorrow, when Needle will be at the tower to tell him I'm not feeling well and turn him away.

Now that there's no thorn buried beneath my skin, that scenario seems as likely as the one I fear. *More* likely. But the roses didn't want me to think clearly; they wanted me to run along back to my prison. It could be they simply have the interests of the city at heart—it *is* dangerous for me to leave, to take such a risk when I am unmarried and the covenant is unsecured—but the vision felt more insidious, the inexorable grip of the vine more possessive than concerned.

As I rub the bruised skin around my new wound, I begin to doubt for the first time in my life what I've been taught about the royal garden. The legends say the roses grew after the first queen's blood hit the ground, a symbol of the sacrifice she'd made and the covenant that would keep Yuan safe.

But what if—

125

"There you are." Gem's voice comes centimeters from my ear, close enough to make me gasp. My ears are sensitive, but I didn't hear a thing until he was close enough to touch.

By the moons, I'm glad he's here. I'm so glad not to be alone with the roses. I'm weak with it. Strong with it. My blood starts to rush again; my bones rediscover their sturdy centers.

"Thank you for coming." I find his chest with my fingers, flattening my palm against the thick fabric of one of his new shirts, hoping he can feel my gratitude as clearly as I feel his heart thudding beneath his ribs.

Ba-bump, ba-bump, ba-bump, bababump bababump bababump. The beating grows faster as we sit in silence, our foggy breath mingling between our faces. Mine is hot, but his is so much hotter and it smells nothing of the cabbage he refuses to eat. Gem's breath is fresh sawdust and sweet smoke, chestnuts and celery root, as sharp and clean as the winter air. It's a good smell, a healthy smell that makes me wonder how breath like *that* would taste on a kiss.

Ba-bump . . . bump. My heartbeat stutters, and I pull my hand away from Gem's chest so quickly that I hit my own throat and begin to choke.

"Are you all right?" He lays a hand on my shoulder, the same shoulder he tore open months ago, the one that bears a tight, sleek scar from the claw that cut the deepest. But now Gem's claws are sheathed and his fingers are careful, gentle.

He's never touched me like this before. We haven't touched in weeks, and even then our only contact was in anger—my fists on his chest, his hands at my wrists, my fingers

126

on his throat, his claws at mine. But this is not anger. This is . . . something else.

"I'm fine." My whisper is hoarse. I clear my throat. "We should go. The patrol—"

"They'll be back soon," he interrupts, his voice gruff. He pulls his hand from my shoulder, leaving my skin colder. "Go back to your tower. If I run, I'll be back in my cell before I'm spotted."

"No!" I say, louder than I mean to. I bite my lip, then whisper, "No. We have to get the bulbs. I know of a secret door out into the desert. No one will see us go, and Needle will make sure we aren't missed."

"And how will she do that?"

"I've canceled your escort to the field," I explain, ears straining to catch the scuff of boots. "No one will come to your room except to bring meals. Needle says she can convince the girl who delivers them to allow her to take over for the next few days. That should be enough, shouldn't it? You said it wouldn't take more than three days. Two, if you were quick."

He grunts. I can tell he isn't impressed with the plan. "And what of the queen? Won't someone notice your absence?"

"I told Bo I don't wish to be disturbed," I say, throat tightening around what I've left unsaid: the crack in the dome waiting to be investigated and the fact that Bo stands at my tower door right now, and all the rest. "He'll honor my wish to be left alone for a few days, and Needle will turn him away if he does not."

Gem makes another dubious sound. When he speaks

again, I can tell he's closer. His breath is warmer. It whispers across my lips, prickling my skin. "If your people find out you took me into the desert with no one to protect you, or prevent me from escaping, they'll think you're more rattled in the brain than they do already. Junjie will lock you away, and you will never rule this city."

"I will never rule this city if I run back to my rooms," I hiss. "I must give the people a reason to see me as—or at least remember me—as something more than . . ."

"More than?"

"The garden will prove I am a good and useful queen," I say, cursing myself for nearly losing control of my tongue. I don't want Gem to know. I don't want him to treat me the way people treat a girl who has been marked for death since her very birth. "The garden will—" A faint thud sounds from the direction of the orchard. I freeze, falling silent, until Gem whispers—

"An apple falling to the ground. There is still fruit on the limbs at the very top." Disgust creeps into his tone. "Your people have so much, you leave food to *rot*."

My answer. I have it. I know how to make Gem come with me. I hate to make promises I might not be alive to keep, but I have no choice. "Help me tonight," I say, "and I will do what I can for your people."

"You can do nothing."

"Not now," I agree. "But if we fetch these bulbs, and the herbs we need later . . . If my garden is a success and my people are healed and learn to love me, they'll respect my judgment. Come summer, when the first of the crops are in,

I'll convince the council to send a portion of what is ours into the desert."

"The herbs may take months to work. My people can't wait that long."

"All right," I say, growing increasingly desperate the longer we linger. "Then I will send food as soon as I can. I'll convince my advisors it's necessary, a peace offering to keep the Desert People from returning to free our captive."

"And who will deliver this peace offering?"

"You will. I'll talk with Junjie. I'll persuade him that you can be trusted to return when your errand is through."

"Can I?"

"You're here now," I say with more confidence than I feel. "You wouldn't be if your father's promise didn't mean something to you. You're honorable. I'll explain that to Junjie."

Gem's laugh is soft but parsnip-bitter all the same. "You think he'll listen?"

"I'll *make* him listen." Tightness flashes in my jaw. "I am *changed*. Things have happened tonight that . . ." I swallow, moistening my lips with my tongue, struggling to keep my voice even. "Things are different now," I whisper. "I won't allow Junjie to rule in my place. When we return from the desert, I will join the council meetings. I will speak to the people and hear their complaints myself. I will not sit quietly by. I will fight for a place in this city, and I will fight for those who have served me well. Help me, and I *will* help your people."

He's quiet for a long moment. "You sound almost like a queen."

129

"I will behave like one. I swear it," I say, ignoring the guilty prickle at the back of my neck.

Gem could never guess how good the chances are that I won't be around to keep my promise. And I can't tell him. I *can't*. Especially with the roses hovering behind us like carrion birds, watching, waiting for a sign that it's time to swoop down and feed.

"Please. I'll beg if I—"

"Where is this secret door?" Gem asks, taking my hand.

My fingers startle open before tightening with a grateful squeeze. I find myself comforted by his calloused palm in a way I never am by Bo's softness. Gem is going to help. He has given me hope, and I swear to myself that I will give the same to his people. I *will*. I will live to honor my promise to him, and hopefully many more.

"This way." I start toward the orchard, still holding his hand. "There's a small gate, the King's Gate, beyond the village green, past the cornfields, near the granaries. It's no more than a door, really," I whisper as we hurry through the trees. "I've never been through it, but I'm told it's hidden behind—"

Gem jerks my arm—hard and sudden—sending a flash of pain through my shoulder. I stumble back, and his arms are suddenly around me, his hand covering my mouth, muffling my rush of breath as our bodies collide. I stiffen but don't pull away. I stand perfectly still, ears pricking.

I press my lips together and nod, and Gem's hand drops from my mouth, but his arms remain around my waist, holding me close as the *scuff, scuff* of boots sounds behind us.

Soldiers. On the path we left only moments ago.

My stomach turns itself inside out beneath Gem's hand. What if we're spotted? I'm assuming it's darker beneath the trees, but that's only a guess. My world is always dark, without variation. I can't know whether it's better to hide in the shadows or run for the green and hope the soldiers don't notice our footsteps. I have to trust that Gem has made the right decision, that standing frozen like statues will keep us safe.

But I do trust him. He doesn't want to be caught. If the soldiers find him with the queen pinned to his chest, they won't hesitate. They'll throw their spears. Aim for Gem's heart. Hope to kill him before he kills me.

They won't take the time to see that Gem's claws aren't extended, that his arms are gentle around me, or that my fingers linger over his. They won't notice that I lean into him, not away, or that my head turns to look over my shoulder, bringing my cheek so near his mouth that his silent breath warms my skin. They would *never* in a *thousand* years imagine that my eyes slide closed and a shiver runs through me not because I fear for my life but because Gem's body is pressed against mine, because his hand on my belly makes it ache, because the longing to taste him is stronger than it was before.

If Gem and I were alone, and I were the kind who cared for nothing but my own pleasure, I would turn in his arms. I would arch my back and tilt my head and press my lips to his. I would kiss him the way Bo kissed me in the royal garden. I would not fear his teeth. I would not think how strange it is for tongues to touch. I would not think about cabbage. I would kiss him until I was breathless.

"They're gone," Gem whispers.

My eyes fly open. I exhale sharply, wondering why the news that we're safe makes my heart beat even faster.

"Isra . . ." Gem's hand curls, and the tips of his fingers press deeper into my stomach, and suddenly my long underwear and two layers of overalls are not enough protection from his touch. I shudder, and the world shifts, and I fill to the brim with a feeling I've never felt before. It bubbles inside me until a soft sigh of pain escapes my lips.

Pain, because I'm not stupid. I *know* what this feeling is.

King Deshi's love songs were the first melodies I learned to play on my harp. My teacher, Biyu, taught me the chords–sitting behind me with her fingers guiding mine–and Father taught me the words. Baba and I would sing some of the songs together before it was time for me to go to bed, but there were some I was too embarrassed to sing with him. Even at ten or eleven, I realized not all love songs are about the way love affects a heart. They're about the way love affects the body, about a hunger that has nothing to do with food. King Deshi's metaphors aren't so clever that I couldn't guess their meanings.

The pelican with its "pulsing beak" was no pelican.

Needle told me how it is with a man and a woman and the "beak" and the "flower" not long after my first blood. Baba thought I was too naïve to understand, but I wasn't. . . . I . . .

Baba.

My lungs turn to stone, trapping my next breath and holding it prisoner. He's gone. It hits me all over again. My chest feels like it's caving in, my throat threatens to collapse, and the only thing keeping the heat behind my eyes from spilling over is knowing how little I deserve to cry.

132

If my father could see me now, he would be *sickened* to the depths of his being. I am even more *wrong* than I suspected. *Wrong.*

The most accomplished lover in Yuan kissed me, long and deep, and continues to do his best to seduce me, and I feel nothing but vague curiosity and more pronounced anxiety. Now a beast from the desert stands too close, and I am dizzy with *wanting* him. I crave his calloused hands on me. I want to be pinned beneath him the way I was that first night. But this time he wouldn't be angry, and I wouldn't be scared. I would be *eager.* Because I am twisted. Tainted. *Wrong.*

My stomach rebels. I taste stomach juices and the beet soup I forced down my throat at dinner, and barely swallow it down.

I twist free of Gem's arms, and stumble to the edge of the green before stopping to bury my face in my hands. I concentrate on the smell of the jasmine perfume at my wrists, the contrast of my breath warming my nose, and my cold fingers pressed against my forehead, struggling to pull myself together.

"Isra?"

When Gem's hand finds my elbow, I pull away. "I'm fine." I cross my arms and hug tightly, holding the miserable scraps of myself together. I can't fall apart. Not now. "I don't need help. I can count my steps to the fields."

Hopefully, by the time we reach the end of them, I will have gained control of my stomach. As for the rest of me . . .

If that other hunger returns, I'll think of Baba and how ashamed he would be. I'll think of my people and the way their lips would curl if they knew the depraved nature of their queen. I'll think of Gem.

He would be as sickened as my people. He loathes Smooth Skins. He would never think of a Smooth Skin woman in *that* way. He put his arms around me because it was practical. That's the end of it. If he knew the unnatural acts that danced through my mind a moment ago, he would abandon me on the spot, though I need his help more than ever.

By the time we find the King's Gate, hidden behind the ivy-covered wall behind the granaries, I'm no longer afraid of going into the desert. I stand calmly by as Gem moves the wooden plank barring the door, my pulse steady. There's nothing out there as scary as the shifting world inside me. I will be safe from Monstrous attack with one of their own by my side, and three days isn't enough to damage my skin.

Not that it would matter. Your skin isn't much to look at anyway. For you, this is no great risk. But for Yuan . . .

I pause with my hand on the ancient wooden handle.

"Hurry," Gem urges in a tight whisper. "There are two soldiers on the wall walk. They'll be over our heads soon."

"I leave my people without a king or a queen," I whisper, a lump rising in my throat. What if the roses were right? What if I'm better off returning to the tower? "If something happens to me . . ."

"Nothing will happen." Gem's heat warms my back as he moves closer. "The desert is a mother to me. I'll keep you safe and bring you home. I give my word."

"*Your* word."

"Yes," he says, his hand closing over mine. "Mine. And I will not break it. You can trust me, Isra."

It's me I don't trust, I think, but there's no time for consideration. I pull my shawl over my head and turn the handle, and Gem and I slip through the heavy door and ease it closed behind us.

And then I am *outside* the dome. *Outside.*

For a moment I can't move. I'm stunned by the strange, dusty, *empty* smell of the desert, by the cold so much colder than anything else I've felt before, by the howling in the distance. It's not animal, not human, not even Monstrous. This howl is otherworldly, a relentless keening more chilling than the cold.

I take a step closer to Gem in spite of myself. "What is that?" My voice sounds smaller out here in the great wide world.

"What is . . ."

"The sound. The . . . moaning."

"Oh," he says, a hint of laughter in the word. "The wind through the dead trees at the base of the first hill. Nothing to be afraid of."

The wind. The wind has a *voice.*

I shove my shawl off my head, and a wind not of my own making lifts my hair from my shoulders, sending it whipping around my face. Strands catch on the chapped place on my lip and lash into my eyes, but I feel no pain. My lungs ache and my throat burns and my eyes sting until I can't stop tears from coming, but I'm not sad.

"You're crying," Gem says in that vaguely horrified voice of his.

It makes me laugh and then cry even harder. My shoulders shake until my shawl falls off. My nose runs, but I don't wipe it. I don't care about my leaky nose or leaky eyes. I don't care about my ugliness or wrongness or the dark fate awaiting me under the dome.

I am not under the dome. For the first time ever, I am free.

TEN

GEM

ʙʏ the time the sun winks its flaming eye and disappears behind the blue hills, I could have killed her ten different ways.

Claws to her throat and her body left outside the dome
for the Smooth Skins to collect if they dared open their gate.
A shove into a zion nest, where venomous insect stings would
stop her heart. A handful of poison milk from the wrong
breed of cactus; a step too close to the cliff's edge as we reach
the foothills and begin to climb. The moments present themselves, and her death plays out again and again in my mind.

She is at my mercy now. All it would take is a broken promise.

I could kill her and put an end to the Yuejihua family's rule. If I were stronger, I could bring her to my chief and hold Isra until her people agreed to give us food and roses and anything else the Desert People desire. I could arrange for Isra to have her turn as captive, let her learn what it's like to be caged, let her tongue grow bitter with shame as she flatters those who hold the key to her chains.

I like the thought of Isra at my mercy—head bowed, no longer giving orders and taking my obedience for granted. I like it very much.

She didn't take you for granted last night. She made a deal. You gave your word.

A twinge near my heart reminds me the organ is still too soft. When I rejoin my tribe, I'll cut my warrior's braid and give it to my father to burn. I don't deserve to stand beside Gare and the rest of the men. I am weak. Kind, when I should be cruel. Gentle, when I should crush my enemy to dust.

"Gem? Can we stop?" Isra pants, tugging at my sleeve. "Just for a moment?"

I turn to see her hunched over, fist pressed to her side, face pinched, and my heart twinges a second time. I've done it again—forgotten that her legs are shorter and that a lifetime of privilege hasn't prepared her for a night and day of hiking in ill-fitting boots across hard ground with only cactus milk to drink and a handful of dried meat to eat.

She brought enough meat in her pockets for one meal, not *three days* in the desert.

I'm not surprised. She has no concept of what it means to be hungry. But after this journey, she will. She'll survive—we're rationing the meat, and cactus milk has strengthening properties—but she won't enjoy it. Maybe that small suffering will be enough to convince her to honor her part of our bargain.

"I'm sorry," she whispers, leaning on the walking stick I found to help her navigate the unfamiliar terrain. "I want to keep going. The sooner we get there, the sooner we get back, but . . ."

Her tongue slips out to wet her lips. She tucks a few loose strands of hair behind her ear with a trembling hand. Despite her sun-pink cheeks, she looks pale, and more fragile than she does in her domed city. I should be pleased to see her in distress. I should push her further for the joy of seeing her break. But I only wish I had my walking pack and supplies. If I did, I could build a shelter against the rocks. I could unroll my grass mat to soften the ground and cover her with a skin.

Puh. I want to make a warm bed. For my enemy.

No, I want to make a warm bed for a girl I *care* for. It's the caring that shames me the most. I don't understand it. How can I feel pity for a queen I've killed a hundred times in my mind? How can I admire the determination of the girl who has held me prisoner? Why do I put my arm around Isra's waist and offer what strength I have, when I should crave distance from her the way my people crave enough food to feed their children?

"Don't." She shies away, as if my arm is a snake she's discovered under a rock. She dances out of reach, closer to the edge of the path, where the wind blows harder than it does near the rocky face of the hill.

A sharp gust tugs her shawl down around her shoulders and lifts her hair, making it writhe like a bonfire made of shadows. Behind her, the setting sun paints the tired desert a hungry orange, the color of vengeance, while far in the distance the dome squats smugly on the horizon, confident the people it shelters will never be held accountable for what they have stolen.

The desert bears their scars. The land spread out below us is all but barren. The desert floor is baked hard. The wind can barely move it. There are no more dust storms here. The ground cracks like eggshells, the pieces moving farther apart with every month that passes without rain. The trees are dead, and the few cacti that stubbornly push their way up from the scarred earth cast gnarled shadows, crooked fingers that would snatch Isra's pant leg and pull her over the edge if they could reach high enough.

I could deliver her into their hands. One firm push, and in an instant she'd tumble down the hill it has taken us an hour to climb.

I say, "You're too near the edge. Let me help," before taking her arm and guiding her back to safer ground. I rearrange her shawl to hold her wild hair captive, brush the dirt from her cheek, warn her to "Be careful. The path drops sharply on your right side," and ignore the way she flinches at my touch.

"I . . ." Her eyes squeeze closed. "I'm sorry. I don't know what's wrong with me."

I know. Now that we're alone, far from the city she rules, with no guards to protect her or chains binding my arms or legs, she remembers that I'm a monster. She remembers to be afraid. I should be glad of that, too, but it only makes my stomach clench and my voice harsh when I remind her, "I gave my word. I'll keep you safe."

"I know you will," she whispers, eyes still closed, her dark lashes fanned out over her cheeks.

I want to call her a liar, but it would serve no purpose, and I'm too tired to fight. I'm feeling how far we've come. We've stopped long enough for my muscles to cool, and the places where the spears pierced my flesh ache more than they have in weeks.

"We'll camp here for the night," I say, turning to assess the trail. "There's a wider place in the path just behind us, and rocks to block the wind. There'll be nothing to drink until tomorrow, but there's enough dry wood for a fire."

"That would be nice," she says with a thin smile. "I haven't felt my nose for hours. I can't believe I thought I knew what it felt like to be cold."

I grunt in response, and her smile slips away.

"I'm sorry," she whispers. "Your people must suffer during the winter."

"They suffer. They starve. You don't care. Remember?"

"I care. Of course I do. That day in the infirmary was a long time ago." When she reaches for my arm, she's trembling harder than she was before.

I take her hand and pull her to me with more force than I intended. "If I were going to kill you, I would have done it already," I growl, not bothering with the Smooth Skin inflection that I've perfected in my months of captivity. We are in my world now, and I will speak the way a Desert Man speaks. "This is a foolish time to lose your courage."

Her breath rushes out, and a wrinkle forms between her brows. "I haven't lost my courage. I . . . You . . ." The wrinkle smoothes, and something flickers deep in her eyes. "You think I'm *afraid* of you?"

"I *know* it." I hate the wounded note in my voice. I must be more tired than I thought, or I wouldn't allow her fear to affect me, let alone allow her to hear it.

"Oh, Gem." She lifts her chin, tipping her face up to mine. I know she can't see me, but in that moment I can *feel* her attention. It prickles the place on my forehead where flesh meets scales, makes my nose itch and my mouth wrinkle. "I'm not afraid of you. I swear it."

I grunt again. "That's why you flinch when I touch you."

"No. I . . . That's not . . ." The wind blows her shawl open at the throat. I watch the muscles there work as she fights to swallow. Ripple, clutch, ripple, shudder.

Seems her lies aren't going down easily for either of us.

"Don't bother," I say, gripping her fingers harder, reminding us both I could snap her bones as easily as the sticks I'll gather for kindling. "Hold your fear close. It will make for poor sleep tonight but peaceful nights back in your tower. If you stop thinking of my people as monsters, how will you ever sleep again? Knowing what you've done?"

ISRA

I'VE done nothing! I want to scream. *It's not my fault your people are starving. I had no idea until I met you that the Monstrous weren't beasts perfectly suited to life in the desert. And a Monstrous killed my father less than three months past. Is it my fault I've been too miserable and angry to think of the good of your people?*

By the moons, I can hardly bear the weight of what's good for mine! I'm only one woman, and most of the time I still feel like a girl. I wasn't raised to rule; I was raised to die. You know nothing about what it's like to be the queen of Yuan, so don't stand there and growl your judgment at me, you stupid, moody thing!

But I don't scream. I don't speak at all.

I endure Gem's less-than-gentle guidance to our campsite and his angry silence as he stomps back and forth gathering wood for the fire without saying a word. I cross my arms and bite my tongue and keep my peace, because if I open my mouth, I'm not sure what will come out.

It could be a reasonable argument, but it could also be something much more dangerous. I could find myself confessing that I'm not afraid of him, I'm afraid of *me.* That I'm afraid of how much I want him to touch me, and keep on touching me, no matter how wrong it would be.

A wicked part of me would like to observe the quality of Gem's silence after *that* sort of confession. I imagine it would be very different from the cold, efficient one I'm enjoying right now. More shocked and off balance. Far less sanctimonious.

The pleasure I'd take in pulling the rug out from beneath his self-righteous feet would almost make up for the shame of his knowing my secret.

Almost.

"Hand me your shawl," he demands, startling me.

"What?"

"Your shawl. Hand it to me." From the direction of his voice, I can tell he's standing. Glaring down at me, no doubt, too sickened to sit and enjoy the fire he's miraculously built. I would ask him how he did it, but it's clear he's not in the mood for polite conversation.

"There's plenty of room by the fire." I leave my scarf where it is, lift my chin, and do my best to look imperious, though I can't remember feeling this filthy in my life, even right after my mother died, when I refused to let anyone bathe me for weeks. But back then I was a little girl locked away in my music room, the only place the tower fire hadn't touched. I didn't spend my days roaming the desert, collecting dirt and grit on my skin, somehow managing to work up a sweat despite the winter chill.

Frozen nose, damp undershirt. *Eck.* I should have taken off a layer when the sun grew warm in the afternoon. At least then I'd be dry right now. I'm discovering the only thing worse than cold is cold and *damp.*

"I'm going down the mountain for something to drink," Gem says tightly, making it clear he's noticed that my nose is as far in the air as it can get without tipping me over backward. He sounds even angrier.

Good. Let him stay angry. I'll stay angry, too, and we'll both be better off.

"If you want me to bring some back for you, I need your shawl to soak up the cactus milk," Gem says. "I'd use my shirt, but I'm sure you don't want to drink from *that*."

His shirt. He wasn't wearing a shirt the night I saw him through the roses' eyes, but I don't remember what his bare chest looks like. I was too focused on his immense size and large, white teeth.

You should still *be focused on his teeth.*

I should. I lick my lips and think of my father, but even imagining Baba's horror is no longer enough to banish the tingling at my fingertips. I would like to see Gem's chest with my hands. I would like to see his face again, to find out if his hair has grown, and if it's still as soft.

Abomination. My internal voice is as venomous as ever, but harder to hear over the wind whistling through the rocks.

I love the wind more than I thought I would, even when it is tangling my hair into fantastic knots and freezing me to the bone. I can't remember ever feeling so alive, so—

"As you wish, my lady," Gem snaps. "But don't complain of thirst come morning."

I reach for my shawl, but before I can hand it over—or tell him I was only *thinking,* not ignoring him—he's stomping down the mountain.

"Ridiculous," I mutter beneath my breath, but it's hard to hold on to my anger for long. *I'm* the one who's being ridiculous.

Why am I letting this madness distract me? For seventeen years I've had close to no interest in the opposite sex. The only men in my life were Baba and Junjie, and what the roses showed me of boys my age did little to pique my curiosity about the rest of the male population. The soldiers were self-important, and the idle nobles were overly impressed with themselves.

I knew Baba would choose a husband for me from one of the founding noble families, so I took a closer interest when the roses showed me those boys, but just close enough to assure myself the possibilities weren't too terrible. That was enough to put the business of boys and husbands out of my mind. I knew love wasn't in my future—not the emotion, and certainly not the . . . other kind of love. I knew I'd have to welcome my husband to my bed until a child was born, but I didn't expect to enjoy the process. It seemed best not to think of it.

Now I can't *stop* thinking about it. Even being frustrated with Gem doesn't banish the awareness of his smell, his touch. When he stood behind me and cupped my hands in his—teaching me to drink from the cactus he'd sliced open—it felt like my entire being was catching fire. It was terrifying.

Is it the tainted part of me that makes me ache for a Monstrous boy? Does this mean I'll never feel this way about Bo? That I'll never learn to enjoy his attention as much as the other women of court clearly do? The thought of being with a man I didn't desire was disturbing before I knew what desire felt like, but now the notion sickens me. Soft hands on my skin, instead of Gem's rough fingertips. Thin lips on mine, instead of Gem's full mouth. My name whispered silkily in my ear, instead of growled against my throat.

Sick. *Sick, sick, sick.*

I huddle closer to the fire, trying to focus on the pleasant warmth thawing my fingers and nose. I don't want to think about the future or my duty or the fact that I am hours and *hours* away from my tower, utterly alone for the first time in my entire life and experiencing my lack of sight in a way I haven't in a long time.

Back home, I know the shape of my world. The tastes and smells and textures of Yuan are familiar, and there's only so much trouble a blind girl can get into in a domed city. Not so out here. I might as well be on another planet. A dangerous planet where millions of unseen things can kill me before I *don't* see them coming.

Ha ha.

I'm able to find the private joke funny until the fire begins to lose its heat and I'm forced to venture away from the rock wall to hunt for more fuel. I know Gem piled the wood close. I remember his repeated huffing and the hollow sound of dry branches tumbling to the ground. But as to where the pile lies . . .

I pat the ground on one side of the fire and then the other, moving a little farther out each time, nerves electrified by every pebble and dip in the dirt I come across, certain that at any moment I'm going to happen upon one of the zions Gem warned me about.

I can't afford a poisonous stinger in the hand or a slow death in the desert. I must return from this adventure with spoils shoved into my deep pockets and ensure the future of my people. I *must.* I can't allow my decision to lead to the fall of my city. The shame of it would follow me beyond the grave, torment me for eternity, never allowing me to forget my irresponsible, unqueenly failure.

And so, after only a few minutes of searching, I give up trying to find the wood. I scuttle back to the place where Gem left me and press myself against the rocks.

All too soon, the fire snuffs out and the wind picks up. Night falls, and the temperature plummets. Within thirty minutes, my nose is as chilled as it was before. Within an hour, the places where my underclothes were damp feel as if they've frozen to my skin. My fingers and toes go numb, then my arms and legs. The chill creeps into my shoulders, licking an icy tongue down to tease at my ribs.

I begin to shake all over in what seems to be my body's attempt to warm itself, but I only grow colder. And colder. I have never been so miserable in my own skin or so tired. Sleepy. So, so sleepy . . . My mind drifts until I'm no longer sure if I'm asleep or awake, hallucinating or remembering. . . .

One moment I'm alone in the desert, the next I'm back in the tower as it burns. I watch the flames leap, and I scream for Mama while the fire rages and my father beats at the door, begging her to let us out.

Mama. Where is she? Why did she lock the door? I can't see through the smoke, and I'm dizzy and sick and exhausted, but I can't sleep. I can't! I have to find Mama. She and Baba and I have to get out. We have to get out!

I look up and see a woman's face in the burning beam

above my bed, watch her eyes go wide and her mouth move urgently, but I can't hear her. I can't hear anything except terrible moans, as if every monster in the world is crying out for my blood.

I open my mouth to scream again, and suddenly I'm back in the desert, wandering along a rocky path without even my new walking stick to guide me, shaking like a pan of popping corn, not sure which world is the dream. With a strangled sob, I tear my shawl from my head and fling it from me, gasping as the wind whips through my hair.

What are you doing, fool?

I don't know. I know only that ridding myself of the thing clutching at my head seemed the right thing to do at the time, and now I'm too frightened to go looking for my lost shawl. I don't know how close I am to the edge of the trail. I don't remember deciding to leave my safe place.

My thoughts are fuzzy. I can't remember . . . I can't . . .

My knees buckle. I collapse onto the ground and decide it's best to stay there. I don't know how to find my way back to the rock shelter, and if I keep walking, I'm sure to find trouble. But oh, it's even colder here. Wherever I am. So cold.

I pull my knees to my chest and wrap my arms around my shins, wishing I hadn't been such a coward. Now it's too late. Even if I find my way back to the camp and the pile of wood, I could never start a fire alone.

But Gem will come back soon. He'll find me. I can't have gone far. Surely . . .

The wind huffs and puffs, its frigid breath making my bare head ache. I curl into a ball around my legs, tuck my face to my chest, and bite my lip, shivering as images from my brief sighted life bloom in the darkness behind my eyes.

I see the pearl buttons on my mother's dress, the ones that dug into my cheek when she let me nap with her on the sofa in her chamber. I see the cabbage fields and the orchards blossoming far below the tower balcony, and the scarlet explosion of the sun setting outside the dome. I see my own pudgy hand—not too tainted then, only dry and a bit cracked—snatching a sticky roll from my mother's tray, and I feel a giddy squeal rising inside me as I sneak with it back to my room. I'd already eaten my morning treat, but my appetite for burned honey icing was insatiable. Mother always slept late and so soundly that not even little feet scampering into her room would wake her.

I'd forgotten that about my mama. I'd forgotten most of those memories. Their recovery warms me from the inside out, makes me smile as I give in to the muzzy feeling tugging me closer to sleep.

I curl on my side in the dirt, arm pillowing my cheek—thinking of those pearl buttons, and wishing I could remember my mother's face—while the cold pulls oblivion over my shoulders, tucks it around my ears, and covers my sightless eyes. Before I consciously decide to go, I am snapped away into something deeper than sleep, but I'm not afraid.

I'm not cold or lost or lonely anymore. I am not a princess or a queen or a sacrifice or an abomination or a disappointment. I am nothing at all, a cup swiftly emptying of all the Isra inside it, leaving nothing behind.

ELEVEN

GEM

I stand at the base of the mountain for a long, long moment, not sure I'll be able to climb back up again.

The place where the soldier's spear pierced my thigh aches so badly, it feels as though the bone there will split in half. A hollow in the ground between two nearby Cross cacti looks more inviting than a Smooth Skin bed of clouds. I think how good it would be to lie down there and stare up at the million stars in the sky and be done with this day. But after a long drink of cactus milk and a too-short rest, I start back up the trail.

As much as I'd like to leave the queen to her lies and trembling up on the mountain, I promised to keep her safe.

Still, I don't hurry. I *can't* hurry with my leg throbbing like a second angry heart, but I wouldn't even if I could. The less time I spend with Isra tonight, the better. I can't remember being this angry since the day she came to my cell and laughed at my starving people and cried her sticky tears onto my chest. I would just as soon wrap my hand around her throat and squeeze as sit by the fire with the queen of Yuan.

How dare she treat me like a comrade at shovel and hoe every day we worked together, only to cower and quake the moment her guards are gone? I'd believed the way she viewed my people had changed. I thought she was different from the rest of the Smooth Skins. I thought she considered me a . . . friend. I certainly worked hard enough to convince her I was worth befriending. Even if every shared story and teasing word and gentle bit of advice was deception on my part, *she* doesn't know that. I've given her no reason to change her good opinion of me.

If she ever had one.

She must have been lying, too. Lying with every lopsided smile and flash of her clever eyes and softly whispered reassurance about my healing legs. She was only pretending to trust me, to feel affection for the beast she kept in chains. I should have known she was false. In her eyes, I'll always be a monster. I suspected as much from the beginning.

So why does the proof of what I've known all along feel like a betrayal? Why does the sight of her shaking hands make me want to hurl boulders down the mountain? Why do I *hurt*?

I feel as bruised as I did the day Meer told me she was choosing another man as her mate. I should have been happy. I didn't want to stay with the tribe and watch the baby growing inside Meer be born into a life of famine and pain. I was a warrior. I had a tunnel to finish digging, roses to steal, Smooth Skin cities to worm my way inside.

But I wasn't happy. There were days when watching Meer love someone else more than she had ever loved me—seeing the casual intimacies between her and Hant at the campfire, catching him with his hand upon her swelling belly and a smile on his face—felt like dying. The same way being captured by Smooth Skins felt like dying, and being ordered about by my enemy felt like dying.

Isra has brought nothing but misery into my life, but when I arrive at the remains of the campfire and see the flames out and Isra no longer sitting where I left her, every hot angry thing inside me runs cold.

"Isra?" I circle the fire, panic sharpening my voice. "Isra!"

The air is too quiet. Even the wind has stopped moaning. It feels like the night is holding its breath, waiting for me to discover the terrible fate that has befallen the queen of Yuan. It has to be terrible. I left a blind girl alone a dozen feet from the edge of a cliff. She could have gone to relieve herself and fallen to her death. She could have decided to follow me and taken a wrong turn on the path and wandered into a zion nest. She could have been discovered by a hunting party and been taken prisoner.

I was certain there would be none of my tribe this close to Yuan, but what of the other tribes? The Desert People from

153

the north have been venturing farther south since they burned the domed city of Vanguard two years ago, only to find that its destruction did nothing to return life to their own blighted territory.

Naira warned my father that if we failed to return with Yuan's magic roses, it might come to war between our tribes one day soon. We must show the northerners that we have harnessed the Smooth Skin magic, and share the power of the roses with them, before their chief convinces his people that the only way to heal the land is to destroy every domed city still standing. We cannot allow Yuan to fall, not until we have secured the secret to their abundance.

Isra knows that secret. I should have been coaxing it from her, not shouting and brooding like a child. I should have thought about my people and my promises. I should have remembered how much Isra needs protecting. The desert might be my home, but it isn't hers. I was a fool to forget that, even for a second.

I think of the first moment I saw her, with her head thrown back and her arms open wide, laughing as she ran through the garden. I thought she was crazy then, but what I wouldn't give to hear her laugh like that right now. I have to find her. I have to. She *has* to be alive. If she's not . . .

"Isra!" I roar, my voice echoing off the rocks. I can't think of her body lying bent and broken halfway down the cliff. I *won't.*

I search the dirt around the fire once, twice, and finally, on the third careful circle, I find an uneven set of footprints.

The moons haven't risen high enough to touch this side of the mountains, but the stars give enough light for me to see the scuff marks leading up the trail. She was walking. Not steadily, but alone. That's something. *Something.*

I start up the mountain at a run, ignoring the agony in my leg every time my left foot connects with the ground. I deserve this pain. I'll gladly take this pain and more if only–

There! An Isra-sized lump, curled on the ground by the side of the trail.

"Isra!" I kneel beside her, expecting her to wake up and snap at me for frightening her. Expecting her to stir in her sleep, or grumble beneath her breath. But she doesn't move, even when I push her hair from her face and cup her cheek in my hand.

Instantly, I know something's wrong. She's so cold. Colder than anything living.

All this time, I thought I was changing Isra's mind, but she was the one changing mine, so much so that I forgot that there *are* differences between us. Serious differences. She has no scales or claws to protect her from the hardships of the desert; she has a body that must be fed and watered more often than mine; she is smaller and more delicate and clearly isn't able to tolerate variations in the temperature of her blood.

The Desert People grow cold during the winter, but there's no danger in it. We are more vital in summer, but we don't lie down and die when the winter nights take hold.

Die. She can't.

"Isra. Is–" My voice breaks as I gather her into my lap.

Her limbs are limp and lifeless; her head rests heavily in my palm. "Isra?" I whisper, throat so tight, I can't speak any louder. "Can you hear me?"

She doesn't move or speak, but when my gaze drops, I see it—the flutter of a pulse at her throat, there, but fainter and slower than it should be. She's alive, but if I don't find a way to warm her, she might not be for long.

The thought has barely formed before I'm on my feet, running back to the remains of the fire, with Isra in my arms. I no longer feel the pain in my leg. Fear has banished the awareness of everything but Isra's life, so close to slipping through my fingers. By the time I fall to my knees by the fire, I'm shaking. I have never trembled with fear, not even on the night we swam up the river and crept into the dome.

I settle Isra across my lap, fold her head into my chest, and hold her there with one hand as I rearrange the wood and tuck dried grass beneath it with the other. I could move faster if I laid her down, but I'm afraid to risk it. I'm not as warm as a fire, but I'm warmer than the night, and my blood is certainly hotter than hers.

"Just a minute or two," I whisper into the hair on top of her head, some part of me certain she can't die as long as I'm talking to her. "You'll be warm soon."

I reach carefully around her limp body, and extend my claws, using them to sharpen the end of one stick and notch a hole in another, before reaching for the wood with my hands. I fit the pointed stick into the notched one and spin it as fast as I can, shaking Isra from my chest in the process and sending her tipping off my lap.

I take only a moment to pull her back to me and shift my position, before starting to spin the wood again. I spin and spin, holding my breath until I smell smoke, and then spinning even faster. My muscles burn and my breath comes fast, but just when I think I can't keep up the pace any longer, sparks fly from the notch and the grass beneath the kindling catches. The grass flames, high and fast, and the slender twigs at the bottom of the pile flare to life. After I add more grass and coax the twigs with a stick, the larger limbs begin to smolder and, finally, to burn.

I am famously quick with a fire, even among my people, who all have a gift for flame, but I don't know if I've been quick enough. I shift Isra, and her head falls limply over my arm. Even in the warm light of the fire, her face looks pale, her parted lips bloodless.

We're sheltered from the worst of the wind by the rocks on either side of our camp, and the fire warms up quickly, but even as her cheeks regain their color, Isra remains terrifyingly still. I whisper her name what feels like a hundred times. I smooth her hair from her forehead, pat her cheeks a bit too hard, rock back and forth and back and forth in the hopes of raising my own body temperature, growing more frantic with every passing minute.

I've made a fire. I'm giving her the heat from my body. There's nothing left to do. I could wrap her in her shawl, but it's no longer around her shoulders. She must have lost it when she wandered up the trail.

"Why didn't you feed the fire?" I whisper, lips moving against her cool forehead. "Why?"

157

I'm suddenly angry, belly-burning angry, but not with Isra. With myself. This is *my* fault. I shouldn't have left her on the mountainside, even for an hour. I shouldn't have taken her from the city in the first place. I should have insisted on going alone. That would have proven I was trustworthy; this only proves I'm a fool. I had no idea she'd be so sensitive to the winter chill, but ignorance is no excuse for what I've done. If Isra dies, it will be for nothing, a senseless waste.

Yes, there are bulbs at the top of these mountains, and they'll take root in her garden and put out a pretty flower that sweetens cactus milk into a treat that makes a man dizzy, but drinking it won't give Isra what she wants. This garden she's desperate to plant will accomplish *nothing*. The hope I've given her is a lie, like every other word out of my mouth since she let me out of my cage, like every smile and laugh I've forced while we've worked the ground together, like everything I've pretended to feel.

And everything I've pretended *not* to feel.

It took this—her nearly lost, and me wanting her back more than I've wanted anything in so long—to make me understand.

If she weren't lying so still, it would be laughable.

It's pointless. Hopeless. Even if she weren't afraid of me, at the core we'll always be enemies. She rules a wicked, selfish city, and my tribe suffers for her people's comfort. She's a queen; I'm her prisoner. I resent her and she fears me, and there are times when I fear her, too. I am her monster, and she is mine. But right now none of it matters.

"Isra, please. Open your eyes," I beg, but I don't think she will. When her lashes flutter, I'm so surprised that my elbow jerks beneath her head, sending her chin jabbing into her chest. Her teeth knock together and she moans, low and grumpy.

It is the most wonderful sound I've ever heard.

"Can you hear me?" I support the back of her head and smooth the hair away from her face in time to see her eyes slit open.

"Gem?" Her voice is sleep-rough and cranky and even better-sounding than her grumpy moan. "What are . . . Where . . ." She blinks, and for a second it looks as if her eyes are trying to focus before they go empty once more.

"Do your eyes hurt?" I ask, hoping her cold sleep hasn't left lasting damage.

"No, but my head does. A little." She winces. "More than a little." Her lids droop, and for a second I worry she's falling back asleep, but then she asks, "What happened?"

"I was about to ask you." She shifts in my lap, and I'm suddenly very conscious of the places where we touch and everything I was thinking before she opened her eyes. Everything I was feeling. When I speak again, my voice is rougher than hers. "I found you on the trail. You were cold and I couldn't wake you. I brought you back here and rebuilt the fire, but for a while I wasn't sure . . . I thought . . ." My arms tighten around her, but Isra doesn't seem to mind.

She turns her head, resting her cheek on my chest with a sigh. "I'm sorry."

"I shouldn't have left you alone."

"I shouldn't have let the fire go out," she says. "But I couldn't find the wood and I got scared, and then I was so cold and confused and . . . I . . . I started remembering things.

About my mother . . . her buttons . . ." Her hand drifts to her chest, but hesitates there only a moment before coming to rest on mine.

"I never meant for this to happen," I say. "I didn't understand. I–I never meant to cut you that first night; I had no idea how fragile your skin was. And tonight, when I left–I thought–I didn't know it was so dangerous for you to get cold."

"I didn't, either," she says. "It's all right."

"It's not all right."

"It is." Her fingers slip between the buttons on my shirt, brushing bare skin. It becomes even harder to breathe. "I forgive you. Can you forgive me?"

I start to assure her there's nothing to forgive, but I can't tell any more lies. "I don't know."

She bites her lip. "Is that why you sound angry?"

"I'm not angry. Not at you. I'm just . . ."

"Just what?"

"Happy that you're alive."

"Me too. And grateful. To you. I . . ." She swallows, and her next words seem to come harder. "I meant what I said. I'm not afraid of you. I'm . . . I know it's crazy . . . but I . . ." She lets out a tired sigh, and when she speaks again, her voice isn't much more than a whisper. "I'd like to see your face again. May I?"

At first I think she means see me the way she did the first night, in the garden, but then she lifts a hand into the air and I understand. She wants to touch me.

"Yes," I say, doing my best not to shiver as her fingers feather around my eyes and down my nose, before her thumb

160

smoothes across my bottom lip. "Thank you for asking," I whisper, lips moving beneath her lingering touch.

She sits up, bringing her face even with mine. Her mouth is close; her breath warms my chin. For the first time, she doesn't smell like roses. She smells like cactus milk—clean and salty and of the desert, like my people—and I suddenly wonder if she would taste like all the girls I've kissed in my life. There were other girls before Meer. After she found Hant, I always assumed there would be more, but I never thought . . .

Even a moment ago when I . . .

I didn't think . . . imagine . . . that *she* might . . .

A part of me still refuses to believe it, but another part knows what a girl wants when her fingers linger too long on a boy's mouth, and it knows better than to hesitate. So I don't. I pull her hand away, and risk a kiss.

Our lips brush, soft on softer, timid and testing, the barest friction of skin against skin, but that's all it takes to know that it's right. Isra sighs and twines her arm around my neck. My blood rushes and my body comes alive and everything in me lights up like a sunrise. Like a night sky spitting stars. Like her eyes when she smiles.

She kisses me again. And then again, harder and longer, and I forget every reason this shouldn't happen. I pull her closer and warm her mouth with mine, moaning when her tongue slips between my lips and I taste cactus and salt, but also a hint of sweet and a dark, velvety spice that isn't Smooth Skin or Desert Woman, that is only Isra.

And for a moment she is *my* Isra, and nothing is impossible.

TWELVE

ISRA

THIS is a kiss. *This.* This, this, *this* . . .

His smoke and wood smell filling my head, his Gem taste bittersweet and perfect on my tongue, his arms around me and my hands everywhere I've been dying to touch, and the memory of the killing cold banished by the way he makes me burn.

I don't care what he is, who I am, what's wrong or right. There is no shame or fear, only the driving need to get closer, kiss deeper, consume and be consumed, to lose myself so completely that I will never be found.

I want to stay this way forever, with his chest pressed tightly to mine, and his lips moving at my throat. With my fingers in his soft hair, his breath warm on my skin, his hand—so hot I can feel it through my clothes—sliding between us, down my ribs, over my stomach, down until—

I gasp and my eyes fly open, and for a bare moment I think I see something in the air above my head—a hint of color, a flicker of light, something strange and unexpected that makes me hesitate to push Gem's hand away. By the time the flicker vanishes and the familiar darkness settles in, I am still . . . hesitating . . .

Hesitating . . .

A quiet, shame-filled voice inside demands I put a stop to *that. Immediately.* But oh, it feels so good. So *unbelievably* good. I had no idea that the ache inside could tighten into such a fierce, sweet knot . . . or that Gem would know exactly how to untangle it.

Untangle *me.*

"Isra," he whispers, making me shiver. I never thought . . . I never imagined that he would feel it, too, this pull, this longing to touch and be touched and oh . . .

I draw his mouth back to mine and kiss him until my lips feel bruised and my breath comes faster. Faster and faster, until my head spins and something overwhelming and frightening and beautiful rises inside me. My fingers dig into the back of Gem's neck and my legs tremble and I shift in his arms, bringing my hip into contact with something I hadn't considered.

Something that—despite what the bawdy ballads claim—feels nothing at *all* like a pelican beak.

I bleat like a sheep and roll off Gem's lap so fast, I nearly tumble into the fire. I try to stand, but my legs are trembling and my knees are liquid and I end up flopping onto my bottom and kicking a foot into the flames, and suddenly Gem is cursing his ancestors—or my ancestors, I can't really tell—and snatching my boot from the fire and slapping at it, and the acrid smell of burned animal skin sours the air, and the warm, beautiful feeling vanishes in a puff of smoke.

I suck in a deep breath, and for the first time since Gem pulled me back from the cold, my head clears. This is *not* a dream or a delusion. This is *real.*

I *really* kissed the Monstrous boy I've been holding prisoner. I really drove my fingers through his hair and tasted his taste and let him touch me for so long my cheeks heat just thinking about it. It's madness, but in the moment the madness made perfect sense. I had no idea it would be like that. I never dreamed how quickly a kiss could get out of hand. It's terrifying. Dangerous. Who knows how far things would have gone if I hadn't accidentally bumped into a pelican beak and come to my senses?

My chest flutters, but thankfully my throat strangles my nervous giggle before it can escape. *Pelican beak.* What a terrible piece of poetry. *That* was nothing at *all* like a pelican beak, or anything like what I imagined *that* would feel like, and . . . and . . .

I can't think about it for another second or my cheeks are going to catch fire.

"Are you all right?" Gem asks in a careful way that only makes me more embarrassed.

"Fine." I pull my knees to my chest and cover my face with my hands and wish that Gem were the blind one. I would very much like for him *not* to see me confused and vulnerable and lost in my own skin. I don't know this skin. It's different from the one I've worn for seventeen years.

"Isra . . . I . . ." He clears his throat, and pauses for a moment so long and awkward that I consider running off again simply to escape it. "I didn't know."

Didn't know? I curl my fingers beneath my chin. "What?"

"I didn't know that you . . . that . . ." He sighs, but keeps going despite his obvious discomfort. "In my tribe, by the time a girl is seventeen . . ."

I realize what he's trying to say, and my face burns even hotter. Was it that obvious? That everything between a man and a woman is new to me?

No, Isra. I'm sure most *girls bleat like sheep and set their boots on fire when they first encounter a pelican beak.*

My stomach drops. I want to bury my head in my lap and never tilt it up again, but instead I force myself to lift my chin. "I'm not a girl. I am a *queen,* and—"

"Yes, I remember. You don't have to put your nose in the air." He has the nerve to chuckle afterward. I consider getting angry—mad seems like a good alternative to mortified—but when he continues, his voice is kind, sincere. "And you don't have to be embarrassed. There's nothing wrong with being . . . new. I just . . . If I'd known . . . It can go more slowly. It can be nice that way, too." His fingers brush the back of my hand. His touch is light, undemanding, obviously meant to be comforting, but I pull away all the same.

I'm not ready to touch him again. Not now, maybe not ever.

By the moons, what was I thinking?

I fist my fingers in my hair and give my head a shake before digging the heel of my palm into my forehead. No matter how good it felt to be close to Gem, no matter how much I want to kiss him again. I can't– We can't– This is–

"Impossible," I mutter beneath my breath.

"Not impossible." Gem scoots closer, until his hip touches mine.

"Yes," I insist, but I don't move away. "Impossible."

"Maybe. But it felt right. You felt right," he whispers, sending warmth rushing in my chest and a hint of that tingling I felt in his arms zipping through the rest of me. Even if every other being on the planet would think we're mad, it's good to know that Gem felt it, too. That I wasn't . . . that I *am not* alone.

I sigh. "There are so many things I wish." I lean into him, resting my head on his shoulder, overwhelmed by everything I want to be different. My life, my purpose, my death. But none of that will ever change, and what we want is more impossible than Gem knows.

"I'm sorry," I say, despair settling in my heart. "I would change the world if I could."

"Then change it," he says, a hint of yesterday's gruffness in his tone, though the arm he puts around my shoulders is gentle. "You're a queen. You're young and strong and clever. And kind, when you want to be. That city is yours to command."

I shake my head. "No, not yet. And even when–"

"Yes. *Yet.* You can change your world. You have that power."

"You don't understand," I say. "Even if the garden—"

"Forget the garden. You don't need the garden." He turns me to him before pushing my hair from my face with a tenderness that makes me ache. "You can make the wrong things right without the garden. You can give the outcasts a place in your city. You can send food to my people. You don't have to wait. Children are starving *now.* My . . . my child is starving."

My lips part. I never even considered. He's only nineteen.

"I don't know his name. He didn't . . . He wasn't named before I left," Gem says, grief clear in his voice. "But I think of him every day. His mother chose another mate, and I'll never be a father to him in the way that man will, but I want to know him. I want him to live to see the first anniversary of his birth, but many don't."

"Please," I beg, the thought of those hungry children, of *Gem's* hungry child, hitting me harder than it has before. He has a child, and I'm still not much more than a child myself. I'm crazy to think we'll ever understand each other. "I'm sorry. I don't want your people or your baby to suffer, I truly don't, but I . . . I don't . . . ." I try to drop my head to my chest, but Gem catches my chin in his hand.

"Then don't back down." His finger traces slowly back and forth across my cheek. "Help my people. Help yourself."

"I can't."

"You can," he whispers, leaning so close I can feel his breath on my face. My lips tingle and my heart beats faster, and all I want to do is taste him again—to lean in and lose myself in the dizzy rush of his mouth on mine—but I can't.

I push his hand away gently but firmly. "I *can't*. The people wouldn't allow it. I'm tainted."

He makes a disgusted sound, but I push on before he can make another grand speech about what his chief would do in my place.

"I know it doesn't make sense to you, but that matters to my people," I continue. "They are repulsed by Monstrous traits, and it isn't just the outer ugliness of the tainted that they despise. We're raised to believe the Monstrous are worse than animals, that they are savages who kill for pleasure, and that their ugliness is a sign of the corruption of their souls."

He sighs, his frustration clear in the sound. "But you *know* that isn't true."

"I don't *know*. I don't know anything for sure," I confess before I think better of it, the pressure of his expectations making me anxious. As soon as I realize how my words sounded, I hurry to explain. "I mean, I know *you* aren't anything like what I imagined a Monstrous would be like, but one of your people slaughtered my father. And I—I'm not like the rest of my people. It isn't just my size or my rough skin or my wild hair. I've never done as I was told. I lie and take chances I shouldn't and think only of myself and—"

"And you think . . ." His breath rushes out. "You think that means your soul is *corrupt*?" he asks, disgust and shock warring in his tone. "Like mine?"

I shake my head, sending my hair flying into my face.

168

"No! No, of course not. I don't think your soul is corrupt. You're not listening."

"*You're* not listening," he snaps. "If you were, you'd hear how rattled you sound."

"I am not *rattled.* I'm trying to explain why I can't rush in and change the world. The world is complicated," I say, feeling more confused with every passing second. I'm not ready for this. I don't know what to say. "I just . . . I know some of what I've been taught is wrong, but you can't deny that we *are* different. You said so yourself."

"Not as different as either side would like to think," he says, before adding in a harsh voice, "Women are women, I can promise you that much. The same tricks work the same way. You even make the same sounds when you—"

"Stop," I choke out, struggling to swallow past the sick feeling rising inside me. For the first time since we touched, I feel ashamed. How could he? How could he be so understanding one minute and cheapen every unguarded thing that happened between us the next? "You're cruel," I say, hating the catch in my voice.

"What did you expect from a *corrupt soul*?"

"Fine," I snap. "Never mind. I should never have—"

"What if you weren't *tainted*, Isra?"

I blink, startled by the change of direction. "What?"

"What if you're wrong? What if you've been wrong your entire life?" he asks. "What if there's nothing *Monstrous* about you?"

"I thought you hated that word," I whisper.

169

"I hate a lot of things."

"I know you think . . ." I pause, not wanting to inspire any further spite, but feeling I owe him honesty in a way I didn't before. Spiteful or not, he saved my life. And kissed me and held me and admitted it felt right, and that has changed things between us. I can't pretend it hasn't. "I know you find your people beautiful," I say, "and I envy you that, I really do. But my people . . . they don't see beauty in mutation. It scares them. They were horrified when they saw me for the first time at my coronation."

Gem snorts as if I've said the most ridiculous thing in the world, and anger flares inside me again. He wasn't there. I was, and I heard the people pull in a collective breath; I felt their surprise when they looked upon their tainted queen for the first time.

"Believe what you want," I snap, "but I know–"

"You know nothing. You're not *tainted*. You're nothing like a Monstrous girl. Any one of them could break you in half, and not one has skin that peels everywhere but their face," he says, making me wince and my fingers curl self-consciously, drawing up inside the long sleeves of my sweater. "Whatever's wrong with you, it's not caused by resembling my people. As far as I've seen, you look almost exactly like the other Smooth–"

"I do not look like them," I snap. "And no matter what you think, I *know* if I weren't queen, my life would be very different than it is now. I might not be tainted enough to be cast out, but I am, *without a doubt*, ugly in a way that puts the state of my soul and mind in question. That's why I can't start issuing bizarre orders. I have to win my people's trust. I believe the garden will–"

"Stop," he says. "I can't listen to it again. I can't."

"I won't talk at all, then!" I turn back to the fire and lean away from him, wishing with every bone in my body it were safe to go for a walk. The last thing I want to do is stay within spitting distance of this stubborn, infuriating creature.

"There's one thing I want to know first." The gravel crunches, and I sense that Gem's moving closer, but I refuse to give him the satisfaction of scooting away. "If I'm hideous, inside and out–"

"I never said–" His arms close around me, and my words end in a sharp intake of breath as he hauls me onto his lap. "Put me down!" I push at his chest, but he ignores me and pulls me close, whispering his next words against my skin.

"If I'm so ugly in every way," he continues, the feel of his mouth moving against my cheek making my blood rush in spite of myself, "then why do you want me, Isra?"

"I–I need your help. And your father promised you would–"

"Don't be stupid. You know what I mean." His hands skim over my body, one teasing the skin at the back of my neck, the other tracing the column of my spine from top to bottom before smoothing around to my hip and squeezing tight, fingers digging in until my belly flutters.

I shiver, and I know he knows the reason why. My lips part and my breath rushes out, but I don't scramble away. I close my eyes and count slowly to ten and try to remember how hurt I was when he compared me to all the other knots he has untangled.

But it's so hard. Because he's right. I *do* want him. I wanted him before, and I want him even more now. I want to banish the ugliness between us with my lips on his. I want to kiss him until his blood runs fast and he whispers my name in his thick, needy voice instead of his tight, angry one.

Words only bring pain; we should use hands instead. I lift my hand to his face, smoothing my thumb across the hint of whiskers on his cheek.

"Answer me," he whispers, fingers slipping into my hair.

"I don't know."

"That's not an answer." His jaw muscle leaps beneath my fingers. "*Why?* Because I'm here, and we're alone? You'd have done the same with any boy?"

"No, it's not . . ." I lick my lips, torn between the painful truth and a painful lie. I decide on the truth. At least there's nobility in that. "I've never felt like this," I confess. "I've never kissed anyone the way I kissed you. No one has ever . . . touched me like that."

"Why not?" he asks, his voice only the tiniest bit kinder. "I can't believe there aren't Smooth Skin boys who would tolerate your *ugliness* in order to have the queen in their bed. Your king will have power. That's the Smooth Skin way, isn't it?"

"It is," I say, blushing in spite of myself at his casual mention of my bed. "And there has been some . . . interest. Bo kissed me once, more than once, I guess." I twine my arms around Gem's neck, unable to resist the temptation of his skin.

"But he didn't make me feel anything like this." I try to move my lips to Gem's, but he turns away, and my mouth bounces off his jaw.

"Why is that? Why do *you* believe you desire me more than you desire one of your own kind?"

I swallow. "I . . ." I'm suddenly sure what he's after, and just as sure I don't want to give him his answer. "I don't know."

"Tell me," he demands. "I want to hear you say it."

I shake my head.

"Is it because you're *tainted*?" he asks, his tone so sharp, I wince. "Because you're ugly on the outside and wicked on the inside? That's why you're drawn to a monster?"

I don't say a word. I don't have to.

He makes a disgusted sound. "I feel sorry for you, Isra. I really do."

I draw my arms back to my chest and slide from his lap, feeling dirty and small and more wrong than ever before.

"You make yourself miserable," Gem says, "and refuse to let anyone keep you from it. I'm a fool, but you are . . . I don't have a Smooth Skin word for what *you* are."

I cross my arms and fight the urge to cry. "What about you, Gem? Why do you want *me*? I thought Smooth Skins sickened you."

He's quiet for so long that I don't think he's going to answer, but finally– "I told you, I'm a fool."

"That's not an answer."

He grunts and falls silent again. After listening to the wood pop in the fire and the wind howl beyond our shelter for what seems like hours, I decide to consider his unwillingness to

173

answer a small victory. Ignoring the tears still pressing against the backs of my eyes and the filthy feeling I know no bath could wash away, I lie down and close my eyes. My body needs the rest, even if sleep seems impossible.

Seems impossible, but obviously it isn't. I'm halfway there by the time Gem lies down behind me and tucks one heavy arm around my waist, fitting his front to my back with such gentleness that I don't startle from my near sleep as much as drift to the surface of myself like a bubble.

"When I thought you were dying . . ." His arm tightens, pulling me closer. "I would have done anything to keep you with me," he whispers into my hair. "Anything."

I put my hand over his and leave it there in silent acceptance of his not quite apology. No matter how much his words hurt tonight, I don't want to fight. I need him too much. And he needs me. There will be no garden for my people, or food for his, if we're at each other's throats.

And what he just said leaves little doubt that he cares for me. No matter how misguided he thinks I am, he *cares*. He really does.

The thought is thrilling.

And petrifying.

I will be married *very* soon, and Bo will come to my bed, and he will give me royal babies and they will become kings or, if they're unlucky, queens, and I won't live to see them fully grown. *That* is my future. It is inescapable.

It makes me want to push Gem away and curl up in a tight, lonely ball.

It makes me want to turn in his arms and shed my two

pairs of overalls and peel off my long underwear and reveal everything to him, *do* everything a man and a woman can do—no matter how the thought terrifies me—because I'm more terrified I'll never have this chance again.

But in the end, I'm a coward.

Leaping blindly from a balcony ledge or walking out into the desert is nothing compared to this. I can't afford to be any more haunted than I am already, and a night with Gem would haunt me, I have no doubt.

THIRTEEN

BO

A dead snake. It's only a dead snake—mangled skin and a bit of dried entrails dropped by a bird as it flew over the city—now stuck to the glass. That's all. No crack in the dome, no danger, no sign that the covenant is weakening. Just a festering dead thing that will be washed away if the rains ever come again.

I give the signal that I've finished my examination, and Father personally reels me back in from my great height above the city. But even when my feet touch down on the stones atop the tallest building in Yuan, I'm still floating inside.

Isra is safe. For now. And now is all I want to think about.

"It's nothing. Just a snake skin," I pant as the other men unhitch me from the wire. "Some guts on the dome. Nothing to worry about."

Relieved laughter erupts as the tension that has followed everyone attending to the inspection evaporates. Lok slaps me on the back, Nan clasps my hand for a hard shake, and Ru has the nerve to ruffle my hair like I'm still a boy, but I don't care, because Isra's blood is staying in her body, and I'm even more thankful than I imagined I'd be.

I can't wait to tell her, to feel her arms around me when she thanks me for handling the investigation personally—and so quickly, too. I am the one who ordered that the crews setting up the rope-and-pulley system work day and night, allowing my inspection to take place a full day and a half early. She will be elated. She'll certainly want more than a kiss on the cheek tonight, and I will most gladly oblige her. I will kiss her until she trembles in my arms and begs me to stay and warm her lonely tower bed.

"Are you certain there was no sign of weakness?" Father asks, pulling me from my thoughts.

He's the only man on the roof not smiling. Beneath his oiled mustache, his cheeks droop solemnly on either side of his mouth; his eyes are as troubled as they were hours ago when he reminded me of my duty to report whatever I found, regardless of how frightening it might be for our people.

"There was nothing." I hold his gaze as I work the buckles on my harness. "It was a dead snake. There wasn't a nick in the glass. I swear it. The covenant is still strong."

"That's wonderful news," he says, before adding beneath

his breath in a voice too soft for the men beginning to disman-
tle the pulley system on the other side of the roof to hear, "But
even if the dome were weakening, it wouldn't change your
destiny. You will be king. She has to live only long enough to
speak her vows."

My fingers grow clumsy. I drop my eyes to the buckles. "I
don't wish the death of my queen."

"Of course not," he says. "None of us do. She's a dear
girl."

He says "dear girl" the same way he'd say "unfortunate
accident," and for the first time I wonder if my father hasn't
grown too powerful. I don't like seeing him eager to spill royal
blood. It feels wrong for him to speak casually about the sacrifice Isra will make.

"She is," I say, choosing my next words carefully. I need
Father to understand that I have no desire to hasten the moment of Isra's death. "I've come to care for her. I look forward
to our marriage and wish her as much life as possible. I know
the day I lose her to the garden will be one of the darkest of
my life."

Father smiles and clasps my shoulder in a rare display of
affection. "You sound like a king already."

"Thank you." I duck my head as I step out of the harness,
grateful for the excuse to cross the roof and tuck the gear back
into the box Nan holds open. I can't look my father in the eye
right now. If I do, I'll see proof that he thinks I'm lying.

Worse, he'll see proof that I'm not.

Baba has known Isra longer and more intimately than

anyone else except the late king, but there is clearly no love in his heart for her. Maybe he knows something I do not, and Isra is a burden I'll have to bear until the day of her death. I admit there have been times when I've worried about the state of her mind, like when I discovered her slippers in the mud outside the beast's window two nights past. Her maid explained the slippers easily enough—Needle dropped them on her way to get them resoled—but there's no explanation for Isra's other odd behavior except . . . eccentricity. Maybe it's harmless eccentricity, or maybe, as my father clearly fears, it's the precursor to her mother's madness.

I'm not sure which of us is right. I only know I can't wait to give Isra the good news.

With a bow to my father, I step into the gondola and lower myself down the side of the building, the seventy-meter drop not nearly as intimidating after dangling three hundred meters in the air to inspect the dome. I reach the street to find a crowd gathered by the baker's shop. Worried eyes meet mine, and I smile, but I don't stop to assure the people that all is well. Isra's subjects will hear the good news from their queen, who deserves to know before anyone else that the danger has passed.

I hurry through the cobblestone streets—past the towering buildings where the poorest citizens live with their children crowded five and six to a room, past the squatter, more decorative buildings where the skilled workers and their families live and run their shops, past the soldiers' barracks, and onto the path leading through the royal garden. I've been avoiding this route through the city the past two days, but this evening the roses hold no terror for me. They're beautiful in the fading pink light, and I find myself lingering near the oldest blooms.

I can feel the spirits of the former queens of Yuan here. One day I hope I will feel Isra's spirit even more intimately.

Possessed by the notion, I drop to one knee in front of the giant blooms. "I will take good care of her," I swear, imagining that the dead queens can hear my promise. "And when she's gone, I will visit her here every day for the rest of my life."

I smile. Father's right; I do sound like a king.

Drunk on promises, I rise shakily to my feet, dizzied by how close I am to being the most powerful man in Yuan. By the time I reach the door to Isra's tower, I'm certain tonight is the night. I'll assure her that death is nowhere in her near future and then make my offer for her hand. Father said he wanted to discuss the betrothal without the potential husband present—as is the custom when negotiating a royal marriage—but I want Isra to remember the moment we decided to marry as something between the two of us.

So I wait until her maid leaves the tower to collect the dinner tray she has fetched for the queen since Isra requested her privacy. Then I dismiss the guards at the door, retrieve the key from its hiding place behind the loose stone, and let myself in.

"Isra?" I climb the stairs swiftly, not bothering to keep my steps soft. I don't want to surprise her. I'm sure she's been worried. A shock is the last thing she needs. "Isra, it's Bo!" I call again, louder than before, but still no answer comes from the rooms above.

She must be out on the balcony. She seems to favor it there, though she can't see the impressive view of the city spread out before her . . . yet.

But by next week, or the following, for certain . . .

Returning her sight. Just another thing my queen will love me for.

With a smile, I push through the door to her apartments, pass her empty sitting room, leaving the door to her private chamber closed—I doubt she's asleep at this hour—and make my way to her music room. From the door, I can see that the balcony on the far side of the room is empty.

The bedroom it is, then, I think, secretly pleased to have an excuse to be alone with Isra in a room with a bed. I turn back down the hall and knock softly on her door. "Isra? Are you awake?"

Silence, but for the soft tick of a clock in the music room.

"Isra? It's Bo. I have wonderful news."

More silence, silence so complete that it's hard to believe she's breathing in the room beyond. But she has to be in there. She isn't in any of the other rooms, and she hasn't left the tower since I walked her here two days ago. The guards outside would have alerted me immediately. I gave strict orders.

"Isra? Are you well?" I ask, growing concerned. "Isra?"

More silence. My stomach shrivels. What if she's ill? What if she's suffering in the absence of the poison the way the wine lovers suffer when our stores run dry? What if I've put her health in danger?

"Isra!" I pound on the door with my fist. "Answer me,

or I'm coming in!" I wait a long moment, giving her one last chance to call out, before I turn the handle.

The heavy wood hits the wall behind with a thud that echoes in the empty room. In the center, Isra's bed is neatly made, the quilt tucked tightly at the edges. In the corner, the maid's narrow cot is also made, but the mattress shows signs that it held a body not too long ago—dips and depressions, a sagging place on one side where she sat as she put on her shoes. Isra's mattress, however . . .

I cross the room to stare down at it. Perfectly smooth. Not a dent or a shadow. Either Needle shakes the mattress out and reshapes it every morning, or Isra hasn't slept here recently.

And if she didn't sleep in her bed last night . . . where did she sleep? And with whom?

"That lying . . . little . . . ," I murmur through clenched teeth.

My hands ball into fists, and it's all I can do to keep from punching the wall near her headboard. Isra's been using me to cover her indiscretions. She could be with another man right *now*, conceiving a bastard to bear after we marry.

I will not raise another man's bastard. I will *not*.

She'd better pray there's another explanation, I think as I slam the door to her bedroom behind me. If Isra loses my affection, she will have very few friends in this city.

And a queen without friends will find herself a dead queen sooner than later.

FOURTEEN

GEM

I woke before the sun, driven by the need to put an end to our adventure as soon as possible. After adding fuel to the fire and waking Isra long enough to assure her that I'd be back before the flames went out, I hurried up the mountain to fetch the bulbs we'd come for. I couldn't risk telling her the truth about the garden.

No matter what happened between us last night, I still need an excuse to leave my cell. Come spring, I must steal the royal roses and return to my people.

Still, I didn't like leaving her alone, even for a short time.

I walked as quickly as my sore legs would carry me and was back by her side by the time the first pink light kissed the desert.

This time, she was where I had left her, curled in a ball on the ground, her sweater-covered hands pressed against her lips. I watched her sleep as I tied the gnarled roots of the bulbs together with strips of dried grass, dreading the moment she'd open her eyes.

The only thing worse than hating Isra is . . . whatever *this* is. Wanting her, wanting her to realize what a fool she is. Wanting all this to be over.

I want to go home. I want to be back with people I know, in a world I understand. I'm sick to death of this upside-down place, where I crave the touch of a girl who holds me prisoner, and every other word I speak is a lie. Half the time I can't even tell who I'm lying to. Her or myself.

I spend the day angry. At myself. At Isra. At the bulbs she insisted on fondling and sniffing before we headed down the mountain, at the rocks on the trail, at the sun and the wind and the dirt in my Smooth Skin shoes and the needles on every cactus where we stop to drink.

I am in a *foul* mood, made fouler by trying to hide it from Isra. The walk back to the dome has been torture. A part of me is eager to be back in my cell. At least there Isra can't cling to my arm, or brush her body against mine, or sigh through her parted lips, or tilt her face up with *that* look in her eyes. The one that makes me want to strangle her. And kiss her. And strangle her some more. And maybe leap off a cliff after the strangling is done, just to put myself out of my misery.

"It won't be long now," Isra says, shielding her face from the setting sun with one narrow hand. "I can smell it."

"Smell what?"

"The dome. I never realized it had a smell," she says, wrinkling her nose. "Like metal when it's cold. And sour nutshells. Mixed together."

I grunt in response.

"What do you think it smells like?" she asks.

"We'll be close enough for the guards to catch sight of us soon," I say, ignoring her question. I'm not in the mood to play her blind-girl games. Not everything has a smell, and if the dome had a smell, it would smell like death. Slow, creeping, unmerciful death. "We should stop here. Wait for it to get dark. There's a mound of rocks just ahead. It should conceal us from anyone using a spyglass."

I don't tell her that my people gathered those rocks, that we piled them high enough to hide a scouting party of two or three. I don't tell her that I came here on my first scouting mission when I was fourteen and stood behind the rocks, seething hatred for the dome that festers like a boil on the horizon.

It's strange, to stand now in this place where my younger self vowed to destroy my enemy at all costs, with a Smooth Skin queen clinging to my arm. I once thought I knew everything I ever wanted to know about the Smooth Skins. Now . . . I know nothing. With every passing day, I grow more and more ignorant. If I keep it up, by the time I return to my people, I'll be as rattled in the head as the queen of Yuan.

"Gem?" She tugs lightly at my sleeve. "Gem?"

"Yes?"

She leans closer, hugging my arm to her chest, making me aware of her, no matter how much I wish I weren't. I want to push her away. I want to pull her closer. I want to punch the pile of rocks until my knuckles bleed.

The pain would be a welcome distraction.

"Are you all right?"

"I'm fine," I snap, then force myself to ask in a gentler voice, "How's your head?"

She tilts her head to one side and then the other, stretching the long column of her neck. "It still hurts," she says. "I've never had a headache like this before. I don't know. Maybe I just need something to eat."

"Soon." I stare hard at the horizon, willing the sun to sink faster. "You'll be back in your rooms not long after dark."

She sighs, a mournful, defeated rush of breath, as if *she* is the one on her way to a cell. "I'll miss this."

"The desert?"

"Well . . . yes," she says, sounding surprised. "I will. The wind especially, even though it's cold. But . . ." Her fingers curl into my arm. "I didn't mean the desert. I meant . . . I'll miss being familiar. Being able to . . . touch."

It's the first either of us has said about *that* sort of thing all day. The closer we get to the dome, the more those moments by the fire seem like a fever dream. I can't believe I tasted her, touched her; that I thought I could reach her with my words. That the real Isra and the real Gem might find a way to be allies. Maybe more than allies.

But Isra isn't real. She's a Smooth Skin. She was raised in an artificial world built on lies, bought and paid for with the

186

lives of my people. The fact that I could forget that for even a moment proves how dangerously close I am to losing my mind. My purpose. My self. If only my father had left Gare instead. Gare would have already found a way to bring the roses home to our people. He would never have let his heart soften toward a Smooth Skin. He would never have loosened his grip on hate.

"Gem?" Isra tips her face up to mine. The dying light catches her eyes and shrinks her pupils to specks of black, leaving nothing but green so bright, I can't stop staring. "What are you thinking?"

"Nothing."

"Liar," she whispers, pinching my arm through my shirt. "It's impossible to think nothing. Even when you're asleep, you're thinking *something*."

I grunt.

"It's true." She closes her eyes, soaking in the last of the sun's fading warmth. "How else would we dream?"

"My people believe some dreams come from the spirit world," I say. "That they're messages from the ancestors."

"Hm." Her eyes slit and her brow wrinkles. "I hope they're wrong."

"Why? Are your ancestors unhappy with you? Sending you bad dreams?"

"I don't know. Maybe. I have this same dream . . ." A strong breeze ruffles her hair, and she huddles closer to my side. When she speaks again, I have to strain to hear her over the howling of the wind. "I dream about the night the tower burned. Over and over again. My mother died that night. My

187

father and I would have died, too, if the guards hadn't reached us in time."

For the first time since I awoke this morning, the tight, angry knot in my belly loosens. Fire is a terrible way to lose a life. And four years old is too young to lose a mother.

I place my hand on hers, warming her fingers. "That doesn't sound like a dream from your ancestors."

"No?" The muscles tighten in her jaw. "Maybe it is. Maybe the dream is my punishment."

"For what? Did you set the fire?"

"No," she says, voice breaking.

"Then stop blaming yourself. You were a child," I say roughly. She seems determined to take on unnecessary pain. It's incredible. Wasteful. It makes me angry at Isra on Isra's behalf, which is just . . . confusing. "Your ancestors wouldn't send a dream to torture you while you sleep," I explain, trying to be patient. "Not without a reason."

"That's good to know." She squints and rubs her fingers in a circle at her temple. Her head has been aching on and off all day. At one point, we had to sit down and rest until the pain passed. It's best we're nearing the dome. Isra isn't made for the desert, no matter how much she enjoys the wind. "I had a strange dream last night. At least I think it was a dream," she continues. "Before you found me on the trail, I dreamed of the fire again, but this time there was a face in one of the burning beams."

"Whose face?"

"I don't know. A woman. I don't think I've met her, but her face was made out of flames, so . . . hard to tell." She lifts her hand, tracing an image in the empty air in front of her again and again. Her fingers are graceful, and I suddenly wish I could see her dance the way my women dance around the fire on the night of the full moons.

"Did the woman say anything to you?" I push images of Isra—dressed in the clothes of my people, her long legs free to kick and leap—from my mind.

"She opened and closed her mouth, like she was trying to speak," Isra says. "But I couldn't hear her over the fire."

I make a considering sound. "That *could* have been an ancestor dream."

She turns back to me, abandoning her air drawing. "You think the woman was one of my ancestors?"

"She could be." I shrug. "Maybe a grandmother. Or great-grandmother, since you don't recognize her face."

"I never met my grandmother, either," Isra says. "She died before I was born."

"Maybe your grandmother, then. She could be trying to tell you something."

"Telling me not to play with fire," she says, with a ragged laugh.

"Do you have a habit of playing with fire?"

Her lips lift on one side. "I suppose," she says, voice husky. "In a manner of speaking."

A memory from last night—Isra's bare throat golden in the firelight, my mouth on her skin, feeling her pulse race beneath my lips—flickers through my mind, making it hard to swallow.

"Maybe that's it," I say. "You should listen closer if you dream that dream again."

"I will," she says. "Thank you."

I grunt. I did nothing worth thanking me for, and I resent her casual gratitude. If she's really thankful, then she should send food to my people the instant we return to the city. She should set me free and tell her advisor and her people to eat their protests. Set me free and . . . come with me. Let me show her that my people aren't animals, let my people see that the queen of Yuan has a heart and a soul and a wish to make things better.

And then we can make love in my hut and fly into the sky to slay the Summer Star together on the back of a golden dragon.

I grunt again. Fantasy creatures will fly through the air before the peace I'm imagining comes to pass.

"What does that one mean?" she asks, tapping my chest with one long finger. "I haven't placed that grunt. It's not the disgusted-with-me grunt, or the preparing-to-say-something-mean grunt, or the trying-not-to-smile grunt."

A smile splits my face before I can stop it. I grunt, and she laughs a laugh like stones skittering down a mountainside, wild and reckless.

"That's the one," she says, still laughing. "I like that one. It's my favorite."

"I like your laugh. You don't laugh in there."

"You'll miss the laugh, but not the touching?" Her smile fades. "That's what we were talking about. I remember, you know. I never forget." Her lips part, begging for a kiss for the tenth or hundredth or thousandth time today.

By the ancestors, I should just give up fighting myself and

kiss her. I *want* to kiss her. I'm dying to kiss her. A part of me even says that my promise to my people *compels* me to kiss her.

Assuming she keeps her promise to send food, playing at being Isra's friend has gotten me closer to helping my people than I could have imagined possible. Who knows what I could accomplish as her lover? If I keep her happy, she might even give me the roses of her own free will. Seduction wouldn't be difficult. Despite the voices in her head that assure her I'm a monster, and assure her that she is something worse for wanting my hands on her, I know Isra wants me. I should manipulate her desire, and forget about the rest. Who cares what she thinks or feels beyond the lust that makes her press her body close to mine? Who cares what *I* feel beyond the satisfaction of serving my people and the pleasure of being with a woman for the first time in too many months?

But the thought of that kind of deception turns my stomach. I won't use or be used in that way, not unless I have no other choice.

"Forget I said anything," Isra says. A nervous shake of her head sends her hair tumbling over her shoulders. She tips her chin down, casting her face in shadow. "You're right."

"I didn't say anything."

"Exactly," she says in a pained whisper, and her pain pains me, too. More evidence of my weakness.

"The sun is down." I take her hand and tuck it efficiently into the crook of my arm, hoping to spare us both any more of this . . . whatever it is. "We should go."

"Wait." She stops, holding tightly to my arm. "I have to—I *want* to tell you I'm sorry for what I said last night. I've been

191

thinking about it all day, and I . . . I wasn't ready for questions about what I thought. Or felt. I know it's best for both of us if we–"

"We should go."

She sighs. "You've made me think. When we get back to the city, I'm going to be different."

I grunt, but this time she doesn't find it funny. Neither do I. "So you said," I say, unable to hide my doubt. I tug my arm, gently pulling her forward.

"So I *say*," she insists. "I know what I've been taught. Now I want to know the truth. I realized years ago the two aren't always the same, but I've never had the courage to say a word to anyone else. But I won't remain silent anymore. I'm going to ask questions. I'm going to pay attention. I'm not going to take for granted that Junjie's opinions or anyone else's opinions are fact until I find proof for myself. I don't care if there is . . . They can't . . ." She takes a shaky breath, and her fingers tighten around my arm. "They can't force me to make decisions before I'm ready. I'll find a way to convince them that I'm good for the city, and that the changes I want to make are in the best interests of all our people."

"All right." I fight the urge to reach out to her again, to try to make her understand the truth about Yuan and the desperate situation of my people. But I can't. I don't trust her. Not yet. But maybe . . . if she means what she says . . . "I'm interested to see this new Isra."

She smiles. "Me too. And I . . ." Her smile grows bigger as she turns to me. "Would you come to the rose garden? With me? Tonight?"

"Tonight?" I ask as I move around the stones.

"Yes." She nods and falls into step beside me."I don't want to wait. Will you?"

Yes! I want to shout, *Yes!—finally,* a chance to learn more about the magic that will save my people—but instead I force myself to wait several long moments before offering a careful, "Why do you want to go there?"

I can't let Isra know how interested I am in her magic roses. There are already guards stomping through the gardens all hours of the day and night. If she adds additional patrols, my odds of escaping with a plant will go from not likely to impossible.

"I want to see you again," she says shyly. "If . . . that's all right."

I ignore the way my chest tightens. "Will there be time?" I ask, not certain how long the magic takes. "The guards come through the royal garden every ten to fifteen minutes."

She hums beneath her breath. "That could be enough time. Or not. It depends on whether or not they're being co-operative."

"The roses?"

"Sometimes they show what I ask to see," she explains. "Sometimes they show me something else. The night we left, I saw Bo knocking at the tower door." Her fingers tap a nervous rhythm on my arm. "Hopefully my absence wasn't discov-ered. I doubt it was. I think the roses were just trying to scare me into staying in Yuan. They've been . . . different lately. I don't like being alone with them anymore."

I walk a little more slowly. The way she talks about the

flowers, it sounds like the roses are alive. Aggressively alive. It makes me remember her words that first night, about their hunger.

"What are the roses hungry for?" I ask.

"What?" She stumbles, but I hold her up, carrying her until she regains her feet.

"That first night, you said they were hungry." I watch her face, barely able to see her features in the increasing darkness. The first moon won't rise for another hour or more. Soon, we'll both be walking in the dark. "You said the roses were hungry."

She licks her lips. "How far are we from the dome? The smell is strong now."

"Is it blood?"

She turns sharply in my direction. "How did you know?"

"I didn't. It was a guess. I saw the thorn under your finger-nail," I say, more disturbed by the confirmation of my suspicion than I thought I would be. Magic fed by blood is dark magic. My people have never practiced dark magic.

Your people have also starved, while the Smooth Skins grew fat in their enchanted cities.

"How often do you feed them?" This might be my only chance to learn how to care for the plant I plan to steal. Dark magic or not, most of my people won't care, as long as it puts food in their babies' bellies.

"I don't feed them," she says. "I mean, I *do,* but that's not what . . . They require a . . . larger offering. Every thirty years. Sometimes twenty. It depends."

"Depends on what?"

194

She sighs. "Oh, I don't know. Lots of things. If the dome is damaged by a storm and the roses have to repair it, that takes a lot of strength. If blight touches the harvest, or children are born sick, or . . . any number of things." She shrugs and lifts a hand in the air. "Any weakness in our city or our people. Correcting those things can make the roses grow hungry again faster."

"But the roses' magic doesn't stop some children from being born tainted." I hate the word, but it's what she understands.

She shakes her head. "No, it doesn't. Which is as good an argument as any that the tainted people aren't a threat," she says, surprising me. "Our covenant has remained strong for almost eight hundred years. The roses take care of us. Surely, if the tainted were something to be afraid of, the roses would use magic to correct their mutation."

"Makes sense," I say, strangely proud of her. And hopeful in a way I haven't been before. Maybe something *is* changing inside Isra.

"I agree," she says. I can just make out her smile in the near dark. "I'll have to remember that when I talk to Junjie about doing away with the Banished camp."

I slow again. "You're going to do it?"

"I am. As soon as I can. After we plant the bulbs tomorrow, I'll go straight to his chambers," she says, squeezing my arm. "But tonight I want to see you."

"All right." I smile down at her, my empty stomach clenching, more nervous than I thought I would be at the thought. I wonder what she'll see when she looks at me tonight? A smile or bared teeth? A man or a monster? "But I want to give the plants my blood. You're already weak."

"No, you can't," she says, sounding faintly horrified by the thought. "It has to be . . . The roses feed only on . . ."

"On what?"

"On women," she says, but there's something crooked in her voice, a sharp edge that jabs at the hope inside me. "It's all right. A little blood won't do me any harm."

"What about a lot of blood?" I ask, putting my finger on what's bothering me most about the roses. "You said the roses needed a larger offering every thirty years. How large?"

She falters again. This time, I don't pull her along. I stop, and turn to her, making sure she's steady on her feet before capturing her face in my hands. I don't want her to hide. I need the truth, and there's just enough light left for me to see her eyes. She can never lie with her eyes. They will answer my question, even if her lips will not.

"How large, Isra?" I whisper. "Do you mean . . . a death?"

Her lips part, and a tiny choking sound escapes her throat. Her eyes tighten and begin to shimmer the way they do before the Smooth Skin tears come. "No, not a death," she lies.

"You swear it?"

"I swear, not one of my people has ever died to feed the roses." This time, her eyes tell me she's speaking the truth. Either she's getting better at lying or there's something that I don't understand.

"Wouldn't be the first time," I mumble beneath my breath.

"What?" she asks.

"Your ways are strange to me." I sigh, feeling every mile we've walked in the past two days. "Some stranger than others."

"They're strange to me, too." She leans her cheek into my hand, and for a moment she looks so young, so lost.

"It's all right." I wrap my arms around her and pull her close, dropping my lips to the top of her head, kissing her wild hair.

"Is it terrible that I don't want to go back?" she asks.

"No," I say, wishing she'd look up.

"Yes, it is. If you knew . . ."

"If I knew what?"

She shakes her head and pulls away, until only her fingers touch my arm. "Nothing. Let's go. At least there's food there. I'm starving. I'm sure you're hungry, too. We can put off the roses until another night if you'd like. Needle set you free once. I'm sure she could manage it again."

"We could eat first and then go," I say, more curious about the roses than ever before. "Could your maid–"

"She could," Isra says. "Or I could crawl up and get us something from the tower. We keep apples and nuts and other things in the pantry in the sitting room for something light between meals. It wouldn't take long for me to fetch some, especially if you tell me when it's safe to climb. I usually have to listen for the guard, but–"

"Why can't you go in the door?"

"I'm sure Bo has put guards outside," she says, her tone souring. "He promised he'd assure my privacy, but I know the

197

way he and his father work. They watch me. They'll want to know if I leave my rooms. That's why I didn't take the door on the way out."

"Then how did you—"

"I jumped," she says. "From the balcony."

"Jumped?" The thought makes my stomach flip. I'm a warrior. I'm not afraid of much. But I've seen the height of that tower. "All the way from the top?"

"Tiered roofs are good for more than decoration. It's only a ten-foot drop each time." She shrugs, but I can hear the pride in her voice. "I've been getting out that way since I was eleven. Getting up takes longer, but there are lots of stones sticking out from the outer wall. It's easy to climb in bare feet."

"You climb the outside of the tower?"

She nods.

"That's . . ." Mad. Outrageous. Courageous. "Impressive," I finally say.

"Thank you," Isra says, grinning.

"Crazy. But impressive." She giggles, and I smile in spite of myself. "You really do play with fire."

"I do." She clears her throat, and her fingers pluck nervously at my shirt. "So . . . food and then roses?"

"Yes. I'd like for you to see me. Give you something to dream about tonight."

I meant it to be a joke, but there's nothing funny about the way she says, "Oh, I've already dreamed about you. This morning, in fact."

My mouth goes dry. "Really?"

"Yes. It was a nice dream," she says. "A very nice dream."

"Isra . . . ," I warn, not sure which one of us I'm warning, or what will happen if the warning is ignored.

"Gem . . ." She mimics my tone so perfectly, I can't help but smile. And grunt.

She laughs as she steps closer, wrapping her arm around my waist. After the slightest hesitation, I put my arm around her shoulders and we walk–hips bumping, her cheek pressed to my chest–and for now we are just a boy and a girl, walking the desert under a sky full of stars.

FIFTEEN

ISRA

CLIMBING is harder than it's ever been before.

My arms tremble and my fingers cramp. My breath comes fast and my toes slip more times than I'd like—especially knowing Gem's watching from below, close to where we've hidden the bulbs beneath a shallow layer of dirt in the fallow cabbage field.

I wanted to impress him, but by the time I pull myself up and over the edge of the third roof, I'm wishing I'd found some way to distract the guards and gone through the wretched door.

I'm starving and exhausted, and not certain I'm going to

make it to the top. It makes me think about my mother, about what it must have been like to jump from the balcony and keep falling and falling. It would be just my luck to tumble off the tower and break my neck right when I feel ready to take on the world.

My world, anyway. Yuan seems smaller after my days in the desert. More manageable, somehow. Even thoughts of the power struggles and hard talks and difficult decisions in my future don't daunt me. I feel strong. In mind. In spirit.

The flesh, however . . .

By the time I drag myself over the balcony ledge, I'm covered in a cold sweat and shaking from head to toe. I collapse on the stone floor in a grateful heap, breathing hard, my heart beating in my stomach, my head throbbing so fiercely, colors bloom in my darkness. My bones vibrate like bells after they're rung too hard, but I'm alive. I made it.

"Thank the ancestors," I sigh, then giggle softly to myself.

I don't know why I find it funny to say things Gem says, but I do. I love the way he talks, his myriad grunts, the rumble in his chest when he laughs. I even love the way he gets grumpy with me and isn't afraid to show it.

But most of all, I love the way he touches me, the way *I* touch *him.*

I've been thinking about it all day, and I just don't see how something that feels so right can be wrong.

"It *does* feel right," I whisper, rolling onto my back, breath finally coming easier. "It feels . . . wonderful." I smile despite the pain still pulsing behind my eyelids. Not even this nasty headache can dampen my spirits.

I stretch my arms above my head and point my toes and arch like a cat, more aware of my physical being than I've ever been. My entire body tingles at the thought of being back with Gem. Unfortunately, my body is also dirty and, a quick sniff confirms, none too fresh-smelling. There isn't time for a bath—though Gem is well hidden behind the bushes on the unguarded side of the tower, I don't want to leave him waiting—but I can at least have Needle bring a bowl of water and a sponge and beg her to do something with my hair before I head back out into the night.

After I ask her to bring me something to eat. I'm faint with hunger.

"Needle!" I call from my place on the ground, too exhausted to bother getting up. "I'm back. I'm on the balcony. Can you bring some fruit and nuts? Enough for two?"

"Who else are you feeding?" The deep, angry *male* voice is completely unexpected, making me bolt into a seated position.

I knock my head on the parapet but ignore the agony blossoming in my skull as my headache becomes something *much* more painful. I spin and spring onto the balls of my bare feet, staying in a crouch, ready to hurl myself at this man's voice and knock him flat the second he proves he's here to hurt me.

Bo's hint that someone in Yuan has been poisoning me comes back in a rush, making me shake as I demand, "Who's there? Who are you?"

"It's Bo," he says, making my jaw drop. He sounds nothing like himself. His voice is so deep and angry and . . . cut-

202

ting. "You're filthy. Get up off the floor. You look like an animal," he continues, barking at me like one of his misbehaving underlings.

"Bo, I . . ." I want to tell him to leave me be, but I can't until I learn how much he knows. "What are you doing here?"

"Better question, where have you been? I discovered you were missing early this evening." I hear his footsteps moving closer, and the hair at the back of my neck prickles. My mind tells me Bo wouldn't hurt me, but something instinctive urges me to run, to fight him if he tries to stop me. "Who have you been with, Isra? What kind of man leaves you looking like that? Like he had you in the dirt?"

"What?" I laugh, even as my cheeks heat. Surely he can't mean—

"You think this is funny?" Bo snatches my arm, and pulls me to my feet. My laughter ends in a gasp of surprise. And pain. His fingers don't feel soft anymore. They bite through my flesh, not shying away when they find bone. "You think it's funny to make a fool of me?"

"Let me go," I order in my iciest tone, doing my best to ignore the fear making my blood race and my splitting head spin.

If Bo decides to abuse me—here in my private chambers, where no one but he and his father have ever dared set foot—there will be no one to stop him. Needle's life will be over if she lays hands on a soldier. The punishment for assaulting a member of the guard is death.

The thought makes my heart beat even faster. Penalty of death or no, she would still defend me. I have to tell her to stay out of this, no matter what. "Where's Needle?" I ask, trying not to wince when Bo's grip grows tighter. "I require my maid."

"Your maid is in your bedroom," he says, his tone openly mocking. "With orders not to set foot outside it until I find out who the queen has been rutting with tonight."

Fury banishes my fear and pain. How *dare* he? *"Get out,"* I snap. *"Now.* Before I punish you the way I would anyone else who spoke to me that way."

Now it's his turn to laugh, an ugly laugh that makes my throat tight. "Are you threatening me?"

"It's not a threat; it's a warning." With a sharp jerk, I wrench my arm from his grasp. Pain knifes through my head in response, but I blink it away, ignoring the throbbing behind my eyes and the pitching of my stomach. I can't show weakness, not if I want to take the upper hand. "I am the queen of Yuan. If I wanted you wrapped in chains and tossed into the river, I could have it done. Within the hour. You forget yourself."

"No, *you* forget yourself," he snaps. "You aren't a queen; you're a disgrace. Everyone knows it. That's why your father locked you away in the first place."

"You have *one minute* to leave before I call the guards."

"I can't believe I felt sorry for you." His anger is a live thing, hovering in the air between us, threatening to dig its claws into me all over again. "I can't believe I defended your life while you deceived me!"

"You're out of your mind." I try to stand tall, but the torture in my skull makes me sway. I brush my hair from my clammy forehead and swallow the bile rising in my throat. "I've never deceived you," I say, voice breathier than I would like.

"But you would have," he says. "When we were married, and you bore me a bastard."

For a moment all I can do is lean against the parapet, gaping in his direction, reeling from shock and trying not to be sick. "We aren't even *betrothed.*"

"But we would have been. It was understood. By everyone, and I don't—"

I cut him off with a hand held in the air between us. "It doesn't matter what was *understood.* There are no papers signed. You never even asked permission to court me. You certainly haven't earned the right to act like a jealous husband."

"I planned to ask you to marry me tonight," he says. "But instead of finding you waiting for news about the welfare of your city, I found the tower deserted and you out spreading your legs—"

"Stop this," I hiss, shaking with anger. "I've done nothing to deserve this, and even if I had, it isn't your place to speak to your queen like a woman you bought for the night!" I shout, regretting it immediately as the pain grows so fierce that tears fill my eyes.

I take a breath and try to blink them away, hating that Bo might think that I care enough to cry over anything he has to say, but the agony only grows worse. The bursts of color return, coming faster, a dizzying barrage of red and green and orange that makes it difficult to focus on his words.

"I wouldn't . . . None of this would have happened if . . ."

He clears his throat. "I came here to tell you the dome hasn't been compromised. I did the inspection myself. It was a snake skin on the glass. I was . . . so happy," he says, a hitch in his voice. "For you. And myself. I couldn't wait to tell you."

"That's wonderful news," I whisper, bracing myself against the balcony wall with both hands.

I'm shaking again. Shaking and sweating, the misery in my head swiftly becoming more than I can bear. I have to get rid of Bo. I need Needle to help me into bed and then hurry down and help Gem sneak back to his cell. I won't be seeing him or the roses tonight. I can barely stay upright, let alone go jumping from roofs.

"Bo, this isn't what you're thinking." I hate defending myself to him, but it's the quickest way to get him to leave. "I was in my garden. Alone. I've been there most of the past two days."

"The guards never mentioned seeing anyone in your garden."

"I hid in the wheelbarrow when I heard them coming," I say, thinking fast. "I didn't want company, but I couldn't stand sitting up here doing nothing. But I did too much. That's why I asked Needle to bring enough food for two. I need to eat. I barely had the strength to get back into the tower."

"How did you get in and out of the tower?" he asks. "The guards never saw you leave, and I've been watching the main stair all evening, and then suddenly here you were, on the balcony. Is there a secret entrance, a hidden passage?"

"Please," I mumble, not having to fake the weakening of

my knees that sends me sliding back down to the ground. "I need to rest."

I close my eyes, but that doesn't make my head ache any less. If anything, it hurts more. I stifle a moan, wishing I were in my bed, wishing I could lie down right here and press my forehead against the cold stone.

"You swear there isn't . . ." He clears his throat. "You swear you were alone? You haven't been with another man?"

I want to scream, but instead I shake my head, just the barest movement back and forth. "No. No one."

Not yet, I add silently, *but if there is any way to manage it, I will make sure I take a lover before I marry you.*

Marry Bo. The thought was nervous-making before. Now it makes me feel like a fish being gutted. But it's unavoidable. Junjie will never go along with any of my proposed changes for the city if I defy him. If I refuse to marry his son, I'll find my chief advisor even more difficult to deal with. And if I relieve Junjie of his duties, my people will be frantic with fear and not inclined to love me for turning their world upside down. They have faith in Junjie; they trust him to keep the city safe. Even before my father died, it was Junjie and his strong, solid presence at the head of the military force that gave the people a sense of security. My father told me as much.

"If that's true . . ." Bo's sigh places him no more than a foot away, his mouth closer to the floor than it should be. He must have knelt beside me while I was lost in the misery of my thoughts. "I apologize. I never meant to upset you. I just . . . I couldn't bear thinking of you with someone else. It hurt me. I care for you, Isra."

I would laugh if I could.

I know what a hurt boy sounds like. A hurt boy sounds like Gem did last night–angry, but desperate for a reason to put his anger away. Bo wasn't hurt; he was embarrassed, and intended to make me pay for shaming him with another man, despite the fact that he has slept with every unmarried noblewoman under the age of thirty, and a few of the married ones besides.

And *this* is the man I will marry. *This* is the man my children will turn to for comfort when their mother is dead.

"I don't feel well," I choke out, breath coming fast as I try to keep from crying, from being sick, from joining the colors flashing behind my eyes and exploding in a burst of pain. "Fetch Needle."

"You don't need her. I'll take care of you." His too-warm, too-damp hand touches my cheek, and I flinch, head rushing with thoughts of how that hand will feel on my body, how that hand will touch places only Gem has touched, places I don't want anyone else to touch.

It sickens me. It's too much. I'm–

I roll onto my hands and knees and retch, bringing up cactus milk–the only thing I've had to eat or drink all day–and continuing to heave even when the last of it is gone. By the time I'm able to stop, Needle's cold fingers are on my forehead, testing the temperature of my skin before pulling my hair back and plaiting it into a swift braid.

I suppose Bo decided he'd rather *not* take care of me after all, if there is retching involved.

I'll have to arrange to vomit every night for the rest of my life.

"Needle," I sob, swiping the sleeve of my long underwear across my mouth. "Are you all right?"

I hold out my palm, and her hand moves beneath my fingers. *I'm fine. Has he hurt you?*

"No. I'm okay. I'm just . . . I'm ill," I say, voice trembling. "I think the eggs you sent with me this morning might have gone bad while I was working in the field."

I know Needle will understand and go along with my pretense, even before she signs, *Pretend I've apologized. Send him away. No one else knows you were gone. We can keep our secret if we're careful.*

"No, it's not your fault. It's m-m-mine," I stutter, the urge to be sick returning as the lights flashing behind my eyes get brighter and brighter. Shapes and colors flash and disappear, shifting and swimming as I turn my head. "Bo?"

"Yes?" He sounds moments from retching himself.

"Will you fetch the healers?"

"Right away." I hear him turn to go, and I dare to hope that Needle and Gem and I will escape this adventure undiscovered.

And then I hear it—a soft grunt over the side of the balcony.

A Gem grunt.

SIXTEEN

ISRA

No. No!

Bo's footsteps reverse direction, moving back toward Needle and me on the balcony. "What was that?"

"Wait!" I turn and grab blindly for his leg.

No. *Not* so blindly. I gasp as I catch a glimpse of a pale, thin hand reaching out in front of me, before the darkness steals it away.

My hand. *Mine.* I *saw* it. With my own eyes. Peeling skin above the knuckles, long bony fingers, and blunt fingertips with dirt under the nails. *My* nails.

"Wait!" I cling to Bo's pant leg, bile burning in my throat as I fumble for his hand and force myself to my feet while the world comes at me in bits and pieces. "My eyes." I swallow, ignoring the vertigo that threatens to claim me as fleeting pieces of the puzzle flash and fade, flash and fade. "The poison . . . I can . . . I see . . ."

I catch a flash of Bo's shoulder, his uniform red and green; a burst of light from inside the tower where the candles burn brightly; a glimpse of Needle's head and the cap she wears over her hair; a fragment of the night beyond the dome, lit up with hard winter stars; movement at the edge of the balcony, large hands, and a swiftly moving shadow.

I have to get Bo inside before he sees.

"We have to go to the healers." I lunge for the door leading into the music room, holding tightly to Bo's hand, but not tightly enough. His fingers slip through mine as he pulls away.

I know the second he sees Gem. His cry bursts from somewhere deep inside him, raw and brimming with such utter surprise that it's clear Gem was the *last* man he expected to find climbing into my tower.

I spin, and the world spins with me. I nearly fall, but Needle tucks herself under my arm and holds me up. I clutch her shoulder and blink furiously as Gem steps out of the shadows.

"How did it get out of its cell?" Bo makes an effort to sound menacing, but fails. Without his spear—which he seems to have left elsewhere—he's helpless against a Monstrous man, and he knows it. Fear makes his voice squeak as he orders Gem to "Stay back. Keep your distance!"

211

"I heard you cry out," Gem says to me, ignoring Bo. "I came to make sure you were safe."

"I'm fine," I whisper, swaying as the darkness I was certain was all I would ever know is ripped to pieces.

"You knew he was free?" Bo practically shouts into my ear, but I don't turn to look at him. "Did you let him—"

"Please . . . wait . . ." My breath comes faster as my aching eyes pull Gem into focus. He's fuzzy around the edges, blooming with black stains that obscure this part or that for a moment or two, but I can see him. I *truly* can.

"I can see." My voice trembles. The rest of me trembles harder. "I can *see*."

I can. I can see Gem. And he is . . . nothing like I remembered. His shoulders are wide and well muscled but hardly mountainous. His mouth is generous, but in proportion to the rest of his face. His high cheekbones are severe but elegant, and his long, silky braid is lovely—a thing of almost feminine beauty when compared to the rest of him. Even the places where orange and yellow scales dust his forehead aren't strange-looking to me now. The scales are nature's jewelry, bringing out the gold tones in his skin, making his dark eyes sparkle even in the dim light from the candles burning inside the tower.

He is beautiful. Beautiful, and a man, no doubt about it. Larger and stronger and different from the men of my city, but a man through and through. How could I have ever thought differently? How could I have thought him a monster, even for a moment? How could I have looked into those eyes that first night and not seen that we are not only similar creatures but kindred spirits? Not because he is Monstrous and I am tainted but because we are both human in the same way. The way Needle is human and my father–for all his faults–was human. The kind of human who wants to make other people's lives better, who is willing to sacrifice for the people we love, who puts the good of the majority before the good of the few.

Bo's voice pricks at my ears again, closer than before. "You see because I made you see. I was the one who told you about the poison."

"The poison," I mutter, realizing the bigger implications of my newfound sight. "How did you know about the poison? Who has been–"

"When I tell my father you let the beast out of its cage, and spent the day in the garden with it with no guards present, he'll wall up this balcony," Bo says, pointedly ignoring my questions. "You'll never leave this tower again."

Yes, Gem is human. Human in a way Bo is *not*.

I'm not surprised; I'm only relieved he thinks gardening is all Gem and I have been doing. But then, why would he suspect anything else? When he considers Gem a monster?

"Isra?" That's all Gem says, simply my name, but I know what it means, what he's offering. His assistance, whatever I need. I can see it in his eyes so intent on mine.

With one swipe of Gem's claws, we could be rid of Bo. With a heave of Gem's strong arms, Bo would go flying over the edge of the balcony, past the edge of the roofs, and down, down, down to his death. I could hide Gem in my room after. I could say that Bo proposed, and when I refused, he was so distraught that he flung himself from the balcony.

I could give Gem the word . . . but I won't.

Because I'm not tainted where it counts. There is nothing wrong with my soul. It's only now, when I have the chance to do something truly wicked and I'm certain I don't want to, that the truth seems clear to me.

"Isra?" Gem caresses my name with his voice, as if he understands what I'm thinking, what I'm feeling, how things are shifting inside me with a speed that makes me grateful for Needle's wiry body bracing mine.

"You let it call you by name?" Bo asks, his horror clear.

I turn, slowly, so as not to disturb my fragile hold on my focus, and look at Bo with my own eyes for the first time. He looks different than he did the night the roses showed him standing at the tower door. Smaller and softer. He's a good half meter shorter than Gem, and a few centimeters shorter than me, but broad and solid. His hair is as black as Gem's, but coarser. Tiny hairs escape his braid to spring around the perfect oval of his face. There, dark, nearly black eyebrows slash down toward the straight slope of his nose, pale brown eyes the color of walnut shells float in shallow sockets, and softly rounded lips perch above a strong but sweetly dimpled chin.

I see at once why women find him desirable. He is strong, healthy, and handsome. But he is not beautiful. Not to me. I will never anticipate his touch. I will never find him anything but repulsive.

And I will regret for the rest of my life that Gem has to witness what I'll do next.

214

"You will say nothing to your father," I say, pressing on before Bo can interrupt. "You will return to your rooms and pretend this night never happened. Then, come spring, when my mourning is over, you will propose and I will accept."

Bo's mouth closes, and his angry eyebrows float away from his eyes. "You will?"

"You have my word," I say, fighting the urge to look at Gem, to see what he thinks about this. What he feels . . .

Bo's gaze shifts from me to Gem and back again. "All right. But in exchange for my silence, you will stop this nonsense with the creature immediately. It isn't a pet. It's dangerous."

"*Gem* isn't dangerous," I say, emphasizing his name, making it clear Gem isn't an *it* in my mind.

"How can you say that? One of them killed your father, Isra."

"Yes, *one* of them did," I admit. "But it wasn't Gem. Gem is my friend."

"Your *friend*?"

"And he's been a great help to me," I say, ignoring Bo's scandalized tone, and hoping I haven't pushed this too far. "I can't get the new garden ready without him."

"Then you can give up the new garden." Bo gives me a stern, almost fatherly look that I can tell I'm going to grow to hate over the course of our marriage, no matter how brief the union may be. "We don't need another garden. Our people are well provided for with what we have already."

"No, Bo. They aren't." I fight to keep my tone even. "Our city's customs are unfair to many of our people. The new garden will grow plants that will provide healing and protection from mutation. I need this. We *all* need it. And Gem has agreed to help me."

Bo puffs out his chest and tips his chin down, but unfortunately for him, it's impossible to glare down at someone taller than yourself. "I won't have my wife playing in the dirt with a monster. The nobles already think you're strange. What if someone had seen you today? Alone with this thing? What if he'd hurt you? Killed you? Where would that have left the city?"

"Please." Anger flares inside me, but I know I have no right to it, not when I've been as cruel to Gem as Bo is being now. In a kinder way, but still . . .

Let him go. You have to let him go.

As soon as the thought races through my mind, I know it's right. I have to give Gem his freedom, no matter how my people will hate me, or how miserable it makes me to imagine my life without him. We'll plant the garden, and I'll send him on his way with a cart full of food and promises to leave more outside the gate whenever I can. It's the very least I can do.

"As your future wife," I say, "I beg you to trust my judgment. If Gem intended to hurt me, he would have done so already."

"You can't know that." Bo scowls again. "You're too trusting."

"You're right. I trusted you, and tomorrow I'll have bruises in the shape of your fingers on my arm." I watch him flinch in shame, and the wonder of sight hits me all over again. I can

Needle slides from under my other arm and steps back far enough for me to look upon her dear face. She's similar to the picture my mind painted all the times I traced her features with my fingers—straight brown hair tucked under her cap, a face as round as a saucer, and enormous eyes. They're beautiful, kind and intelligent and sad, but determined and just . . . everything I imagined Needle's eyes would be.

I'm scarcely aware the tears are coming before they're slipping down my cheeks.

"Thank you," I say. "For everything."

I know she understands that I mean more than everything she's done the past few days. I mean every day she kept me from being so desperately alone. Every minute she spent teaching me to understand her special language. Every little-girl tantrum she tolerated when I was too young to understand what a blessing she was to my life, and she not nearly old enough to bear the burden of raising me.

I know she understands because she starts crying, too. Smiling and crying and touching my arm, my shoulder, my cheek—all the places she would touch to communicate her concern when I was blind.

By the ancestors, I'm not blind. I can see her. I can *see*.

I lean down to hug her with the arm not wrapped around Gem's shoulders, and end up bumping my forehead into hers. Not hard enough to hurt, but hard enough to make us both laugh. Me, a soft giggle; her, a silent shake of her shoulders.

"Sorry. I'm not judging distance well," I say, pushing my hair—which has already escaped from Needle's quick braid—from my face, remembering how terrible I look. I glance down, shocked by just how rumpled and dirt-streaked my overalls are. Bo must be desperate to be king if he can still stomach the thought of marriage after seeing me tonight. Even dressed up and freshly washed, I'm far from a Yuan beauty.

My heart lurches, and my knees go weak. *Myself.* I'll be able to see myself. Finally, I'll know what made every soul in Yuan gasp when I stepped out onto the dais after my coronation.

But not now. I'm not strong enough. I need food and water and . . .

I need . . . to sit down.

As if reading my mind, Needle motions Gem and me inside, shooing us over to the low couch where I sit to practice my harp, while she rushes into the other room. The couch is black and blue. Black silk, with midnight-blue flowers and black thread binding it to a frame so polished, I could see my reflection in it if I tried.

I don't.

I look up at Gem, studying his profile as he settles me on the couch and sits awkwardly beside me. The seat is so low that his knees nearly touch his chest. He looks out of place, but no more out of place than I do. My filthy overalls and ratted halo of hair are from a different world than the silk we sit on.

I lift my hand and pull one of the less fuzzy tendrils in front of my eyes.

"Red," I mutter, hand shaking as I pull the curl straight, before letting it pop back into a coil.

"Brown," Gem says, his voice as careful as it always is under the dome. He sounds like a citizen of Yuan again. It glass and knock it over. Before I can try again, Needle has poured a glass and placed it in my hand.

"Thank you." I take great gulps of the cool water with the lemon rinds floating at the top. Yellow seen through my own eyes is more glorious than I remember, bright and dense and cheery enough to make my teeth hurt.

Needle nods, and gestures out to the balcony before turning back to me with one eyebrow raised, communicating more with one look than in seven or eight of her hand gestures. I'm suddenly not surprised that my father seemed to understand Needle almost as well as I did, though we never told him of our secret language.

"Yes. Gem and I are fine," I say, then remember what Needle will be cleaning, and wince. "I'm sorry. Leave it. I can clean it up later."

Needle dismisses my protest with a wave of her hand and goes to fetch water and soap and towels from the washroom. I still feel terrible, but I suppose I shouldn't. Queens don't clean up their own messes. At least, they never have in the past.

I reach for the plate of cherries and one of the bowls of nuts and pull them into my lap, munching as I think. Now that I can see, I'll be able to walk among my people and form my own opinions much more quickly. Maybe I can right the wrongs of the past and repair the wreck I've made of my first months as ruler of this city.

But first, I have to clean up a different mess.

I start to call for Needle but shut my mouth with a sharp clack of teeth as I realize I don't have to. I can *see*. I can pick out my own clothes to put on after my bath.

I stand, suddenly eager to get on with it, to tidy myself and confront the demon of my reflection and move on to more important battles. "I'm going to wash up and change," I tell Gem, setting my plate down on the tray. "I'll be quick."

"Do you want Needle to take me back to my cell?" he asks, his voice strangely guarded as he sets a now-empty dish back on the tray and reaches for an apple.

"No, I want you to stay," I say, suddenly feeling shy. "I'd rather not be alone."

"You won't be alone. Needle is here."

If I couldn't see him, I'd think he wanted to go. He sounds cold, disinterested, but his knee jiggles up and down, his fingers twist the stalk on the apple until it snaps. His elbows are on his knees, his shoulders hunched as if protecting himself from an anticipated attack. His long, thick braid hangs down his back like a weary pet in need of a brushing.

I step closer, and touch the top of his head ever so softly. He glances up, surprised, unguarded. "Please stay," I whisper. "I want *you* to be here."

He nods, rather unhappily I think, and turns back to his apple.

"There's a washbasin and towels in the sitting room down the hall. By the pantry," I say. Though, aside from his dusty shirt, Gem doesn't seem to be in nearly as bad a shape as I am. "If you want to freshen up, feel free."

"All right," he says, eyes still glued to the fruit in his hand.

"I won't be long," I say, hoping both of our moods will improve once this is done. I've felt my own face and my peeling flesh. I have a fairly good idea what I must look like. Strange, different, big-featured and rough-skinned, but not altogether hideous. The truth can't be much worse than what I've imagined.

Or so I tell myself as I turn toward the washroom, half hoping Needle neglected to haul up the usual supply of water in my absence, and I'll have a good excuse to fall into bed filthy and deal with facing my face in the morning.

SEVENTEEN

GEM

I eat everything left on the tray. I drink all the water and then the tea.

Tea in the desert is bitter and smoky, the way a drink intended to get you out of your hut on a winter morning should be. Smooth Skin tea tastes like crushed flowers, so sweet it made me gag the first time I put a cup of it to my lips. I detest Smooth Skin tea, but I drink the honeyed liquid anyway. I'm on edge. Drinking gives me something to do with my hands.

Isra, Isra, Isra. Her name knocks around inside me as I

wash up and return to my seat on the tiny couch. *Isra*. It hurts and heals and makes me hope. . . .

I can't hope. Not yet. It's too dangerous.

I don't know what will happen when she looks at herself, but I know there's a good chance she'll hate me. I didn't lie, but I didn't tell the truth, either, and my halfhearted attempt last night was worse than no attempt at all. I don't want her to hate me. I want her to keep looking at me with eyes that confess all her secrets.

I thought seeing me would remind her of our differences, but instead she looks at me like . . .

Like I look at her.

"Gem?" She's suddenly standing in front of me, her freshly combed hair tumbling around her shoulders, her body encased in a black skirt and a long-sleeved green shirt with silky ruffles at the throat. I smile despite myself. It's a playful shirt. It suits her better than her silkworm dresses.

Her fingers tangle nervously in the ruffles. "This was my mother's," she says. "It was one of the few things of hers to survive the fire. I've never tried it on, but I thought . . . It seemed right to wear it."

"I like it."

"I do, too." She fidgets, frowns. "I can't believe it fits."

"Your mother must have been tall like you."

Isra nods, but her brow remains wrinkled. "I suppose. I don't remember her as . . . Father never said anything about my mother being tainted, but I suppose I–"

"Where is the mirror?" I rise. It's time.

"Needle said she has one by her bed." Isra takes a breath

and tucks her hand into the crook of my arm, despite the fact that she no longer needs anyone to guide her.

She leads me down a narrow passage to a bedroom where a giant bed with a scarlet quilt the same color as the royal roses stands proudly in the center. The bed is too big for a girl alone. It's a bed built for two, solid and sturdy and meant to withstand the use of generations of men and women.

Of Isra, and her soon-to-be husband.

"Wait." I stop inside the door, unable to pull my eyes from the bed. I have to reach Isra before she decides I can't be trusted. "You don't have to keep your promise. Once I'm back in my cell, it will be your word against Bo's. No one has to know you let me out. You don't have to marry him if you don't want to."

"Do you think I want to?" she asks, voice shaking.

I look down at her, at her parted lips and her shining eyes, and immediately I hurt. Because she hurts.

I cradle her face in my hands. "Then don't do it."

"I don't have a choice," she whispers. "I have to be married by spring."

"Why? You said seventeen was young to marry."

"It is, but it doesn't matter." The tears sitting in her eyes roll down her cheeks. "I'm queen. I'll be married as soon as my mourning is through."

I catch a tear with my thumb and rub it gently into her skin. "Why?"

"There are reasons. I'd rather not explain them, but they're real. Inescapable." She drops her gaze to my chest with a sigh. "There isn't time to get out from beneath Junjie's thumb. If

I'm going to change anything for the better, I'll need his support, and he won't give it if I refuse to marry his son."

"Find someone to take Junjie's place."

"There isn't time," she repeats, lifting troubled eyes to mine. "He was at my father's side for twenty years. He makes the people feel safe. I'd never find someone fit to take his place in a few months."

"Then put off the marriage," I say, fingers tightening, pressing lightly into her jaw. "Have a . . . I don't know what you would call it. In our tribe it's a trial."

"A trial?"

"Two people spend time together, sometimes even live together, but nothing is official until the woman claims the man in a ceremony before the tribe."

"The woman does the claiming?" Her eyebrows lift. "Interesting."

"The man has to agree, but the decision to end the trial is the woman's."

She hums beneath her breath. "If my father had lived, he would have chosen my husband. He might have even chosen Bo. Whoever he would have picked, I wouldn't have had much say about it. That's how it is for most noblewomen. We marry within the descendents of the founding families, being careful not to marry too closely. I've heard some of the common women marry for love, but . . ." Her eyes shift to the side, as if she's suddenly become very interested in the door frame. "Did you ever . . . *Were* you ever . . ."

"No," I say. "Meer and I . . . it was never a trial. At first I thought we might, but . . . She chose someone else."

"Oh." She plucks at her shirt. "Women in Yuan aren't supposed to . . . I mean, I know some *do,*" she says, her voice dropping to a whisper. "I've heard there are herbs they take to make it possible to"—she waves a hand nervously in the air—"without any babies. For Yuan women, a baby is only supposed to come after marriage. It's scandalous otherwise." She tilts her head back and blows air through her pursed lips. Even in the dim light of the lamp burning by her bedside, I can see how pink her cheeks have gotten.

"Different from our ways," I say, trying not to smile.

It's strange to me that she's embarrassed by something my people consider natural. But then, for my people, there is no shame in it. No man or woman is forced to be with someone not of their choosing. No baby is left unloved because it came from one man and not another.

"Yes," she says, casting another glance toward the corner of the room, where a narrow bed sits next to a chest of drawers with a blue and white washbasin on top. Above the basin, a mirror hangs on the wall. "We don't have trials. A couple will be betrothed for a time before they're married, but I can't have a long betrothal. I must be married. It's the rule." She turns back to me as I'm opening my mouth. "And don't tell me to change the rule. This isn't a rule I can change. It's not a rule anyone can change. Some things just are the way they are."

I grunt—because I was going to tell her to change the rule—and she smiles a sad smile.

"But thank you," she says, with another peek at the corner. "It was good of you to try."

I catch one of her curls and twine it around my finger. I know why she's looking at the corner. She's ready, but suddenly I'm not. "I'm a good prisoner, then?"

"You've become a good friend," she says, lifting a hand to my face. Her fingers are cool, but that's not why I shiver. "And you won't be my prisoner for a second longer than necessary. I'll let you go, Gem. I promise I will. And I'll send food with you, and put more outside the gate for as long as I live."

"Isra . . ." This wasn't what . . . I never thought she'd . . . "What about Junjie? And your people? You said they would never—"

"I'll give Junjie what he wants. In return, he'll give me some things that I want." She steps closer, engulfing me in the smell of roses. Roses on her skin from her bath, roses on her breath, roses lingering in her hair. The perfume mingles with her Isra scent and becomes something darker, more dangerous than any flower.

I thought I couldn't want her more than I did last night, but now, with that soft look in her eyes, and brave words on her lips, I want her so badly, it hurts. I more than want her, and that hurts even more.

"Junjie will free you," she continues. "Or I will refuse to marry Bo."

I wrap my arm around her waist. "I won't let you pay for my freedom with yours."

"I'm not free. I've never been free."

"But you could be." I move my hand to her back, skimming my fingers up the length of her spine. Her bones are like beads on a necklace, delicate but strong. "With the right clothing, the desert might hold no danger for Smooth Skins. You could come home with me. At least for the rest of the winter."

"And then who would send food to your people?"

My eyes squeeze closed as I drop my forehead to hers. She's right. If she came with me, she would starve right along with the rest of my tribe. Maybe before winter is through. She's already thin.

"My fate was decided a long time ago," she whispers, fingertips tracing a path up my chest. "But you can still have a future. With your people. I want that for you. When I'm married, I want to imagine you happy. I *need* to imagine you happy."

When she wraps her arms around my neck, a wretched heat fills my head, pushing behind my nose and eyes, as if my soul is trying to find a way out of my body.

"I hated you," I say, voice breaking. "Until a few days ago, I hated you. At least, I thought I did."

"I know." She *does* know. I can hear it in her voice, feel it in the way she touches me. She knows that I . . . that I'm so close . . . and I only want closer.

"I'll take the food to my people and come back," I say, threading my fingers through her hair.

"You can't." The salty, hopeless smell of her tears fills my head, making the pressure behind my eyes even worse. "I can't know that you're here . . . when I . . . I don't want to be with him," she says, words coming faster as her tears fall harder. "I don't want anyone but you."

My head feels as if it will collapse from the heaviness

building inside it. I can't talk anymore. I can't listen. I can't imagine Isra with that soldier. I *won't.*

I draw her to me, tasting her tears before she opens her mouth and I taste honey and roses and Isra. All the dark and light of her, all the fear and selflessness, all the innocence and daring of a girl so determined not to be caged that she leapt from a balcony to find her freedom.

But now she'll be worse than caged. Her love for her people—and whatever it is she feels for me—will steal the last of her freedom away. Bo and his father will get what they want, and Isra will lose control of the city before she has a chance to rule. If she does this, she'll destroy not only herself but any chance for change—for my people or hers.

I pull away, breath coming fast enough to stir the hairs falling into her face. "I lied to you," I say, cupping her cheeks, forcing her to look at me and see what I really am. "The garden is a lie. It was always a lie. There are no plants or herbs that will stop mutation, and even if there were, I wouldn't know a thing about them."

"Wh-what?" Isra's lips part, but she doesn't pull away.

"I'm a warrior," I say, determined to make her hate me. "I was raised as a warrior from the time I was ten years old. I was raised to hate you. I stood outside your dome when I was fourteen and swore I'd tear the city down with my bare hands if that's what it took to save my tribe."

She pushes my hands away and takes a step back. But only a step. It's not far enough.

"Those bulbs we brought back won't do anything to help your people. Every day we spent digging in the dirt, preparing the field, was a waste. You gave Junjie control of your people in exchange for nothing. You almost died last night for *nothing.*"

She blinks, but no new tears fill her eyes, and when she speaks, she sounds calmer than she has since we entered the room. "You lied to get out of your cell."

"I lied to get out of my cell and kept lying every day we worked together," I say, as cruelly as I can with the taste of her still sweet in my mouth. "I pretended to be your friend while I dreamed of opening your throat."

She doesn't flinch. She just . . . stares at me, gaze flicking from my eyes to my mouth, down to the fists balled at my sides, and back again. "You wanted to win my trust so it would be easier to escape." She nods slowly. "So . . . why didn't you escape while we were in the desert? I can tell your legs are stronger than you led me to believe."

My mouth opens, and the truth gets dangerously close to coming out. If I tell her about the roses, that I've been planning to steal them all along, she will hate me for certain. She'll give up the idea of sacrificing herself for me, and turn her attention to work that will truly help her city.

But she'll also make sure I never get my hands on what my people desperately need. I can't risk that, not even for her. I can't.

You've already risked it.

My hands ball into fists. I *have* already risked it. There will be no reason for her to let me out of my cell now. I should fall on my knees and beg her forgiveness. I should tell her I stayed with her because I care—it wouldn't even be a lie—but I can't.

I can't lie. I can't tell the truth. I don't know who I am or what I'm supposed to do next. I only know that "You can't marry him," I say, sounding as desperate and angry as I feel. "You can't. It will kill you."

"I'll be dead sooner than later, anyway," she says with a strange smile. "I've lied to you, too."

"What?" My eyes wander down her long, lean body, the one that seemed strong until last night in the desert. "Are you sick? Is there—"

"My family are the keepers of the covenant that protects the city. We sustain the roses. We make an offering of ourselves for the good of our people. The . . . queens make an offering. *Only* the queens."

The larger offering. Only the queens.

She wasn't lying when she said none of her people have died to feed the roses. None of *them* have. Only her female ancestors have died. Only Isra will die.

Only Isra.

EIGHTEEN

ISRA

"My mother died when I was four. Thirteen years ago." The words float easily from my mouth. This night feels like a dream—too much has happened for it to be anything else— and the consequences of this confession seem distant, unreal. "I could have another seventeen years. I could have ten. The advisors could come for me tomorrow if they believe the city to be in danger."

"How long have you known?" Gem asks, a stricken expression on his face.

"Forever." I brush my hair wearily from my forehead. "I

can't remember a time when I didn't. It was never a secret. I always knew that if my father didn't remarry and give the city another queen—"

"Why didn't he remarry?" Gem demands, his anger hot and immediate.

"He was doing what he thought was best for me," I say, more exhausted with every word. "As future queen I was protected. I don't think my mutation is severe enough to send me to the Banished camp, but—" My words end in a yip of surprise as Gem snatches my hand and half drags me across the room toward the mirror on the wall.

Instinctively I dig my heels into the carpet. I'm not ready. Not like this. "No," I say, squirming my fingers, panic making my voice high and tight. "I'm not ready."

"You need to see yourself," he says. "You need to see the truth."

I shake my head and throw my weight backward, fighting harder to free myself from his grip. "In a minute. Wait! I—" He drops my hand, only to scoop me up in his arms. "Stop! Please," I beg, shoving at his chest. When he stops in front of the mirror, I squeeze my eyes shut and turn away.

"Look at yourself," he demands. "Look!"

I press my face against his shoulder, inhaling the smell of the desert and Gem on his shirt, hating that he can still smell good to me even when he's dirty and bullying me like everyone else in my life. "You're no better than Bo," I say through gritted teeth.

"I'm only trying to help!"

"Sh!" I stab his chest with the tip of one finger. "You'll

scare Needle. She's mute, not deaf. If she comes in here and finds us like this, she'll bring the bed pot down on your head. It's copper. It will hurt." I peek at him through slitted eyes. "Even someone with a skull as thick as yours."

"You're one to talk," he says. "You're the most stubborn person I've ever met. *Stupidly* stubborn."

"Then put me down and go away," I say, voice breaking. "If I'm so stupid."

"I don't want to go away. I want to help," he says in a softer voice. "Please, let me." His arms gentle around me, no longer holding me prisoner, just holding. Waiting.

"This doesn't help," I say, relaxing in spite of myself. "Not like this."

He presses a kiss to my forehead. "I should have told you before," he whispers, making my skin tingle.

I wish we'd never stopped kissing. I wish Gem would give up on saving me, and give me something to remember when my life is out of possibilities.

"I would have," he continues. "If I'd known. I swear I would have."

"Told me what?" I let my fingers play along the scales at the back of his neck, mesmerized by their smoothness.

He looks down, catching my eyes, the emotion in his making my heart beat faster. "I would have told you that you're beautiful."

My stomach flutters and my chest gets warm and tight. I fist my hands and hold his gaze and my breath, determined to bind this moment tight inside me and never let it go. He

240

means it. I'm beautiful to him. To Gem, who is beautiful to me. Does it really matter what anyone else thinks?

"You're beautiful," he says again, kissing my eyebrow. It's a strange place for a kiss, but nice, an offering meant to comfort me, taking nothing for itself. "And you know it. You said so yourself."

My brow furrows. "I never said that."

"You did," he says. "That girl in the painting isn't a goddess. She's a queen."

His meaning hits, and my lungs forget how to draw breath. "That's cruel," I choke out, pushing at his chest. This time he lets me go, dropping my feet to the ground and spinning me to the mirror so quickly, I don't have time to avert my eyes. I catch a glimpse, and a glimpse is enough for the glass to take me prisoner.

My lips part. The girl in the mirror's lips part, too, and any lingering doubt vanishes in a dizzying wave. That's me. *That* is what I look like. The shoulders that burst the seams of every dress are the perfect size in my mother's shirt. My slender throat flutters delicately as I breathe. My face is not a perfect oval or a moon, but its angles aren't hideous. There is elegance in my sharp chin and strong jaw, and my nose that isn't shy about being a nose. It pokes proudly from the center of my face, ending in a tip shaped like a square, as if I ran into a wall with it and the skin never popped back into place.

It's large, and might be distracting if it weren't balanced out by my eyes. Enormous, unflinching eyes as green as summer grass, fringed with dark lashes, blinking beneath brows a bit too wild. My hair is even wilder, curling and coiling and running amok above my forehead and down my back, creeping wiry fingers over my shoulders, gluing stray tendrils to my damp cheeks. But it's lovely, too, in its untamed way.

But there's still the other . . . the part I keep hidden . . . I was careful not to look too closely in the bath, but now . . .

I lift my hand, and pull up my sleeve, revealing the peeling skin beneath the green fabric. There, where I thought scales lurked below the surface, is simply dry red human skin. Peeling and flaking and messy, but not hideous.

Sickly-looking, but not unnatural. Damaged, but not tainted.

I am . . .

I am *not* . . .

"There may be some way to treat it," Gem says carefully, as if he senses how fragile I've become. "It might be irritated by something you're eating or . . . washing with. A certain oil, or . . ."

He trails away. I don't say a thing. I don't know what to say.

This is my body—sickly, not tainted. This is my face. *This* is my face. The face of the girl in the painting. I remember sitting for a portrait on my sixteenth birthday, but I was never told what happened to it. Now I know. I am the girl in the painting, that beautiful girl. I don't look like the other women whose faces I've felt—the proportions and structure and shape are completely different—but there is nothing Monstrous or ugly about me. I know it, Bo knows it, Junjie knows it. My father knew it.

My father *knew* it.

My heartbeat slows; my lips go numb. My throat cramps, and my ribs petrify. I feel the air in the room turn against me, pushing into me from all sides, threatening to turn my bones to dust.

Never, in my wildest dreams, would I have imagined that finding out I've been wrong would feel like this. That I would want to pull my beautiful face off the wall and hurl the mirror to the floor, stomp on the pieces until my feet bleed, scream until I lose my voice. That I would wish with every fiber of my being to go back to the way life was before, when I believed myself ugly, when the world and my place in it were perfectly clear.

But I do. I wish. But I can't go back. Not ever.

I watch the girl's face—*my* face—crumple in the reflection, see the way her upper lip pulls up, the way the cords on her slender throat stand out garishly from her skin, and her large nose turns red as she begins to cry, and I am momentarily comforted.

I can be ugly, after all. I can be as wretched-looking as I feel.

Gem turns me gently and pulls me into his arms. I fist my hands against his chest, bury my face between them, and sob as if the world has come to an end. "I'm sorry," he mumbles into my hair. "I'm sorry I didn't tell you."

I shake my head, my forehead rubbing against the stiff cotton of his shirt, but I can't talk. I don't blame Gem. It wouldn't have mattered if he'd told me. I wouldn't have believed him. I was certain I knew the truth, that I knew it all. At least when it came to the who and why and what of Isra.

But I knew *nothing. Nothing.* I am worse than the emperor without clothes. I am the biggest fool in the world.

"You were right," I say, forcing out the words. "I *am* stupid."

"You're not. You were ignorant, and you didn't stay that way on your own."

He's right. I didn't become this fool alone. Baba made me this way. My father hid me away in this tower, and provided me with a mute maid incapable of telling me about myself. By the time Needle and I learned to communicate, I was older and unwavering in my beliefs, the reality of my world set so firmly in my mind that Needle's compliments trickled in through my fingers and out through both ears. She was a servant, she was obligated to flatter me. I never imagined . . .

I *couldn't have* imagined. If I had, if I for *one second* had thought I was nearly as whole as any other citizen of Yuan, then I would have known there was no excuse for any of it. No excuse for keeping me prisoner. Or for not, *at the very least,* allowing me visitors aside from the rare music tutor, sworn to silence about her time in the tower. If my father had been worried only about my safety, he still could have brought friends. Girls my age to play with when I was younger, to gossip and make music with when I was older. I didn't have to be alone. I didn't have to grow up feeling like a disgraceful secret.

But I did. No matter how much time Father spent with me, no matter how many times we laughed together or sang together or how many times he said he loved me, I always believed he was ashamed of the tainted girl who was all that remained of his family.

But I'm not tainted. I'm not. And as Gem said, there might be some way to treat my skin if I ask the healers for help. But Father never called the healers, even when it became obvious that Needle's honey baths and creams weren't making me better. I didn't imagine it was possible to get better, not until Gem came to the city.

"I don't understand," I say, fists tightening until my nails sting my palms. "Why did my father do this? Why did he keep me here? Away from almost everyone? Why did he let me think . . ."

"I don't know."

I shake my head again, struggling to breathe past the rage burning white-hot inside me. I'm devastated and hurt and betrayed, but most of all, I'm furious. I want to hit something. Someone. I want to bloody them. *Him.*

A sense memory rises from somewhere deep inside me. My hands clawed, my nails torn, and blood—some mine, some not—hot and sticky on my stinging fingertips. The memory has the cold, silent terror of all my earliest memories, of those days when I was newly blind, but somehow I know it's older. It's something I've forgotten. Until now. Until suddenly it's all right to remember flying at my father in a rage and raking my fingers down his face.

But why was I so angry? Did I know that what he was doing—holding my mother and me captive—was wrong? Did I try to fight back, only to give up and give in and forget? To trick myself into believing a story that made it okay to love the only person I had left?

"If he'd remarried, then that woman would have been the offering?" Gem asks.

I sniff, and lift my head, slowly. It feels heavier than ever. It weighs more than all the rocks in the desert. "And if they'd had children, one of them would have been the next king or queen. I would have been safe. The crown would have reverted back to me only if they'd had no heirs. I would have had, at the very least, more time. More . . . life."

Gem curses beneath his breath as he tucks the hairs stuck to my cheeks back into the mess from which they came. The *lovely* mess. I am a lovely mess now. That should matter, I think, but it doesn't.

"I know I shouldn't wish for someone else's death," I say, sounding broken. "And I don't. Not really. I just wish . . ."

"That your father had wished for it," Gem finishes, proving once again that he is clever and human and privy to at least some of the secrets of my heart.

I smooth the wrinkles from his shirt, trace the damp circles with my fingers where my tears wet the fabric. "I wish he'd told me it wasn't easy to decide I would die for my city."

"He never said anything?"

I shake my head. "And he knew what I assumed. About myself. I told him. He's the only one I talked to . . . until you." I look up, wishing Gem were the only one I had ever told.

Gem's eyes narrow, and for a moment I see the terrifying creature I encountered that first night in the garden. I know he would rip my father open right now if the other Monstrous hadn't done the job for him already. "*He's* the monster you should have been protected from," Gem says.

Tears fill my eyes again, but I refuse to let them fall. "He was my father," I say, voice lurching as I try to regain control. "He was all I had. He taught me everything I know. I don't . . ." I take a deep breath that comes out a terrifying little laugh. I don't know that laugh. I don't know myself.

"Who am I now?" I ask. "I don't know that girl in the mirror. I don't know how to be her. I don't know how to think her thoughts or—"

Gem lays his hand on my cheek, so gently, I can barely feel his touch. "You are Isra. And now you'll be the person you would have been without the lies. His lies, or mine." His eyes swim with regret. If Gem hadn't told me it was impossible for Desert People to produce tears, I'd think he was about to cry.

"I don't blame you." I put my hand over his, pressing his warm palm closer to my cheek. "I think only good things about you. Except when you're making me angry. Or being bossy. You're very bossy."

"You have to stop this," he says, his expression grimmer than ever, refusing to let me tease us out of this terrible moment. "You shouldn't have to give your life. No one should."

My hand falls to my side. "This is the way things are, the way they've always been," I say, acutely aware of how exhausted I am. I'm a rag that's been wrung out, leaving only a few drops of me left behind.

"This is dark magic," Gem says. "Blood is bad enough, but death . . ."

"One death, to preserve thousands of lives. Without that

one death, the crops would fail, the dome would fall, and the city would crumble," I say, crossing to the bench at the foot of my bed and collapsing gratefully onto its cushioned seat. "Every man, woman, and child living here would die." I run my fingers over the needlepoint flowers embroidered on the fabric beneath me. Roses. Fitting.

"I can't let that happen," I whisper. "I will remain queen, and when the time comes, I will do what queens have always done."

"Your mother didn't," Gem says, the heat in his tone making me look up to find him pacing the thick carpet in front of Needle's bed.

"Yes, she did."

"If she burned in this tower, then how did–"

"She didn't burn," I say, stomach lurching. I've known the truth for a long time, but it sits differently now that I know it wasn't only my mother who wished me dead but my father, too.

Gem stops pacing, and turns to me. "But you said–"

"She set the fire, but she didn't burn."

NINETEEN

ISRA

"SHE . . ." Gem shakes his head, and keeps shaking it, as if doing so will cause what I've said to make sense sooner or later.

"She set the fire." I lift my hand to my throat and feel it ripple as I swallow, finding myself comforted by the rush of my blood beneath my skin. "One night, when Father was reading to me before bed, Mother came in to light the little lamp I liked to leave burning while I slept.

"Baba had mentioned something about a strange smell in my bedroom earlier, but neither of us knew what it was until my mother threw the lamp at the curtains. Apparently she'd soaked them with oil earlier in the day. They went up with a rush that sucked all the air from the room. I can't remember what my mother looked like, but I remember seeing her silhouetted against the flames, how white her nightgown looked next to all that red and orange."

"Why?" Gem asks, his voice breaking.

"She had decided the royal family had to die. Together," I say, piecing together what little I remember with what Baba told me of that night. "As soon as she lit the curtains, she ran from the bedroom. She locked me and Father inside, and went to set another fire in the sitting room. Father slammed his fists against the door and begged her to let us out, but she wouldn't. She . . . She said she loved us, but that fire was the only way."

My brow wrinkles as the unfamiliar piece of the puzzle fits into place. I don't know if it's seeing my bedroom that's helping my memory, or the fact that I'm telling the story aloud for the first time, but I can suddenly hear my mother speak, as plainly as if she were in the room right now. I can hear the tears in her voice, the genuine grief over what she felt, for some mad reason, she had to do.

"I didn't remember that last part before," I continue, "but I'm sure I heard her. It was right before my nightgown caught fire."

I press my fingers to my lips, concentrating until I swear I catch a whiff of smoke. "I screamed for Baba, and he ran back to the bed and threw me to the ground before the fire could touch my skin." I point to the spot on the floor, only a few feet from where I now sit.

"My head hit the stones beneath the carpet and . . . everything went blurry. I don't remember much after that, but I know soldiers arrived and broke down the bedroom door. Father gave me to one of them and went to find my mother. She was in the music room, but she ran out onto the balcony when she saw Father and the guards. Baba said she refused to come back inside. When she realized her plan had failed, she leapt over the parapet, down onto the top of the first roof, and threw herself from the edge. I heard her scream as she fell.

"My father and Junjie took her body to the rose garden the next morning." I glance at Gem, who stands frozen on the other side of the room, as horrified by the story as the people were in the days after my mother's suicide. Suicide was always expected of her, but not like that, not anywhere but in the garden.

"They slit her throat and spilled her blood on the soil." I drop my hand to my lap. "According to the terms of the covenant, the queen should do that herself—make the first, fatal cut before the royal executioner finishes the job—so it wasn't the way things were traditionally done, but it was a suicide, and the covenant was satisfied. The city had been running low on water for months, but that very day, the water came surging back into the underground river at full force. For the next three years, the harvests were so abundant, Father had to have additional granaries built to contain the bounty. He named one of them after my mother. Not the greatest honor for a queen, but it was all he felt proper for a woman who'd tried to burn her family alive."

Gem curses. It's a Desert People word, but there's no doubt that it's a curse.

"She was mad," I say, defending Mama out of habit. "My father and mother were married for almost twenty years before she became pregnant. I was a complete surprise. Mama was forty years old when I was born. Needle tells me the gossips say she was strange before my birth, but afterward . . ."

I sigh. "She started to talk about leaving the city. She even took me outside the gates once when I was four. It's one of my earliest memories. We were spotted by the guards and brought back inside almost immediately, but . . . My father couldn't trust her after that. He moved us both to the tower. Father said Mother didn't mind. Court life had always been a misery for her, and going out into the city center gave her fits. She'd get so upset, she'd forget to breathe, and faint dead away on the street."

"Was she sick?" Gem asks.

"Not in body," I say. "Father said the illness was in her mind but that she seemed happy in the tower. He never thought she'd . . . do what she did. I didn't, either." I lean back, resting against the mattress. "I don't remember much about her, almost nothing, really, but I remember feeling loved. I'm sure, in some part of her mind, she did what she did out of love."

Gem crosses the room, his steps soundless on the thick carpet. He's learned to be as silent in his boots as he is in bare feet. He has adapted well to my world. If only I could have

252

the chance to see if I would adapt as well to his. I already miss the desert, the wind, the moaning of the dead trees. I'd never be alone in my sorrow out there. There would always be the wind to commiserate with.

"I'm sure she did," he says as he stops in front of me. "It's not hard to believe."

I look up, up, *up* at him in surprise. "It's hard for most people. It was hard for me when I was little."

"She was trying to spare you a life spent preparing to die."

"We're all preparing to die."

"Not like this." He squats down, resting his hands on my knees. "You know it's not the same."

"I know," I whisper, running my fingers over the ridges on the backs of his hands, down the top of each finger, tracing the places where his claws go to hide. They're solid, sturdy chambers, like a second set of bones on top of the first, barely contained by his thick skin. I've felt them before, but I never expected them to look like this, so . . . natural. Not scary at all, really.

I lift his hand, studying the tiny puckers above his finger-nails that must open in order to let his claws out. "I would like to see your claws."

"No."

"Please. Show them to me," I say. "I want to see what gave me the scar on my shoulder."

Gem fists his hand before pulling it from my grasp. "I wish I'd never touched you," he says, dropping his eyes to the floor. "I wish I'd never come here."

"I'm glad you came, and I'm glad you touched me. I wish

you would . . ." My words trail off. I'm still too shy to state it plainly, but surely . . . I reach out, my hand trembling only slightly as I slip my fingers into his open shirt, resting them over his heart. "Can't we stop talking?"

Gem's eyes flick to mine. There's no doubt he understands my meaning—it's clear in the way his lips part, in the way he braces his hands on either side of my hips, fingers digging into the rose upholstery—but instead of kissing me, he says, "There has to be another way."

"There is no other way." My lips prickle with disappointment as I withdraw my hand from his warmth. "The covenant is a binding contract, signed in blood by the founding families of Yuan. Its terms are nonnegotiable."

"It's the covenant that's the source of the magic, not the roses?"

I nod. "The roses grew after the first sacrifice. They're a symbol. Part of the magic, but not the source of it."

"A symbol of what?" Gem's expression is so intense, it makes my head start to hurt again just looking at him. "From what?"

I close my eyes, and rub the space above them with my knuckles. "What do you mean?"

"What has entered into this contract with your people?" Gem asks. "The magic of the planet has been quiet for hundreds of years. So, what magic is this?"

"I don't know." I cross my arms over my chest, suddenly colder. And tired. "It's just . . . magic."

"But whose magic?" he asks. "Who or what accepts the offering of a queen's blood and grants Yuan vitality in return?"

I start to argue, but the words I need won't come. What he's saying makes sense. Magic has to come from someone. Or something. I know the roses grew after the first sacrifice—it's the most written about and sung about event in our city's history—but as far as who or what made them grow . . . what inspires the flowers' hunger for blood . . .

"I don't know," I say in a small voice.

"You don't know," he repeats, as if I've confessed that I don't know how to feed myself or put on my own shoes.

"No, I don't know," I say, defensive and anxious at the same time. "I know the legend, but I— The stories say the noble families arrived in one of the fifteen great ships. They were in charge of supervising the building of Yuan, making sure the dome would protect the colonists until they knew if it was safe for humans to live outside. Everything went well until the eleventh year of building. That's when the workers constructing the dome—the ones who spent the most time outside the ship—began to change."

"To mutate," Gem says, as if he's heard the story before, making me wonder how much history we share.

"Yes." I worry my earlobe between two fingers. "But they mutated more quickly than people ever had on our home planet. Massive changes within a month or two, instead of gradually over thousands and thousands of years. Even the scientists had no explanation for it except magic."

For the first time, it strikes me how strange that must have been for my ancestors, for people from a planet with no magic to suddenly be trapped on a world ruled by it.

"The mutated people turned violent," I say, keeping my

eyes on Gem's chest. "They attacked the ship where the colonists had been living, and tore it apart, killing the people who hadn't been transformed, destroying all the books and the machines that stored the ancient knowledge, and scattering them across the desert."

I glance at Gem's eyes. His expression is neutral, patient, waiting for the rest. "The noble families escaped with a few dozen others whose mutations were still minor," I continue. "Together, they ran into the city, and locked the gates behind them. They were safe inside—the dome was finished and the central buildings constructed—but the city wasn't ready to support life. The animals they'd brought from their home planet were still very young, the seeds hadn't sprouted, and most of their medicines and supplies had been left aboard the ship. They had water, but not much food, and they were too terrified to venture outside the walls. The people were starving to death when, one night, the woman who would become our first queen had a vision."

"A vision of what?" Gem asks, the intensity returning to his voice.

"I don't know." I lift my shoulders and let them fall, before tucking my feet beneath my skirt. "Just . . . a vision. Of how to save her people. Of the covenant," I say, ignoring the prickle at the back of my neck I've always associated with telling a lie. I'm not lying—not as far as I know, anyway.

So why does it feel like I'm telling Gem a fairy tale?

"All right," he says, clearly unsatisfied. "What happened after the vision?"

"The queen woke her husband and representatives from

the other noble families. They walked to the center of the city, where the king transcribed the sacred words of the covenant from the queen's dream onto parchment. They all signed the covenant in blood and spoke the words aloud. Then, as the sun rose beyond the dome, the queen . . .

"As soon as her blood hit the soil, the first bed of roses sprang up from the ground. By the end of the day, crops that should have taken months to grow were ready to be harvested. Yuan was saved," I say, though with less enthusiasm than my father used when telling this story. "The king remarried that evening, and since then the city has never been without a queen, or a daughter in line to be queen, for more than a single night. There are similar stories about the other domed cities. Each one felt the call and formed covenants of their own."

Gem grunts his dubious grunt.

"That's the story as I know it." I turn my palms over to stare at the lines creasing the skin, embarrassed without really knowing why. "The covenant came to the queen in a vision, and the king wrote it down. No mention of who or what made the roses grow. I suppose I've always thought . . ."

"Thought what?"

"I don't know. It seemed to me . . ." I peek at him through my lashes. "Maybe it was the power of her sacrifice that created the magic."

"I've seen sacrifice," Gem says. "I've seen old men wander into the desert to die to give their hut one less mouth to feed. I've seen mothers choose between two babies when there isn't enough milk for them both. No magic roses sprang up when their blood was shed. There's something darker here."

"What do you mean?"

He studies me a moment before saying, "My people have legends, too."

"I know that," I say with a tired smile.

"I don't mean legends like the girl who loved the star. I mean history. Stories from when our tribe was young and some still remembered—"

A knock at the door makes us both turn our heads. Needle stands in the doorway with the rope she took to Gem the night we left for the desert, and an expression that clearly communicates she thinks it's time for him to go.

"Just a few more minutes," I say, profoundly relieved Gem preferred to talk instead of kiss. I can't believe I didn't think about the open door. If Needle had come to fetch Gem and had found us kissing, or worse, she would have been scandalized. She would be scandalized if it were any boy, but a Monstrous boy . . .

I pause, studying Needle as she studies Gem. What does she think of him? She set him free, and sent me out into the desert with him. She must trust him, or at least trust me enough to have faith in my judgment. And she didn't seem afraid when he crawled onto the balcony. She seemed more afraid of Bo, so . . . maybe . . .

"We'll join you in the music room when he's ready," I say. The hope that I might be able to talk to Needle about the way I feel about Gem lifts my spirits. At least a little.

Needle moves a hand to her lips and then rubs the same hand in a circle on her stomach, but I shake my head. "No, we don't need anything else to eat or drink," I say. "Thank you."

She takes a step back into the hall, but I can tell she's reluctant to go. Every minute Gem's here is another minute we could be discovered. Bo could be fetching his father and a team of guards right now. I don't think he would risk his future—he wants to be king and understands how stubborn I can be if I don't get my way—but Needle's right. We won't be safe until Gem's back in his cell.

"Don't worry," I assure her. "We'll be quick. I promise."

Needle smiles—a grin that transforms her simple face into something truly beautiful—and nods before disappearing down the hall toward the music room.

"She's happy you can see her," Gem says.

"I'm happy I can see her, too." I turn back to him. "I never understood how much I was missing. We have our own language, but she says a hundred things at once with her face."

"She does. And she's right. I should go. We can—"

"Not yet," I beg, wishing he never had to go. "Tell me your people's version of the story. It won't take long, will it?"

Gem's forehead wrinkles, the scales there crinkling like tissue paper. "Not too long . . ." He takes a breath, and his forehead smoothes. "The legends of my people say the old ships brought too many colonists. They expected many of the settlers to die in the first years here, falling prey to predators or disease. But this world was good to them. Their numbers grew, and by the time the domes were complete, there wasn't enough room inside for everyone. The people who organized the expeditions, those in power, the people you call the nobles, saw what was coming and took steps to protect themselves. They crept into the domes in the night and locked the other colonists out."

"Because they had mutated?"

"A little, but back then my people still looked more like the Smooth Skins," he says, taking my hand in his and turning it over, running his finger over the flaky skin where my claws would be if I had them. "They didn't fully mutate until months later. . . . The summer heat was brutal that year, and brought new predators from the mountains. My people were dying of sunstroke and animal attacks. They left their settlement and returned to New Hope to–"

"One of the first cities," I say, pleased I paid attention to my history lessons. "But that's hundreds of miles south, past Port South even."

"My people were originally part of the New Hope settlement," he says. "So they returned there, begging to be allowed in until the heat passed, but the people inside refused to open the gates. That's when my ancestors started north. They hoped the summer would be easier here, but it wasn't. They made it as far as Yuan before being taken in by another group of outsiders. They had built shelters with the remains of their ship and were weathering the heat a little better."

He crosses his arms, emphasizing the breadth of his shoulders. It was hard for me to imagine him being descended from the same people as the small, narrow men of this city. Learning that half of his people came from somewhere else makes sense.

"The real changes started not long after," he continues. "But my ancestors were grateful. They considered the mutations a blessing. Mutation allowed them to survive the heat, and fight off predators. In those days, there were still giant horned cats hunting the lands here."

I blink. "Horned cats?"

He nods. "At first, the creatures left us alone, but when the land outside the domes began to die, their usual prey died along with it and they began hunting people."

"It's strange to think of the world being so . . . different."

"But it *was* different," he says with a passion that assures me this isn't just a story for him. This is his history, the legacy of his people. "There were forests and grasslands and fruit and game. In the early days, there was no reason for my people to envy the people in the domed cities. We had everything we needed. Even when the forests died and the grassland turned to desert, we survived. After the mutations, our children were all born larger and stronger than Smooth Skins, with scales and claws and other adaptations that allowed us to survive."

"Then why . . ." I hesitate, knowing I'll have to phrase my question carefully. "Why did your people and the others outside the domes attack the cities? I understand you need food *now*," I hurry to add, "and it's a matter of survival, but the first of the domes fell four hundred years ago."

"That's when the tribes began to realize the truth," he says. "That while our land was dying, the land beneath the domes grew more and more fruitful. Our elders said it was bad magic, and some of the more violent tribes decided it was time for the cities to be destroyed."

"But if that's true," I say, finally understanding all his talk of Yuan robbing the land beyond our walls, "then why hasn't the desert come back to life? Almost all of the domed cities have fallen. There are only three left. Shouldn't the world beyond the domes have recovered with fewer cities . . . draining the lands outside?"

Gem looks away, watching the lamp on my bedside table burn, uncertainty clear in his eyes. "Some of the tribes to the north think *all* of the cities must fall before the planet will begin to heal."

"What do you think?"

"I don't know," he says. "Maybe they're right. My chief thought . . ."

"She thought what?"

"She thought . . ." When his gaze returns to me, his eyes are so full of pain, it summons a sound from my throat.

"What's wrong?" I ask, coming to my knees on the floor in front of him.

He shakes his head. "I can't . . ."

"Tell me." I run my fingers down his cheeks, over the whiskers on his chin. They're black, even blacker than his hair, and sharp enough to tickle the skin around my mouth when we kiss.

A kiss. It seems the thing to do. I lean in, pressing my lips to his forehead the way he pressed his to mine, offering comfort, but after only a moment he takes me by the shoulders and sets me gently away.

"I should go." He rises from the floor in one effortless movement and starts toward the door.

"All right," I say, trying not to be hurt by his eagerness to leave. He's right. We've already been longer than the "moment" I promised Needle.

"I'll send the guards at the usual time tomorrow." I come to my feet much less gracefully, struggling with my skirts, and follow him down the hall to the music room. "We can talk more while we work in the garden."

He casts a narrow look over his shoulder.

"I know what you said about the bulbs, but it will give us an excuse to meet." I clear my throat, pushing down the sadness rising inside me as Needle hands Gem the rope and gathers her sweater.

It doesn't matter that the garden is a lie. I'm not tainted, and Gem isn't a monster. There might be no need for herbs to impede mutation. If the people in the Banished camp have scales or claws or other mutant characteristics, there's nothing wrong with that. What's wrong is the way the rest of the city treats them. I'll find a way to convince the whole citizens that they have nothing to fear from those who look different.

"Tomorrow, then?" I ask, voice rising sharply as Needle hurries past me to the tower stair and Gem follows without saying a word.

What have I done? Why does he suddenly seem so cold?

"Gem?" My voice breaks in the middle of his name, betraying how much it hurts for him to leave this way.

He stops, his entire back rigid, before he turns and walks back down the hall toward me. He looks angry, furious, and for a moment I'm afraid of what he'll say, but he doesn't say a word. He pulls me into his arms, lifting me off my feet, silencing my breath of surprise with a kiss.

Kiss. The word is inadequate for urgent hands and bruised lips and his taste filling my mouth and his breath in my lungs and need strong enough to rattle my bones, shake me to the core until all I can do is dig my fingers into his shoulders and hope to survive being so close. It's wonderful and awful and all I ever want. Forever. I don't want it to stop. I never want him to leave.

He has to leave. I know that, but knowing doesn't keep my chest from aching like it will split in two when Gem sets me back on my feet.

"Don't go," I whisper, my arms still tangled around his neck.

"Find the covenant," he says. "If it's written, you should be able to read it for yourself. There has to be some way."

Some way to save me without destroying my city. Some way to spare his people without sacrificing the safety of mine.

"I'll ask Junjie to bring it to me tomorrow," I promise. "We can read it together."

He smoothes my hair from my face. "But I'm still learning. I–"

"That's all right. Needle can read. She can–"

Needle. Oh, no. Oh. No . . .

The blood drains from my face as I peek around Gem's wide body to find Needle standing at the door to the stairs, her eyes fixed on the carpet and the ghost of a smile on her lips. There's no chance she missed that kiss, and still, she's smiling.

I didn't think it was possible to love her more, but I do. Instantly.

"Bring it to me, then," Gem says, backing away. "If there are words I don't know, Needle can help."

I nod and warn them to be careful as they start down the stairs. As soon as they're out of sight, I hurry to the balcony to search the moonlit world far below for soldiers, but there are none in sight. Not on the path that runs by the tower, not in the cabbage fields, not in the browning stalks that are all that's left of the autumn sunflowers.

When the two shadows—one slight and swift, one tall and broad but no less swift—emerge from the tower, they cross the road unobserved. Well, almost unobserved.

I observe them. I watch them with the miracle of my new eyes until they disappear into the field of dead flowers, bound for the orchard beyond and the royal garden beyond that, where the roses will see them race by, hurrying to get Gem back into his cell before he's discovered.

I imagine the way the blooms will twist subtly on their thick stems, turning their unblinking eyes on my friend and the mutant who kissed me, and I shiver. What was it Gem said? Something darker . . . Something darker was at work.

It isn't hard to imagine something darker at work in the earth beneath the roses, something greedy and so desperate for blood that it refuses to sustain life without taking life in return. Perhaps the covenant will shed some light on that dark thing's identity. I will ask Junjie to bring me the document first thing, before the sun has a chance to rise or his son has a chance to come knocking at his door telling tales.

And then I will ask for a tour of my city and watch his face very carefully as he realizes the queen is no longer blind.

TWENTY

GEM

QUEENS. Only queens. Only Isra.

The words repeat over and over as I lie on the hard bed in my cell with my hands propped beneath my throbbing head. I watch the moonlight move across the ceiling, and remain sleepless even though my body aches with exhaustion.

The magic of Yuan might still save my people, but—

Queens.

—if Isra's right, then the magic doesn't lie in the roses at all, it lies in—

Only queens.

–the covenant, and the blood of the queen of Yuan. Once I read the covenant and learn the sacred words Isra spoke of, I could take her. I could take her *and* the roses–

Only Isra.

–to be safe. We could marry according to the Smooth Skin tradition. From what she's said, it seems that would be enough to join me to the magic, allow me to carry on the covenant when she's gone.

If she's going to die to save a nation, why shouldn't it be mine? Haven't my people suffered enough? Isn't it time we had abundance, even at the cost of a life now and then? Better one life than many. And if she's going to die . . .

If she's going to die . . .

Only queens.

I don't want her to die. By the ancestors, *please* . . .

Isra.

–there has to be another way.

ƁO

"I'M sorry." My voice is unnaturally loud in the silent room. Father hasn't said a word for the past half hour. He simply sits there, turned in his chair, studying the moonlight shimmering on the lake outside his window, while I stand at attention before the fire until my shoulders cramp and sweat runs down the valley of my spine. "Baba, please–"

"You aren't a child," he snaps without bothering to look my way. "Stop using childish words."

"I'm sorry, Father," I say, then, "Captain," because I'm not sure which he'd prefer now that I've disappointed him so completely. I shouldn't have told him the truth.

But I had to tell. There was no avoiding it. Isra can see, and she wants to know why. I wouldn't be surprised to find her on Father's doorstep first thing in the morning. Father would have known soon enough. Better that he heard it from me.

"I thought I was doing right by my future wife," I say. "That's all. I never meant to defy you."

He finally turns to me, but I wish he hadn't. The utter absence of feeling in his eyes makes my heart lurch. He has never looked at me like this, even when he used a switch to express his displeasure with his only son.

"You disobeyed an order from your father, who is also your superior, and violated the wishes of your former king," he says, every word as crisp as the folds ironed into his uniform. My mother irons his clothes herself. The maids never get the creases quite right, and everything must be exactly right in my father's house. Perfect. If not, everyone under his roof pays the price. "That is the definition of defiance."

"I–I'm sorry," I stammer again, hating the whine creeping into my voice. Father's right; I sound like a child.

It's Isra's fault. I never should have told her about the tea. I should have let her live out the rest of her life in the darkness. What difference will it really make? Will sight make her happy, and even if it does, does her happiness matter? The kingdom doesn't require her happiness, only her blood.

"You're impulsive, Bo. That isn't a good trait in a king." Father rises from his chair and crosses to stand too close, the way he does when one of his soldiers has stepped out of line. I've seen Father break men with nothing more than a stern look, but he doesn't stop with a look when it comes to his son.

He hasn't struck me in years—not since I joined the military force when I was sixteen—but I can tell he wants to now. My jaw clenches; my teeth ache. Beads of sweat form on my upper lip, but I'm too afraid to wipe them away. It's best not to move when Father gets this way.

"You didn't stop to think that she'd want an explanation?" he asks, his voice terribly gentle, like the slaughterer's hand when he takes a sheep tenderly by the scruff of its neck.

"I thought . . ." I swallow. "I plan to tell her I heard a rumor."

"She'll want to know where you heard it."

"I'll tell her I don't know," I say, "that I heard two people talking, but it was dark and—"

"You're a poor liar," he says, watching me like I'm an insect found swimming in his bed pot. "The girl isn't a complete fool. She'll know you're deceiving her. She'll decide you're not trustworthy, and what girl wants as a husband a man she can't trust?"

I'm tempted to tell him Isra has already promised to marry me, as long as I keep quiet about her activities with the

Monstrous, but I bite the inside of my lip. If Father finds out I disobeyed him a second time by speaking about the marriage when he expressly forbade it, and then left Isra alone with a monster . . .

I shudder to think how he'd look at me after that. I don't want to remember what it feels like to cower at his feet.

"You've made this far more complicated than it needed to be," he continues, eyes so cold it makes me shiver despite the blazing fire at my back.

"I'm sorry." I drop my gaze, staring at the lines on either side of his mouth, just visible beneath his mustache. In the firelight, his wrinkles are more defined. He's an old man. He can't live forever, and when he is gone, I will truly be king. I'll make the decisions for this city, and they will be good ones. I'm not impulsive. It was affection that made me foolish, but I won't make the mistake of caring for my queen again. Isra isn't worth the trouble.

I'll hold my tongue until the day we're married, and then I'll show her how a true ruler gives orders.

"Yes, well . . . I suppose we'll have to tell her the truth," Father says, a hint of hard humor in his tone. "I'll tell her I placed the herbs in her tea every morning," he says, bending to toss another dung patty onto the fire, though the room is already stifling. "But only because her father begged me to continue doing so once he was no longer able to administer them himself."

I hesitate, but can't keep from saying, "She won't believe you."

Father grunts as he returns to his chair. "I'll show her the official order, signed in her father's hand." He sits down with a soft groan.

I imagine the pain Isra will feel when she realizes it was her own father who sentenced her to darkness, and some weak part of me wants to feel sorry for her, but I clench my jaw against it. Pity is what got me into trouble in the first place. I can't afford pity. A king must be made of sterner stuff.

"And then I'll tell her the story of her poor mother," Father continues, "and I'll reveal to her all the terrible sights that her father wanted to protect her from."

My lips part. He wouldn't. "But, Father . . ."

"But what?" He snaps, setting my nerves on edge all over again.

"I'm not sure how she'll take it," I say, careful to sound suitably submissive, though I'm horrified by what he plans to do. I don't care for Isra the way I did, but this isn't right. She's been living in a dream world. If that dream is ripped away, who knows what will happen? She might go as mad as her mother. She might be the next queen to hurl herself from her balcony. If she takes her own life before we're married, she will bring about the fall of Yuan. Isra isn't completely rational as it is. It's dangerous to test her sanity this way. "She truly has no idea, and I–"

"She will have a very good idea by the time tomorrow is through."

"But I–"

"You what?" he asks, standing so abruptly it startles me into a step backward. "You thought you'd give her eyes and not have her see?"

271

"Please," I say, holding up my palms in an instinctive plea for understanding. "I have a plan. We'll keep her in the nobles' village. There's no reason the queen should go into the city center or the Banished camp. She's already been presented to the people. After we're married, I can handle all interactions with the common people and–"

"You can't keep your piss in the pot," he spits. "All you had to do was keep your mouth shut and wait for the kingship to be delivered into your hands, but you ruined it. You destroyed what I've sacrificed so much to ensure."

"What have you sacrificed?" I ask, suddenly angry. "You won't have to marry a woman marked for death. You won't have to watch her die. You won't have to know your children will meet the same fate if they're born female."

I pull in a breath, fighting to regain control. I've never spoken like this to Father, but I've never been on the verge of sentencing my entire family to death, either. I don't love Isra, but I don't hate her. I don't want her to die. I don't want my next wife or my daughters to die. The sacrifice of the queen seemed like a sad but noble act growing up, but now it is a black, twisted thing squirming its way into my life, poisoning every thought and feeling.

I brace myself, expecting Father to strike me, to shout at the very least, but instead he sits back down in his chair. He sighs, and the rigid lines of his shoulders relax as he bows his head over folded hands.

"I didn't mean to sound ungrateful," I whisper, not sure what to make of his response. "I want to be king. I just never expected it to be so . . . difficult."

"Maybe I've . . ." Father runs his hands over his head, pushing springy gray hairs back into the smooth black of his braid. "Maybe I've made a mistake."

"No, Father," I say, panicking at the thought of having my new torment taken away. I don't want to be king, but I can't stand the thought of *not* being king, either. "You don't make mistakes."

"Don't I?" He lifts his face. The shadows there seem darker than they did even a moment ago. "I thought you were ready. I thought I was ready. But . . . there are things . . ." He takes a breath, and his fingers tighten on the arms of the chair. "The king was planning to marry again."

"What?" I ask, genuinely surprised. "But it's been thirteen years since Isra's mother died."

"Yes, and as time passed, the king grew increasingly certain that he couldn't bear for his only daughter to meet the same fate as her mother. He planned to wed Suyin, Rune Lee's widow. She's only twenty-seven, and has already borne two healthy children. A new heir was assured." He sighs. "No official paperwork was signed, but I discussed the match with Suyin on the king's orders. She was agreeable. Her husband left the family with nothing. They've been living with his sister for two years, but it's obvious there's no love lost between Suyin and her sister-in-law. Suyin was willing to lay down her life in exchange for a way out of her sister-in-law's home and a richer future for her existing children. It was only a matter of time."

Father leans back, folding his hands in his lap once more. "As I said, she already has children. The line of succession would have been ensured for another generation. Her eldest is a daughter, but the girl is only five years old. She wouldn't have been old enough to marry until you were nearly thirty, Bo, and who knows how the political climate would have changed by then? The only way I could ensure your place on the throne was for the king to die before he could marry again, while I still had the power to convince the other advisors my son should be the one to marry the queen."

A sour taste fills my mouth, and the floor beneath my feet goes as soft as sand, leaving me nothing firm to stand on. My legs tremble and my heart beats faster, but for a long moment I can't understand why I'm frightened. Even when my brain sorts out the meaning hidden in Father's words, I can't believe it. Surely I'm missing something. Surely . . .

"The king was killed by the Monstrous," I say, my voice as weak as my knees.

"It appeared that way." He stares me straight in the eye, not flinching when he adds, "But only because I made it so."

I reach out to brace myself on the mantel above the fire. "I don't believe you."

Father ignores me and continues, "The Monstrous was on the path by the lake, near the garden where the flowers for the court tables are grown. I had planned to poison the king, but as soon as I saw the creature, I knew my moment had come. I killed the guards first, to make certain there were no witnesses. Then I killed the king, cutting him open to make it look as if the Monstrous had done it."

"No," I say, sounding more like a child than ever. Tears burn the backs of my eyes, and sickness rises in my throat. If I hadn't skipped dinner, I know I'd be ill all over Father's finely carved fireplace.

"Thankfully, it was one of the creatures without our language, who couldn't reveal what I'd done." He rises slowly from his chair, looking older, wearier, than I've ever seen him, and comes to stand beside me, gazing into the fire. "If it had been the other one . . ." He shrugs and slips his hands into the pockets of his pants. "Not many would have listened to the ravings of a monster, but there are always those who pause to consider the absurd. If they'd paused long enough, they might have found reason to believe it."

Isra might have paused. Isra might have listened to the monster. Tonight she called it her "friend." If she ever learns the truth . . .

"She'll have you killed," I whisper. "She's not as fragile as you believe. If she finds out, she'll—"

"She'll never find out," Father says, his strong hand coming to rest on my shoulder. "Not unless you tell her."

I turn to him so quickly I lose my footing and knock my shin on the marble step of the fireplace. "I would never. *Never.*"

"I have your loyalty, then?" he asks, uncertainty lurking in his eyes.

"Yes," I say. "Of course. I'm your son."

He nods stiffly. "I spent my entire life serving another family. I wanted you to rule your own life, to be your own man," he says, mouth weak around the edges, the muscle in his cheek leaping. I've never seen him out of control. He has never appeared vulnerable in any way. I've imagined Father weak, and thought I'd find the sight thrilling—but this isn't thrilling. It's terrifying, a god falling from the sky, his wings on fire. "I did this for you, Bo."

"I know, Father." I take him by the shoulders and give a firm squeeze, willing strength into both of us. "I won't fail you. We'll manage Isra. Together. I'll be king by springtime, and I will never forget that I owe everything I am to you."

He's quiet for a long moment, before whispering, "Thank you, Son." Then he smiles. Really smiles, a proud smile, a grateful smile. Proud of *me*. Grateful *to me*. The sight firms up every trembling, doubting bone in my body.

Great men aren't afraid to do dangerous things to tip the hand of fate in their favor. My father is a great man and he did a brave, dangerous thing to give me a chance at a future I couldn't have had without him. I would never have asked him to kill the king, but . . . it's done now. There's no going back. We can only go forward, and make certain we prove that the end justifies the means.

I will be a great king. I will do great things for this city, and I won't let a girl who'd rather play in the dirt with a monster than devote herself to her people get in the way.

"Let me do it," I say, giving my father's shoulders one final squeeze before dropping my arms to my sides and standing tall, determined to show him I'm man enough to handle the queen. "Let me show Isra the truth about the city tomorrow. I'll find a way to make her love me for it. I swear I will."

Or hate me less. I will be the only one who's ever told her the truth. She'll have to respect me for that, at least enough to honor the promise she made tonight.

"All right," Father says, with a slow nod. "You'll be her

husband. You'll have to learn how to manage her sooner or later."

"Thank you," I say, the rush of being treated as my father's equal for the first time making me certain I could climb the tallest mountain in the desert if it were safe to leave the city. "I'll make you proud."

He cups my cheek in his hand, his touch gentle for the first time in longer than I can remember. "I'm already proud."

My throat grows so tight I can do nothing but nod in response.

"Until tomorrow." Father bows. I bow lower, keeping my head tucked to my chest until he has left to join Mother in their bedroom.

Even when he's gone, I can feel his faith in me lingering in the air, warming me to the core, making me certain there is nothing I can't do. Nothing I won't do to ensure our family's success.

TWENTY-ONE

ISRA

ONE, *two . . . five, six . . .*

Seventy-five . . . one hundred and twelve . . . eighty-eight . . .
eighty-nine . . . ten . . . two . . .

I can see, but I find myself counting my steps all the same.
Counting to stay calm, to retain control, counting until numbers lose their meaning and my mind is a jumble of circles and
curves and slashes. The hourglass of an eight. The dangerous
corner of a seven. The soft belly of a six. I trace their shapes in
the air as I walk, my fingers busy at my sides, frantically trying
to bring order to the world.

278

But even numbers are powerless against chaos. Disorder. Madness.

I'm beside myself, outside myself. I watch my long body glide down streets filled with the twisted and the wrong, and everything is . . . upside down. Inside out. I look down, expecting to see the sky beneath my feet and my heart settled on the skin outside my chest, but there is only the shimmering green of my dress, tight at my bust, tighter still at my waist, but loose enough near the ground.

Loose enough for hands with missing fingers to reach out to brush the fabric as Bo and I pass by.

This particular hand belongs to a child, a girl with only three fingers, a wee thing with silky black hair that hangs over her face, partially concealing the fact that her nose is missing . . . pieces. Pieces of skin. Maybe bone. Skin and bone. I don't know. I can't look too closely. Not at her, or her parents, or all the others gathered by the side of the street to kneel as I walk by. I just can't.

I lift my eyes and find a tiny rectangle of blue sky high above the laundry lines zigzagging between the intimidating buildings of the city center. These towers make mine look like a child's toy. They are breathlessly tall, and each one overflowing with people. The people must live three or four to a room, at least, if the amount of laundry is anything to judge by. Hundreds of pants and shirts and dresses and overalls and underthings hang like uninspired flags, blocking most of the sun's light, drooping limply toward the street, where their owners were ordered to assemble this morning to meet their queen and let her look upon them with her new eyes.

I demanded that the royal gong be rung and messengers be sent throughout the city. I insisted on walking through the city center, the better to see my people. I would not be swayed.

Now it's all I can do not to turn and run back to my tower. I long for the comfort of my darkness, my ignorance. I want to go back and undo it all. I want to be the Isra my father worked so hard to create. If only I'd known how easy I had it in my cage, with my velvet blinders always in place . . .

My scrap of blue sky vanishes, and my gaze drifts down to the street ahead, where a woman without arms or legs sits propped in a chair beside several little boys. A mother who can never hug her sons or hold her babies. How did this happen? *How* . . .

A choked sound escapes my lips, bursting free before I can contain it.

"Are you all right?" Bo asks from his place beside me.

"No," I whisper. "Of course not. Of course, of *course* not." I press my tongue to the roof of my mouth, stopping the stream of babble. I can't lose control in front of my people. I can't show them how unprepared I am. I can't be like my mother.

"The tower. My mother." I pull in a labored breath. "That's . . . *This* is why."

"Yes," Bo says. "In her home city, the nobles lived within a second wall at one edge of their dome, kept entirely separate from the common people. She had never seen a human who was not of noble blood before she came to Yuan." Bo's hand is firm at the center of my back, guiding me relentlessly onward, through the city center to what lies ahead, to what I've demanded to see.

I want to twist away, to order him to keep his hands off me, but I can't. His touch is the only thing keeping me going. If he withdraws, I'll stop walking and be stranded in the middle of the nightmare.

Nightmares upon nightmares. I had the fire nightmare again this morning, saw the woman's mouth opening and closing in the burning wood. But this time I listened harder, the way Gem told me to, and I would have sworn I heard her speak. She was saying something about the truth . . . about hope . . . something important. . . .

When I woke, I couldn't remember exactly what she'd said, but I was bursting with happiness anyway. I could see the golden miracle of the sunrise shining through my window, the brilliant bleeding red of my quilt, and Needle's tightly curled smile as she brought my breakfast tray. My life and my dreams were changing, and I was certain my city wasn't going to be far behind. This morning, Yuan was a riddle I was confident I could solve.

But this is . . . a disaster. A tragedy. Hopeless.

"Now you see why your father felt he had to take such extreme measures," Bo continues, increasing his pace until I have trouble keeping up. My dress is wider at the bottom than my other dresses, but it's tight at the thighs. Still, I don't complain. I don't care if I have to wiggle and wobble down the street like a fool. The sooner we leave the city center and all the damage behind, the better. "He was only trying to protect you. He thought if you remained unaware of certain truths that you would be spared your mother's madness. It was only after she came here that she became . . . strange. She grew even worse after you were born. At first the healers dismissed it as the sadness that sometimes comes over new mothers, but then she began talking of going into the wilderness to speak to the Monstrous. Father says she set the fire not long after."

I don't say a word, though I want to ask Bo if he knows *why* my mother wanted to speak to the Monstrous. I've always known Mother was Father's second wife and foreign—a noble from far away who married my father to escape a city on the verge of collapse—but I've never heard anyone speak of her expressing the desire to make contact with the Monstrous. *Why would she want to do that?* I want to ask, but I don't trust myself to speak without breaking down.

When Bo first told me it was my father who had ordered the poisoning of my tea, I nearly slapped him. I was certain he was lying. I refused to believe that my father would steal the sight from his own daughter, even when Junjie showed me the signed order bearing the king's seal. I just couldn't believe Baba hated me that much.

Now I understand. My father didn't hate me. He was trying to spare me from the heartbreaking truth.

"I wanted to protect you, too," Bo says, louder now that we've reached the edge of the city center and only a few citizens kneel at the sides of the street. "I planned for you to remain in the nobles' village, where the people are whole. There was no reason for you to see this particular truth." His hand slides around my waist, his familiar touch becoming openly intimate, making my breakfast gurgle angrily in my stomach.

I swallow hard and step away. "Yes, there is. I needed to

know. I . . . had . . . to . . ." My words dribble away as we pass by the final knot of people.

Beyond them, the world opens up, the wide dirt road continuing on through the fields. I want to rush ahead into that open space, but instead I force myself to nod and smile a brittle smile at the subjects kneeling in the grass at the edge of an orchard of bare-limbed pear trees. There are three men and five women, all wearing orchard workers' overalls, all with missing parts. They are ripped pieces of a dozen different puzzles that will never fit together, and I don't understand it.

I don't. I can't . . . I thought . . .

"The Banished camp is . . . worse?" I whisper when we've finally passed the last woman. I find little comfort in the even rows of fruit trees on one side of the road and the perfectly ordered grape trellises on the other. Beyond these tidy fields, at the end of this road, lies the place where the Banished—the people deemed too grotesque to inhabit the city center—live out their abbreviated lives.

"Far worse," Bo confirms, hesitating at my side. "We can go back to the great hall if you like. I can—"

"No." I lift my chin, and move past him on stiff legs. "I need to know the truth."

"I can tell you the truth. Let me do that for you," he says, hurrying to catch up, what sounds like real compassion in his voice. He's been unfailingly kind this morning—like the Bo I knew before last night—but I'm not fooled. I will never trust him. Not ever, no matter how helpful he tries to be.

"Thank you, but no." I pull my shawl tight around my

shoulders and aim myself toward the royal carriage waiting for us by the side of the road. The driver is an elegant old man with silver hair, supposedly a commoner like all noble servants, but without damaged parts—at least, none that I can see. His defects must be hidden inside, like Needle's. Selfishly, I'm glad of it. I need a moment. Just a moment.

"Please, Isra." Bo stops me with a hand on my arm. "Let me spare you any more of this."

"Why?" I subtly shake off his fingers as I glance back over my shoulder, finally able to pinpoint what's been plaguing my mind, now that I have some distance from the city. "Why are—"

"I care about you. I told you that last night."

"No. Not that," I snap, unable to bear talking feelings at a time like this. "Why are the people damaged? How has this happened? I thought the covenant was strong."

"The covenant is strong," Bo says. "It's been this way since the beginning. You know the legend: those families who refused to sign the covenant did not receive equal protection from its magic."

"I thought that meant they had fewer goods, smaller houses," I say, voice louder than I mean it to be. "I didn't think it meant they—"

"It means they suffered from this planet's dark magic. They weren't made Monstrous, but their humanity was not preserved in the same way that those of noble blood are preserved. They suffer from a different sort of mutation."

My brow wrinkles, and for the first time in more than an hour, my thoughts begin to organize themselves. "But the

Monstrous look nothing like that. What's happened to our people isn't mutation. It's . . . something else."

"Something like what?" he asks.

"I don't know. Something . . ."

Something dark. Something unnatural.

Yearning for Gem grips me so fiercely it feels like my stomach is climbing up my throat. The thought of talking this madness through with him gives me strength and, more important, reminds me—

"I'm not sure." I turn back to Bo. "But perhaps the covenant will offer some insight. I'd like it brought to my rooms this afternoon."

He blinks as if I've snapped my fingers between his eyes. "The covenant?"

"Yes, the covenant," I say. "Have it delivered to the tower immediately. I'll be keeping it overnight." That should give Needle and me time to sneak over to see Gem.

By the moons, I can't wait to see him, to feel his arms around me, his chest warm and solid beneath my cheek, making the world feel steady and possible again. Night can't come quickly enough.

"We should go," I say. "The driver's waiting."

"But . . ." Bo's mouth opens and closes as I circle around him and climb into the royal carriage for the first time in my life. I was looking forward to the ride this morning—the wind in my hair, the fields rushing past on both sides—but now I can't imagine taking pleasure in simple things, not when there is so much suffering under the dome.

"Isra, I can't have the covenant delivered." Bo climbs up

beside me, clearly deciding he deserves to sit in the carriage rather than ride on the step at the back with the other guards. "It's impossible."

"What's impossible?"

"The covenant was lost," he says. "Hundreds of years ago. Not long after King Sato died."

"What?" I want to believe he's lying, but he seems genuinely confused, completely at a loss.

Lost. The covenant is lost. How could that be? How could something so important be *lost*?

"King Sato hid the covenant for safekeeping," Bo says, giving the signal for the driver to start the horses. The silver-haired man flicks his whip, and the buggy lurches forward, throwing me back against the seat. Bo steadies me with an arm around my shoulders. I'm too horrified to push it away. "He died before he could tell his last wife where it was hidden."

"But that's . . ." King Sato was our third king. That means . . . "No one's read the covenant in six hundred years?" I squeak. "Or more?"

"It's all right." He has the nerve to smile. "Our history isn't lost. There are other texts that tell us all we need to know, and the sacred words spoken at each royal wedding are engraved on a gold tablet we'll hold between us on the day we take our vows." Bo pulls me closer, until I'm wedged beneath his armpit, my spine crunched and my dress straining across my back. "Don't worry. The covenant is strong. The damaged people have been that way for generations upon generations. They don't suffer from it the way we would. They aren't like us."

"Then what are they like?" I squirm free, and scoot to the other side of the buggy.

Bo's expression hardens at the sarcasm in my voice, but to his credit, he maintains his patient tone. "They aren't Monstrous, but they aren't human the way we are, either. They don't know any other kind of life. They're happy with what they have, to be a part of our city, to be safe, fed, and protected."

He sounds like he's telling the truth, but that doesn't mean anything. He could think he's telling the truth—the way I did every time I assured Gem I was tainted—and still be telling a lie. I know for a fact he's wrong about my people's suffering. I could see the pain in their eyes. I could feel the hard facts of their life weighing on me as I walked among them, dragging me down until it felt like my feet were moving beneath the surface of the ground.

"You said there are other texts?" I ask, brushing a lock of hair from my face, finding no joy in the wind that whips it back into my eyes.

"There are," he says. "Would you like me to have those delivered to your rooms?"

"Yes, right away." I try to feel optimistic about what I'll learn in the texts, but I can't. Something deep inside insists that all I'll find in those writings are more lies.

I have to find the covenant. I have to discover where it was hidden so long ago, and I can think of only one place to look for help, one thing that's been around for more than six hundred years and still has eyes to see.

The roses have deceived me as often as anyone else has,

but tonight I'll make it clear that I won't tolerate lies. They will give me what I want—the truth and nothing but—or I will . . . I will . . .

Or I will refuse them their offering.

Even the thought is enough to make my head spin and my heart thrash against my ribs, but I can't help but think . . .

What if the stories of Gem's people are true? If so, wouldn't my people be better off in the desert? Better off transformed than forced to live with missing pieces? The nobles and soldiers and some of the merchants are still whole, but the overwhelming majority of my people are suffering, not thriving, under the dome.

Maybe if Yuan is abandoned, if the other domed cities are abandoned as well . . . Maybe if we all go into the desert together . . .

Maybe I don't have to die. Maybe Gem was right. Maybe there *is* another way.

The thought should renew my flagging hope, but it doesn't. My entire life I have been afraid to die, but at least I thought I had something worth dying for.

Now I have . . . nothing. A terrible mess I don't know how to clean up, and the certainty that I will find no help from those in power in this city. The whole have beauty, pleasure, comfort, and abundance, and they've convinced themselves they deserve it. Because they are more human than the people who suffer in the city center, or the Banished in their lonely camp, or the monsters starving in the desert.

I'll never be able to convince them differently. Yuan will never change, not unless I can find proof that something is

wrong with the city. The nobles are spoiled and soft and inclined to gossip, but they are not evil people. I must convince
them that Yuan is rotten at its core. I must find the covenant
and discover why it was hidden away.

ƁO

THE morning lasts forever. The afternoon is even longer. By
the time I finally sit down on the carved wooden bench outside the court meeting chambers, I'm exhausted.

Isra insisted on seeing every part of the Banished camp—
the shelters, the feeding troughs, the burial pit, even the trench
filled with their bodily waste. It was . . . unspeakably repulsive.

The other soldiers stayed at the perimeter with the guards
charged with keeping the Banished contained in their corner
of Yuan, but I was forced to walk among them. I couldn't
leave Isra's side for a moment, not if I want to be seen as her
equal, and, someday soon, her better.

Today's insanity shouldn't make *that* very hard.

What kind of queen willingly walks among the Banished?
What kind of queen tries to talk to people who aren't much
more than monsters, and all of them out of what's left of their
minds?

Even Isra learned that quickly enough. By the time the
fourth or fifth Banished ran, screaming nonsense when she

tried to approach, she learned to keep her distance. Still, she refused to leave right away. She stayed and asked questions about their treatment, their feeding schedule, their living arrangements, and, finally, why the Banished weren't allowed into the city center with the rest of the people, since many of them seemed less damaged, physically anyway, than the people she'd seen there.

I was shocked that she needed an explanation.

It's obvious to anyone with eyes—even new eyes—that the Banished display Monstrous traits. They have patches of scales and huge teeth and hands with pieces of claws exposed outside their skin. They creep and crawl and cower like the beasts they are. They run from any whole citizen in fear, sensing, I suppose, in some part of their wretched brains, that we are their enemies. That *they* are *our* enemies, that the Monstrous they resemble want to destroy us, and our way of life, forever.

"They're lucky we let them live," I finally said, too astonished by Isra's complaints about the mistreatment of the creatures to mind my tongue. "Other cities smother them at birth. Or put them outside the gates to starve. Or worse. We are the gentlest of the domed cities, Isra. We always have been."

Isra went pale at that, as if she couldn't imagine anything more terrible. She's spent too much time with that creature. It's more clever than most—it speaks our words and plays at being like us—but the beast is feral beneath the façade. It plots the downfall of our city. I can sense it. I saw it in his face last night on Isra's balcony. He wanted nothing more than to kill me, the way his people have killed mine for centuries, though

I have done nothing but treat him with a civility a prisoner scarcely deserves.

But he'll be taken care of soon enough. I spoke with Father before Isra went into his meeting chamber to discuss her tour of the city. He agreed the Monstrous would have to be disposed of as soon as I am made king of Yuan. The safety he affords isn't worth the risk he poses. The entire court has been on edge since the day Isra insisted on working with the creature. He hasn't hurt her yet, but we'd be fools to think he isn't planning to. We'll kill him before he gets the chance and deal with the—

"Yes, I agree." Isra's voice drifts from the shade of the arbor covering the front entrance to the court offices. In the spring, purple flowers will hang down far enough to tickle the top of her hair as she walks beneath. Bees will hum and the air will be warm and sweet and we will be married.

And I will have the power to tell her to go to her tower and stay there if she refuses to listen to reason.

The thought makes it easier to smile as she emerges into the watery afternoon light, followed closely by my father. He's dressed in his faded amber advisor's robe, the one with the slightly frayed sleeves worn by three generations of chief advisors to the royals of Yuan. The robe softens his rough edges, makes him seem more approachable than his soldier's uniform.

I'm sure the choice of clothing is no coincidence. He wanted Isra to feel comfortable with him today, to feel confident that he was listening to her concerns and opinions.

"I'll start organizing the documents at once," Father says, stopping less than a foot away, but not cutting his eyes in my direction. He tilts his head back to look Isra full in the face, as if he has never found anyone more enrapturing. "I'll send them to the tower for your review as soon as they're finished."

"And when will that be?" Isra asks, fingers twirling absent-mindedly at her sides the way they have all day. I grit my teeth and force my eyes away from her fidgeting. It's enough to drive me mad. If I'd fidgeted like that as a child, my father would have bound my hands in cotton. "I want to start the process as soon as possible. Things can't continue as they have."

"Certainly not." Father nods, but I see his eyebrows draw tightly together. "I'll have the first drafts of the amendments to the code drawn by late tomorrow. The next day at the latest."

"That isn't soon enough." Isra's fingers move even faster, tracing an elaborate, repeating pattern I can't begin to sort out. "I need them sooner. At least the amendment related to the treatment of the Banished. I'd like to see a draft of that tonight."

"Tonight it is, then." Father's forehead smoothes, and the hint of a smile gentles his lips. He looks as pleasant as he ever does—even more so, actually—but I'm not fooled. "I'll work through dinner and have the amendment delivered to you in the great hall as soon as I'm finished. The texts you requested on the covenant should already be waiting in your rooms. I ordered them sent before we sat down to chat."

"Thank you." Isra's breath rushes out, and her fingers finally still. "But have the amendment sent to my rooms as well, please. I won't eat in the hall tonight. I need some time. Alone. It's been quite a day."

"Indeed." Father smiles. "I've never discussed this many amendments to our code of law in the course of a year, let alone one afternoon."

Isra bites her lip and shoots Father a wary look from beneath her long lashes. "I know this must seem strange, but I'm certain this is right, and the only way to move forward. I think Baba . . . what he did . . . giving me the herbs for all those years . . ."

"Your baba loved you very much," Father says, apparently not minding if Isra uses childish words. "Never doubt that."

"I know. I believe he did," she whispers in a trembling voice, but when she lifts her chin, her expression is calm, strong. "I was shocked, at first, but I think the choice Father made was for the best. He gave me fresh eyes. He allowed me to see Yuan and our people in a way those who have lived in the midst of this . . . confusion no longer can. Being an outsider, and ignorant of many things, has allowed me to see where our city has gone astray."

Father inclines his head in a gesture so subservient, it makes my jaw drop. "An interesting and wise perspective."

Isra glances my way, and I hurry to return her hopeful smile. "Thank you," she says, turning back to Father. "I'm glad we could come to an agreement, and I'm grateful for your support. I know the other advisors will find the changes easier if you're there by my side when I announce them."

"Certainly," Father says. "Change, even drastic change, can sometimes be the only way to move forward."

Isra's smile is . . . dazzling, and for a moment I remember why I wanted to marry her. She's lovely in her happiness. So lovely it makes me ill to know this moment isn't what she thinks it is. I know my father hasn't been won over so easily. I *know,* even before he puts a hand on my shoulder and says, "Bo, would you join me in my chamber? I have some business I'd like you to attend to while I draft the amendments Isra and I discussed." He shifts his attention to Isra with another kindly smile. "If that's acceptable, my lady? If you'd rather Bo escort you back to your rooms first, then—"

"No, no, don't worry about me," Isra says, her smile still lighting her face. "I have my guards, and Needle is waiting for me." She watches with a satisfied expression as Father and I bow. "Until later."

And then she turns and glides away, the confidence in her new walk making her seem like a different person from the girl who scurried across the field to her tower rooms a week ago. I watch her greet her guards, with a hint of guilt worming its way into my heart. I told myself I didn't care about the queen anymore, but I can't help but feel bad for her, to fear for her.

She's barely out of sight when my fears are confirmed.

"We'll have the wedding tomorrow," Father whispers. "Prepare yourself. It might be an unpleasant ceremony."

"But her period of mourning isn't over." Mourning rituals are strictly observed in our city. It's bad luck to go against them, such bad luck that the advisors decided it was better to leave Isra unmarried for several months rather than go against the grieving customs.

"I know, and it may bring dark days to Yuan to have her married while still wearing green, but there's no help for it. The girl is out of her mind." Father waves a weary hand through the air. "The other advisors were listening in on my conversation with Isra. They sent this just before the conclusion of our meeting." He hands me a note on parchment paper, written in the unmistakable cramped, slanted hand of Tai, the late king's oldest advisor and the man second in power only to my father.

The girl has fallen prey to her mother's weakness. She is no longer fit to rule. Arrange for the marriage to your son to take place tomorrow morning. We'll compel the union if we must. The law allows it in cases like these. We must secure the safety of our city first. Once a new king sits on the throne, we'll decide how best to keep Isra safe from herself.

"They think she's mad?" I ask, shocked, though I shouldn't be. I've had similar thoughts all day, but when the word "insane" flitted through my head, I didn't mean it. Not really. Isra is odd and stubborn and strange, no doubt, but she's not out of her mind. At least not in a dangerous way. "But, Father, I don't—"

"You should have heard her, Son," Father says with a sigh, plucking the parchment from my fingers. "She wants to put an end to the Banished camp and bring those pitiful creatures into the city center to live with our people."

I lean in, certain I've heard him wrong. "But she saw them. They're animals. They barely speak our language, they lack the sense to keep their waste in the assigned trench, and ran from us every—"

"She thinks they're afraid." Father sighs again before shuffling over to the bench and easing himself down. He looks older than he ever has before, as if the meeting with Isra has aged him ten years. More. "She saw bruises on their bodies. She thinks the guards beat them, and that's why they run from whole citizens."

"They beat them because they attack each other," I say, pacing in front of the bench. "They'd tear each other apart if the guards didn't keep them in line."

Father lifts his hands in the air. "I tried to tell her, but she wouldn't listen to reason. She thinks the Banished could learn to speak our language and behave properly if they received different treatment."

"She's stubborn." I curse myself for not making the facts clearer to her. I'm willing to go against her wishes once we're married, but I wanted our marriage to be her decision. I know Isra well enough now to realize that marriage to her won't be pleasant if she's forced into it. "Let me talk to her. Maybe I can convince her to change her mind."

"It isn't only the Banished," Father says. "She wants to improve conditions for the commoners in the city center as well. She wants to build more housing and provide nurses for those with the worst deformities and no family to care for them."

Now it's my turn to sigh. "Where will we get the resources to build? We can't cut down trees. We need them to refresh the air."

Father shakes his head. "She thinks we should tear down

the king's cottage and a number of the other noble cottages and use those materials."

"What?" I laugh. The idea is ridiculous. "And where would the nobles without homes live? In the barns with their horses?"

"She thinks the noble families can learn to be comfortable sharing a home with another family."

"She what? She's out—" I almost say "out of her mind," but bite my tongue at the last moment. "She doesn't understand. She's been kept separate from our people. She doesn't know how things work or that no one is bothered by it but her. At least give me one day to make her see reason."

Father's head stays down when his eyes lift, emphasizing the brown shadows beneath his eyes. He's exhausted, and I can't help but feel responsible. If I hadn't told Isra to stop drinking her tea, all of this could have been avoided. "She also wants to send food into the desert," Father says. "To the Monstrous tribes."

It's as if he's struck me. "She . . . she doesn't. She can't."

"She says she'll send the Monstrous boy with a wagon. She believes he'll come back if he's released."

Exhaustion settles in my bones, and I wish Father would ask me to sit beside him. There's no hope, then. Isra might not be mad, but she's wandered too far outside the realm of what even *I* will tolerate. The Monstrous deserve *nothing* from our city. Isra's ideas are too radical, and she herself is too different to be good for Yuan.

"I'm sorry," Father says as he rises from the bench to stand beside me. "I know you had hopes for a different sort of marriage, but I was prepared for this from the beginning. Your mother and I will help you through the ceremony, and everything that comes after."

"What do you mean?"

"She can't be allowed her freedom," he says, regret clear in his eyes. "She's a danger to herself and to the people. To the city itself. We'll have to keep her contained in the tower."

I nod, but my stomach roils inside me. I threatened to lock her away myself, but I didn't really mean it. I don't want my wife to be a prisoner. If only Isra could see reason. If only she could be less . . . Isra.

"It won't be too terrible for her," Father says, as if sensing how much I loathe the idea. "She's spent most of her life there. She'll have her entertainments and her maid as her companion, and you may visit her anytime you wish."

"She won't want me to visit her. She'll hate me."

"No, she'll hate me." Father grips my shoulder. "Let me bear this burden. I'll make it clear this is my decision, not yours."

"No, it's my fault. All of it. If I hadn't told her—"

"If you hadn't given her sight, we would have had more time," Father says. "But the end would have been the same. I knew that, Bo. I knew it the day she insisted on working side by side with a monster that could kill her in an instant. She's put the entire city at risk. She's selfish and childish, at best. At worst, she's on the path to becoming as mad as her mother." He sighs, and his arm drops to his side. "The king should never have married an outsider."

"Were all the people of New Persia mad?" I know the

story—that King Yuejihua married a woman from across the planet who arrived in the last of her people's flying carriages, fleeing a city on the verge of collapse in the wake of Monstrous attack—but I never thought to wonder anything more.

"No, not that I know of. It was a small city, but they kept their technology functioning throughout the centuries," he says, motioning to the servant waiting in the shadows beneath the arbor, indicating we're in need of drink. "In the beginning, the king was more interested in the technology than the wife. He wanted to see what our ancestors had given up when they'd adopted our more primitive way of life. He agreed to marry the king of New Persia's youngest daughter only if the flying machine used to deliver her was also his to keep."

"He kept the flying machine?" What would it be like to see something like that? Something from long ago, built on another world? "Where is it?"

Father's brows lift, clearly disapproving of my interest in the machines our ancestors chose for us to live without. They believed technology was evil and led to the destruction of our old planet.

"It's in pieces," he says. "Its parts put to other uses. The New Persians failed to send fuel. Without it, the machine was useless. There was no way to lift it off the ground, or to send Queen Kanya back to where she'd come from." He turns, fetching a goblet of peach juice from the tray the servant has brought. When the tray is shifted before me, I wave it away. I'm thirsty, but it seems wrong to sip something sweet at a time like this. "But by then the king didn't want to send her away," Father continues. "Kanya was a beautiful woman. Very tall, bold-featured. Nothing like our women, but beautiful. As Isra is beautiful. And she was kind and gentle, before the madness took her."

I think on that for a moment, of Isra's mother, and madness, and beauty, and other things passed down from parents to their children. "There will be no children for Isra and me," I say, unable to imagine Isra tolerating me in her bed.

"It's for the best," Father says. "Better to wait and try to be a true husband with your second wife."

My second wife. I haven't even taken my first. It's . . . too much. I can't think about it. Not now. I'll think about it tomorrow night, when Isra and I are married and I am king. Surely all of this will seem more manageable then.

"If you don't need me, I'll go back to the barracks," I say, with a deep breath. "I could use some time to myself."

"Go. I'll have dinner sent to your room." He drains the last of the liquid. "After dinner, we'll discuss how you'd like to take care of the other matter."

"The other matter?"

"The Monstrous." He holds out his goblet. The servant and tray magically appear to claim it and whisk it away. "You should kill it tonight. Now that Isra's been deemed incompetent, there's no reason to wait. The marriage will go forward with or without her consent."

I swallow. I didn't think Father would expect me to kill the Monstrous myself, but I should have. "You're right," I say, refusing to show how unnerved I am by the prospect of slaughtering the beast, the night before my wedding no less. "I'll choose my best men. We'll go to the creature's rooms tonight and . . . kill it in its sleep. If possible."

Father smiles, that same smile from last night, the one that assures me he's proud of who I'm becoming. "A wise plan. And a merciful one." His voice is as silky as it was when he praised Isra for her keen perception, and for a moment I wonder . . .

I stop the thought before it can find its other half. I don't wonder anything. I know what must be done and I will do it, and come tomorrow night, all the terrible things will be over.

TWENTY-TWO

GEM

I wait for her all day and long into the night, staring out the window at the royal garden, watching for a shadow slipping from the orchard, but she doesn't come.

My prison gets smaller by the hour. The bars more hateful. I prowl the confined space a hundred times. I do every one of my exercises a thousand. By the time the three moons rise high in the sky, I should be too exhausted to stay awake, but I'm not.

I can't sleep. I can't rest until I know what's happened. If someone's hurt her . . . If they've locked her away . . .

I'll break through these bars with my bare hands. I'll kill every soldier who stands in my way. I'm not sure if this is love or madness, but it doesn't matter. It's real. True. And as inescapable as this wretched cage.

I growl and slam my balled fists into the door of my cell. It rattles on its hinges, but doesn't break or bend. Outside, there isn't a sound. The guard from my early days is asleep in his own bed. The Smooth Skins are so sure of their doors and locks. But Isra found a way out of her prison. If she can do it, I can do it. I *will* do it.

I spin and stalk back to the window, claws slicking out as I move. I haven't tried my claws on their bars. I wasn't ready to escape before, but I am now. I have to make sure she's all right.

She's not all right. She's marked for death, and refuses to fight for her life. If she had someone else read the covenant and it offered no hope . . .

I clench my jaw, grinding the thought to dust between my teeth. It doesn't matter. Isra would come if she could. Even if it was only to say good-bye.

I won't let her say good-bye.

My claws strike the bars hard enough to send pain shooting up the backs of my hands into my forearms. I curse and shake my fingers at my side, moaning as my claws draw painfully back into their chambers. Every nerve in my arm is on fire, and the skin above my nail beds is ripped and bleeding, but the bars don't have a nick on them.

I curse in my language, adding in a few foul Smooth Skin words I've picked up from listening to the soldiers. I kick

303

the wall beneath the window hard enough to bruise my toes through my thin boots, and curse again, but manage to keep myself from further self-destruction by wrapping my fingers around the bars and shaking them with all the strength in my body. I shake and shake, tensing until the muscles in my neck threaten to snap. By the time I'm finished, I'm even more exhausted than I was before.

Maybe enough to sleep. Or at least to rest . . .

I'm turning to my bed when I see it. The shadow near the garden.

A woman's shadow, winding her way through the orchard. She seems familiar, but I can't place her until she steps onto the paving stones and the moonlight catches her curls. It's Isra, but she doesn't walk the way she did before. She doesn't reach with her toes before she steps; she doesn't hesitate before allowing the rest of her body to catch up with her feet. Her eyes have changed her. It will take time for me to recognize her in the dark, time I don't know if we'll have.

I want to call out, but I don't dare. The guards will be through the garden soon. I have to wait.

I stand at the window, wondering how she plans to reach my cell—through the main entrance or by climbing through the window down the hall the way I did when Needle returned me to my cage. I expect her to hurry down the path toward the barracks, but instead she stops on the far side of the roses, near where the vines have crept from their bed. She goes utterly still for a moment before her hand darts out, reaching for one of the low-hanging vines.

Above her bowed head, the roses rustle awake, rotating their obscene blooms to peer down at the queen.

I open my mouth to howl her name, but something stops me—a sudden throbbing in the places where my skin tore above my claws, a pain that shoots up my arm and into my chest, squeezing my heart, heating my blood, making the room spin and the blue night pulse before my eyes.

I try to step away from the window, but I can't move. I can't breathe. I can't scream, even when the night air comes alive, whipping in to beat at my face, stinging at my skin like sparks from a funeral fire, hot and full of magic.

I fall to the floor, gasping for breath, and begin to crawl toward the door.

Something is happening in the garden. I have to get to Isra, before it's—

ISRA

——TOO late. It's too late to pull away, even if I wanted to.

"What happened to the covenant?" I demand, fighting to keep fear from my voice. I've never felt such a powerful presence in the garden before. It feels bigger than the roses, older and darker and deeper, a cold, unblinking eye staring straight through my skin. "Where is it? Show it to—"

My words end in a pained cry as fire courses through my fingertips, shoots through my arm, trapping the breath in my lungs, making my ears ring with the sound of a thousand voices screaming at once. Agony explodes on either side of my head, and my eyes roll back.

The thorn in my finger digs deeper, while another darts out to stab my arm, jabbing deep. Something primitive inside me snatches control of my muscles. My legs push away from the flower bed, but when I move, the thorns move with me, digging into my skin. The roses are hungry, starving, they—

No, it's not the roses who hunger. It's the other *thing*—the ancient presence coiled like a snake beneath the flowers—that is hungry. Gem was right. There is something else. The roses are only the teeth that creature uses to chew its food, a mouth that will pull me into the belly of the beast.

Come to the Dark Heart, girl. The voice in my head is a tongue made of ice licking at the frantic pulse at my throat. *Come to the Dark Heart and join your mothers and grandmothers. There is peace in sacrifice.*

The Dark Heart. That is its name.

I go utterly still, overwhelmed by the vastness of the being speaking in my mind. It is bigger than I first assumed. As tall as the mountains beyond the dome, as deep as the violent ocean the roses showed me on my thirteenth birthday, as big as the planet itself.

It is a god, and I am only one small person, so briefly alive that my death is practically not a death at all. I should be content to lie down in the fertile soil, to join myself with the Dark Heart, to give my blood to the one who sustains my city.

The roses' gnarled stalks and their thorns—as big as my hand, bigger, how could I not have noticed how deadly they could be—reach for me, ready to pull me into their embrace, to the center of their bed.

To my death.

The haze clouding my thoughts departs in a frantic rush of blood.

"No!" I pull away, but the roses loop a toothy arm around my wrist and squeeze tight. Smaller thorns slice through my skin, creating a bracelet made of blood, igniting my body with lightning flashes of pain.

"Help me!" I scream, hoping the guards will hear. I bat at the flowers with my fists, kick the vines that snake close enough to snatch at the legs of my overalls. "Help me! I'm in the royal garden!" I scream, but no one comes. The one time in my life I'd be breathlessly grateful to see a soldier, and none can be found.

And the thing controlling the roses, the Dark Heart, knows it. Of course it does. The Dark Heart knows everything that happens under the dome, and it knows that I've learned too much, that it must take me before I ruin it all, before I steal the lifeblood from the splintered, wicked thing my ancestors have fed for generations.

But my ancestors weren't murdered; they were *willing* sacrifices. Even my mother took her own life when she jumped from the tower. But I'm not going to lie down and die. I won't!

"I don't give myself to you. I don't!" I shout as I knock a vine away with the back of my hand, earning myself another deep scratch. I pause to survey the damage for less than a second, but a second is all it takes for a vine to snap around my other wrist, as quick as a whip. I scream and tug on both arms, but the vines only squeeze more tightly.

"I'm not a willing sacrifice," I sob, heart racing as the thorns get closer and closer to my face. "I'm not married. I have no children or brothers or sisters or anyone." I feel the vines' death grip loosen the slightest bit, and I know I've hit upon the only thing that might save my life. The Dark Heart is starving, but it doesn't want me to be its last meal. "If you kill me, you will never feed from this city again. The covenant will be broken forever. Forever!"

When the vines stop moving, there's a thorn longer than my finger a whisper from my eye.

I force myself to face it, ignoring the sweat rolling down the sides of my face, the frantic racing of my pulse, the pitching of my stomach. "Let me go," I say. "Let me go! You have no choice."

But they do, *it* does, the Dark Heart. It could decide that one last meal from our city is better than none at all. It could take comfort in the fact that there are still two domed cities alive and well and filled with women willing to die.

Everything in my being screams for me to fight, to get away before it's too late, but I can't. The force controlling the roses will have to choose to let me go. There's no way I can free myself without cutting my arms from my body. I'm already hurt badly. The muscles and nerves in my wrist are shredded, and my blood spills with a steady *smack, smick, smack* onto the dirt. I can feel how much the Dark Heart craves more of it. Its need echoes inside me.

If only I'd gone to Gem before coming to the garden. He could slice through the vines with his claws in an instant. But I was afraid he'd try to stop me, that he'd say it was too dangerous, now that he knows the truth about the roses.

Now I may never see him again. I may not live to tell him how much I care, how much I—

I gasp as the vines suddenly clutch more tightly, as if the Dark Heart can read my thoughts and disapproves of the way I feel for Gem, as much as any citizen of Yuan would.

Death, the Dark Heart whispers inside me, making me shiver and my arms go numb. My eyes roll toward the sky, but instead of the dome and the moons hovering above it, I find myself seeing through the roses' eyes.

But this time they show me something new. They show me . . . fires.

Fires in the desert, scaffolds made of long-dead tree limbs holding the corpses of Monstrous men and women and children. There are a dozen of them, more than a dozen. Twenty. Thirty. Fires all around, and at the center of them, an ancient-looking Monstrous man shaking with grief. His shoulders convulse, his chest heaves, but no tears spill from his eyes. The Monstrous can't cry, but they can obviously feel tremendous pain, pain that takes over and has its way with a body.

I watch him, feeling his agony as my own, and then suddenly I am somewhere else, in a time before the fires, standing beside the old man as he places a shriveled black root into the hands of devastatingly thin Monstrous people. Old men, young children with distended bellies, boys Gem's age with their wide shoulders concave with starvation, girls my age with glassy-eyed babies clinging to their necks. One of the girls is even thinner than the rest. Her baby still has the strength to wail, to squeeze his eyes closed and scream as his mother slips the root between his lips.

He's dead almost instantly.

"No!" Heat floods my face; tears spill from my eyes.

The scene changes again, going back even further, showing Monstrous men and women gathered around a fire. Their faces flicker with orange and red from the flames, but their backs are kissed by pale blue winter moonlight. It's a night like tonight—it could even be tonight—and the people are thin, but not dying.

It's not too late. It's not too late to help them, to save them. Gem and I can go into the desert. We can bring food and—

A growl—loud and deep and fierce enough to make the hair on my arms stand on end—shatters the scene playing behind my eyes. I land back in my body with a jolt and wrench my neck toward the sound, a relieved breath already bursting from my lips.

Gem! He's here. He'll free me, and together we'll—

"Ah!" I cry out as the roses jerk me closer to the flower bed, hauling me over the retaining wall and into their midst, surrounding me with thorns, crowding my eyes with blossoms fattened on centuries of blood.

TWENTY-THREE

ISRA

Red floods my vision. The smell of rot and metal and bitter herbs sweeps into my nose. My skin crawls as sharps mean as needles press at me through my clothes. I squeeze my eyes shut and scream as I cower closer to the ground.

"Let her go!" Gem shouts. I hear a whistling sound and a muffled thud as something soft, but heavy, falls to the ground. Before I can turn and see what's happened, the roses are moving, their thorns piercing through my clothes, making me howl like a trapped animal.

"No!" I beg. "They'll kill me! Don't touch them!"

"I have to get you out," Gem says, sounding so fearful and desperate that I know he cares for me. Now I have to prove I care for him as much.

"You have to go," I say, panting against the urge to be sick. The pain is too much, coming from everywhere all at once. "Your tribe. They're in trouble."

"How do you—"

"I saw it. In a vision."

"A vision." He lets out a shaking breath. "From the roses? Were there—"

"Please, Gem. Half your tribe will die if you don't go." I grit my teeth, refusing to whimper, to do anything to make Gem feel compelled to stay with me. "Needle prepared a pack for you this afternoon. It's waiting by the King's Gate. Take it and go. Now."

"I won't leave you," Gem says, voice breaking. "I can't."

"You have to," I say, and then add silently, *But you can come back. Oh, please come back. Oh please, oh please.*

If he comes back . . . If he cares enough to come back . . . maybe we can find a way to end this, to escape from the Dark Heart and make a better life for both our peoples.

The thorns press deeper, and I can't keep a soft cry of pain from escaping my lips.

"Isra . . . they're killing you." His hand finds mine. I can't turn my head to see him, but I know he has risked his life to reach out for me. I cling to him, selfishly needing to touch him one last time.

"They're not killing me. They're keeping me here. They

312

know my thoughts. They know I wanted to go with you." I close my eyes, memorizing the feel of his fingers threaded through mine. "They'll release me when you're gone."

"You don't know that."

"I do," I lie, knowing that Gem will refuse to leave unless I properly convince him. "They need a willing sacrifice, a suicide. They can't murder me," I say, hoping it will be enough to make Gem go before he's caught. "How did you get out of your cell?"

"I broke the lock on the door. After I . . ." His breath shudders out, and his grip on my fingers gets tighter. "I saw you coming into the garden and I tried to call your name, but–I felt something, a terrible magic."

He has no idea *how* terrible, and I can't tell him. Not now.

"There's no time." I release his hand, pushing him away. "Go. Run. Hurry."

I hear a rustle in the leaves, and when he speaks again, he sounds farther away. "I'll come back as soon as I can," he says. "If you're not alive, I'll burn this city to the ground. Starting with this garden." The blossoms closest to my face rotate on their stalks, moving out of my line of sight as they turn to Gem.

I lift my head, meeting Gem's worried eyes through a jumble of leaves and thorns. I want to tell him how beautiful he is to me; I want to tell him everything I've held back. I want to share everything that's happened since he left the tower last night, because only after sharing it with Gem will it seem real.

I want to tell him that, too, but instead I say, "Please go."

313

He has to go. There's no time. "I'll watch for you on the wall walk. Every night. Set a fire by the gathering of stones. I'll come as soon as I can."

"You're bleeding," he says, throat working. I can see it, even in the moody blue light of my least favorite moon.

"Don't forget me," I whisper. "Please. Don't forget."

"I'll come back," he says. "If I have to drag my body across the desert. I swear it. On my life."

I nod, squeezing my eyes closed to keep the tears at bay. By the time I open them, he's gone.

"Let me go," I whisper to the roses after several long moments have passed. They've gone as still as any plant now, but I know they're listening. "You've gotten what you wanted." The Dark Heart clearly wanted Gem to leave the city. There's no other explanation for why it showed me the suffering of the Monstrous out in the desert. It wanted Gem—and the risk he poses to the continuation of the covenant—removed from Yuan.

But he'll come back to me. I know it. I haven't lost yet, not if I gain my freedom tonight.

"Let me go." I try to straighten my legs, but the ancient vines lie heavy and motionless across my thighs. "Let me go! I won't be held like—"

"What have you done to yourself?" The voice is soft, shocked, and so unlike Bo's that I don't guess who it belongs to until I look up to see him standing where Gem stood a few moments ago.

"Who were you talking to?" Bo asks again, in that same

314

numb way that makes me more nervous than his angry voice ever has.

"No one. Myself." I lick my lips, taste my tears, and shiver despite the fact that the night is the warmest we've had since autumn. Why is Bo here? How much has he seen?

"The Monstrous is out of his cell, Isra," Bo says. "Do you know anything about that?"

"Y-yes," I stutter, my heart beating faster. "I needed him to take care of a few things in our garden. He's going there now," I say, hoping to buy Gem more time to reach the King's Gate by sending Bo in the opposite direction. "He's trustworthy. He'll be back in his rooms within the hour. There's no need to–"

"There's every need," Bo snaps, anger creeping into his tone. "There's every need to do . . . something." He shakes his head, his expression bleeding from anger to confusion to utter bafflement. "What are you doing here? Why have you hurt yourself?"

"I didn't do it deliberately. I tripped and fell," I say, lifting my chin. "And it seems to me you should be more interested in helping your queen than interrogating her." I can't tell Bo that the roses attacked me, or he'll think I'm more rattled than he does already, but I don't have to endure being treated like a fool. "Now. Help me out. Use your sword. Cut the vines if you have to."

Bo's lips part, and a horrified look creeps into his eyes. "You want me to desecrate the royal garden? Are you mad?" He laughs, a single *baw* so loud that it makes me wince. "Of course you're mad. *Of course* you are. And to think I . . . I felt for you," he says, gravel in his voice. "Even today. I thought my father and the other advisors were being unfair, but he's right. You've lost your mind."

"No, I haven't." My forehead wrinkles, but it doesn't hurt. At least the roses didn't attack my face. "Your father supported every measure we discussed today. He sent the amendment concerning the Banished to my rooms a few hours ago. It was exactly–"

"He's lying to you, humoring you until tomorrow morning," Bo spits. "He and the other advisors are going to force you to marry me and give Yuan a ruler who's not out of his head. They say the law allows them to compel your marriage, whether you consent to the union or not."

My stomach clenches. "But I . . . I'm still in mourning. It's against our–"

"Sometimes big changes are necessary to protect the city," he says, mocking his father's kind words from this afternoon perfectly, setting fire to the last tattered shreds of my hope. "I tried to convince him to wait," Bo continues, swiping the back of his hand across his mouth. "I wanted you to choose to marry me, but clearly you aren't capable of making wise choices."

"You don't decide what I'm capable of! I'm the queen. My word is law!" I sound like a child having a tantrum, but how can I help it? What other option has Bo or anyone else in this city given me, when they treat me like a small girl or an invalid or a madwoman?

"I'm *not* mad," I say, fighting tears. "This *city* is mad. All of you! You and your father and the advisors and all the rest. Gem is three times the person any of you will ever be!"

Bo sighs, but when his gaze meets mine, he doesn't seem angry. He's gone numb again. Numb with a hint of . . .

Pity. He pities me. He's so sure of the legitimacy of his hate that he can't consider for a moment that the Desert People might be human like us. Or that *I* might be the only one in Yuan *not* out of my mind.

But maybe that isn't possible. Maybe the mind of the majority is always the healthy mind, simply by virtue of its numbers. Maybe it's the definition of madness to believe I'm right and everyone else is wrong, to find my thoughts rational and reasonable when almost the entire world finds them damaged and flawed.

The thought makes me want to cry all over again. Cry, and beg Bo to listen to me, to try to understand. Despite his cruelty last night, Bo isn't as terrible as his father. He cares for me—or cared, at least a little. He has a gentle side, too.

"Bo, please," I whisper. "I'm not crazy. I swear I'm not. I—"

"Did you mean to hurt yourself tonight?" he asks, ignoring my protests.

"Of course not!"

"You're bleeding," he says, as if breaking a scary bit of news to a child. "Those wounds are deep. You'll have scars. Why did you do this?"

"*I* didn't do anything! They pulled me in. They were trying to kill me," I say, regretting the words the moment they pass my lips.

"Who was trying to kill you?"

317

"The . . . roses," I mumble, digging my nails into the dirt, wishing I had fingers big enough to uproot the roses with my bare hands. "I don't expect you to believe me, but it's the truth. They aren't what they seem. Nothing is what it seems."

Bo glances down at the vines, now lying, limp and lifeless, across my legs. No one but Gem knows what the roses can do, and now no one else ever will. The roses won't help me prove that I'm not insane. My allegedly weak mind stands to gain them a king and a captive queen and continuation of life as the Dark Heart that caused them to grow prefers it.

For a split second I consider telling Bo about the Dark Heart and the wicked magic supporting life under the domes, but before I can think of a way to break the news to him that won't sound mad, two breathless soldiers appear behind him.

"The Monstrous has been spotted from the wall, sir," the short guard with the crooked teeth huffs. "Running toward the King's Gate."

"Go. Take the ten men waiting by the—"

"No!" I shout. "Please, let him go. If you let him go, I won't fight any of it. I'll marry you tomorrow morning." I begin tugging the thorns from my flesh, refusing to wince as the stickers pull free. "Just let Gem go."

"Take the ten men waiting by the tower," Bo continues as if I haven't spoken. "Tell them to kill the beast on sight."

"No!" I stagger to the edge of the rose bed. "You can't! I forbid it! As your queen!" But the soldiers refuse to look at me, let alone listen.

"Bring his body to the dungeon!" Bo shouts as the men rush away through the orchard, the *scuff, scuff* of their boots

318

transforming to a *shush, shush* as they hit the grass beneath the trees.

"Run, Gem! They're coming!" I scream, even as I hope he's too far away to hear me. "Run!" I scramble off the edge of the bed wall, moaning as I hit the ground, and every place where the thorns tore my muscles cries out at once.

Bo takes my arm with a tenderness that startles me. I glance up to see sympathy in his rich brown eyes.

"It's for the best," he says. "When he's dead, the unnatural feelings will fade. I'm sure of it."

"They aren't unnatural." I'm too exhausted to scream the words. It wouldn't make a difference, anyway. Bo doesn't think he's ordered a murder. He thinks he's asked for an animal to be put down. Raging at him for the wicked thing he's done is pointless until he understands how wrong he is.

"Gem is like us, Bo," I say, pleading with him to understand. "He feels and thinks and hopes and dreams. He loves his family and is devoted to his tribe. He's no different, not in the ways that count."

"Let's get you back to the tower," Bo says, ignoring me. Again. He starts back toward the tower, cradling my elbow as if I'm made of glass. "I'll have the healers sent to attend you."

I dig my heels in. "I'm not going," I say, jaw tightening as I stare through the trees in the direction where Gem disappeared. I can't see him or the soldiers any longer, but I swear I can feel him. He's still in the city. "Not until I know Gem's safe."

Bo heaves a tragic sigh, but he doesn't try to force me to keep walking. He stands beside me, as silent as I am, though

I'm certain he's not straining as hard for a sign that the soldiers' mission has failed.

"It could have been good," he finally whispers. "You and I."

I don't say a word, though I agree with him. In a way.

We *could* have had a very different relationship if Gem hadn't come into my life. If not for Gem, I might have mistaken faint stirrings and budding friendship for something more. I might have thought love could grow between Bo and me. I would have agreed to marry him and would be looking forward to however many years we'd have together before I made the ultimate sacrifice for my city.

Sacrifice.

"I don't have to do it," I whisper, my reprieve finally seeming real now that I'm free of the roses. I will never lie down in that wretched bed and slit my own throat. The realization makes my breath come faster, makes my ribs shake with something too hysterical to be laughter. "I don't have to do it."

"I'm afraid you won't have a choice," Bo says, watching me from the corner of his eye, clearly seeing my relief as another sign of madness. "Father says the law allows the advisors to compel you to marry."

My ribs grow still, even as my heart beats faster behind them.

Junjie will kill me if I refuse to go to the roses. I know he will. As soon as Bo and I are married and the city begins to fail, he'll slip poison into my food or slit my throat while I sleep. Then, once I'm dead, Bo will remarry and that poor girl will pay the price for my refusal to honor the covenant. She will be a bride in the morning and a dead woman by nightfall, and the wicked thing at the city's core will never be stopped.

I can't let that happen. I have to find some proof of what I felt in the garden tonight. I have to convince my advisors and my people that the power sustaining our city is evil.

"But how?" I mumble, biting my lip.

"I don't know," Bo says, continuing to labor under the delusion that I'm speaking to him. "I suppose one of the advisors will say your vows and the sacred words for you if you refuse to say them yourself."

So refusing to speak won't be enough. . . . What if . . . What if I . . .

"Take me back to the tower," I say, gripping Bo's arm. "I want to see Needle."

"But I–"

"My arms and legs hurt. Needle will tend to them," I say, not bothering to explain myself any further. A woman has a right to change her mind, and a madwoman even more so. There's nothing I can do for Gem here and now, but if I can rid myself of Bo and move quickly, while the guards are distracted . . .

"I'll send for the healers as soon as you're safe in your rooms," Bo says as he leads me through the orchard.

I start to tell him no, that Needle is the only attendant I need, but I think better of it. I don't want to make him suspicious, and his mission to fetch the healers will keep him

321

busy while I throw together what I'll need for my journey. *Our* journey. I'll go with Gem. Tonight. I'll leave the city and not come back until–

Never. I'll *never* come back. If I'm not here, no one can force me to marry. And if I never marry, then the curse ends with me.

But where does that leave your people? Needle? All the innocent and the damaged who have already suffered so much?

Dead. It leaves them dead. Sooner or later.

I swallow, blinking back tears as Bo and I make our way through the withered stalks that are all that's left of the sunflowers. Soon, the remains will be plowed under, and bone meal and sheep dung added to the soil, and next autumn's flowers planted in the enriched dirt. *Sunflowers are feeders,* Father said. They'll suck the life from the land if you're not careful.

I'll suck the life from this city if I leave it. Innocent children will die. Needle will die. But if I stay, it never ends. It never ends and all our lives are paid for with blood and hate and fear, and the Desert People will die and I will die and I will never see Gem again.

I can't leave. I can't stay. I don't know what to do. I don't know what's right; I've never felt so ripped apart inside.

"Don't cry," Bo mumbles beneath his breath. "Please."

I swipe the back of my hand across my eyes, hissing as salty tears sting into the cuts at my wrist. I didn't even realize I was crying, but I am. Weeping as if my heart is broken. Which it is. Broken in two. One half here in Yuan, with the city I was raised to serve. One half with Gem as he—I hope—runs into the desert to save his people.

Everything is happening so fast. I need more time!

"It won't be a miserable life for you when we're married. I won't be cruel," Bo says, motioning aside the soldiers guarding the door of the tower. The two men stand gaping for a long moment without moving, before first one and then the other scrambles out of the way.

Bo and I are climbing the stairs by the time I realize why the guards were so surprised. They have no idea how I got out, let alone came to be covered in my own blood.

Get out. I can still get out. There's time between now and when I'll be forced to marry Bo tomorrow. I'll let Needle bandage me up and do some serious thinking. I'll tell her everything that's happened and see what she believes I should do. Needle is more practical and selfless than I'll ever be. She'll have advice. Good advice.

"Needle, bring the medicine kit," I call at the top of the stairs. "And water, please, with two cups."

Poor Needle. She's going to be beside herself when she sees what's happened to the skin she's fussed over all these years. I wipe at my face again, trying hard to pull myself together.

I'm so busy worrying about the look on Needle's face when she sees me that it takes me longer than it should to realize she didn't come when I called.

"Needle?" I call again.

A strange cawing sound comes from the music room in

response. I pull away from Bo and race down the hall as fast as my aching legs will carry me. I fling myself through the doorway at the same moment Needle flies through it in the opposite direction. I cry out as we collide, but when my hands find her shoulders, I don't let her go. Her face is streaked with tears, and one cheek bears an ugly red handprint.

"Who did this to you? Who's here?" I demand, searching the room behind her. At first I see nothing, but then, movement on the balcony. Three pairs of wide shoulders shifting, six big hands lifting, two hand trowels busy spreading sluggish gray mortar between heavy red bricks.

They're building a wall. A wall to take away the world.

I tried to stop them, Needle signs beneath my hand. *I tried.*

"I'm sorry," Bo says from behind me. "They shouldn't have struck her."

"What is this?" I ask, unable to turn to look at him, unable to glance away from the wall already rising as high as my thighs.

"It's to keep you safe. I wanted to make sure the beast couldn't enter your rooms," he says. "And Father was worried. I didn't tell him about last night, but after what happened today, and with your mother . . ."

"No," I whisper, breath coming faster, feeling more trapped than I have in my entire life. It's been years since I was truly a captive in the tower, and I've never had so many reasons to gain my freedom.

"It's not forever," Bo says. "Once we're married, and you start feeling better . . ."

No. No, no, *no!*

I'll never feel better. I'll never feel the wind in my hair again. I'll never race through a damp field in bare feet. I'll never sneak away to the King's Gate or the desert beyond. Even if Gem sets a fire burning by the gathering of stones, I'll never see it. I'll never see Gem again.

I'll never leave this tower, not until the day they lead me to the garden to die.

My knees give way and I crumple to the floor, but I don't cry out. I don't sob or scream. There's no point in it. Bo is here by my side, three strong men occupy my balcony, and guards with spears and sleeping darts wait at the bottom of the stairs. There is no way out. There is nowhere to run. It's over. Everything is over. I am over.

The world goes soft around the edges, my mind softer.

I don't remember rising from the floor. I don't remember Needle tending my wounds or mixing a sleeping draft or tucking me into bed—though she must have, because when I come back to myself hours later, I am bandaged, and the bitter taste of valerian root is strong in my mouth.

I don't remember throwing off my sheets or dragging the chair in the corner across the room. I don't remember ordering Needle to help me lift it on top of my bed, or threatening her with dismissal if she refused to assist me. I don't even remember climbing up to stand on top of the tower of furniture and nearly falling in the process.

Later, when Needle asks me how I knew the diary was there, I tell her it must have come to me in a dream, but the first thing I recall between my falling to the ground at Bo's feet and the slender volume dropping into my hand is reaching for the beam above my bed, fingers prickling as I released the secret latch I was certain I'd find on one side.

I tell Needle it must have been an ancestor dream, like Gem said. My father was always proud that we could trace our ancestry all the way back to King Sato and his third queen.

I don't know what he'd feel if he were alive to read our ancestor's words now. It takes more time for Needle to read and sign each word than it would if I could read the diary myself, but still it doesn't take long to learn that the volume belonged to that very queen. Or that everything I've been raised to believe is a lie.

TWENTY-FOUR

GEM

I hear the heavy footfalls and turn to see soldiers rushing around the granaries, but the men scrambling through the tall grass inspire more relief than fear. I'm already at the King's Gate with the pack of food and supplies strapped to my back, and they're coming from the direction of the royal garden. They must have found Isra and freed her from the roses. I know these people have no issue with killing a queen, but only after she's married, and that day is still months away. Isra should be safe until I return.

Please let her be safe.

With one last glance back at the tower, the peak of its highest roof barely visible over the rise, I step through the door and walk away from Yuan.

I walk. There's no need to hurry. It's too dark for their arrows to find me, and the soldiers won't dare follow me into the desert.

I walk until the dome is a faintly glowing speck on the horizon, on through the darkest part of the night, and into the next morning. I walk until the sun bakes my head, and the straps of my pack rub blisters on the scale-free flesh on the undersides of my arms, on through another night and the pale blush of a second morning, before exhaustion hits like a rock slide crushing me into the ground. I collapse into a hollow between two cactus plants, but I don't sleep for long. I don't know which is stronger, the need to reach my people, or the need to return to Isra, but both drive me like nothing has before.

I walk until my good leg throbs and my bad leg screams for mercy. I walk until both legs go numb and my joints begin to creak like the wheel of an overloaded cart. I walk until my entire body is a collection of aches and pains and my mind exists outside it all, lulled by the endless rhythm of my footfalls, stubbornly refusing to acknowledge the misery of my flesh. I drink little; I eat even less, determined to save as much food for the others as I possibly can. The pack is brimming with dried fruit and nuts and salted meat, enough to keep the hundred souls still remaining in my tribe from starvation for a month if the food is rationed carefully.

I think of how wonderful it will be to see my father's face, my son's smile as he gums a piece of dried fruit, the relief in my people's eyes as they eat well for the first time in months. I think of Isra, of her lips on mine that night in her tower.

I can't be without her. Seeing her held captive by the roses settled any question about that. I can't accept her death as a necessary evil. I won't have her blood spilled. Not for Yuan, not for the Desert People, or anyone else.

Gare will never understand. Father, maybe, if I explain myself well, but Gare . . . never. He'll never forgive me for caring for a Smooth Skin. He'll hate me until the day he dies, and he'll go to his funeral pyre with a curse for me lingering in his soul.

I'm sure most of my people will feel the same way. The Smooth Skins are the enemy. Our rage against them has been building for centuries, a bonfire stoked and fanned by every loved one lost too soon, every night spent listening to a child cry out in hunger, every morning a mother rolls over to find her baby starved to death on the pallet beside her.

I know now that most of the Smooth Skins have no idea how their actions have affected my people, but I still have hate for them in my heart. I hate Bo and his father and the soldiers who damaged my legs, but I care for Isra more than I loathe them. I . . . I love her. And love is stronger than hate. I believe that. I believe Isra and I can change our worlds. Together. If we are brave.

I finally feel brave. I won't ask Father to cut my warrior's braid. I'm not a coward. I'm a different kind of warrior, one who will fight with my heart instead of my hands, and I'll start by telling my people the truth. It would be easier to lie, but lies will never change the way they see the Smooth Skins, and we've all told too many lies. I'm sick of them.

Sick . . .

I'm nearly half a day's walk from my tribe's winter camp when I smell it. Smoke. Funeral smoke. In the middle of the day. My people burn our dead at night, but there's no mistaking the smell—charred and oily, bittersweet, musky . . . terrible. The smell of burned hair and melting flesh and all the dreams the dead will never dream going up in flames.

I start to run. My leg buckles and bends the wrong way, and my bones knock together with a sick crunch. Pain and heat explode behind my kneecap, but I don't stop. I run toward the smoke billowing on the horizon, with my leg burning like fire. I run until my ankle turns and my run becomes a hobble. I hobble until my good leg fails me and I fall to the ground and crawl.

I come into the midst of the fires on my hands and knees, and I'm glad. This isn't something to see standing up. It isn't one fire or three or even five. There are a *dozen*. No, more. Fourteen . . . fifteen. A city made of funeral pyres, flaming houses eating up their lonely residents with no mourners gathered below to cry their souls into the next world.

Where are they? Where are the families? The mates? The friends?

My breath comes faster. Pain and fear and dread swell so big inside me that it feels like my cracked skin will have to tear wide open to let it all out.

I look up. I force myself to look to the top of each pyre, guessing at the identity of each burning corpse. Any one of the adult-sized bodies could be my father or my brother. My friends. Meer.

And that one, that tiny one on the right . . .

It could be my son. It's a baby. A tiny spot of dense and dark at the center of a fire too big for a person with so few memories to burn away and no life magic to gift to those left behind.

My son. That could be my son.

My eyes squeeze shut. *Oh, please. By the ancestors, please, let my son be alive*, I beg, though I know my prayer is selfish. If my son is spared, then that means it is some other baby burning on that pyre. Someone's baby is dead. Fourteen other mothers, sisters, brothers, lovers, fathers, are dead.

Why is this? And where are the rest of my people while their loved ones burn?

I emerge from the city of fire, and my question is answered. A line of my people stands before our healer, their heads bowed in defeat. I see the medicine man hand something to a young mother at the far end of the line, and I try to scream—

"Meer!" But my throat is raw from the smoke, tight from dread, strangled by terror. She doesn't hear me. Her head stays down as she slips whatever the medicine man gave her between our listless child's lips and rubs it back and forth across the baby's tongue.

Instantly, I know what she's holding. Poison root. Poison root. Poison root in my baby's mouth.

"No! Stop!" The words explode from deep inside me as I scramble across the dirt on my hands and knees, the pressure inside my body threatening to make my heart explode. "Meer! Stop!"

Meer's arm jerks, pulling the root from my son's mouth. From somewhere farther down the line, a cry rises into the air. And then another, and another, but there is no hope in the sounds. No celebration. I'm too late. I know it; everyone knows it. Everyone knows I saw. I *saw*.

No. *Please, no.* I can't have gotten here just in time to watch my son die for no reason. When there is food here on my back and hope so close.

"Meer." I gasp, but she doesn't respond. Her eyes are wide and empty in her painfully thin face, her jaw slack. Without emotion she watches me crawl toward her for a long moment, before her head snaps down and the arm cradling the baby lifts him closer to her face. She drops the root and pats his cheek. She smoothes his hair away from his face. She places one skeletal hand over his heart and holds it there for what feels like an eternity.

And then she screams. She screams like her heart is being cut out.

He's dead. He's dead, oh no, please, *no*.

A strangled sound bursts from my throat. I push to my feet, only to fall immediately back to the ground. No amount of will can make up for how broken my body has become. Broken. Everything broken. My tribe, my baby, my life, my heart.

Meer's wail ends with a sob as she looks up, meeting my eyes with an expression so terrible, I instantly feel what she feels. The pressure building inside my chest and my head, crushing against the backs of my eyes, becomes unbearable. Meer. My friend. If I could spare her this pain, I would.

I'll hold her and tell her I forgive her. I'll tell her it's my fault. I'll—

Suddenly, Meer's legs bend and her fingers reach for the dirt.

"No!" I scream, but it's too late. The root she dropped is already in her mouth, her teeth are already biting down. She's already falling to the ground, her eyes closing, her mouth falling open as her soul leaves her body.

I watch her fall. I watch the limp bundle that was my child roll from her dead arm, and then there is nothing but red.

Red behind my eyes as I scream and scream until my throat is raw and I taste metal on my tongue. Red as I pound my fists into the ground until my knuckles break open and weep blood onto the desert floor.

I howl until there is nothing left inside me. Until my head buzzes and my muscles lose the last of their strength and I collapse onto the ground with my too-late salvation still strapped to my back and the red world goes black.

SPRING

TWENTY-FIVE

ISRA

I am married. I wear a black dress and a black cap over my hair, breaking mourning tradition and wedding tradition, making it clear I consider the ceremony the blackest of rites. Bo holds my hand during our vows, but he doesn't stay in the tower that first night, or the next, or any thereafter. I understand that he means to keep his promise not to be cruel, and am grateful for small favors.

I'm grateful for big ones, too. As the world beneath the dome begins to fade and falter, I know Bo is all that stands between me and death. He begs the advisors to give me more time to come to my senses.

I beg the desert to send Gem back to me before it's too late.

Needle sneaks to the wall every night after returning my dinner tray. She watches for a fire by the gathered stones, while I stand by the door, waiting for news of Gem, hoping so hard, it hurts.

I am always disappointed.

Winter ends and the days grow longer and warmer, but the crops refuse to grow. The cows cease giving milk, and—as our stores are used up and milk is replaced with water and wine—I learn what has caused the sad state of my skin. An allergy to the milk I've drunk every morning and been bathed in twice a day, every day, since Needle came to care for me. She blames herself for not realizing the milk and honey baths were hurting more than helping, but I assure her I'm not angry. I'm elated. Gem was right about that, too. I add it to my list of things to tell him, but weeks pass and he doesn't come, and things only get worse.

The chickens refuse to lay eggs, and half the livestock fall over dead in the fields. The orchard flowers rain to the ground, but no leaves or fruit grow in their place. Beneath Yuan, the underground river becomes a narrow stream. Water is rationed and the city's worry becomes an ever-present, buzzing fear. I know what game the Dark Heart plays, but I refuse to panic. Gem will come. He will come and we will end this madness. Forever. We can do it. I've read the queen's diary. I know the secret now.

For a month I believe.

338

And then the month becomes two months. More. I stop waiting by the door, no longer certain the black night outside the dome will ever be broken by the light of Gem's fire. I retreat to my bedroom to sleep the rest of my life away, to dream and keep on dreaming.

I dream all the time.

There is nothing to do in my prison but sleep and dream, wake and dream, sit staring at the scrap of sky visible through the mostly walled-up window in my room, and ache for my freedom like a missing limb, and dream and dream. . . .

I learn to speak the language of midnight, to communicate with phantoms. I have long conversations with the burning face in the beam, my ancestor, Ana, King Sato's third wife. Reading her diary has opened a door between us, and now we speak freely, without needing sleep as a meeting place.

She tells me of Yuan at the end of its first hundred years, before the Dark Heart was forgotten, when every soul in the city knew the roses were the teeth of the monster they had created. She tells me of growing up yearning for the world outside, watching from the wall walks the giant cats roaming the grasslands, and longing to run free the way they did. She tells me of her fourteenth birthday and the meager meal she shared with her family at the end of a summer when the crops had refused to grow, the day it was decided that the queen must die and Ana's father promised her to the king.

King Sato was tired then, already finished with two wives, and decades older than his new bride. The king promised Ana's father that he, the king, would take his turn under the blade when it became necessary, and he and Ana were married. Years passed and three children were born. Then, just before Ana's thirty-sixth birthday, the crops once again began to fail. King Sato was nearing his ninetieth year, but when the advisors agreed the time had come for a sacrifice, he refused to go to the roses.

Ana was told to kiss her children good-bye and prepare herself for the ceremony the next morning.

Terrified, Ana ran from the tower, through failing fields begging for blood, to the King's Gate and out into the desert. She hid in the tall grass that surrounded the city in those days, praying she wouldn't be found by wild animals, hoping the king would take his own life within a day or two and she would be able to return home.

It was there, sleeping in the grass with her cheek pressed to the earth, that she spoke to the Pure Heart of the planet for the first time. She'd been raised to fear the Dark Heart's other half, the magical force that had caused the deformity of most of Yuan's citizens, but she found the Pure Heart anything but cruel. It spoke kindly to her; it offered her life instead of death. It told her how to break the curse and restore the health of the planet and all the creatures living upon it.

Ana was transformed, frightened, but also filled with the certainty that her people must change their ways and end the division of the world.

She returned to the city and to her tower, where she wrote her last diary entry, the one explaining how to break the curse, and why the people of Yuan must reach out to the monsters in the desert.

The diary ends there, but Ana's spirit shows me the morning the guards came to escort her to the royal garden.

King Sato and the heads of the noble families were gathered around the roses. The royal executioner was already wearing his hood. Ana begged the king to listen to what she'd learned outside the dome, but he wouldn't. No one would. Just as no one would remind the king that—according to the covenant—his life would serve as well as hers. The king threatened to kill Ana and marry another if she refused to offer herself to the roses, while, beneath the soil, the Dark Heart called to her, promising her peace and rest, assuring her there was no choice but death.

Finally, Ana gave up. She knelt down. She took the knife in her hand and opened her own throat. The executioner ensured that her death was swift.

After the ceremony, King Sato buried the covenant beneath a paving stone in the royal garden and ordered all copies of the text burned, hoping to ensure the ignorance of his fourth wife. Unfortunately, the king didn't live to enjoy his new wife for long. Only two days after giving Ana's bloodless body to the river, the king suffered a heart attack in his bed and died. His new wife—barely twenty and unprepared to rule—married Ana's eldest son the next afternoon and went on to give the city many sons and daughters.

Ana had died for nothing. Her soul lingered to see that painful fact, to see her diary hidden away by her maid, and to see the truth of the covenant and the dark magic it nurtures lost to the people living beneath the dome. Her spirit lingered for centuries, reaching out to Yuan's rulers in their dreams, hoping one would discover her diary. She was a part of the city, but a piece that didn't fit, the keeper of a secret even more important than the location of the covenant, the keeper of the truth about the Dark Heart and the only way to end the nightmare of life under the domes.

Love. The secret is love.

A citizen of the domed cities and a man or woman of the Monstrous tribes must love each other more than they love anything else. When they do, the cities will fall, life will return to the desert, and every creature dwelling on the planet will be made whole and strong. All it takes is love.

My mother must have also somehow discovered the truth. That *had* to be why she took me into the desert, and why she attempted to destroy our family when she was locked in the tower and denied a way out of Yuan. She wasn't crazy. If she'd succeeded in burning the three of us to ash that night, there would have been no blood for the Dark Heart. Murder would have succeeded in destroying Yuan, but only love will heal our world.

I love Gem. I grow more certain of that every day. I also grow more certain that Gem is dead.

He would have returned by now if he weren't, I know he would. He must have died out there in the desert, and now I will never be able to tell him how much he means to me. At least, not in this life.

I ask Ana's spirit if I will see Gem in the afterlife, but that is one question she refuses to answer. She doesn't want to believe I will share her fate; she wants to believe Gem and I will end the curse, but I know better. Yuan is failing. I awake each morning certain I'll find Junjie and the guards waiting outside my bedroom, prepared to kill me if I continue to refuse to give my life for my city. Bo can hold them off for only so long. They will come. Soon.

My time grows shorter than the thorns on the royal roses.

I tell Needle about the secret location of the covenant, but warn her to stay away from the garden. Still, I'm not surprised when she returns one evening with a scroll wrapped in cloth so ancient that it falls apart in my hands.

I unroll the paper carefully. Needle reads and signs each word. I follow along, flinching when she reaches the final line and I learn that Ana was telling the truth. Our city's bargain with the Dark Heart calls only for the death of "one bound by oath of marriage to the first sacrifice."

One bound by oath. Not a *woman* bound by oath. Not a queen. A king would serve just as well.

It's a little betrayal in a world ravaged by centuries of hatred and suffering, but it doesn't feel little. It feels like proof that there is nothing good within the human heart. How could there be? If an entire generation could condemn Yuan's daughters to death because they found that preferable to the death of Yuan's sons?

What is there worth fighting for? Worth dying for? What have any of my dreams ever been worth?

That night, I tuck the covenant beneath my mattress, lay my head on my pillow, and dream of the day my mother took me walking outside the dome. I smell the wild scent of the desert; I feel the sun hot on my cheeks. I hear a whisper on the wind, a voice begging me to stand up *to* my people and *for* my people, to force the darkness to end with me, to save my daughters, to save myself.

To be brave.

I wasn't brave. I was as afraid of that voice as I was of death itself. So afraid I buried every memory of my life before I heard it, in an attempt to keep myself from remembering what I had been asked to do. But I'm not afraid anymore.

I am finished with my fearful heart. I am ready. I am brave.

Are you certain? Needle mouths.

"Yes. But I want you to go first," I say, refusing to meet her sad eyes.

I look at the pile of bricks in the corner instead. Needle has been gathering them—one by one, two by two—for the past month. As soon as Bo left this afternoon—lips pressed into a thin line after all his pleading won him nothing but a pat on the shoulder and a walk to the door—she began pulling the bricks from their hiding places.

Tonight is the night. Tonight I will build my own walls.

First, a barrier to cover up the entrance to the tower, then a wall in front of my bedroom door, and finally another behind. It should be enough to hold the soldiers until tomorrow morning. And maybe even a bit longer. It will be enough.

The city is on the brink.

Suddenly, this very morning, Yuan went from ailing to falling to pieces. The walls began to crumble. Above our heads, the dome groans like a field animal that's swallowed

344

something foul. Needle says only the nobles still believe the city can be saved. The people from the Banished camp, the farmers and their remaining livestock, and all but a few of the commoners from the city center are fleeing into the desert, bound for Port South.

I hope they make it there safely. I don't wish them any pain, but the cost of saving Yuan is too great. The Dark Heart will not feed from this city again.

I've failed to end the curse and heal our planet—either Gem is dead or he never loved me the way I love him; I suppose I'll never know which—but I won't fail in this. I'll take one city away from the darkness. Yuan will fall, and there will be only two cities left. And maybe someday, in one of those cities, a girl or a boy will look out into the desert and see someone who makes him or her want to change the world.

I close my eyes and see Gem's face as clearly as ever. Nearly three months, and I can still remember the way his eyes reflected the candlelight, the warmth of his skin, the feel of his lips.

Bo didn't mar that memory. He has been a better unwanted king than I could have imagined—he has never stolen so much as a kiss. He has refused to take what wasn't freely offered.

Not a kiss, and certainly not my life.

I knew he'd been sent to kill me today. I knew it before he said a word, before he fell to his knees, begging me to save the city and spare at least one woman's life. He warned me that his father would come tonight with his own knife. Bo can't protect me any longer. This evening, Junjie will arrive at the tower to slit my throat, and Bo will marry another. The woman has already been chosen, a woman older than Bo with two children she'll leave motherless, the oldest a five-year-old girl who will become next in line for sacrifice if Bo never marries again. The woman's wedding dress is sewn and her mind made up. She will say her vows with a blade in her hand, and willingly give her blood to the roses as soon as she is made the queen.

Bo was so genuinely troubled by it all. It made me glad the covenant is hidden in my room and will remain there until the city falls.

When I first learned the truth, I wanted nothing more than to throw it in Bo's face, to make it clear his blood would serve the roses as well as mine. But in the end, I had to keep the ancient king's secret. If Bo knew he could feed the roses, he might pick up the knife and do so, and I can't have that. I need the Dark Heart to starve. I need the city to fall. Soon. Tonight, if I'm lucky.

"You have to go." I turn back to Needle, who has yet to budge. "You have to tell the people of Port South how to end the curse."

Her bird hands flit from my shoulder to my cheeks, but her kindness offers no comfort.

There was a fire in the desert again last night, Needle mouths.

My stomach flutters. "It's probably some of our people," I say. "Camping by the dome, waiting to see if the city will be restored."

It could be him, she mouths. *Let me go and see.*

Him. *Gem.* Even thinking his name makes my heart do strange things in my chest.

"It's too late," I whisper. "If he loved me, he would have come sooner."

Needle's fingers move beneath my hand. *Maybe he was prevented from returning.*

"How?" I ask.

Maybe he was hurt or grew ill. Maybe his people did the same thing to him that yours have done to you.

"I don't think the Monstrous have towers or walls made of stone."

Needle scowls. *Don't make jokes. Junjie will kill you.*

"Only if he can get through my walls before the city crumbles."

Then the city will kill you.

"The city was always going to kill me," I say. "At least this way I will take Yuan with me."

But what if Gem—

"Leave," I snap, unable to bear thinking of Gem right now. "I have to get started. Even the fast-setting mortar will need an hour to gain strength. I must have the first wall built before sunset. You're wasting my time."

Needle's lip trembles and her eyes shine with unshed tears, and I immediately feel terrible. Poor, tired Needle, my dear friend.

"Please, love," I say, taking her sweet face in my hands. "You have been my mother and my sister and my slave and my keeper for too long. Take your bag and go. Go to Port

347

South and live. Find people you can trust and tell them the truth. There can still be a future for this planet. All hope is not lost."

Except for me.

It doesn't matter if it's Gem who's been lighting those fires by the stones these past two nights. It's too late. Even if I let myself believe in Needle's excuses for his long absence, there's no way I can join him in the desert. If I set foot outside the tower, I'm a dead woman. The soldiers have been ordered to kill me on sight. Bo warned me of as much this afternoon. Junjie is determined that I will die before sunset and has enlisted every remaining citizen of Yuan to his cause.

Save one.

"You've been so good to me," I say. "I want you to live and be happy."

I would rather stay, Needle signs, *but I'll do as you ask.* She picks up the pack we've filled with food and clothes and all of my jewels. No need for them to be buried along with me, not when they could help Needle get settled in her new home. I'm not sure how the people of Port South treat their damaged people, but I know a rich mute woman has a better chance than a penniless one.

I will miss you, my friend, she mouths, refuting my claim that she's been a slave or a keeper, with the same firm grace with which she's always handled me.

What would I have done without her?

"Good-bye," I whisper, eyes filling as I stand and hug her tightly. After a moment, she moves out of my arms and down the stairs without a pause in her step, without looking back.

I tell myself I'm glad. And then I cry the tears I've refused to cry all day, but only for a minute. There isn't time to waste. When my brief cry is over, I wipe my nose on my less-than-fresh overalls and get to work. It doesn't take long to lay the first row of stones. The quick-drying mortar is already mixed and ready. By the time my tears have dried on my cheeks, I have the beginnings of my wall.

Unfortunately, beginnings are not the same as endings.

I'm not even close to an ending when I hear footsteps on the stairs. Heavy steps, two pairs of boots, two men's voices arguing in harsh whispers as they circle around to the top of the tower. When they reach the last stair, Junjie pauses, clearly surprised to see me and my half wall.

"What is this, Isra?" Junjie's eyes are sad, but not nearly as sad as his son's.

"I tried to stop him," Bo says from his place behind his father. "I wanted you to have a few more hours."

A few more hours. Then he means to do it, to help his father kill me.

"No," I whisper, shaking my head. I can't have failed, not when I'm so close.

"This doesn't have to be painful," Junjie says, holding out his hand. "You can still change your mind and make your death a meaningful gift to your city."

"It's no gift. Not for you or Bo or anyone else." I back away, my trowel falling to the floor with a dull thud, smattering mortar across my bare feet. "This city is built on evil. It has to end with me," I say, voice rising until it rings with desperation.

"You will give your blood, or we will take it," Junjie says, as stern as he's been with me since I was a little girl. "This city will stand and prosper and flourish for another seven hundred years. You know this is the way things are done in Yuan."

And the way they will always be done. Nothing I say now will change that. Nothing I do will accomplish anything but putting off the inevitable. Escape is impossible, but still, I turn and run. I skid into my room and slam the door behind me, throwing the lock seconds before Junjie throws his weight against the door.

I back away from the trembling wood, hands shaking at my sides.

I won't let him take my death. It's the only thing I have left, the only thing that matters. My death will be mine. I will have my revenge against this city and the monster beneath the ground so eager for my blood, and I will finally, finally, *finally* be free of it all. Of life and fear and love and loss. Free of my responsibilities. Free of my failures. Free of this love that's been nothing but another curse, another stone around my neck pulling me to the depths of an ocean of pain so deep that I will never hit bottom.

I want to be free. *Free.*

"Isra! Open the door!" Junjie shouts.

"Free," I say aloud.

I've always craved freedom more than anything else. *Anything.*

If even one citizen of the dome and one Monstrous can love the other more than they love anything else . . .

If I'm brutally honest with myself, do I really love Gem

350

more than freedom? Have I ever loved anything more than that elusive, seductive unknown? If I had the choice—Gem or freedom, even the freedom that will come with death, when all my obligations have been honored and I'm free to exit on my own terms—what would I choose?

Gem is strong and brave and clever and good, and he makes me feel things I never dreamed I could feel, but he is also difficult and frustrating and impatient and . . . overwhelming. His arms feel like home, but he represents everything strange and uncertain and unknown. Loving him means gathering up all of those things, and carrying them with me. Forever. Love means being vulnerable and beholden. Love means embracing the pain I've been holding apart from myself for all the months that I've waited for him. It means taking that pain and claiming it and knowing it might not be the last of the pain he'll bring into my life.

Love is pain, and pain is the opposite of freedom, and freedom is all I've ever wanted, but I've never really stopped to wonder why. Why do I want my freedom so desperately? Why do I dream of the wind instead of something solid or permanent that I can hold in my hands, my arms?

Maybe I . . . Maybe . . .

"Isra! Isra!" Junjie is still shouting loud enough to rattle the door, but his cries seem muted, drowned out by the roar of the revelation taking place inside me.

"I had nothing better," I whisper. Back in the time before Gem, back in the darkness, in my cage, in my narrow world with Death waiting with His arms outstretched and only my father to help me prepare for the long walk to greet Him, there was nothing better than the dream of having no ties to bind me.

But Gem, with all his flaws and complications and high expectations, *is* better. His love, his faith in me, his belief that I can be as strong and brave as he is . . . The way he makes me feel and think and try harder than I've ever tried . . .

All of it, all of *him,* is better than anything else. Anything at all.

I take a breath and let the pain and love and admiration and everything I feel when I think of Gem fill me up, soak into my soul, break my heart wide open. It hurts—so, so much—but it's also a relief. It's also warm and peaceful and safe. Beautiful. This kind of love is weightless, limitless. . . .

And almost exactly what I imagined freedom would feel like.

If only I'd known sooner. If only I could thank Gem for helping me find the only thing I've ever wanted as much as I want him.

TWENTY-SIX

GEM

I'M too late. Yuan is falling before my eyes.

Cracks as wide across as my body snake up the surface of the dome. Stones tumble from the wall walks, making skittering sounds beneath the moaning of the buckling metal that once fused the glass to the rock.

Bizarrely shaped Smooth Skins unlike any I encountered during my captivity, partial mutants that I assume are the Banished that Isra spoke of, and a few starving animals stream away from the once-healthy city in a seemingly endless ribbon

353

across the desert. The last of them emerged from the Desert Gate less than an hour ago.

Isra was not among them. But I didn't expect her to be. There's a reason the city is crumbling to pieces. Isra is gone.

Not gone. Murdered, and the city along with her, while you walked away. And stayed away, wallowing in your weakness. You might as well have slit her throat that first night. You're the reason she's dead.

Add another name to—

I begin to hum beneath my breath one of the songs Isra taught me, a complicated tune with as many ups and downs as the path over the mountains that brought me back to Yuan from the wilds where I had lost myself for months.

Singing drowns out the terrible thoughts. Sometimes I imagine I'm singing to Herem, the son I held for the first time the day I lifted him onto his funeral pyre. Sometimes I imagine Father singing along in the deep, steady voice of my childhood, banishing from my memory the confused whimpers of his last days.

By the time I returned, Father no longer knew me. He called me by his brother's name. He asked where our sisters were. He smiled and told stories about his new mate, as if he were a young man and he and Mother just married. He cried like a child, begging me to bring a light into the hut because he was afraid of the dark.

He died in his sleep a week after I returned. I never got to say good-bye to the man I remembered.

Gare blamed me for that, too. He blamed me for Father's broken mind. He blamed me for the twenty dead before I brought the food. He blamed me for the hopeless future when the carefully rationed provisions inevitably ran out. He said I should have taken the roses and Isra and made Yuan's dark curse our own. He called for a war party to be formed to return to Yuan and capture the roses and the queen at any cost, to kill every Smooth Skin we could kill and avenge our tribe. Our usually peace-minded chief agreed, but the final decision for war is always taken to our people.

It failed by one vote. Meer's mother said no. She said Meer wouldn't have wanted to live if it meant binding our tribe to dark magic. She said Meer wouldn't have wanted her son to be raised under the shadow of evil or for me to lose the woman I love.

I told my people what I felt for Isra. Most of them assumed my head had been damaged by my time spent under the dome.

I close my eyes now, and let my head fall back against the warm rock behind me. *Isra.* Thinking her name is enough to rip me apart. I was sure I was done with these feelings. I thought I'd known the worst pain any man could imagine, but I was wrong. There is still more pain. New pain. The worst pain. I am a broken man. Without Isra, I will never be whole again. There is nothing left to hope for, no reason to keep living.

I imagined that the worst thing awaiting me in Yuan would be explaining to Isra why it took me so long to return, asking her forgiveness, hoping she could understand how lost I was. But this . . .

By the ancestors . . .

I should have known it was possible. I should have prepared myself.

You knew. You refused to prepare. Coward.

"I'm not a coward," I whisper. I never betrayed her. I never lied, I never took the easy way, even when Gare, the last living member of my family, disowned me before the tribe, when he said a lover of Smooth Skins would receive no death wails from his throat, and vowed to let my body rot on the ground if I were foolish enough to die before he does.

He won't give me the release of a funeral fire. He hates me that much.

I don't hate him, but I would have fought him if he'd tried to hurt Isra. I would have killed him if I'd had to. My own brother. I'm no better than he is, but I'm—

"Not a coward," I choke out.

"No, you're not." A soft voice. A girl's voice.

My eyes fly open—some desperate part of me hoping I'll see Isra, though I know her voice is deeper and richer than the one I heard. Instead I find Needle standing at the base of the rocks I climbed last night and haven't bothered to leave all day. She looks up at me, her golden skin rosy in the fading light, her black eyes glittering with wonder. She looks . . . complete.

"I can speak." She blinks, sending twin streams of water racing down her cheeks. "For the first time in my life. I was born without the parts I needed to make words, but a few minutes ago I felt . . ." Her fingers touch her throat, her awe clear in their trembling. "It's magic. Isra was right. Everything in the queen's diary is true. The curse is breaking."

Isra.

"Is she . . ." I falter and start again. "Is she–"

"She's in the tower."

My chest explodes with a relief brighter and purer than anything I thought I'd feel again. "She's alive," I say, just to hear the words out loud. Then again, "She's alive!"

"We must return to the city. Quickly." Needle drops the pack slung over her shoulder onto the ground and backs away toward the dome. "She thinks you're dead and she's determined to die, too," she says, sending my heart plummeting into my stomach. "She wanted to stay with the city until it falls, to put an end to the covenant, but now that you're here–"

As if in response to her words, a terrible sound–like thunder, but a hundred times sharper and closer–erupts from the direction of Yuan. Needle wheels to look. I lift my eyes in time to see a chunk of the dome as big as the stones I'm standing on break away from the rest and fall . . . farther . . . farther . . . until it finally collides with one of the buildings at the center of the city, sending the structure tumbling to the ground. A little farther to the left, and the thick shattered glass would have destroyed Isra's tower.

I jump from the rock, and hit the ground running.

"Wait!" Needle calls as I race by her.

I glance over my shoulder to find her already running after me.

"There are soldiers still in the city," she says. "They have orders to kill Isra if she leaves her rooms."

"Why?" I ask, slowing just enough for Needle to keep up.

"Junjie forced her to marry his son," she says, making my

357

stomach knot. But there's no time to think about what Isra's marriage means for us. I have to save her life. That's all that matters. I can't be too late again; I won't survive it.

"Once she's dead, Bo can marry again," Needle continues, moving quickly for someone so small. Though . . . she seems larger than I remember her. Larger and stronger, with muscled calves peeking out from beneath her simple gray dress. "Isra was walling herself inside her room to try to protect herself, but if you hurry, you can reach her before she finishes. Go," she pants. "You can run faster. I'll wait for you both by the stones."

I've just started to push harder, when Needle cries out—

"Get her out, Gem. Kill the others if you have no choice."

I stop for one precious moment, and turn back with a nod.

Needle sighs with a mixture of relief and fear I completely understand. "Isra has to live. She has to see this," she says, arms sweeping out as if she'll embrace the entire desert. It's only then that I notice the color. Color in the desert.

Patches of green and gold and black and blue prick at my eyes. Golden grass pushes up from the crumbling earth; green teases the branches of trees that have been dead for decades. Bruised blue and black storm clouds sweep over the mountains, smelling of sweating metal and new grass and the sweetness that comes just before a rain.

I can't remember the last time it rained. I can't remember the last time I saw a storm cloud. It's been years.

Something's happening, something miraculous, and Isra has to see it. She has to know the world can change, no matter how hard the road has been to get to this place or how viciously the old world will fight to keep us from walking out of that dying city.

There is hope. For her, for me, for all of our people.

With one last glance at the clouds rolling across the sky, blanketing the sizzling desert with cool promise, I run for the dome. I run faster than I have ever run. I run to her, for her, my Isra.

TWENTY-SEVEN

ISRA

I have to get out. I can't let this be the end. I have to know if Gem was the one lighting the fires at the gathering stones. I have to know if he's alive, and if he is, I have to tell him the way I feel. I refuse to die without at least *trying* to—

"Father, please," Bo says. "Let me talk to her alone."

"You've talked enough!" Junjie shouts. "The world will end, and you'll still be talking! Open the door, Isra. Show that you are more than a blight on your family's good name."

I laugh in response, a mad laugh that sends me dashing on tiptoe deeper into the room. I spin in a circle, looking for a way out, though I know there is none. The window is bricked closed, save for a sliver of an opening too small for me to fit more than my fingers through, and there is no other window, no door, no way out.

But one. Maybe. One.

"Isra? Please, listen," Bo says. "The dome is falling. We'll all die by tomorrow morning without your help."

You might die sooner than that.

I press my fist to my mouth and hum a tune I don't recognize as I throw open the trunk at the base of Needle's bed and pull the knife with the jeweled scabbard from beneath a stack of lavender-scented sheets. I found the blade among my mother's things when Needle and I were searching for places to hide the bricks. I don't know why Mother had it or if she ever put it to use, but I swear I can feel her spirit within me as I take it in my hand.

"Your father would be ashamed," Junjie says. "He didn't raise you to be a coward."

I'm not a coward. But can I really . . .

I can't even think the thought. I've never wanted to take a life. Never. Not even Junjie's, and certainly not Bo's. He's wrong and more blind than I ever was, and jealous and trapped in the deep dark of his father's shadow, but he's not wicked. He doesn't deserve to be murdered.

Neither do you. They've given you no other choice.

"Get the key from behind the stone. It opens every door in this tower," Junjie orders beyond the door, before adding in a gentler voice, "This is your last chance, Isra. It's not too late to die with honor."

361

My last chance. He's right. This is my last, and only, chance.

My fingers tighten around the knife. I ease the blade from its sheath, toss the heavy gold scabbard onto the bed, and walk on cat feet toward the door, my breath heavy in my lungs, my fist clenching the hilt of the knife until its jewels dig into my flesh.

With an unexpectedly steady hand, I reach for the lock. I'll wait until I hear Bo start down the stairs. Then I'll throw open the door. Surprise will be my only ally. Junjie is shorter than I am, but stronger and trained to fight. I'll have one chance, one moment to–

"No," Bo says. I pause, hand hovering over the lock. "I won't."

"Then I'll get the key myself," Junjie says.

"No, Father." There are shuffling sounds outside, and then Bo continues in as strong a voice as I've ever heard from him. "She's my wife, and I'll decide what to do with her."

I'm about to tell him he has as much right to decide my fate as the ants I found in my fruit tray this morning, but Junjie beats me to it.

"You have no rights. You lost the right to decide anything when you–"

"I won't see her murdered," Bo says. "That's not the way of our city. It never has been. The queens gave their blood as a gift to Yuan. Even Isra's mother chose to jump from that balcony. I wish Isra would give us that gift, but that's *her* choice."

My hand drops to my side; my fingers loosen on the hilt of the knife. Bo truly does have a heart. Not enough for me to love him, but enough for me to respect him more than I thought I could.

"Her choice will be the ruin of the city," Junjie says, pain thickening his voice. "Yuan will fall, Son. Forever. There is no going back."

"I know." Bo's whisper is so soft that I must lean in and press my ear to the door to catch the rest of his words. "But there's nothing we can do, not if we choose to be the kind of men who deserve to be kings and leaders of kings. We can't make the same mistake twice. Murder isn't the way."

Can't make the same mistake twice . . . Murder isn't the way . . .

"What does that mean?" My voice is loud enough to hurt my ears, so I know that it penetrates the wood, but there is no answer. Not from Bo, and not from his father, whom, until now, I've never known to be at a loss for words. "Who else did you murder?" I slam my hand into the door hard enough to make my palm sting. "Who?"

Bo told me Gem escaped the night Bo sent the soldiers after him, but what if he was lying? What if the soldiers killed Gem? What if that's the reason he hasn't come for me the way he promised?

"Tell me who you killed!" I shout, trying not to panic. "Tell–"

"You should go, Father. Take the soldiers with you for protection and head south with the others," Bo says, ignoring me as he's always done when what I have to say is inconvenient. "I'll stay here with Isra."

What? All the angry words ready at my lips fall away. What does he mean he'll "stay with Isra"?

"No," Junjie says. "That's ridiculous. You'll come with me."

"I'm king. I will stay with the city through all trials. It's what I swore to do when Isra and I were married."

"No, Son, please." Junjie's words end in a barking sound and then another. It takes a moment for me to realize the sounds are sobs, that Junjie—the most intimidating, respected, terrifying man in Yuan—is crying. "I never wanted this."

"It's all right," Bo says, then whispers something too soft for me to hear, something that makes Junjie's barking become a pitiful moan.

I would feel for him, but it's impossible to feel for a man who lied to me, betrayed me, held me captive, and—if not for his son's intervention—would have killed me without a second thought.

"I'll tell the story to the people in Port South," Junjie says, pulling himself together enough to speak. "They'll know my son died a hero. A true king."

"Tell Mother I love her," Bo says, his voice muffled. I imagine him embracing his wretched father, and I have half a mind to throw open the door and stab them both.

But I don't. I wait until Junjie's footsteps fade away down the hall, before I say, "I want you to leave, too."

"I can't." Bo sounds wearier, more fearful now that his father is gone. "I made a promise."

"You can keep your promise as well outside as you can here by my door," I snap. "I don't want to die this close to someone I despise."

Bo sighs. "I could have loved you, Isra. If you'd let me."

"Who did you kill?" I ask, refusing to confess that I appreciate his decency, or that–vow or no vow–I see no reason for him to die with me, until I know what he's done.

"I didn't kill anyone. It was . . . someone else."

"Your father."

"Yes." Bo sighs again.

"Who did . . . Is it . . ." I bite my lip until my flesh feels bruised, but that isn't the reason tears gather in my eyes. "Is Gem dead?"

"Gem?" After a moment of silence, Bo laughs. "Even now, your monster is all you can think about."

My monster. I wish Gem were mine; I wish it with everything in me.

"Your monster might be dead, but my father didn't kill him," Bo says, sending a shiver of relief through my body. My breath rushes out and my forehead falls against the door with a thud. "He did something worse. At least I believe it's worse. Who knows what you'll think, since you obviously don't care for your own people anymore, but I–"

"I care for them more than you ever will. I've told you the truth," I snap, sick to death of this same argument. I told Bo about the queen's diary. I even tore out a few pages for him to look at–those I knew wouldn't give the secret of the covenant away–but he refuses to believe in the Dark Heart. "The power sustaining the domed cities is evil. The people are better off."

"You're mad. At least half our people will die of exposure or Monstrous attack before they reach Port South. You've sentenced hundreds of innocents to death."

"Better death than life paid for by the suffering of others."

"The suffering of the Monstrous, you mean," he says, bitterness straining the words. "I almost hate to tell you what Father did. If you love them this much while you believe a monster killed the king, how much more will you love them when you know the truth?"

Despite the still, humid air in my walled-up room, I'm suddenly cold. He can't mean . . . He can't . . .

"It was my father who killed yours," Bo whispers. "He made it look like the Monstrous, but . . . it was him."

No. *No*. I pull away from the door and step back, staring hard at the wood, half expecting it to catch fire and burn, showing me Bo's face on the other side. I have to see his face. I have to know if he's telling the truth.

I reach out and twist the lock, fling open the door. He steps back quickly, shooting the dagger in my hand a wary glance, but when he lifts his eyes, there is more shame than surprise in his expression.

"It was the only way for me to be king." Even Bo's soft voice seems too loud with the door no longer between us. Or maybe it's the terrible truth in his words that makes my ears ache. "Your father wanted you to be spared. He was planning to marry again, the same widow I was going to marry tomorrow morning. She already has children. The line of succession would have been insured for another generation. So my father decided to dispose of the king before he took another wife. If the Monstrous hadn't invaded the city, he would have found another way. I didn't know about any of it until afterward, but . . . it's the truth."

I shake my head. Father was going to remarry. He wanted me to be spared the burden of being queen of Yuan. He loved me after all.

And Junjie killed him. He killed his king, his friend, a man who trusted him with every secret in his heart, with his life. With *my* life. Junjie would have taken them both if he'd had his way, all so that his family could have more power, more prestige.

I suppose I should be shocked, and in a way, I am, but deep down inside . . .

Isn't this what Yuan is about? Killing for what we want, what we've convinced ourselves we deserve? The nobles living in obscene luxury at the expense of the common people, the common people clinging to their small comforts at the expense of the Banished, and all of us stealing life away from the land and the people outside the dome so that we can have feast days and harvest festivals and surplus and more and more and more when even half of what we have would be more than enough?

Junjie was only doing what the people of Yuan have always done. He was paying for what he wanted with someone else's blood.

But not anymore. Not ever again.

"Thank you," I say, feeling closer to Bo than I ever have. "For keeping your promise to the city."

"Didn't you hear what I said? My father–"

"I understand." I glance down at the dagger in my hand, grateful I didn't get the chance to use it. I don't want to know what it feels like to pay a blood price. "It's all the more reason for this to end with us. I know you don't believe what I've told you, but—"

"I don't know what I believe anymore," Bo says. "It was so clear before, but now . . ." He braces his hands on either side of the door frame, his head sagging wearily between them.

I glance at his bowed head, at the pale hairs weaving their way in among the black. His short time as king has taken its toll. Bo's not a boy anymore. He's a man, maybe even man enough to be trusted with the truth.

I'm parting my lips, debating whether or not to tell him the entire truth, when a great screech and a shattering fills the air, as if every plate in the royal kitchen were dropped at once. The tower walls vibrate, and Bo and I cover our ears with twin cries of pain. A moment later, a dull boom rocks the stones beneath our feet.

The floor tilts, sending me staggering back into my bedroom. My dagger falls from my hand and scuttles across the stones, only coming to a stop when it hits the far wall with a clank. My arms wheel and my feet spread wide to steady me, even as my heart screams that it's pointless to fight, useless to resist. The tower will fall and I will fall with it. This is the moment I thought I was ready for.

But I'm not. I'm not! How could I be? How can anyone ever be ready?

Mercifully, after several endless seconds, the floor steadies and the stomach-flipping tilting stops. My breath rushes out and my heart pounds fast enough to make me dizzy as I turn in a careful circle, taking in the crooked new world left behind in the wake of the quake. My bed curtains list to the left, and my dressing table has fallen on its face, while the pictures on the walls hang at disturbing odds with the room, now that gravity has taken the room one way and pulled the pictures the other.

"Are you all right?" Bo asks, drowning out another faint but troubling sound.

"Sh," I hiss, ears straining. Outside, the air is still once more, but from somewhere deep within the tower comes a crumbling, crunching . . . loose sound. A faltering sound; a falling sound.

"Go! Run!" I shout, dashing on bare feet to the door, where Bo stands braced against the frame, wide-eyed and as panicked-looking as I feel. I duck under his arm, snatching at his shirt as I dash for the stairs, dragging him after me, praying the way out is still passable.

It's one thing to say I'll die with the city; it's quite another to climb into bed and let the tower collapse beneath me. That's too close to giving up, and giving up is too close to drawing a knife across my throat. I'll fall with Yuan, but I won't go down peacefully. I'll go fighting for my life every second of the way. I am a warrior now. Gem made me this way, and I won't betray him or myself by giving up without a struggle worthy of the last queen of Yuan.

TWENTY-EIGHT

GEM

THE city is a monster, screaming and frothing and losing teeth in its frenzy to feed one last time.

The soldiers run like frightened children into the desert, dropping spears and dart blowers and swords in their haste to escape. The few still left inside shove each other as they fight to squeeze through the narrow opening that is all that is left of the King's Gate now that the walls have all but collapsed. Even before I'm close enough to see the sweat and tears on the men's faces, I can smell their terror, sour and filthy on the wind, tainting the fresh air crashing over the mountains like waves of redemption.

The men are so afraid of their city that they don't notice their old monster running toward them until I'm close enough to kill them with a sweep of my claws. Two short, soft boys scream and put on a burst of speed, darting closer to the wall to get away from me, before racing back toward the desert, while the man wedged half in and half out of the opening in the gate cries out and lifts his arms in a desperate—and useless—attempt to protect himself.

If it's necessary to kill him, he'll be as dead with those arms up as down, but I'll leave that decision to him.

"Leave now and I won't hurt you. Stay to fight me, and you die," I growl as I pull him through the opening by his arm-pits and fling him onto the ground. I wait half a second—long enough to see that he has scrambled to his feet and followed his friends—before turning back to the opening and hauling at the rocks blocking my way.

I'm bigger than the men of Yuan. I won't be able to fit unless I make the opening larger. I dig my fingers into the stone, until they bruise. I wrench at the rocks until my muscles scream with effort. I curse myself for allowing my body to grow thinner and weaker in my weeks wandering the wild. I dig in and dig down and give everything I have and more, but the last colossal stone refuses to move. Not a centimeter, not a fraction of a centimeter.

I grit my teeth and howl with effort, refusing to fail now. Above me, the city howls more loudly, twisted metal and crumbling glass wailing a miserable, selfish cry for blood and suffering and death. But beneath it all is the rush of the clean wind and, finally, a wondrous smatter-patter, the sound of raindrops on desperately dry earth, the remarkable rhythm of rain falling harder and harder until the drumbeat of hope pounds all around me.

The drops kiss my bare shoulders, soak into my skin, bringing me to life like a seed waiting for a miracle.

The stone gives beneath my fingers, rolling away, falling to the ground with a thud. Heart racing, I shove my shoulders through the opening and tumble into Yuan. I roll back to my feet and run, around the granaries, through the barren fields, past fallen trees and massive shards of glass, cresting the final hill in time to see the tower fall.

And fall . . . and fall, loose stones scattering like bones thrown from a medicine man's cup, foretelling the death of anyone still left inside.

ISRA

BY the time we reach the base of the tower, my childhood home is crumbling all around me. With barely a moment to spare, I fling myself through the door to the outside world and out onto the path, with Bo close behind me. As I dash for the barren sunflower patch, my bare feet crunch through the clods of dirt that are all that remain of the cabbage field.

My breath comes fast and my arms pump at my sides; my lungs are raw, but the salty taste in my throat only makes me feel more alive. I'm alive. Still alive!

We're going to make it out. We're going to make it!

It's my last thought before a stone fist punches me between my shoulders, knocking me through the air. I fly—a bird with broken wings and a belly full of pain—only to fall to the earth with a pitiful moan. My breath rushes out, but I can wheeze only a little air back in. It hurts to breathe deeply. There are too many sharp things inside me, fighting for a place to exist in this soft, bleeding body. My vision swims with red, my fingers flinch at my sides, instinctively grasping for things I'll never touch.

I blink, pulling the world into focus, to see Bo standing a few feet away, staring back at me, hunks of rocks falling to the ground all around him. I try to tell him to run, but I can't speak. Even if I could have made words, it would have been too late.

It's a stone no bigger than a child's ball that hits him, but it makes contact in the worst of places, colliding with his skull, shattering him in the blink of an eye. I see more red, and then Bo is facedown on the earth. Not moving. Not breathing.

My chest burns, and I know I would cry for him if my body weren't full of knives made of broken bones. He's gone. As gone as I will be soon.

Soon I will not be Isra anymore.

I could find peace with it, I think, some kind of peace, enough to close my eyes and move away from the pain, at least, but a moment after the last stone hits the ground, he's there. He comes running through the wreckage, his expression as fearful and hopeful as I imagine mine was a few minutes ago.

Gem. *Gem.* Every part of my being screams his name.

I know it's him and not some vision created by my dying mind. He's the same as he always was, but also very different. Altered from the boy I knew. He's leaner, with sharper cheekbones and shadows smudging the skin beneath his eyes. Eyes that are hollow and haunted, but charged with energy that reaches through the air between us, electrifying my body the second his gaze meets mine. He loves me. I see it. I know it the way I know the darkness from the light.

My heart pumps desperately against my broken ribs, heedless of the pain it causes as it celebrates seeing our beloved, too innocent to understand how terrible this meeting is. But I understand. I'm dying. And all Gem can do is watch.

Gem's gaze travels down my body and back up again, and his steps falter. His lips part, and the hope drains from his face, replaced by understanding and agony and regret so sharp that I see it twist inside him, making his desert-tanned skin pale beneath his scales. He's staggering by the time he falls to his knees beside me.

"Not again," he says, his voice the rawest thing I've ever heard. "I can't lose you. Please, Isra. Please. Stay with me."

I suck in a breath, but all that comes out is a whimper too

soft and pitiful to be called a sound at all. I can't speak. I can't even tell him I love him.

"Isra?" Gem brushes my hair from my face. "Can you hear me?"

I blink and blink again, before slowly, deliberately lifting my eyes to his and forcing my mouth to curve at the edges, hoping he can see that his being here makes everything hurt a little less.

Gem presses his lips together, but doesn't speak. Or move. Or seem to notice when a piece of the dome plummets from the sky, crashing into what's left of the tower. I twitch my fingers, trying to point away from me, to let him know he has to leave me and get out, but he isn't looking at my hands. He's watching my face with eyes that shimmer in the murky gray light.

"You can't die," he says, the shimmer becoming a shine. "You have to see it. Needle is waiting for you. The desert is alive. Grass is growing; the trees are budding. It's raining. There . . . there's so much. You have to see it with me."

I smile so big, it hurts, but I don't try to stop it from taking me over. Then we did it. Gem and I. We loved enough. The planet will be made whole. There will be no more domed cities, and our people will have a second chance. I hope they will choose peace, forgiveness.

"Needle can speak. She's the one who told me to come find you," Gem says, breaking through the fog settling over my mind. "When she stepped into the desert, she was made whole."

As soon as the words leave his lips, I see the dream form

behind his eyes. A part of me wants to dream with him, but I know better. I won't live to see the desert again. I know it even before he scoops me into his arms and one of the sharps inside me shifts and lifts and punctures, and suddenly I can't breathe at all. Not a whisper, not a sip.

The pressure builds in my chest, and my eyes slide closed, but for a few moments I can still feel my body bouncing in Gem's arms as he races for the gate, hear him begging me to stay, telling me it's not too late.

And then there is nothing but the slowing of my heart and the quiet in my head and blessed numbness and separateness and softness, pierced only by one regret. I wish I could know that Gem is safe before I go. I wish I could tell him to lay my body down and go and be a champion for the world the way he was a champion for me. I wish . . .

I wish . . .

I . . .

stop . . .

wishing.

TWENTY-NINE

GEM

HER body goes limp, but I don't stop. I run for the gate while the city does its best to kill me before I can escape. Chunks of glass as big as houses ram into the dirt, sending soil exploding into the air and raining down on my shoulders. I clutch Isra closer and run with her head held to my chest, hoping to protect her from the worst of the debris.

Trees uproot in my path, reaching gnarled roots out to catch at my legs, but I leap over them. I'm starting to believe we'll make it to the desert, but when I reach the King's Gate, the hole I crawled through isn't there. There's nothing but rubble and an impenetrable shield of broken glass blocking the way.

With a curse and a prayer to the ancestors, I turn and race back toward the Hill Gate. It was larger to begin with. There has to be some of it left, some way out.

I run through fields planted with glass and twisted metal, through trees ripped from their orchards and left to shrivel in the rain now falling through the holes in the dome. I run past the rose garden, where the flowers screech and writhe in their bed, tossing their great heads back and forth, reaching with vines like clawed tentacles to try to snatch Isra from me as we pass.

But I'm too far away and they are too late. This city will never rise again. The world outside is reclaiming its power. It will be healed. It will heal Isra. It will. It *will*.

I run on—lungs burning, legs aching, but I force myself to move faster. There's no time. Isra is moving further away with every moment. I can sense her soul separating from her body, considering flight the way I did that night in the dungeon.

"Stay, Isra," I pant. "Stay with me."

By the time I reach the Hill Gate and squeeze through the last space big enough for a man carrying another person, she's more than limp. She's as still as the stones on the ground.

I want to stop right away and lay her down, let the rain kiss her face and bring her back to me, but we're too close to the city. Most of the wreckage is falling inside the walls, but there is still danger near the gate. I have to keep going.

I run until we are at a safe distance, and then a little safer still, and then farther than we really need to be, and still I don't put her down. I don't want to put her down. Somewhere deep inside I know. I know like I knew Herem was dead before he rolled from Meer's arms, like I knew Meer was gone before she touched the ground.

Isra's gone. Too far gone for even magic to bring her back.

"No, please," I beg as I finally fall to my knees and settle Isra on a patch of newly grown grass. "Please, please, please."

I brush the wild curls from her face, smooth a bit of dirt from her cheek. I let my hand linger at her waist, hoping and praying to feel her body stir as she draws breath, but there is no breath. There is nothing, even when I cup her face in my hands and press the softest kiss to her lips, even when I tell her I need her, even when I beg and beg the Desert Mother to bring her back to me. Even when I throw back my head and howl up into the pounding rain, there is nothing. Isra only lies there, until her lips pale and her cold skin is dotted with raindrops.

I sit on the ground beside her, holding her hand as the last of the storm clouds roll away and the setting sun makes one last glorious crimson appearance, casting the newborn desert in rose and gold, making our world look like paradise.

Inside me there is nothing but misery so fierce it burns. Burns my heart, my throat, my eyes. . . .

My eyes. Something hot and wet and *impossible* pushes at my eyes, through my eyes, to burn two desperate paths down my cheeks. Tears. From the eyes of a Desert Man. It's impossible. Never in the world, never in my life . . .

But here they are, as wet and salty as Smooth Skin tears, pouring from my eyes as I grieve her. I feel them drip from my chin, watch them land on Isra's pale hand, still cradled in my lap, and I understand. This is what the desert gave me. It gave Needle a voice. It gave me tears, a place for all the pain to go, a way for it to leave my body and be swept away, but it will take forever. Years of weeping, rivers of tears. I can't imagine ever standing up again. I can't tolerate the thought of building a pyre and placing Isra on top and setting it aflame.

I can't. I won't. I will sit here and cry for her until my body runs dry and I turn to dust. I will cry, and each tear will be another miracle she didn't live to see.

"Isra, please," I whisper. "Don't leave me here alone. I love you."

It's only when the words are out that I realize I never told her. I felt the words, but I never said them aloud. There was never the right time or place, and now there never will be. Never. Isra is gone, and she never knew. Not for sure.

I cry harder. And harder, until my vision swims and I can barely see.

But I can feel. I can feel the ground shake as the last of Yuan crumbles to the ground behind me. I can feel my soul thrashing inside my body, beating at the walls of my flesh with tight fists, determined to escape the torture of living through losing her. I can feel my teeth grind together as my jaw clenches, trying and failing to hold back the moaning-keening-growling-suffering sounds vibrating in my throat. I feel it when more tears fall onto my hands, sliding onto her hand, sealing us together.

I feel it when her skin warms and her fingers brush–ever so slightly–against mine.

I suck in a breath, and look down to find her . . . glowing. Not some trick of the setting sun reflecting off her skin, but light beaming from within her, painting her bare arms a soft orange, lighting the hollows of her eyes, illuminating her lips until they are redder than the roses dying in the city behind us.

"Isra?" I whisper, with equal parts fear and hope. "Isra?"

With a soft moan, her chest lifts, her throat lengthens, and the fingers still twined through mine squeeze tightly. I clutch her hand with both of mine, wishing so hard that I'm afraid to breathe as her head tilts back and her lips part. She sighs, and gold and orange sparks fly from her mouth.

Instinct tells me to move back, but I stay, refusing to be frightened away as more and more sparks fly with each breath until Isra is breathing fire, but showing no signs of burning. Instead of feeding on her flesh, the fire is nourishing her, transforming her.

Ribbons of flame whip out to tease at her chest, her arms, all the way down to her knees and bare toes. Her legs grow longer, her hips and shoulders wider. The bones of the hand still clutched in mine shift and reshape, while above her eyebrows and down her cheeks orange and gold scales unfold like cloth laid across her skin.

The light shining from within her glows brighter, the flames between her lips rise higher, and higher, until I can't resist the urge to reach out and touch them. I brace myself for pain, but my hand passes into the center of the fire without a single burn. The flames are hot, but they don't hurt. They . . . heal.

Warmth and sweetness stitch up things inside me, soothing and reassuring, kneading and molding, taking and giving. My teeth grow smaller and slicker against my tongue, my tongue creeps farther back into my throat, and, for a moment, it feels as if my jaw will melt off my face before it firms up again in a different, more delicate shape than it had before. My shoulders and arms grow looser and lighter. My fingers splay wide, the muscles of my hands rippling uncomfortably before relaxing into their new shape, a rounder shape, without any dangers hidden beneath the skin.

I stare at my new hands, surprised, but not missing my claws. They are a part of the past. This is the future. My future. *Isra's* future.

She's going to live. I know it even before the fire fades away, leaving us alone in the cool, bluing light of early evening. Even before Isra opens her eyes and looks up at me and smiles a smile more beautiful than the one she had before. She's even more breathtaking now. Not Smooth Skin, not Monstrous, but something in between, a strong, stunning, living, breathing beauty with scales all the colors of fire, and eyes as green as they ever were.

"I love you," I say, needing it to be the first thing she hears.

"I love you, too." Her smile grows impossibly wider as she reaches for me.

"I don't know what I would have done without you." Tears rise in my eyes again as I pull her into my arms and hold her tightly. But they're different tears. Grateful tears I don't try to hide as I hug her even closer, burying my face in the soft curve of her neck, smelling her Isra smell, reveling in the way her wild hair tickles my cheek.

"Are you . . ." She pulls away, her new hands cupping my face. Their shape is different, but the way her touch makes me feel is exactly the same—alive and hopeful and happier than I could ever be without her.

"You're . . . different. And tears . . ." Her lips part as she brushes a tear from my cheek with her thumb. "How?"

"The magic of the planet. The desert is alive again, and I've changed. *We've* changed," I add in a careful voice, uncertain how Isra will take her transformation.

She only recently became accustomed to seeing her old self. How will she adjust to this body? Will she be able to see the beauty that I see? Or will she be troubled by her scales and new size and feet no longer white and thin but wide and light brown with orange and yellow scales freckling their tops?

"I can feel it." Isra lifts a hand to her face. Her fingers feather over her forehead and down her cheeks to her throat, farther down, past the strap of her overalls to feel her bare shoulder, gingerly exploring the scales that will shield her skin from the harsh light of the sun, hold in heat during the cold nights, and protect her from other natural dangers of this world. "I'm like you."

"No. You're like you, with a little of me." I watch her discover her new legs and feet, grateful she doesn't seem disturbed by what she sees. "And I'm me, with a little of you," I say, holding out my hand, letting her see that the chambers that once sheathed my claws have vanished. "We're something . . . new."

She points her feet and flexes them, giving her toes an experimental wiggle. "My shoes would never fit now."

"You hate shoes anyway," I say, heart breaking when she looks up at me and laughs her throaty laugh. It's terrifying to think how close I was to living without that laugh, that smile, all of my sweet, brave, maddening, perfect Isra. I swallow, fighting another wave of emotion as she wraps her arms around my neck.

"I do hate shoes," she whispers, leaning into me until her forehead touches mine and her heat warms my lips. "Why are you so sad, love?"

"You almost died," I say, voice breaking. "Maybe you did die. I don't know. I was so scared. I was . . ."

"It's okay." She presses soft kisses to my cheekbones, the tip of my nose, the skin between my eyes. "That's part of what makes it real."

"Makes what real?" I ask, breath coming faster as she kisses the corner of my mouth, making it twitch.

"Love, of course. You're not stupid, Gem. Don't pretend to be," she says, mimicking her queen voice from our time working in the garden so perfectly that I can't help but smile.

"Yes, I am stupid," I say, holding her more tightly. "I should have come sooner."

"You came when you could, and everything is as it should be. The planet is whole again." She moves closer, angling her head to fit her lips to mine. "That's all that matters."

"No, it's not." My hands mold to her ribs, holding her away from me. I need to tell her the truth. I need her to know everything before I can be sure the worst is behind us. "I could have come months ago, but I . . . Terrible things happened, and . . ." I moisten my dry lips, and force myself to speak the miserable truth. "My son is dead. And my father. And many of my people. I was too late. At first I hated myself for it, then I hated you, and then I hated the planet and the ancestors and . . . everything and everyone.

"I started walking into the desert," I continue, getting the words out as quickly as I can. "I walked until I stopped feeling anything, and then finally . . . something. I still loved you. Love was there, hidden beneath the suffering. I started back to Yuan, and finally started to hope again, because I was doing what I should have done before. I was coming back to you."

She smiles a smaller, sadder smile that fades quickly. "I'm sorry about your family," she says, eyes shining. "So sorry. You were right to hate me."

"No, I wasn't."

"Yes, you were," she says, bowing her head. "I could have done so many things differently, better. And if I had, maybe—"

"So could I. So could most of the people on this planet and all of our ancestors. You did the best you could."

"Isn't that what I just said to you?" She lifts her chin, sticking her nose into the air in that way that drives me mad and makes me love her even more because it is so *her*. So Isra. "You should listen to yourself, if you won't listen to me."

"I will listen. I will always listen."

"Me too." Her forehead wrinkles. "I have so many things to tell you, things I should have told you the night you left, and things that have happened since then that—"

"Do I need to know those things right now?"

She arches a brow as my hands travel up her back, pulling her chest tight to mine. "No. . . . They can wait," she says, relaxing into me, fingers teasing at my braid as she looks up. "Assuming you're going to kiss me."

"I'm going to kiss you," I whisper, and then I do. I kiss her and taste a world where miracles can and do happen. I kiss her, and for a moment there is only Isra, my Isra, and she is the loveliest person in the world, no matter what skin she wears.

"We should find Needle." She pulls away, her breath rushing hot against my lips. "She'll be scared to death until she knows that we're all right."

"That *you're* all right."

"*We're* all right," Isra corrects. "She likes you. Maybe more than she likes me. She's been frustrated with me lately."

"You're a very frustrating person."

"You're one to talk." She smiles and kisses me on the cheek before jumping to her feet and reaching a hand down to me. I take it and hold tightly as I lead the way back to the gathering stones.

To our right, an imposing mound of rubble and a cloud of lingering dust is all that remains of the city of Yuan. I wonder, for a moment, if the sight makes Isra sad, but when I glance at her, she's staring out at the newly living desert, a peaceful look on her face. Where the land was once cracked and barren, grass waves in a light breeze, birds sing in trees lush with rain-damp leaves, and night flowers lift pale faces to the darkening sky.

Soon, the stars will come out and Isra and I will sleep beneath them, our first night together in the new world. I will hold her tightly and tell her I love her, last thing before she closes her eyes, and first thing when she wakes in the morning. I will tell her every day for the rest of our lives, and more important, I will show her.

I will show her that loving her is my greatest truth, and the most beautiful thing I have ever known.

IN THE BEGINNING

IN the beginning was the new world and hope brighter than the stars.

The broken were made whole, the Banished were welcomed home, and all people—Smooth Skin and Monstrous—were transformed by the planet that loved them.

There were, of course, those who feared the sudden changes in their world, who cursed their new skins and their old enemies, but there were far more who celebrated, who were grateful and eager to live in peace.

In this particular beginning, there were also a girl and a

boy whose love had saved the world, and who refused to let the world slip back into darkness. Together they became the king and queen of a new nation, and led their people as wisely as they could. Sometimes that meant leading them into hiding. Sometimes it meant leading them into battle, and when it did, the boy and the girl fought their enemies fiercely. But when the battle was won, they remembered to be merciful, to begin again with love for their enemies as well as their friends.

Love was the gift they gave their world. Love made them happy for many, many years, until it was time for yet another beginning.

On the night their souls slipped away—within moments of each other, surrounded by children and grandchildren and great-grandchildren and the first great-great-grandchild with green eyes like the queen's—the Summer Star split down the middle, leaving two stars in its place.

One was white and as pale as Queen Isra's skin when she was a girl, the other a luminous orange like King Gem's scales when he sat before the fire. They were celebrated and named Beauty and Beast, but none of the king or queen's people would ever say which star was which. They would only look kindly on the stranger who'd asked and say, "Beauty is wherever you find it, and Beast is there when you need to defend it."

Centuries passed and cities rose and fell, wars were fought and lives were lost, but every summer, when Beauty and Beast appeared in the night sky, somehow the people remembered to love a little harder, and never again did their planet fall into darkness.

ACKNOWLEDGMENTS

Many heartfelt thanks to everyone who helped in the birthing of this book. To my agent, Ginger Clark; my editors, Michelle Poploff and Rebecca Short; and to the entire team at Delacorte Press, who are amazing at all they do. Thanks to Julie Linker and her daughter, Annabelle, my awesome friends and beta readers. Thanks to my family for their unfailing support and encouragement, and to my husband for bearing with me through my typical drafting angst (you have my fret cycle down to a science now, my love, and always help me through it). Last, but not least, thank you to my readers. Every email and letter means so much. I am honored to have the chance to tell you stories.